IN GOOD HANDS

IN GOOD HANDS

Bonne Parish

IN GOOD HANDS

iUniverse books may be ordered through booksellers or by contacting:

iUniverse
1663 Liberty Drive
Bloomington, IN 47403
www.iuniverse.com
1-800-Authors (1-800-288-4677)

Because of the dynamic nature of the Internet, any web addresses or links contained in this book may have changed since publication and may no longer be valid. The views expressed in this work are solely those of the author and do not necessarily reflect the views of the publisher, and the publisher hereby disclaims any responsibility for them.

Any people depicted in stock imagery provided by Thinkstock are models, and such images are being used for illustrative purposes only. Certain stock imagery © Thinkstock.

ISBN: 978-1-4917-5831-1 (sc)
ISBN: 978-1-4917-5830-4 (e)

Library of Congress Control Number: 2015901000

Print information available on the last page.

iUniverse rev. date: 05/18/2015

For Dar and Sally Rose -
Thanks for your love and support.

1

Darius Steele is standing in the doorway to the crowded great room of the father of the bride, financier Blake Stone's house. The man has definitely filled out nicely but still looks fit and trim and as handsome as ever. The only flaw to his otherwise perfect appearance is his choice of date. A tall, skinny brunette scantily dressed in a short, tight black sheath is hanging on his arm like she'd fall over if she let go of him. She is teetering on five inch platform strappy sandals making her the same height as Steele. I wonder if anyone heard my heart break, time doesn't heal all wounds, but perhaps he won't see me...

Standing beside me is my dearest friend and escort for the evening Mokie Joe, or Joseph Mokena. He looks down at me as I tense up watching the former love of my life socialize with the bride's father. Mokie looks over and sees why I've suddenly stopped talking.

He slips his arm around my shoulders and turns me away from the line of sight of the man that damn near wrecked my world. My brain has stopped functioning and as I see our reflection in the bank of windows I think to myself, why I couldn't I have fallen for Mokie Joe instead of the Rottweiler across the room. We compliment one other in temperament, likes and dislikes, as well as our love of cooking. We have the same sense of humor, and we're only three years apart in age.

Mokie is wearing a perfectly tailored black tuxedo suit with a white shirt and burgundy tie. His long, black, thick mane is pulled back into a queue, making his Native American heritage even more obvious. His obsidian eyes under his dark brow take in our surroundings as his hand slides down to the small of my back resting comfortably above the swell of my backside, naturally just not sexually.

I know my red dress with the soft draping neckline and the peplum running diagonally down my hip is a knock out, my red leather clutch and open toed pumps are the perfect touch to my ensemble. My own shoulder length blonde hair is swept up in a soft up do and the diamond earrings and matching cuff bracelet finish the look. My most cherished piece of jewelry, a red ruby ring surrounded in diamonds sets my hand on fire, flashing its brilliance as I move my champagne flute to my sheer pink glossy lips. I bought this ring myself when I started my own catering business six years ago and whenever I'd start to doubt myself I'd look down at the blood red gem and find my center.

"Let's get some fresh air," he whispers in my ear and steers us through the open double French doors leading out to a magnificent courtyard strung with what appears to be tens of thousands of small lights hanging down from the branches of the trees. My staff them around the trunks and draped them over the rafters of the arbor as well as all the shrubbery. Every surface has softly flickering votive candles; the strains of the string quartet can still be heard from here lending to the ambiance. I let out a sigh. It does look magical. Smiling at his consideration I lean my head on Mokie's shoulder and he kisses the top of my head in a brotherly fashion.

"Thanks I needed to get out of there," I tell him and we walk over to the loungers placed all over the patio nestled between huge royal palms and fichus trees in cache pots the size of my car. We sit down on one of the chaise lounges and look around at the opulence surrounding us. It's a whole other world, a far cry from where we came from.

My brother Jonathan and I grew up in a small town in southern California called Lakeside about twenty minutes out of San Diego which is where Mokie Joe is from. We lived in a small house at the base of a mountain until our parents divorced then we went to stay with our Grandmother Kate Mosier. Our parents couldn't be bothered with raising the two of us. The courts awarded temporary custody to my stoic grandmother and we simply never left her place in Willow, even when our parents cleaned up their acts, remarried, and moved on with their lives. Jon and I have three half-brothers and one half-sister from their combined new marriages, but we don't see them, rarely exchange emails or phone calls. It's always been just me and my brother and then Mokie Joe joined our group.

I met Mokie Joe at Community College when I was a freshman and he was getting ready to transfer to UCLA on a sports scholarship. My older brother Jon had finished his second year and had no intention of furthering his education. Mokie grew up a navy brat, but an unwanted one not only due to his mixed race, but because he appeared to be in his own world, not interested in joining the military like his father. He was an only child and preferred his own company, a real loner by choice. He and I connected immediately in a cooking class the college sponsored.

Mokie nudges me with his tuxedo covered shoulder, bringing me back to the present. I look over at him and smile, making him roll his eyes when he sees the far-off look on my face.

"Wake up goober," he says, "Stone is heading our way, probably wants to thank you for producing this amazing display of gaudy wealth and circumstance."

I look up and see Blake Stone walking over towards us with his wife in tow. We stand up and look at our fun hosts. She is gorgeous, well turned out, and with only a discrete nip and tuck here and there. She is dressed in a stunning silver gray floor length sheath and appears to have been enjoying herself. He is fit and trim, maybe a little work done, but nothing obvious, they're just a nice couple. They look like a wedding cake topper that has been preserved, a little brittle up close.

"There you are," Stone says, "I lost track of you. Are you having a good time? I have to say this is exactly what our Randi wanted, isn't it hon?" he says to his wife who smiles and nods her well-coiffed head at me.

She takes my hand in her perfectly manicured one and says, "Carrie Anne you're a Godsend. A magician I swear to God. I didn't think anyone could pull off a fairyland reception and not make it feel like a theme park... but you did!" She hugs me sloshing her champagne as she sways with me.

Blushing at her high praise I start to tell her it was my pleasure when Dare walks through the doors and suddenly stops when he recognizes me. Crap! This is just great.

There is no way to pretend I didn't see him as we connected immediately. Everyone probably saw the sparks fly out of the top of my head.

Up close he looks harder now at thirty two than he did seven years ago when I met him in Paris. Mokie tightens his hold on my hand, giving me his physical as well as moral support. Mrs. Stone releases her arm from around my shoulder and steps back to see who walked over to our group.

"Darius Steele," she says smiling and holding out her bejeweled hand, "I'm so glad Blake talked you into staying for the reception." She leans over and kisses his freshly shaved cheek, "Let me introduce you to our bridal consultant/caterer and her date.

"We've met," Dare says and raises his flute in silent salute, taking in every aspect of me and Mokie Joe. "I don't believe I've had the pleasure of meeting her escort for the evening."

Mokie holds out his glass to me to hold, not relinquishing my other hand as he shakes Dare's extended palm.

"Joe Mokena, The Escort," he says, "and you are?" The sardonic grin on my friend's face is enough to make me burst out laughing at his attempt to make Steele jealous.

Dare looks into Mokie's black eyes and grins, causing fine lines to appear at the corner of his clear blue eyes. He reads my friend loud and clear.

"I'm Darius Steele, an old friend of MS Mosier, from her time in Paris…" he says implying we were intimate, which is the truth but no body's business, "This is Miss Rhonda Starr."

His date simpers and holds out her acrylic tipped hand, hoping Mokie will be impressed, he is not. He barely touches her hand before he releases it and takes his glass back from me.

"Good to see you again, after all these years." I tell him noticing the gleam of mischief popping into his eyes as he looks down at our clasped hands. "We were just on our way to the buffet line, have a nice time." I tell him and look over my shoulder, catching him staring at my backside, "It was nice seeing you, take care." I nod at the Stones, "I'm glad En Bonnes Catering was able to make your daughter's dream wedding come true. I'll speak with you later."

I walk away feeling those artic blue eyes drilling into my spine. Forcing myself not to pick up the pace and leave his sight, I stroll away in style. Mokie slowly runs his hand up and down my spine knowing Steele is watching us as we walk back inside the house. It's all I can do not to bend over and laugh at my date's antics.

"You are a nut!" I tell him and hug his waist, feeling his arms close around me as we stand in the back of the food line.

"That cowboy is trouble," he says, "when an Indian tells you that," he jokes, "you can take that to the bank. He'd love to get you alone, have his nefarious way with you… again, it was written all over his face."

"Mokie shut up and fill your plate." I tell him handing him one of the white china plates and helping myself to a delicious assortment of puff pastries, my own recipe naturally. The girls did a wonderful job of laying out the display, and of course making the food as well. My staff is a dream to work with, looks like they'll be wanting a couple days off after they clean up tonight's success.

Normally I work the floor when it's a big gig like this, but because I had a full staff all five of my crew are here and Mokie was visiting I decided to play boss and let them show me what they've got. I've had the same crew for the last four years and we work like clockwork. They've become my extended family and earned a large bonus for their work tonight. I'm impressed and from the look on everyone else's face, it's unanimous; *En Bonnes Catering* has another success under our belts.

Mokie takes our loaded plates outside through another set of open French doors, this time onto a different patio set up with small intimate tables, as I get fresh champagne for us. Together we sit down at one of the small back tables not reserved for any of the guests. The cake has been cut, the toasts have been made, and everyone is enjoying the great food and the carefree atmosphere.

As chef's we discuss the seasonings on the roasted shrimp, deciding to adjust the heat when I glance up and see my nemesis and his toothpick girlfriend heading our way. Crap!

"Mind if we join you?" he asks, pulling out a chair for MS Starr before either of us can respond. "I didn't want to take someone's seat and cause a fuss in this otherwise well turned out event."

Such high praise coming from someone that likes 'beer dogs' but I let his opinion and tone slide off my back; I smile and wave my hand to the extra chairs. My company has made our clients extremely happy and that's all we care about.

"How are you enjoying your evening, MS Starr?" I ask the sullen woman who is nibbling on a wedge of lemon.

"Its okay I guess," she says looking around, "I was kind of hoping to see some celebrities, but they're just bankers and realtors not movie stars."

I look over at Dare and notice the smirk on his lips, and I can't help but smile back at him. His own date just insulted him and she has no idea she did so.

I raise my glass and say, "to the lighter side."

Mokie starts laughing as he raises his glass, touching his rim with mine. I look over at Dare and see him raise his glass, "To the uncomplicated side."

I start to drink but then understand his toast, he is saying I complicated his life when we were together, and now he prefers things a bit more 'easy' which is fine with me. I raise my glass to my lips and drink to his veiled insult.

While MS Starr twists and turns in her chair looking for the paparazzi no doubt, Mokie engages Dare in a number of safe conversation gambits.

"How do you know Mr. Stone?" he asks Dare, "are you a developer or a banker?"

Looking over at me he winks and says, "Just a glorified realtor these days."

"Don't let him kid you dear," I look up at Mokie's smiling eyes and say, "he is a land developer, a speculator making his way in the high-finance crowd, right Darius?"

I can't help but feel a small amount of resentment at his downplaying his career choice, as he chose it over us. I feel if you chose a career over a relationship, it had better be very important to you, otherwise you're just playing with someone else's life, like he did with mine.

Steele stops chewing long enough to narrow his eyes, signaling he isn't happy with my question. I tilt my head at him, waiting on a response but before he can reply one of my wait staff approaches me with an anxious look on her face.

"Excuse me Carrie Anne," Naylah says leaning down to whisper in my ear. "There are several groomsmen that are harassing Gina at the bar, and I can't find Saul to relieve her, do you mind handling them?"

My best sous chef likes to bar tend when given the chance even though she is barely legal herself. Gina Barone is a drop dead gorgeous girl, Italian and hot headed, so it's in my best interest to intervene.

"No problem Nana," I tell her and lean over to whisper to Mokie, "If I'm not back in ten minutes come get me." I nod my head at our table mates and laying my white linen napkin on my seat I walk back to the bar area with Naylah.

"The best man and the groom's brother are hitting on that girl something fierce," she hisses, practically running to keep up with my longer stride.

Nana as we call her is a mother hen type, a bit on the plump side, but one of the best cake decorators I've ever come across, at least without any technical training. I love Nana dearly and know she doesn't exaggerate so I'm prepared to deal with the drunken jerks.

Gina looks up from the makeshift bar with a look of relief, but I know she'd love to have a go with the two booze hounds. She is my martial arts partner and we've missed two classes this week due to scheduled receptions. I nod my head at the gorgeous brunette and walk up to the glass topped bar.

"Is there a problem here?" I ask in my best Director's voice, "Are you gentleman causing a problem? Do we need to have you removed from the bar room?" I cross my arms under my breasts, practically tapping my foot at their obvious sloppy drunken behavior.

"Yes there's a problem," the best man says, slurring his words and spilling his beer, "this chick won't give me her phone number and I've got a bet going I can get it as well as cop a feel before the hour ends."

This causes the younger groomsman to burst out laughing and sloshing his beer onto the best man's arm. They argue with each other and start pushing and shoving, ending up on the floor. I look around hoping to find Mr. Stone when I see Mokie followed by Dare walk over to join the ruckus.

"Take it outside Gentlemen," Mokie says, "don't cause a scene on your bud's big day."

"Fuck off, Cochise." The Best man says as he stands up.

He pokes his finger in Mokie's chest; A big mistake.

"Get on back towards the reservation 'Low'", the other drunk yells, making other guests turn to see what the shouting is about.

"Stop it this instant," I snap at the two jerks. "Walk away from this area or I'll call security."

"Why don't you walk us out... to our car," the best man leers at me.

I decide to end the situation with the quickest and most effective method I can.

"Fine, let's go." I tell him and see Mokie shake his head, silently laughing at what I'm about to do to Mutt and Jeff. "Don't break anything," he jokes, "remember you're only hirable as long as you're insured." He waves my red leather clutch back and forth letting me know he is holding it for me.

"Thanks," I tell him making a face at my friend, "After you gentlemen."

As the three of us walk past Dare he grabs my arm and pulls me into his chest.

"What the hell are you thinking, going outside with these two jerks? Let me handle this, like your boyfriend should have done." He snaps looking back at Mokie who is talking with Nana and Gina at the bar.

"Don't worry about it," I tell him removing my wrist from his grasp. "I've been taking care of myself and my business for the last six years, no make that all my life. Please go on back to your 'date' and let me do my job."

I walk away and join the two men at the door leading to a private garden I noticed earlier today during our set-up. Stepping up to the younger groomsman I give him one last chance to sober up somewhere else.

"I'd love to sober you up, maybe take that stick out of your ass and have a party." He laughs loudly and leans into my side.

I take a step back and hold the door open to allow him to go ahead of me, which like the clueless moron he is walks outside and then turns to face me with his hands on his hips. I turn to the best man.

"Last chance," I whisper and he shakes his head at me. "Okay, but let me get rid of junior and then I'll be back for you."

He smiles that self-assured grin and nods his head for me to step outside, he's going to wait. Dare tries one more time to get me to let him deal with these two jokers.

"Don't do this," he whispers, "I'll take care of them, run and get security, I'd hate to break anything in Stones house, I need to be invited back in the near future."

"Steele, I'm only going to say this one more time," I tell him starting to lose my patience with him. "I don't need your help, I don't want your help, and don't expect you to lift a finger in protecting me. Now get out of my way or I'll be compelled to show you what I've learned since you and I went our separate ways. Move it."

"Fine, make a fool out of yourself," he says releasing my arm, "You never listened to anything I ever said in the past, I see now you haven't changed, have you?"

"Oh don't worry little man," I tell him letting the iron shine through in my tone, "I've learned a lot since you left me. The main item being not to depend on a man to handle any problems I might incur."

I turn on my heel and walk out the door grabbing a hold of the groom's brother and walking around one of the tall potted shrubs. I slip out of my shoes, hike up my dress and before he can remove his jacket I send a back kick to his solar plexus, and down he goes. I balance my weight on the balls of my feet and just as he starts to rise I kick him again and he stays down this time.

I turn around to find the second drunk taking a leak in the hedge. While his attention is diverted I slam him in the back with my elbow causing him to fall forward through the hedge. Shouting obscenities he struggles to get back on his feet, but when he does he is beyond angry and starts to charge at me. As I find my center I prepare to flip this jackass over my shoulder but he is lifted off the ground by Darius, twirled around and meets the knuckle end of Dare's fist. He is out for the count.

"Impressive," I tell him, tugging my dress back down over my knees. I slip my heels on and tuck a stray curl behind my ear.

Dare just stands there, shock written on his face, and then it's replaced with anger.

"You could have gotten hurt and not just broken bones. What the hell were you thinking? If the second guy had shown up you'd be in a world of hurt right now," He snaps at me and reaches towards me, intending to drag me back inside. "You're welcome for my saving your ass."

"I didn't ask for your help nor did I need it wise ass." I cross my arms under my breast fuming at his need to set me straight. "For your information, the other guy is laying on the other side of that zebra grass over there, counting the stars circling his head."

Dare looks around the cluster of exotic grasses and frowns when he sees the patent leather shoes of the downed man.

"Furthermore," I tell him as I walk past him, "my ass is my own business, remember? You left me six years ago to fend for myself, I've never forgotten nor do I intend to. You're not my lover, my brother, my employee, or my friend so back off."

I slip back inside the door and walk straight over to the bar.

"Give me a shot," I tell Gina who is looking at me kind of strangely, "Now!" I hiss at her knowing her hesitation is due to Dare walking up behind me.

"Make it two," he says, "I would like a word with you MS Mossier, if you don't mind."

I toss back the bourbon down my throat, letting the burn fuel my anger and set the glass back down on the bar. Turning to Mokie I nod my head I'm ready to leave. He hands me my purse and holds out his arm.

"I don't have the time or the desire Steele," I tell the demon of my dreams, "maybe in the next lifetime, but certainly not in this one."

Mokie smiles down at me and waits for Dare to move out of our way.

I look over my shoulder and tell Gina, "Find Saul and tell him if he values his job he'll take shorter breaks, close the bar at exactly eleven and make sure all the soiled linens are tagged and put in the van. I'll handle everything once it's back at the studio. Have all the dishes accounted for and ready for pick up tomorrow, and please make sure nothing gets broken, or you'll have to deal with Jim this time."

Gina nods her head and smiles, knowing how distasteful a confrontation with our lead rental supplier can be when his merchandise is not taken care of properly, he is a drama queen. Naylah walks up to me, waiting for me to give her direction.

"Make sure Kit and BJ clean this place up before they leave. Our contract states we leave the place in pristine order, we'll be back tomorrow for the thorough cleaning, but have them get a head start if you can… Your detail, your ass," I tell her and she smiles at my confidence in her.

"Done," she says and turns back around to help find Saul, "I miss Roz at times like these."

I laugh out loud, knowing my Office Manager Rosalyn Cannon can be a beast to work for, but she is a whiz at organizing people. She is visiting her father up in Oregon for the weekend, but should be home on Monday. He was in a fender bender, nothing serious she said, but he's bruised up and sore.

Dare steps in front of me and before he can speak I tell him, "Good to see you again Steele, take care, and let's make it another six years before we see each other again."

2

Mokie leads me over to the Stones who are embarrassed at the drunken display of the wedding party, but are clueless as to how I handled the men. I assure them En Bonne has things under control and I'll get with them tomorrow and settle up the final third of the bill and remove all the lights from their garden, pick up the table and chairs as well as all the other rental items.

Once we're outside I can finally breathe. I look over at Mokie and he is waiting on me to say something, anything. He starts smiling and then laughing at the way I behaved earlier.

"What?" I ask, "That man was so out of line, I wanted to flip his ass too."

Mokie throws his arm around my shoulder and he hands the valet our ticket while we wait for his white Jeep to be brought around. He helps me up inside the vehicle due to the tightness of my gown and trots around the front, handing a tip to the young attendant and soon we are racing along Highway 101, with the wind blowing through my shoulder length blonde hair, whipping it loose from the pins it took me forever to secure. I love the cool night air, I feel so free...

I kick off my shoes and scoot down in the seat, prop my feet on the dashboard and together Mokie Joe and I sing to the amazing sounds of Eric Clapton, who shot the sheriff but not the deputy. Together Mokie and I sing through the entire CD, laughing and cutting up at each other's off key notes. As we exit off the interstate and slide into the sleepy little town of Elk I stretch the kinks out of my back and take in the beautiful town my best friend has lived in for the last seven years ever since his mother died and left him the place.

Elk is breathtaking during the daylight hugging the majestic pacific coast line. In the dark however it becomes magical. I can hear the surf breaking on the cliffs and smell the saltiness of the ocean. There is a great deal of light this evening due to the near full moon casting its silver beams on the rocks flashing past my window. Every time I come here I'm amazed at how beautifully untouched the area appears. The quaint shops whizzing by are filled with clothing boutiques, gourmet food shops and restaurants all lending to the charm of a small town but in no way detract from the rugged terrain.

Pulling into the drive of his contemporary wood and glass home on the other side of the village I lean over and kiss his cheek, silently thanking him for being there with me tonight, not just to make sure the reception was a success, but throughout the evening with Steele. I can't believe that man just walked back into my world, no notice, no apology... just Dare being Dare.

Grabbing my shoes and purse I follow Mokie who has my overnight bag on his shoulder, up the front walk and then through the front entrance of his gorgeous beach front home. He flips on the light, turns to lock the door and reaches for my hand.

"Let's have a night cap." He suggests, "It's only ten thirty; let's catch up on what's been happening with each other, like the old days." He sets my bag on the wooden bench he built himself.

"I need a drink and a big one if I'm to rehash tonight's ups and downs." I joke and we walk through the living room into the wide open kitchen space and I set my evening bag down on the table, waiting on a glass of wine from my host. Mokie's kitchen is spotless and like the owner streamlined and extremely efficient. Opening one of the cabinets he removes two champagne flutes while I grab the sparkling wine from the restaurant grade stainless steel refrigerator. Once he pulls the cork from the green bottle I hold the tubes out to be filled.

"Here's to success and failure, one is worthless without the other." He says, and we clink our glasses together and drink to his enlightening toast.

"Let's go in the living room, or do you want to go to bed," he says suddenly realizing what a stressful time this evening must have been for me, "I'll understand if you're not in the mood to talk about Steele," he says in his most caring manner.

"There's really not much to tell you, at least that I haven't already shared." I tell him knowing there is one element I have refused to discuss with anyone; it's just too painful even now, six years later I can't say the word out loud. That one incident cleaved my heart in two, and it never healed completely. I lost a piece of myself that horrible day, and even though Dare wasn't to blame for me losing our baby, he wasn't that upset about it either… he was probably relieved the 'complication' I brought to his plan was gone, like he said earlier this evening and that is something I can't get past.

"Let's talk about you and your next project," I change the subject, "So you're the chef in high demand for Sonoma County, good for you."

He grins and takes a sip of his wine then says, "The article in *Bon Appetite* did wonders for Arnie's place, and it opened a few doors for me as well. I thought Roz's sister Desiree captured my true greatness in the photo layout, don't you?" he jokes tossing his black mane over his shoulder and striking a provocative pose.

I laugh and snuggle up to him, sitting on his huge gray flannel sofa, looking out the wall of glass at the breathtaking view. The moon sheds light on the breakers as they crash to shore, lulling me into a calmer realm. I yawn and rest my head on his broad shoulder and feel myself unwind.

"Dez is a whiz behind the camera," I agree, "I wish she wasn't so busy. It'd be great if I could get Roz to sign her under contract with us for the events we cover. She's too much of a loner if you ask me, but then I understand her need to create, however she does it."

We're silent for a couple of minutes and I know when he has had enough of my evading the topic of discussion that is Darius Samuel Steele.

"Tell me what Steele did to you baby," he says knowing I'm keeping the rest of the story from him. "I know something terrible happened, not just you two breaking up… tell me the truth, did he abuse you?" he asks and I can feel his chest muscles tense under his unbuttoned white shirt.

"No, he wasn't abusive, not like that," I tell him, "we simply wanted different things out of our relationship, such as it was." I look up into his black eyes and see the worry. "It's been six years ago, I'm fine, or will be when I get some sleep."

Setting my wineglass on the walnut coffee table I lean back and kiss his lips, softly but tenderly.

"I love you, thanks for caring but I'm alright, I promise." I tell him standing up and reaching for my discarded shoes, "Thanks for being there tonight; it meant the world to me. Wake me for breakfast."

"Coffee's on you baby doll." He tells me as I walk toward his guest room, "I don't get up at the crack of dawn like you. Please be quiet until ten o'clock, we high demand chef's need our beauty sleep," he jokes, "goodnight Carrie Anne. I love you."

I open the guest room door, step inside and toss my shoes towards the closet, unzip my dress and start to get ready for bed. Mokie takes the minimalist approach to decorating but it works. The bedroom contains a queen size four poster bed in a driftwood finish, white carpeting, gray and white grass cloth wall coverings and one white dresser and two matching nightstands with nickel finished chrome lamps attached to the wall. The bathroom is all white marble and streamlined as well. Brushing my teeth I look in the mirror at the woman staring back at me wondering if Dare thinks I've changed in six years. My eyes are still cornflower blue naturally rimmed with dark brown lashes like my eyebrows. The slightly crooked front tooth still shows when I smile too wide. I bite my full lower lip as I take stock in the image reflecting back at me. My figure is a bit fuller now but I like to think of my curves as hard won and looking good on my slightly taller than average frame. Have there been that many changes in six years, I wonder? I feel much older now, like that time happened decades ago…

3

I'm running late today, my last day of intermediate course at Le Courdon Bleu in Paris. Catching the Metro I arrive at Vaugirard in the 15th arrondisment with minutes to spare. I hate being late and dread the look on my instructor's face. Thinking about my last presentation I'm not paying attention where I'm going and run into someone's chest. Looking up, ready to apologize I'm stunned, knocked speechless at the most gorgeous man I've ever seen, who happens to be holding both my arms in his large hands.

Crystal blue eyes twinkle back at me and a grin to stop anyone's heart appears on his face. He has near black hair so thick and wavy I have to fight the compulsion to sink my fingers into the mass, wickedly arched brows rest on a high forehead, a nose straight off a Roman statue, and a sexy as hell van dyke surrounds full and smiling lips. I can't think until he releases my arms, leans down and whispers in my ear.

"Nice running into you, but you need to be more careful." He says in a glorious American accent.

I didn't realize how much I missed that sound and to have it escape from between his full lips is too much. My power of speech flies out of my head so I simply smile and nod. His companion, an older man looks down at his expensive gold wrist watch, and motions with his hands for my prince charming to hurry up.

"Don't worry about him," he says, "are you alright? Say something so I know I didn't do any permanent damage to you."

I smile and relax enjoying that sexy grin he is wearing.

"I'm sorry," I tell him, "it was totally my fault, but I'm fine."

"Good, I'm Dare Steele, from Sonoma California," He says holding out his hand.

"Nice to meet you, Dare is it? My name is Carrie Anne Mosier, and I'm from California too."

We laugh and he says, "Small world and getting smaller by the minute. Where are you staying? I'd love to grab a coffee or a café as they say over here." He jokes but glances down at his watch. "I've missed hearing the sound of an American speaking English."

"Please don't let me keep you," I tell him remembering my own lateness and pulling away from him. "I'm late for class anyway. Sorry again for crashing into you, au voir."

I turn and run down to 8 Rue Leon Delhomme. Thankfully I'm not late for class but I'm feeling out of sorts now. Having met the worlds sexiest man tends to do that to a person, at least I imagine others would be affected the same way if he gave them all of his attention like he did me. God he was divine. It's a shame I'm so busy, which in itself is a strange thing for me to think. All my life I've wanted to go to Paris France and attend Le Cordon Bleu and finish all six courses. I received my Diplome de Cuisine and have the advanced level of de Patisserie to finish. That leaves the Grand Diplome to go.

I love the hectic pace, the quick thinking, and the hustle and bustle of Paris, and when I've finished my internship I planned on staying in France, but having met Mr. Steele makes me homesick for my family and our American way of life. First I have to graduate so I buckle down and concentrate on what our instructor is saying.

Five hours later I walk outside and join my flat mate for a cigarette, not that I smoke but she does and hates to be alone in this strange city she doesn't like. Diane is from London and misses her boyfriend to the point of distraction. Before today I never understood why she couldn't concentrate on her courses, but if her guy makes her feel a fraction of what I felt with the blue eyed stranger, I'm starting to feel sympathetic towards the irritating girl.

We return to our small apartment around ten o'clock that evening, which is normal time. We're in class all day long and by the time we are able to kick back, relax a while we both fall asleep and wake up the next day and start the draining process all over again.

But tonight, there is a bouquet of pale pink roses sitting by our door in the run-down apartment we share, with a hand written note stuck in the gorgeous blooms. I assume they're for Diane but she reads the front of the card and hands the vase over to me, then unlocks the door and walks inside; flipping on a lamp she smiles over her shoulder.

"Keeping secrets from your flat mate?" she asks before she disappears into her room.

I drop my bag and purse on the small sofa and place the heavy arrangement on the old trunk we use as a coffee table. Picking up the card I flip it over and almost die from shock.

I enjoyed running into you, would love to have that coffee,
Call me; I'm staying at the Ritz,
Dare.

Should I call him? I'd love to get to know this man better, which is strange as I don't usually make time for a social life... but something is compelling me to pick up the phone and call his hotel. I pour myself a glass of wine, sit back on the blue slip covered loveseat and stare at his handwriting. It's bold, but not flourishing. He knows what he wants and appears to take a chance or two... maybe he's married and in the city with his five children and wife... or not. I finish my glass of wine, set back and decide to take a chance. I call information, get the number of the Ritz and call for his room. He picks up the phone after the fourth ring, one ring before I was going to hang up.

"Steele," he says sounding like he was asleep. "Hello?"

"Uh, hi this is Carrie Anne Mosier," I'm practically whispering, "I hope I didn't wake you but I just got home from class and found your flowers, they're beautiful, thank you."

"I'm glad you liked them. What do you mean you just got home from class? Have you been in school all day?" he asks and I swear I can hear him sit up in bed, rustling the sheets...

"Yes, I am attending Le Cordon Bleu, going for my advanced level 'patisserie' which will last ten weeks, then I'm done and should receive my Grand Diplome." I tell him hoping I don't sound like I'm bragging.

"I'm impressed; tell me what you're planning on doing after you complete your courses." He asks and we spend the next hour talking about my plans to open a catering business.

He is a great listener, asking the right questions, encouraging me to talk about my plans. I hear him yawn and look at the clock on the shelf and see I've kept him awake for over an hour.

"I'm sorry for rambling on," I tell him, "but if you're interested I'd love to have that coffee with you. But I'm busy for the next two days, and then I'm free for the weekend, that is if you're still in the city."

"I'm here for the next three months," he says laughing at the sigh of relief I unwittingly let out. "I'm flattered, and let's have that coffee, here at the Ritz and then we can spend some time sightseeing, if you want to."

God yes! My mind shouts but I pause for effect and then take a deep breath.

"That sounds lovely. Let's make it café at nine on Saturday at your hotel, sound good?" I ask hoping he can't hear my heart pounding in anticipation.

"Perfect. I'll see you then." He says, "Bonne nuit Carrie Anne Mosier."

"Good night Dare Steele of Sonoma California." I tell him and hang up the phone to the sound of his sexy chuckle.

Falling back onto the loveseat I hug my pillow I made from an antique tea towel and slip into what will become a happy pattern for the next couple of weeks.

4

Sitting out on Mokie's deck the next morning, I'm enjoying my second cup of coffee, loving the sun on my bare arms, the sound of the surf in its never ending battle to reach the shore and stay there. The sounds of the gulls that are soaring then dipping down into the water is hypnotic. I hear Mokie open the large sliding glass door and he bends down and kisses my lips with his soft touch.

"Good morning baby doll," he says, "sleep well?"

Surprisingly I did once I stopped dreaming of Dare. I turn to face him as he sits across the table from me, his back to the ocean and he blows across the hot brew before he takes a sip. He is every woman's exotic dream, from his free flowing black hair, his black diamond eyes and that buff body encased in tight dark blue jeans cuffed at the bottom, his white V-necked T-shirt, open black chambray shirt and bare feet, he's a walking orgasm... to everyone but me.

"Yes I did," I tell him, "the sound of the ocean is so hypnotic, I swear I didn't dream once."

"Liar," he says and starts laughing at the face I make at him. "Seriously, I hope you're over that chunk of granite, because that is one hombre I'd not want to mess with, but then again, you're the 'nth-degree' black belt in the family, I'm just a cook."

We sit and enjoy each other's company for over an hour before I hear my cell phone ring. I get up and grab his cup for a refill and pick up the phone without reading the screen, knowing it will be Nana wanting to know what time I'm coming over to the Stone's for her final inspection.

Smiling I answer the phone, "Keep your pants on, I'll be over in about an hour."

A deep laughing voice replies, "I'd be happy to keep them on until you get here, then all bets are off."

Oh God, Dare in a good mood, first thing in the morning is hard to resist. I remember waking up to his kisses, and lovemaking, putting us both in a good mood. He was better than a hot shower, or a burst of caffeine to get me going in the morning.

"Hello? I can hear you breathing," He laughs then softly says, "say something Cam, I miss hearing your voice first thing in the mornings."

His use of the nickname he gave me seems unfair, too assuming. We're not lovers any more, not even friends, yet he seems to think it's alright to be so familiar with me. Not anymore.

"Sorry about that Darius," I tell him in my best professional tone, "Good morning, what can I do for you?" I ask putting the conversation back on a non-personal level.

"Oh Camy there are so many things you could do but I know you won't do any of them." He says in that sexy, lazy tone of voice I used to crave. "I'm calling to see if you'd like to get a coffee, catch up on old times… scratch that," he says chuckling at his turn of phrase. "I'd like to see you today if possible, before I head back to Sonoma. Are you free?"

Free and clear is what I want to say but I put the distance back in my voice and say, "I'm sorry but I'm going to be tied up today, clearing up the Stone's place and heading back to my studio, maybe some other time," I tell him knowing hell will freeze over before I have a coffee with him again.

"Suit yourself," he says, "I also wanted to apologize for my behavior last night, I had no right to come down on you," he says, "Saul and BJ told me you have a black belt in karate and I should watch myself and not piss you off."

"Good advice, but I'll have to remind my crew not to gossip about their boss to strange men." I tell him, knowing he doesn't consider himself a stranger, but after six years, that is all he will be to me.

"Well, if you're sure you don't want to meet, I'll let you go, tell Mokena to take good care of you… I miss you Cam, goodbye." He says and ends the phone conversation.

I stare down at my phone as if it can answer the thousands of questions running through my mind.

What did he want to talk about?

Does he really miss me?

Is he sorry for leaving me to deal with the miscarriage?

Why didn't he contact me before now?

What has he been doing all this time?

"Sweetheart, call him back and ask him." Mokie says snatching my phone out of my hand and looking up Dare's number.

I try to grab the phone away but he holds it out of my reach, laughing at my attempts to get it. He stops laughing when I elbow him in the ribs and take the phone from his

29

hand but it starts to ring before I can hit the end button. Maybe Dare didn't hear it ring…

"Joseph Mokena!" I shout at him while he rubs his injured side. "I can't talk to that man and you know it."

I start to storm off to my bedroom when he reaches out his arm and pulls me into his embrace. He pushes my head to his chest and I feel the flood gates open, tears from six years ago come crashing down my cheeks like the never ending surf outside.

When I've dehydrated myself, I look up into Mokie's eyes and surprisingly feel better. He kisses my lips, offering solace not passion and I hug him close to me, resting my head on his chest.

"Thanks," I whisper and I feel him smile into my hair as he leans his cheek on the top of my head.

"Anytime," he says, "but lay off the Joseph Mokena bit, you say it just like my mother used to do."

We laugh and start back up on an even keel. After breakfast of an out of this world omelet, he drives me back to the Stone's Spanish style mansion and drops me off out front. He is going to park his jeep and meet me around back to help take down the lights from the patios and pool.

I walk up the steps, feeling slightly under-dressed in my favorite faded jeans, my over-sized, white gauze shirt, and my white leather thong sandals. Slinging my black leather bag over my shoulder I run my fingers through my wind swept shoulder length hair, press the doorbell, and look back down the wide expanse of the concrete drive lined with palm trees and flower beds. The heavy double oak doors open and I'm surprised when Mrs. Stone greats me dressed in a pair of black slacks and a peach blouse, her hair and make-up done to perfection.

"Carrie Anne, come on in my dear," she says hugging me and pulling me inside. "Have I got a surprise for you," she says.

"What kind of a surprise?" I ask, hopefully not the 'we're not going to pay the balance of our bill' surprise.

I look around the grand foyer and see my crew has removed all trace of last night's revelry, which is what I pay them to do, but it's always good to see they did such a good job. The two story entry to the Stone mansion is open and breezy with the gleaming white stucco walls and deep red and white patterned Moroccan tile. The curving staircase is a gallery of world class art leading a person towards the second story. Wrought iron balustrades and railings lend an authenticity to the home's old world charm.

"Remember your old friend, Dare Steele?" she asks not waiting on my response, "well he said he was so impressed with your services last night he was going to see about hiring your company for his firm's annual picnic... isn't that the greatest?"

Pasting on a smile I hope doesn't convey my dread I nod my head and let her steer me to the sun room and the patio. BJ and Kit are taking stacks of chairs through the bank of open French doors and out to our box truck parked on the pavers. Gina and Saul are busy loading up cartons and crates of dishes and stemware to be returned to the rental agency tomorrow. The soiled linens are riding on top of the glass crates to be returned as well. Everything looks great, no mishaps, no broken dishes... its perfect, just like I planned.

I turn to hand Mrs. Stone the rest of the bill when I hear her husband speaking to someone out in the hall.

"…I'd love to get in on the ground floor; I don't have very many dealings in Sonoma. This deal sounds like a gold mine, keep me posted on the buy-out and we'll discuss Stone, Inc.'s buy-in option," He says then sees the two of us and heads our way. If it's possible Steele looks even better in his charcoal dress slacks, French blue button down shirt and burgundy wingtips, his aviator sunglasses perched on top of that dark wavy hair than he did last night in his formal tuxedo.

Dare is looking right at me, devouring me with his eyes. That wicked little grin he seems to be wearing lately is making me uncomfortable. Again I decide to brazen it out and put a big smile on my face for Stone and Steele, letting them know I'm not afraid. At least I hope that's what my smile implies.

"Carrie Anne, good of you to come by and oversee the cleanup although with your crew, there doesn't seem to be much left to do." He says looking around the room. "Did you tell Carrie Anne that Dare is interested in hiring her?" he asks his wife who nods her head and turns to look back at me.

"We'll have to get together and work out a plan," I tell him, "My office manager is out until Tuesday, but we can set up a time for an initial meet today, then she'll confirm everything with your office." I tell him and the Stones who are watching our exchange.

"Sounds good," he says, "but maybe we could have a coffee, have a quick meeting just the two of us, I don't have to head back until later this afternoon, how does that sound?"

Not liking the way he has put me on the spot in front of my clients I smile and say, "let me check my schedule, excuse me please." I give him my 'I know what you're up to' face and turn to hand the envelope to Mr. Stone.

"Let me cut you a check for the balance," he says, and walks out of the room.

"Dare, did you know Carrie Anne started her catering business all by herself? She was first a personal chef to a couple celebrities, but she always wanted to run a catering business, and here she is doing just that." Mrs. Stone is pitching my business to the one person in the world I would never want to service.

"You're being too kind," I tell her and look up at Dare, "excuse me a moment while I check my staff."

"I'll come with you," he offers, "I met the rest of them last night after you left. Quite a talented group you have working for you." He turns to Mrs. Stone and says, "Phyllis, it's been good seeing you again, hope to see more of you and Blake in the future."

"Look forward to it Dare; Carrie Anne, Blake will be right out so if you'll excuse me I need to see about our guests accommodations. Thanks again Carrie Anne, you're the only caterer we're using from now on, see you soon."

She flits out of the room leaving me alone with my nemesis. I decide to ignore him and walk through the open doors and onto the patio where Mokie, Saul, and Gina are loading up the chairs. I haven't seen Nana yet but I know she's here, it's her crew.

"Sorry I missed your call back this morning, but it only rang once and you'd already hung up when I answered. Have cold feet or butt dial me? What did you want to say that you so quickly changed your mind about?" he bombards me with his questions, closing the space between us just as quickly.

Before I can answer Mr. Stone walks into the room waving the check and smiling at me.

"This is a hefty sum, but totally worth every penny," he says handing me the check. "Phyllis informed me last night you're our new caterer so I hope you realize Phyl put you on speed dial."

I can't help but smile at his openness and laugh as he shakes my hand.

"Call whenever you need us, you're in good hands with us, pun intended." I tell him.

The men shake hands and then Mr. Stone leaves the room, and I'm alone again with Dare.

"So are you going to answer any of my questions?" he asks brushing a stray lock of my hair behind my ear. "I like the shorter haircut, it looks good on you, and you do look good, I can't believe it's been six years since I saw you last."

"Like I said last night," I tell him suddenly feeling him crowding me, "I can go another six before I need to see you again, maybe longer. I have to help my staff so if you're serious about having En Bonnes Catering serve up your next function, please contact the number listed on my card," which I reach into my back pocket and hand over to him. "Or Roz can email you the particulars we offer, buffet, casual picnic, whatever plan you want, she'll set it up for you. See you around." I tell him and turn to walk outside but he wraps his arm around my waist, pulling me back into his body, letting me feel his strength.

"Don't ever try to pass me off to someone else." He hisses in my ear. "You and I will deal with each other one-on-one. Now I can carry you out of here over my shoulder or you can walk out the front door beside me but either way, we're going to have that coffee, and hash things out between us, now."

"Let go of me Dare." I whisper, "I don't want to talk to you now, tomorrow, or for the next sixty years. Are you really that thick headed or maybe you're still just as callous and self-centered as before, but know this, I won't be able to meet your needs, any of them, so let go of me or I'll have to remind you of my other talent, the one where you end up flat on your back with my foot across your throat," I tell him knowing exactly when he takes my threat seriously.

"You win this round, but I'll have my day, count on it." he says and removes his arm from around me and spins me around, crushing my lips under his, letting me know he is still a force to be reckoned with, then he softens his kiss, coaxing a response from me against my will. I hear myself whimper at the unwanted feelings he is pulling from me before he pulls away, gives me a soft peck on my bruised and swollen lips. "I'll call your office for an appointment, see you later Camy."

He waves at Mokie who is heading my way. He walks out of the room, leaving me stunned and dazed, and a little aroused. I quickly help finish the clean-up just to keep from having to answer Mokie's questions.

5

Once the van and box truck are loaded, I turn to tell my best friend goodbye, "I'll be over to get you next month for the Cartwright gig," he reminds me of our standing date.

The Cartwright Gala is a charity auction to help feed meals to children during the summer months when school is not in session. So many children depend on those meals as their only real source of nutrition. When school is out they can get free meals at the Cartwright House which is a youth club for under privileged children in the San Diego area. I have been his date for this event for the past three years. He is one of the prizes. Mokie donates a week of his Chef services to the highest bidder, and he rakes in the cash. I love watching him squirm on stage as the rich women in the audience try to outbid each other. Last year he was shocked when an eighty year old Grandma won the bid, but was pleasantly surprised when she gave him over as a gift to her maid. He said the fanciest dish he prepared was macaroni and cheese, but he had a blast with the lady's children, and the mother was thrilled. Mokie will make a wonderful father someday, once he gets past his fear of being responsible for anyone.

He always picks me up and we drive down together, staying the weekend, being tourists. I never book a function on that date. I slide behind the wheel, lean out the open window, and kiss him goodbye.

"I wish we could have spent more time together, but duty calls." I tell him and he smiles and looks around the paved drive way.

"It looks like Steele is hanging around, waiting on you to leave," he says lifting his hand in a wave to Dare, who is indeed waiting on us to leave.

He waves back from his black Land Rover parked on the edge of the circle drive. I hope he isn't planning on following me back to Willow. Saul honk's the horn on the box truck, letting me know he is getting impatient.

"We better go before he rear-ends us," Nana says from the passenger seat. "you take care of yourself young man," she directs Mokie, "Or I'll be force to buy your services at the Gala, then you'd be in a world of hurt, me telling you what to do, what I want… wait a minute, I may have to start saving up my resources so I can afford you."

He laughs and says, "I'd give you a week for free old woman, but then you'd be ruined for all the rest that follows."

She laughs out loud, shaking her head at him and nodding her head, "you'd probably kill me after the second day, but what a way to go."

"Whenever you're through we can go," I admonish the mother of three adult children. "Besides, I'd never get any more work out of you," I tell her, "you're the stalker type and you know it. Watch out Mokie, she'd be the one looking through your bedroom window, the pervert."

"Stop! That's so wrong," Gina says from the back seat, "I still have to work with the woman. She'll be shot by the time we get home."

"Goodbye ladies," he says patting my arm which is hanging out the window. "I love you; call me if you need to talk, okay?" He says looking at me, reading my eyes through my sunglasses.

"I will, but you better start planning your kiddie's menu for the Cartwright Gala," I tell him, "I'll bet Granny is going to win again."

"I'd love it," he says, "no pressure from the little rug rats. Drive carefully, bye girls."

We pull around the wide drive and I stop when I reach Dare in his vehicle.

"I'll have Roz call your office Tuesday, if you'd like." I tell him leaning over Nana's lap.

"No, what I'd like is for you to call me, not the office." He says, "But I'll take what I can get. I'll be seeing you, soon. Drive safely Cam."

I nod and know I'm going to get bombarded with questions for the next hour and a half. Surprisingly enough the girls are quiet, Gina napping, Nana texting her grandchildren. I turn up the CD of the Eagles on my stereo and the time flies. Soon we turn into the studio parking lot in an unassuming neighborhood of my favorite place to be, Willow.

En Bonnes Catering operates out of an old two story farm house that I and my staff converted into a top notch catering facility. The white clapboard structure and large oak trees reminds me of my grandmother's house where I currently live. Pulling around to the garage we begin the process of unloading. Saul is dropping off BJ and Kit, who actually live here, at least while BJ is working through his internship. He is working his way through the on line courses of Le Cordon Bleu out of Pasadena. They work for me only when I need their muscle which works out well for both of us, plus they get to use my facility whenever they need to. Kit is happy doing what he does.

"Saul, don't forget to get a receipt for the goods." I holler at him as he drives off.

He waves his muscular arm out the window and drives away to make his drop off. He'll return the truck tomorrow when he reports to work. Without Roz around I've got to remember our next function - a Chamber of Commerce luncheon on Wednesday. The girls help me unload the van along with the guys and soon we're done for the day.

"Sleep in." I tell my crew, "Roz won't be back until late Tuesday, so we'll be slow tomorrow. But please don't forget to check the messages on the phone, fax, as well as email in Roz's office, I'll handle my own. Love you all, great job, and take a load off."

Laughing at their exhausted faces I park the van in the rear garage and get into my cherry red 1969 Mustang convertible. I love this car, with the stereo blasting, the top down, I'm carefree and flying down the road until I reach my turn off, which is just on the outskirts of town, maybe fifteen minutes from the studio.

Pulling into the driveway I smile at my safe haven, Grandma Kate's house, with the volume turned up. Last year I had to replace the roof, and decided to upgrade the place as well. I had a tin roof installed. I love the sound of the rain striking the metal and look forward to those rainy evenings, but my cat, Mouser does not.

The male of the house is sitting on the front porch railing taking a bath, waiting on me to feed him a can of tuna, but he is the best roomie I could ask for; he's around during the day, but goes out on the hunt in the evening. He is the perfect male companion. Feed him and he wraps himself around my legs, but when he's through he takes off, but doesn't lie on the sofa, drink my booze, or demand I spend all my waking hours with him.

I pull into the new double car garage I had built; the old one was made at the same time as the house, when people had one car, and didn't use the garage as a storage unit. But the extra space is a blessing. Grabbing my purse and overnight bag I open the door and walk into the house gladly shutting out the rest of the world. Hanging up my keys on the rack and tossing purse and bag on the old farmhouse table, I kick off my shoes and walk over to the state of the art refrigerator and take out a bottle of dark ale.

Padding into my office I check voice mail, as well as email. There are three emails: One from Roz reminding me of Wednesday's appointment with the Willow Chamber of Commerce. The next email is from a supplier of mine checking to see if I needed updating, and the last one is from Mokie Joe, telling me he is thinking of me and hope I'll call him if I need to talk.

Smiling at his worrying I press the play rewind button on the answering machine. The numeral four flashes on the digital readout. Two are hang ups, the third is from my brother Jon reminding me of Uncle Walter's birthday next weekend, and did I think I'd make it this year? And the last is from Dare, which I'm not surprised.

"Hey Camy, wanted to make sure you made it home safe and sound, I know it's crazy but since I saw you I feel responsible for you again. Sorry old habits are hard to break… well shit that didn't come out right. Just call me when you get home, humor an old friend. Call me on my cell," he says and gives me the number.

I frown at the machine, what does he mean he feels responsible? He didn't feel very responsible when I needed him six years ago, and what does he mean I'm an old habit? Who the hell does he think he's talking to? Like hell I'll call him back, he's no old friend of mine.

I walk into the kitchen, check out what's in the fridge and decide to order a pizza with everything on it. It costs a bit more to have it delivered out here, but I crave the solitude. I place the order and tell them to deliver it in an hours' time.

Finishing my beer I walk upstairs and change into my work out clothes of black yoga pants, black sports bra and a purple tank top with my black cross trainers. Opening the door to my dojo I wrap my hands, slip on my gloves and walk over to the punching bag suspended from the rafters and pound the crap out of it. I see Dare's smug face grinning at me, remember all the asinine comments he made and take out my frustrations on the leather bag.

Next I hit the boards, smacking them with my callused hands as well as my full impact kicks. Thirty minutes later, exhausted, sweaty, and generally feeling gross I take off my gloves, unwrap my hands and walk into my bathroom for a hot shower. Feeling infinitely better afterward I slip into fresh underwear, a short cropped striped T-shirt, a pair of coverall shorts and my white converse court shoes. Twisting my hair up into a loose knot I know I'm not going to win any glamour contests but I'll get honorable mention in the comfort category.

Reaching for another beer my cell phone rings. I walk over to my bag and setting the beer on the table I pull the phone out, read 'Steele, Inc.' on the screen. Do I answer it or let it go to voice mail? I've never considered myself a coward before now. I let it go to voice mail and set the phone down on the table wondering if I should just pick it up when the doorbell rings.

Letting out a sigh of relief I walk over and look out the window, see Mama Rosa's pizza delivery van in the drive. I open the door and smile at the pizza boy.

"How much do I owe you?" I ask making him stutter the amount, "wait here," I tell him and walk into the kitchen for my billfold and take out enough for the pie as well as a substantial tip for making the trip out here.

He smiles at the bill and says, "Thanks! This is fantastic. Ask for me anytime lady," he says, "my name is Cal. Thanks again, enjoy your pie."

Smiling at having made his day I take my heavenly smelling pizza into the kitchen and decide to eat a slice right out of the box, so hedonistic. With a mouthful of the spicy treat I pick up my phone and listen to the voice mail from Dare.

"Hey sweetheart, just wanted to talk to you, see if you made it home alright. Call me back, let's talk like we used to, anyway call me on my cell, you got my number." He ends the call and I know he won't stop until I call him back but I can't seem to muster the desire for the drama that will ensue.

I eat two more slices of the pie and know that's my limit, putting the entire carton in the fridge I open a can of tuna for Mouser, set it on the back porch and lock up the place, intending to make an early night of it. With the traffic, the reception, plus the Dare drama I'm beat. Flipping on the TV in my bedroom I strip down and slide between the sheets, folding my arms behind my head I watch an old sitcom from the eighties and soon I'm dozing off and immediately I'm transported through my dreams to a happier time…

6

Dare kisses me awake, as he leans forward on the sofa in his hotel suite, he smiles and says, "It's getting late, so unless you're planning to spend the night, you better get up before I forget how to let you go." He teases.

We've been talking about taking our ten day relationship to the next level, and since I don't have classes tomorrow, tonight is the perfect night. I roll over and hug him around the waist, pressing kisses along his jaw, feeling his arousal against my stomach.

"I want to stay here tonight," I whisper to him, making him stare at me like I spoke in another language. "Unless you don't want me to, then I'll go of course."

He continues to stare at me for a couple more seconds then rolls me underneath him, pinning me to the soft cushions, letting me feel his weight, his desire to make love to me. I need to tell him he's the first but he is already unbuttoning my jeans, pulling my T-shirt over my head, he is light years ahead of me but I hate to slow him down so I start to undress him as well.

"Let's go into the bedroom," he says kissing my eyes, my jaw, my lips. Devouring me and making me want to rip his jeans off of him and have my way with him.

"Dare, I want to make love to you, but I need to tell you something first." I say to him as he pulls me by the hand into the bedroom, where he is tossing the throw pillows onto the floor, tugging the duvet to the foot of the bed and whipping back the sheets.

"Talk fast baby because I've been dying to have you for the last ten days." He says pulling his black T-shirt over his head, exposing his gorgeous abs and chest muscles.

"Well, I've never really done this sort of thing before, so I was hoping you'd sort of guide me through the process." I tell him but he is busy removing his sketchers and socks.

"Sure, we'll take it slow, or at least as slow as I can manage our first time, but we've got all night, so don't sweat it." he says standing up to remove his jeans, "are you on the pill?" he asks.

"What? Yeah of course, but I need you to slow down," I mumble as I watch his jeans and jockey shorts hit the floor.

Oh my God he's magnificent is the only thought I seem to be processing at the moment. He is well endowed and extremely proud at the moment. There is no way that thing is going to fit inside me, it's not physically possible, but I want to try to make it fit.

I turn away and slide my jeans and panties down, kicking out of them with a bit too much force since they fly up and land on the bed. I turn around and see Dare already under the sheets, watching me undress with the lights on and everything. Suddenly I feel as shy as a butterfly and once I remove my bra I dive under the sheets and bury my face in the crook of his neck and shoulder.

"Don't be shy sweetheart," he whispers running his hands up and down my spine, making me tremble from passion, not fear.

I love his smell, the taste of his skin, and feel of his body lying next to me. I lean up on my elbow and smile into his sexy eyes.

"This is all new to me, so I'll follow your lead." I tell him making him shake his head and laugh.

"There's nothing new on me that you haven't seen before but I like a woman that wants me to take the lead… just let your body relax and let's play." He says.

His lovemaking is wonderful, from his wet kisses, to the callused palm of his hand sliding down my trembling belly, to his hairy legs sliding over mine. He makes me so hot, so wet that I can't think of anything right now except joining with him. I wrap my arms around his waist and pull his lower body into mine. Opening my legs he traces the crease between my legs and torso with his fingers, then dips between my folds, tweaking my nerve center, back and forth he coats his fingers in the dew he's creating.

He shifts over to lie between my legs; nudging my thighs wider apart he settles himself in my cradle and slowly eases the head of his shaft inside my opening. The pressure is incredible, uncomfortable and constricting. He continues to stretch me until he pauses and kisses my lips.

"Baby you got to relax, you're too tight, I don't want to hurt you so let go, think of me sliding inside you, stretching you, making room for me. You're as tight as a virgin, or so I'd imagine." He jokes making me hold my breath as he pushes further into my unyielding body.

"Maybe this isn't a good idea, at least not yet," I try to tell him but he is determined and chuckles at my words.

"It's always worked before," He says and I can hear the laughter in his voice, "hold on, it's just that you're so small…"

Then he grabs a hold of my hips and drives his steel rod straight through my spine, or so it feels like. I let out a shout as he seats himself to the hilt in my protesting body. He is not moving, just hovering over me, then I feel his arm muscles tense and he remains stiff and rigid and then he groans.

"Tell me it's just been a long time for you, and this is not your first time." He says through clenched teeth. "Tell me you're not a virgin… shit, you're a virgin."

He drops his chin on his chest and lets out a long breath and stares down at me with a look of sheer disgust on his face. I had no idea men were disgusted with virgins, granted they are few and far between at my age, but I'm only twenty, not some spinster sitting on the self. I decide then and there I want nothing more to do with Darius Steele.

"If you'll just slowly back out of me, I'm sure they won't count this time against you. Your track record of 'no-virgins' is still intact. Get off me." I snap at him.

"Hold on Cam," he says, "I need a minute to regroup and we'll sort this out. I'm sorry for rushing you but I'd never have guessed you'd never had sex before."

Not only is he disgusted by my lack of sex, he just told me I looked experienced. This evening just went from bad to worse in three seconds.

"Pull out of me or I'll do it for you." I hiss at him, pushing on his chest, tugging his waist.

47

"Stop moving or I'll come," he snaps then says, "too late… oh God…I'm sorry but I got to move."

He starts sliding back and forth inside me, building up speed and strength. I feel every scrape of his penis as it drags across my sensitive tissue. It's like someone is rubbing salt in an open wound and its all I can take. I start crying, pressing against him, trying to dislodge this beast off of me but it only incites his passions and soon he tenses and shoots his semen deep inside me, pumping his life force into my screaming body.

Finally after what seems like an hour but was mere minutes he collapses on top of me. His sweaty body weighs a ton and I feel suffocated by him. A few minutes later he slides out of me, rolls over on his back and covers his arm over his face, trying to make his breathing become normal. All I can think of is escaping but he rolls over on his side, rises up on his elbow and places his large hand on my wet, sticky belly.

"I'm sorry your first time was uneventful," he says smiling down at me, "but I'll make it up to you later, just give me a breather and we'll make the next one work for you, okay?"

He's crazy, certifiable if he thinks I'm letting him climb on top of me again. But he is waiting on me to agree so I nod my head, and he falls backwards onto his side of the huge bed and pats my wet thigh. Soon he is sleeping and I see my chance to escape.

I roll over on my side, pretending to be sleeping, which makes him roll over onto his side as well; thankfully his back is facing me. I ease out of bed, gather my clothes and rush out to the living room. Quickly I dress in what clothes I can find, feeling his essence wet and sticky between my legs, grab my purse and slip out the door. I run to the elevators at the end of the hall and almost get away free and clear when I hear Dare shout my name just as the doors close.

Once I hit the lobby I hail a cab and soon I'm on my way back to my flat. Hopefully my roommate is out, looking at my watch I see it's only after ten. I pay the exorbitant fare and trudges up the steps to my third floor apartment, and as luck would have it, my roommate's boyfriend is here and the door chain is latched preventing me from entering my own flat.

Not wanting to sit on the stoop I walk up to the roof, and sit back on one of the lounge chairs the tenants in the apartment above us left up here. The evening is mild, but there is a chance of rain. Hopefully it will hold out until morning. I huddle in my sweater and must have dozed off because the next thing I know I'm being lifted off the lounger and held in a pair of strong arms.

I'd know Dare's touch, his scent anywhere. I turn to cuddle into his chest when I remember what he did to me and I start to fight him in earnest.

"Let go of me." I hiss at the man, "I want nothing to do with you, let me go dammit."

"Stop it or you'll hurt yourself." He says, "I'll sit on top of you all night if I have to, but you will listen to me, let me apologize for screwing up your first time, then allowing you to end up on the rooftop in a not so secure part of town."

I stop fighting him and just lay against his chest, hoping he can't see how red my face is, how embarrassed I am over his disgust. Tears fill my eyes and soon he is wrapping his arms around me, comforting me, pleading with me not to cry.

"Baby let me make it up to you," he whispers, "I swear it won't be like the last time, I promise."

"You're disgusted at my being a virgin, why would you put yourself through that again." I tell him knowing it must not have been so bad for him if he's willing to go through the process again.

"I was disgusted with myself, not you," he says, "I swear it's all on me, I'm to blame for ruining our first time together, let me make it up to you, please."

His sincere request is making me waiver, but in fairness to him I was enjoying the whole ordeal up until he tried to slide his huge member into my small body. Everyone else likes it, so maybe I should give it another try, it can't be any worse than the first time.

"Okay, but my roommate has locked me out so we'll either have to make love back at your hotel or do it in this lounger." I tell him loving the smile I get.

"My place, no question about it." he says kissing my ear, "We'll go nice and slow I promise, just try to relax, I don't want to hurt you and I know I already did." He says tugging me up off his lap and walking down the stairs and out into the street.

"Let's walk," he says, "it's only a couple miles without all the usual traffic, okay?"

Smiling up at him I tell him, "fine by me, but don't complain if you're too tired to perform, it was your idea."

He laughs out loud and after a couple blocks he sees a cab and hails it down. In no time we're riding up to his room in an empty elevator. I feel myself starting to tense up when the doors open and he ushers me down the hall to his room.

"Relax, just go with the flow," he coaxes, "I swear I won't jump you, at least not yet."

"I'm sorry for making such an ordeal out of this." I tell him and he leans down and kisses me, deeply, thoroughly until I'm leaning into his chest, wrapping my arms around his waist and moaning for more.

"Let's get undressed, again." He jokes and I notice the bed is trashed, like he jumped up on the mattress, ran across it as I ran out on him.

"We're going to pretend while ago didn't happen, but just so you know," he says, "You're my first too. I've never been the first for any woman, so we're even."

I bark out a laugh, "Not by a long shot, I didn't try to cleave you in two."

What I thought was a catchy comeback he is taking literally.

"Are you alright, do you need to wait?" he asks, "I hope I didn't hurt you too bad, but just so you know it's supposed to hurt the first time, or so I've been told. We'll take it easy just to be safe."

I grab a hold of his hand and pull him over to the unmade bed, push him down onto the mattress and straddle his thighs.

"Make me forget my first time, give me the climax everyone is always talking about, make me yours in every way." I tell him and kiss him as deeply as I can.

He stirs and picks me up, twists around so I'm underneath him and he continues to kiss my neck, my jaw, and then lifts my T-shirt to kiss my naked, swelling breasts.

He lathes them, suckles me, twists my nipples until they distended and then he moves lower.

He unbuttons my jeans and slides them down my legs along with my panties. He runs his long fingers through the soft triangle of curls at the apex of my thighs, making me moan in delight. Dare slides his finger between my folds and slips inside my channel, stretching, widening me, trying to ease the pain of our next joining. It hurts for a second or two, but then the strangest thing happens.

My body releases a natural lubricant, keeping the friction off my swollen muscles. The more he works my passage the wetter I become until I feel a tightening in side. He presses my clitoris between his two fingers, pushing and tugging as he continues to suckle my breast. My body is coiling, constricting but not in a painful way, but in anticipation.

He continues to tease and please me until I need more; I actually want to feel him inside of me, moving, creating the good tightness from earlier. I press on his shoulders, and finally he releases my breast.

"What's wrong baby," he asks, "am I hurting you? I'll go slower just relax."

"No Dare I need to feel you inside me, make me yours, now." I tell him and immediately he releases me, jumps out of bed, strips off his clothes and joins me once again.

"Trust me not to hurt you," he whispers and slides the engorged head of his shaft just inside my outer lip. "Take a deep breath and when you feel too full, or you're hurting in any way, let me know, okay?"

"Kiss me," I tell him and when he leans over me, touches his lips to mine I press his lower body into mine, and he lights up like a lightning rod taking a direct hit.

"Yes," he groans and slides all the way inside me, clear to the base of his shaft. "God you feel so good, so tight. Can you stand me moving a little?" he asks so afraid of hurting me.

"Please, move a lot," I tell him and he laughs making his shaft jump inside me. "You're so snug; your body is hugging me so tightly, like a fist."

He starts to move a bit faster, then deeper with each stroke until I start to feel that spiraling sensation again. I lift my bottom off the bed as he lunges towards me, creating a friction neither of us was expecting. I clench my delicate inner muscles and feel him have to work a bit harder. He grabs my hips and starts pummeling me and I feel myself unwind, like a spring in a clock, I snap loose and soar across the sky, shouting his name.

He continues to slam his body into mine until I feel him tense up and soon he too shouts out his release, groaning and pumping his life force inside me for the second time this evening. I can't believe how great I feel, how free and elated, all because I accepted my Dare.

We both are hot and sweaty, panting like dogs, but feeling like a million dollars. He slides out of me and rolls over on his side, scooping me closer to his body.

"Are you alright?" he asks trying to catch his breath. "No pain, no soreness?"

I shake my head and kiss his neck then his jaw, and finally I run my tongue over the crease of his lips, until he opens his mouth and lets me inside. I deepen the kiss and suck on his tongue. When I release him we're both out of breath and if we weren't exhausted we'd be going at it again.

"Pace yourself newbie," he jokes, "I'm five years older than you, that may not seem like a lot but in dog years I'm ancient."

"Are you saying I can't teach this old dog a new trick- If I had a new trick that is." I laugh at him.

"So long as I'm the only dog in your kennel, you can teach me anything you'd like." He tells me, "seriously I don't share, I'm not a player by any means, I want monogamous, exclusive rights, ownership, pink slips…" he goes on, "I have a plan for my future and look forward to including you, if you're interested."

I continue to stare at him unsure what he is saying. He sighs and pulls his pillow out from underneath his head and wallops me across the head, making me laugh at his antics.

"Will you be my girlfriend?" he shouts like he's back in junior high.

"Yes, I'll go steady with you." I tease him making him start to tickle me in retaliation.

Out of breath he lies on top of me and leans down to kiss me softly on the lips.

"I've enjoyed these last ten days like nothing I've ever experienced before. It's too soon to say how we feel right now, but I want you to know, we belong together, now and always."

Smiling up at him I know this is the exact moment I fell in love with him. He is my world, and I'm pretty sure he feels the same way. Our futures are joined as of this moment…

I open my eyes and feel the tears run down my cheeks at the bittersweet dream. Punching my pillow I roll over, grab the remote control and turn off the TV and try to fall back asleep without reliving anymore of the past…at least for this evening.

7

The next morning I wake feeling refreshed and ready to face the day's challenges. Monday's are usually pretty light in my office so I should be able to get caught up on my personal errands. After showering I pull out a pair of faded jeans, an orange and white striped T-shirt, wrap a beige scarf around my neck and slip on my favorite rust colored cardigan, since the morning is a bit cooler, it feels like rain, but you never know. Saturday's weather was perfect, hot during the day but still nice enough in the evening not to need too much of a jacket.

Sunday was more of the same, but today I'm cold, and can't seem to get warm. Looking in the bedroom mirror I appear tired, so I add some mascara to my lashes to make my blue eyes sparkle, slide some lip gloss on my full lips and pinch my high cheekbones for a touch of color. I put on a pair of gray sneakers, grab a traveler mug from the cabinet, and fill it full of the dark French roast I love. I have errands to run, groceries to shop for, as well as making sure my crew starts on the Chamber's luncheon. I pick up my phone, slip it into my bag, take the car keys off the peg and start off on what's going to be a busy day after all.

Stopping by the studio first I unlock the front door, right away I know I'm the first up. Looking at my watch it's already nine thirty, so I go into the kitchen, start a pot of my coffee, no one else prefers the dark blend I crave, but first come first serve. I walk into my office, drop my bag in the side chair and sit back in my black leather chair and enjoy my refill on caffeine. Still disconcerted from my trip down memory lane last night I jump when my cell phone rings. Malcolm Cannon's name flashes on my screen.

"Good morning Roz," I answer the phone, "how's your dad?"

"Cranky, irritable, and as bossy as ever," she replies "He's back to normal."

We laugh at that accurate description of her father. He is in a perpetual bad mood, and insists on sharing his dark thoughts with anyone within shouting distance. But at least he was there for his two daughters, unlike my parents. Shaking my head, clearing my own dark thoughts I only catch the last part of my Office Manager's rant.

"… and like always Dez is gone, traipsing through the back woods of who knows where, searching for the 'just out of reach' shot. If she wasn't such a brilliant photographer I'd make her stay here with Dad and look after him, they're so much alike it's scary. We're supposed to be taking turns but the little snipe took off and I can't reach her."

Man oh man Roz is pissed. She is normally unflappable, but spending a week with her perpetually angry father is taking its toll on her.

"Sweetheart, calm down," I tell her, "take a deep breath and tell me what's wrong."

I hear her sigh into the phone.

"I hate to ask, but I need another week up here," she says, "Pappy is still not as mobile as the doctors would like, and since Desiree is 'unavailable' I'm stuck, do you mind? I'd be happy to work on my laptop from the little café in Silver Shore Lake."

"That's not necessary," I tell her, "take as much time as you need, but I will need you back in time for the Anderson's Fiftieth Anniversary, that's in three weeks, is that enough time? Think of it as an unplanned vacation, but don't worry about us, just take care of yourself in the wilds of Oregon."

"Thanks, but I keep remembering why I left Oregon," she says, "it's so rugged, I see why Mother left, honestly between the rough country, isolation, and my old man it's a wonder she stayed long enough to have us girls."

We both laugh at her observation but I can hear an undertone of the truth. Roz fills me in on this week's jobs, and I was right, we're light for the next seven days so I know we'll be alright.

"I'll take care of contacting our suppliers but when you get to the internet mecca in Silver Shore Lake, please email anything I might need to address during your leave, okay?" I ask her knowing she runs her office as well as her life like a well-oiled machine.

"No problem," she assures me, "how did the Stone Reception go? Did you enjoy your time with Mokie? Did you spend the whole weekend with him?"

I hear something in her voice, I'm not sure what it is but I'd swear it was a hint of jealousy... Man oh man my best friend is in for a world of hurt if Roz and he hook up. That could be great or a potential disaster.

"No, it turns out since he was the featured chef in Bon Appetite his time is too valuable to spend goofing around with old friends. But he was my escort for the reception and we had a good time, and the Stones are making us their exclusive caterers, how about that? Pretty good for a couple of small town girls don't you think?" I joke.

"There's nothing small town about En Bonne, and don't you forget it missy." She laughs, "I got to go, Pappy just walked in and hates for me to use the phone, everywhere you call is long distance, so I'll email you later when I head into town. Love you girl, take care."

We end the call and as I walk into the kitchen for a refill I see BJ standing at the huge commercial fridge, looking for something to eat. He turns around when he sees me and as always I'm stunned at his male perfection. He could be a high paid model or even a movie star with his dark brown hair, clear hazel eyes and marvelous cheekbones not to mention his trim lithe build but he is so shy, almost backwards when he meets strangers, which makes his choice of career a bit harder.

Chefs are notorious for being prima donnas, very temperamental, and this sweet, shy boy is likely to get eaten in this field if he doesn't develop some grit. But I love him dearly and he is one of the best sous chefs I've ever worked with, next to Gina. Hopefully he'll be happy when he completes his courses and will want to stay with us. I love my crew, but I'd never stand in anyone's way of fulfilling their dreams.

"Good morning 'Camy'," he laughs in his soft, silky voice with a hint of a southern drawl in the background, "is that your real nickname?"

"Little man, if you want to make it through breakfast you will refrain from repeating that blasphemous moniker. I hated it all those years ago and I hate it even more at this moment." I raise my eyebrows at him and he looks down at his feet, but is still grinning.

"I was shocked when Mr. Steele called you that," he admits, "but Saul and Kit thought it suited you, but I didn't." He looks up at me through his ridiculously long lashes and says, "you'll always be 'Tough as nails Mossier' to me, just like Roz is '44 magnum Cannon'."

I laugh at his silliness and walk over to the fridge.

"What's left in there for us to fix?" I ask changing the subject. "I'm starving and my refrigerator at home appears to be on a diet. Oh good, some left over ham, cheese, peppers… what would you make with these ingredients, tell me what first pops into your head."

"Quiche," He says then smiles when my eyes light up.

"Good choice lets have brunch. Go call Kit down; it's after ten o'clock, time to join the living." I tell him and he turns to head up the stairs, but stops and turns around to face me.

"Sorry if I was out of line earlier," he says in his heart felt tone, "Are you and Mr. Steele dating? The only reason I ask is he was plenty upset when he found out you spent the night with Mokie Joe. Apparently he didn't know about your relationship with Mokie, but Saul and Kit set him straight."

I stare at my friend, shocked to the core my team has been gossiping about me to a total stranger as far as they're concerned. This is not going to happen again I vow to myself.

"No, Mr. Steele and I are not dating, or even good friends," I tell him, "I'm only going to say this once. Do not talk about me to that man or any man for that matter. I need to trust the people in my employ, and even though I think of you all as friends, I will not tolerate gossip, okay?"

He ducks his head and says, "I'm sorry for my part, it won't happen again."

Running up the stairs I can hear him speaking to his best friend and roommate. Kit's real name is Clint Jacobs. BJ is shy and quiet, Kit is forward and loud, put him and Saul in the same room, and it's a free for all. Kit is my go to guy. The best idea man I've ever met, a jack of all trades, but he can't cook to save his soul. He and BJ were best friends throughout school and have remained so. At first I thought the two were a couple, but they immediately set me straight; they're just soul brothers.

Saul walks in the back door as I start frying up some shallots in butter. He is one big dude. At six feet four, around two hundred and forty pounds, he is tall and powerfully built, but all muscle. His black hair is cropped close to his head and he is always in need of a shave, but when he turns those piercing gray eyes at you, you're either afraid he is concentrating on you or you're wanting him to be concentrating on you...He is my head of security, my main bartender, a sparring partner, and as stubborn and hard headed as a Missouri mule, which is fitting since he is originally from De Soto, Missouri. My staff is all about the same age, mid to late twenties with the exception of Nana, who is in her early sixties with the energy of a teenager.

"Are you working or making breakfast?" Saul asks as he hangs up the box truck keys on the peg by the garage door.

"Hungry?" I ask smiling to myself as he is constantly eating.

"Starving, Mel is spending the day with her Mother, so there was nothing to eat at home," he tells me, snitching a handful of the diced ham I'm getting ready to add to the onions. "You'd think she would know by now how to treat me right... but she just doesn't get it." He grins before continuing his playful rant, "Good things she's hot in bed or I'd be on the prowl, like a certain Mr. Steele was Saturday and Sunday. Care to share?"

I point my wooden spoon at the hulk and snap, "if I ever catch you or any of the rest of my crew gossiping about me I'll fire the lot of you and go to the nearest staffing agency and replace you all. Got it?"

He holds his hands up in front of his chest, warding me off and starts laughing.

"Sensitive situation, huh?" he continues to poke at me, "just give him what he wants and he'll leave you alone... it's not like he asked you to marry him, start a family for God's sake..."

I drop my spoon, and it clatters to floor, splattering grease everywhere.

"God dammit Saul," I yell at him feeling my nerves stretching tighter, "get out of my kitchen," I tell him grabbing some paper towels and mopping up the mess on the terra cotta tiled floor.

"Hey, I was just kidding," he says kneeling down beside me, running his hand up and down my back in a comforting motion, "what's wrong kiddo? You and this guy have a history don't you?"

We both stand up and I turn to look at him and I feel the tears start to well up. Drawing me into his arms he holds me with his powerful embrace, swaying me back and forth until I get myself back under control.

"Sorry, are we interrupting a private clench or can anyone join in?" Kit says as he and BJ walk into the room grinning like the Cheshire cat.

Saul flips the wooden spoon at an unsuspecting Kit, hitting him in the head and that makes us all laugh, breaking the tension. Of course Kit is now getting in the swing of things and starts smacking Saul with the same utensil, making sharp, cracking sounds as the wood hits solid muscle.

I grab another paper towel and dry my eyes, but see my shallots are on the edge of burning. Quickly removing the sauté' pan to the back burner I turn back to my over six foot preschoolers and with hands on my hips I address the trio.

"The next one of you that throws something, smacks someone, or makes a wise crack is on KP duty for two events. And that means no dishwasher, but hand washing," I tell them.

They freeze at my threat. BJ just stands there, grinning from ear to ear trying not to laugh. Saul is still fuming at the red welts Kit left on his arms, and Kit blows me a kiss. This is my crew, my motley crew… I start laughing at them.

"Now if you expect to eat, I expect you to work. Snap to it." I direct them.

Kit and Saul head for the coffee maker, while BJ grates the cheese we are going to need for our cheese pie. As I scoop out the onions and add the ham to the hot skillet Kit starts picking on BJ.

"You little suck up," he jokes as he laughs at the big pile of cheese my sous chef brings over to me. "Don't think she'll exclude you from KP just because you can second guess what she needs before she can tell you."

BJ picks up the wooden spoon again and hands it to Saul who flips it on Kit's head one more time, making Kit yell in pain.

"God dammit Saul that stings," he whines rubbing his forehead, "Now you both are on KP duty, so there!" He throws the wooden spoon in the sink and turns towards me and moves his hand through the air, like he is presenting the two guys for punishment.

"I'm sorry, I didn't see a thing." I tell him and the three of us start laughing at the look on Kit's shocked face.

"Bullshit, you stood right there and watched Saul do it. BJ had to lean over you to reach the spoon for crying out loud…" Kit argues with me his laid-back surfer look in conflict with his snapping blue eyes and pressed lips.

"I guess she likes us better," BJ slowly drawls, "besides you're the one that started the whole argument this morning. She got mad because we were talking to Mr. Steele about her."

"That's no reason to cause a riff between your work staff," Kit reasons, "besides, you looked hot Saturday in that red dress, nobody could blame the man for hanging around Sunday…"

Smiling at Kit's off the wall compliment I decide to end the speculation concerning Dare and myself.

"I knew Darius Steele when I lived in Paris, we became… friends." I stammer on the word friend but keep going. "It didn't work out, end of story. Now the next person I catch gossiping about me is fired. End of story."

I scoop the heated ham out of the skillet and turn the stove off. Turning back to face my staff I see sympathy in their eyes. Great, they're going to turn protective of me, now that they know Dare dumped me. I can't seem to catch a break on this topic.

"Let me also state that as much as I appreciate your loyalty, and want to protect me from the man, it's really not necessary, I promise. We're simply old lovers that met recently and have both moved on. So please drop it." I nod my head at each of them and they nod back accepting my request.

"Now, Kit go help Saul unload the truck since he's already dropped off the rental companies items, so everything on there needs to be washed, sorted, and put away. Hop to it and we'll call you when breakfast is ready." I turn back to the stove and pick up the plate of ham and onions.

Saul walks over to me and whispers in my ear, "I'm sorry for that stupid comment I made earlier. I was just jerking your chain."

"Sweetheart, I know you didn't mean anything by it, but I'm still going to mop up the floor with you tonight. Are we back on Mondays, Wednesdays, and Fridays schedule? I miss beating the crap out of you, and I know Gina does too." I laugh at his affronted expression.

"Mel is back on her regular rotation at the hospital, now that her Mother is back on her feet, well Alice has a walking cast now, but Mel might need me to cover for her a couple nights, I'll let you know." He says and pinches another handful of my ham as he walks away. "And neither of you girls has ever gotten the best of me in the gym."

His mother- in-law broke her leg a couple weeks ago in an automobile accident and his wife, who is a Registered Nurse, took some time off to help her mother get situated. Saul loves the older woman like his own mother and willingly has been helping out whenever he's needed. For all his macho ways he's a marshmallow when it comes to his wife. He adores her, which is how it should be since she is crazy for her Missouri Mule. Nana calls her Saint Melinda of the Willows.

Half an hour later we're sitting in the 'bull session' room, eating quiche, a field green salad, and raspberry sorbet for dessert. My men eat quiche, whether they're real men or not. There is never a speck of food left over when the guys are in the studio. They're discussing what needs to be done concerning Wednesday's schedule when my cell phone rings. I push away from the table and walk over to my purse and look at the screen. I know Dare is going to continue calling me so I answer the call.

"Hello?" I respond.

"Hey Cam, just checking in to see if your office manager received my emails; I sent them last night but haven't heard back from her. What was her name, Rosalind or something? I didn't write it down." I can tell he is in business mode, when he starts rapid firing questions.

Looking over my shoulders I notice the trio has stopped talking and are watching me. I wiggle my index finger at them and then look pointedly down at the dishes on the table, and then look over at the sink. They catch my drift and take their plates and cups to the kitchen, but once their dishes are in the sink, the guys bail on me and race outside to the garage. Smiling at their shenanigans I return my thoughts to Dare.

"…the least you can do is talk to me. I've apologized for my behavior, cut me some slack here." He is saying and I haven't a clue what he was talking about while I was messing with the guys.

"Dare, sorry I didn't catch all that," I tell him, "about your emails, Roz is still in Oregon on a family matter, and will be out of the office for the rest of the week. Please resend them to my email address and I'll look them over and get back with you."

"Great, maybe we can get together, go over your thoughts, and plan the picnic together." He says smiling into the phone, "I recall we had some fantastic picnics when we were together, remember? I especially recall how they always ended. The one we had in the Jardin des Tuileries almost got us arrested… remember how close we came …"

I interrupt his trip down a painful memory lane before he sidetracks me completely.

"Dare, I'm having a busy Monday and I need to go," I lie, "please resend the emails and I'll check our schedule and set up a time to meet, okay?"

He is quiet for a couple of seconds then softly says, "I dreamed about us last night. I miss you Carrie Anne, I want to get together, talk about us, and please baby don't pretend you haven't missed me too."

Deciding to end this conversation my way I tell him, "I missed you when I woke up that morning and you were gone, I missed you when I needed help getting my thoughts in order after I miscarried our baby, but I really missed you the most when I'd lie in our bed, trying to figure out what I did to make you leave me without so much as a phone call once you got stateside."

"That's not fair," he snaps, "I buried my brother. I was a little upset myself, then his girlfriend committed suicide and I couldn't leave because of my …"

Again I cut him off.

"You could have called me!" I shout in the phone, "No word from you spoke volumes, so don't make excuses for not returning my phone calls. I left you more messages than I care to remember. I practically begged you to come back but you remained silent until I received your check, to cover Paris expenses… I believe that was what you had written on the memo line." I pause, trying to get my voice back to normal.

"I need to see you, now," he says, "don't put me off, Cam. Give me directions to your place. I can be there in a couple of hours."

"No, there's no reason to meet," I tell him. "I apologize for yelling at you. I can assure you I don't generally bark at my clientele. I'll expect your emails within the hour. Goodbye Dare." I tell him and hang up the phone.

Resting my arms on the table I drop my head on them and try to get my breathing back to normal but I feel like I've ran a marathon. I need to work off this aggression. I need Saul. I walk outside to the garage but the three guys are nowhere to be found. I walk around to the brick patio and see Nana holding one of her grandbabies. Her daughter is standing beside her with a cloth diaper on her shoulder. The guys are clustered around the infant, amazed and instantly charmed.

"It's good to see you Pam and your little boy," I tell her walking over to join them. "Let me hold him Nana."

She places the two month old baby in my arms and the feelings of loss come crashing down on me, making me hold my breath so I don't shout out my pain. I wanted a baby so bad, no I wanted Dare's baby. It broke my heart when he didn't want either of us. His conversation is flitting around my brain and I hear bits and pieces of what is being said.

"...Mel anywhere near to that little guy, at least not for a couple of years."

"...cry a lot or does he sleep through the night?"

"...I'd love a big family someday, but not anytime soon."

"...looks like a natural holding little Tony."

Smiling down at the little cherub staring up at me I know someday I'll have a family of my own, but until then, holding and coddling other people's kids will have to do.

"Hey Carrie Anne, Roz is on the phone." Kit shouts from the back door, "She's kind of hard to understand, I think she's in the woods or something."

Handing Tony back to his proud grandma I walk back inside and head to my office where my land line receiver is laying on its side. Kit knows nothing about phone etiquette; he could have put her on hold instead of giving her dead air space.

"Roz, what's up?" I ask her.

"Can you hear me? I'm in the middle of Woodlawn's café so I need to make it quick." She says then she starts cutting out on me.

"... emailed me but I can't...Maybe you can call Steele, Inc....."

"Roz, listen, I've already handled that part, so don't worry about responding, okay? Can you hear me?"

"...can't hear but every other word...hope to be back next...take care, love..."

Shaking my head I can't believe there are still places in our civilized world that has no cell phone reception. Sitting at my desk I pull up my emails and see three from Dare. Opening the first one I see a scheduled outline of what will be done at the picnic, the next is a list of dates which would work best for Steele, Inc. and the third email has an attachment, but the text just says, "I remember."

8

I click on the attachment and know instantly I made a mistake. I see a photograph of the two of us, lying in the grass, our heads together and we're smiling into the camera he is holding at arm's length. We were so young, so happy and carefree... at least I was.

I close the attachment but can't bring myself to delete the picture, since I have very few keepsakes of my time in Paris, this one I'll save, maybe crop him out of the picture. I answer his emails letting him know our free dates; I send him several PDF files with possible menu plans and ask for a headcount.

I start to ignore the third email but know I can't do that. I pick up the phone and call his direct line he listed in the footer of his email. He answers on the second ring.

"Thanks for calling me back." He says, "I got your files and will have my assistant go through them and we should have a head count and a menu selected by the end of this week, is that soon enough?"

"That's fine, but we need to know a date as soon as possible." I tell him, "I can't hold open any particular weekend for too long, especially with the holiday season's coming on. People that plan early get what they want."

"True, did you get the photograph?" he asks waiting on me to answer.

"Yes, I did," I reply, "we were so young. My time in France seems like a lifetime ago."

"It was the best time of my life." He says, "I wish you'd meet me, talk things through. I hate that you're still upset with my leaving, but I explained it all in the letter I left you. You act like I just deserted you but that's not true," he says with a bit of edge on his voice, "I had no choice in the matter, my family needed me and I had to go."

Not wanting to hash this out over the phone I decide to set up an initial appointment with his assistant and get him on the books.

"Can I get the contact information of your assistant? Maybe she and I can speed things up deciding on a date, then once you're on the books Roz and your office will finalize your choices and the En Bonnes can get down to business." I tell him hoping he takes the change of subject.

"Sure, I'll email you her info but I still want to get together with you, on a personal level." He says making my heart beat erratically at the notion of getting on a personal level with him again.

I clear my throat and say, "No, it's best if we just leave well enough alone. You did what you felt you had to do, and I've moved on as well. Let's keep this as a purely business relationship and that way no one gets hurt."

"I never meant to hurt you dammit," he snaps, "why you don't believe me. Oh forget it, you're right, business only is for the best. I'll expect to hear from Roz in a week's time. Take care." And he ends the phone conversation.

I want to cry again, which is silly since I'm the one that wanted nothing to do with seeing him. My hormones are running amuck. There must be some chocolate somewhere in the pantry. I decide to go look when I run into Gina walking in from the garage wearing skin tight jeans and a red cropped t-shirt that does wonders for her body. She is a bombshell with a wickedly sharp tongue and I'd be lost without her.

"Hey girlfriend, what's wrong?" she asks, "What did Kit do now?"

Laughing at her assumption I hug her around her slender waist and walk to the pantry with her. She shares my views that chocolate cures all ills so we pull out several rich Swiss chocolate bars and peeling the wrappers back we toast our bars like champagne glasses.

Walking into the living room she joins me on the white slip covered sofa. We prop our feet on the antique blanket chest we use as a coffee table and savor our fix. Saul walks into the room and sits down in one of the accent chairs then leans forward and snatches my candy bar out of my hand.

"Saul you big beast that's mine," I yell at him but he has already broke the bar in half and tosses it back at me. "You suck," I tell him and look over at Gina who gives me a warning look before she covers her bar with her hands, protecting it from me and Saul.

"There's more in the pantry," I tell him, "you owe me half a candy bar."

"Think of it this way," he says around a mouthful of my treat, "it's just fewer calories you have to work off later."

I grab one of the throw pillows and send it flying at him, but he catches it before it hits its mark. We sit around brainstorming for the Steele picnic for the next hour and a half. BJ and Kit took the shopping list to the warehouse store and should be back in a couple of hours. Thankfully BJ offered to get my personal groceries too so now I won't have a skinny fridge.

"What kind of picnic are they having?" Saul asks, "Is it a large corporation? Who is Steele, Inc. and what do they do?"

Good questions I think to myself. I decide to find out so we adjourn to the bull session room, pull out our tablets and we all do some research on the company. Gina is the first to find anything.

"They're speculators, or developers whichever one is politically correct these days. They buy property, piece it out, and resell it for a small fortune. Steele Inc. is a solid Fortune 500 company, recently going head to head with several European Brokerage houses and coming out on top. Says the company is still family owned, and there are several photos of the three generations of Stones. Take a look," she says, turning her electronic tablet around to show us.

I'm not grasping the obvious here. I see an older man, dressed in a beautifully cut Italian suit, his salt and pepper hair brushed back revealing a high forehead. His eyes are sparkling, like Dare's always did when he was happy. Standing beside him is Dare, dressed in an almost identical suit, but his hair is shorter, darker, and his eyes aren't twinkling. The smile on his face looks a bit sardonic but his hand is resting on the shoulder of a little boy who is the spitting image of Dare.

The child's hair is lighter, but his eyes are just like Dare's. The caption under the photograph reads, 'Three generations of Stones gathering no moss'.

Dare has a child? The boy looks like he's about five or six? But how can that be? Again it takes me a while to decipher what I'm seeing but when I do; I feel the top of my head explode.

"Hon, are you alright? You look a bit pale," Saul asks, "Gina get her a glass of water, quickly and a couple of painkillers, she's got a migraine coming on."

No sooner than he said it, I see white spots before my eyes, my nerves are jumping, and I feel nauseous. He is holding my hand, rubbing my shoulders and whispering to me.

"Hold on Babe, take your pills and I'll help you upstairs where you can lie down for a while. Don't collapse, not yet."

Gina returns with bottled water and two tablets. I gulp them down then turn to look over at my two friends. They're both worried but not sure what to do about it.

"I'm okay." I tell them, and take steadying breaths, trying to shift the pain in my heart to the pain in my head. If only those two pills could deaden the pain inside my chest…

"I'm going to go lie down, like you suggested, wake me in an hour okay?" I ask Saul.

Gina says, "I've got to make a run to the bank for Roz but I can come back by if you need me to."

Saul shakes his head, "I'll run her home if she isn't feeling any better, go ahead and make the deposit while the bank is still open. I don't trust the after hour deposit."

Smiling at my lead man I have to agree with him. I like seeing the people who are handling my money, see them face to face, eye to eye. That way you can judge their character… well not everyone can be read that clearly. I close my eyes and see the little boy with his grandfather and father, looking as proud as a peacock… Man oh man how could I have been that stupid?

Saul walks me upstairs, each step creaking as we put our combined weight on the riser and we turn to the first guest room, facing away from the street. The bedroom across the hall is the one BJ uses, and that is where I put the wrought iron bed Dare and I bought at a local flea market and I had it shipped back to the states, why I'll never know. But I can't look at the bed and not think of the fun times Dare and I shared, lying side by side, talking about our future…

Closing the door behind him Saul walks back downstairs. I can hear his heavy tread on the wooden steps. When I can longer hear his footsteps I let go of the tears I've been holding back. My head is splitting, along with my heart. How could he have a child, five years old when he was with me, setting the plans for our future in motion?

Once he found out I was pregnant, he became withdrawn. I thought at first he was just afraid of becoming a father, taking on the responsibility of someone else's welfare. But according to the news article, he is proud of carrying on the tradition of sons taking after their fathers. A Legacy he called it. I hate him with all my heart. He chose another woman to bear his son. It wasn't fatherhood that scared him; it was being tied down to me that set him off. I close my eyes and relive the exact moment when my world started to crumble.

9

I had been fighting the flu for over a week, had even gone to the doctor for a shot to try to end my misery sooner, but in the end, it took me a full three weeks to get back to normal. Dare and I had just moved in to our small apartment, completely furnished except for the bed. We spent an entire weekend traipsing around the countryside looking for that perfect find, and once we located it, we ended up paying twice what the merchant was asking for it, but the old man agreed to deliver it to us.

We spent hours lying together, making love, joking, whispering, but mostly sleeping. I was deep into my courses and would arrive at school at nine in the morning and wouldn't get home until ten or eleven o'clock at night. Dare was always waiting for me after class, driving me back to our place where he'd have either toast or croissants waiting on me, then we'd shower, make love, and fall asleep.

After my sickness, I jumped back into my schedule with gusto, finally seeing the end of the session in sight. I had two weeks to go when I woke up one morning and felt nauseous. I barely made it to the small bathroom before vomiting into the toilette. Dare leaned down and helped me back on my feet, handed me my toothbrush and a glass of water then sent me back to bed. I slept that whole day and by the evening was feeling fit as a fiddle as my Grandma Kate used to say.

But the next day I went through the exact same thing, throwing up, and then fighting the nausea for the next couple of hours. Luckily Dare had already left for his meeting and wasn't there to see me sick again. I made it to class with minutes to spare, but instead of the three hour lunch I normally endure I went to a pharmacy and bought a pregnancy test. Something told me I didn't have the flu again.

I hid the box from Dare and when he left for his meeting the next morning, I climbed out of bed, used the test and sure enough, I was pregnant. Once again I got to class on time, and made it through the long day and started to get excited about telling Dare we were going to be parents.

He picked me up at the usual time but instead of heading back to our place, he took us to a small tavern, ordered a couple glasses of wine and looked like he wanted to say something. I kept smiling at him, waiting on him to speak so I could share my news with him.

"What's wrong with you? You seem so nervous." He laughed and squeezed my hands, "Will you please sit still so I can tell you my news."

I licked my suddenly dry lips, took a sip of my wine and tried to do as he asked but he was fidgeting and taking his sweet time in telling me his news and I couldn't hold it back.

"I'm pregnant." I told him and clasped my hands together, then held then over my mouth, hating that I blurted out the news, but so happy he knew.

He sat there staring at me, the smile he was wearing earlier gone, and as a matter of fact he was no longer showing any emotion. He had a sort of 'shell-shocked' expression on his face, so I decided he was scared, or anxious. I took his hands in both of mine and squeezed them.

"We're going to be parents." I told him laughing at the joy in my heart. "Say something, sweetheart; tell me what you're thinking."

He looked down at our joined hands and said, "This is going to fuck up everything."

I felt like he just punched me in the stomach. Then it was my time to sit and stare at him.

"Sorry, that didn't come out the way I meant." He said pulling his hands from mine and leaning back in his chair. "Are you certain? Did you go to a doctor or do a home pregnancy test? How far along are you? When did you find out?"

I felt my heart being crushed by his callousness. I took my glass of wine, upended it and walked away from the table. He joined me at the car and together we drove back to our apartment in silence. I stripped out of my clothes, slid into bed and tried to find some peace, but only dozed off. That was the first time in almost three months we didn't sleep together.

I woke the next day, got ready for school and as I was walking out the door I saw the note on the table. Unfolding the single piece of paper I read his short note.

We need to talk. D.

I folded the paper in half and put it in my back pack, then headed out the door. At least my courses were almost through and I was at the top of my class. I muddled through the day and half expected him to not be out there waiting for me, but he was so we drove back to our place once again, neither speaking.

Once we were inside he took my hand and pulled me into our small seating area. Leaning back on the loveseat I waited for him to speak, no longer feeling the need to speed him along I let him ramble on about his plans for our future, how a baby was going to change all that. He was worried about our careers, and what a drain a child would be on our resources. I heard the fear in his voice, and wished I could take it away, but I still loved the idea of having a child, someone I could love and would love me back unconditionally.

He gathered me in his arms and held me tightly, kissing the top of my head. Maybe he'd work his way through his fears, rework his 'plan' and come to grips with it. I decided to trust in his character, knowing in my heart he'd step up to the plate. Our relationship changed that night, good or bad, we were different people, and we were someone's parents. Looking back now I should have known it was too good to be true.

The next day was Saturday, so I didn't have school, he didn't have to work and we planned to spend the day together in our favorite park, near the Louvre. I packed a picnic, a bottle of wine, and a blanket in my straw tote. He said he had an errand to run and wanted to meet me at our favorite spot over by the huge, black oak tree we'd lie under, read out loud, sip wine, and just while away the hours.

As I was boarding the Metro I noticed a couple of young men get on the bus behind me. I settled in my seat and watched as the bustling city went about its business.

When the bus pulled over at my stop I grabbed my bag and started down the steps when one of the guys I noticed earlier punched me in the stomach, pushed me down hard onto the pavement, grabbed my tote, and took off running. I felt a sharp cramping in my abdomen and immediately felt the blood trickle down my legs.

Keeping my knees together, hoping and praying I wasn't losing my baby I felt people's hands on me, trying to help me stand up but all I could do was lie on the pavement in the fetal position, crying out for Dare, for my baby, for God to let me keep my child. A wave of dizziness washed over me and then all went dark.

When I woke up I was lying in a hospital bed, an IV hooked to my arm and a deep searing pain in my heart. I knew I lost the baby. There was no one in the room with me, Dare wasn't around, I had no close friends to call, and my fellow classmates sort of left me alone when I stopped hanging out with them in my free time. I was completely alone and afraid. I wished Mokie Joe was with me.

The next time I woke up Dare was sitting in a chair, flipping impatiently through an old magazine left behind by the staff. He kept looking at his watch, then at the door, and his leg was doing that irritating jog thing he'd do when he became anxious.

"Is there someplace else you need to be?" I whispered, barely able to keep the anger at bay.

"Thank God you're alright." He said leaning over to kiss my forehead. "The nurse said to let her know when you came around, I'll be right back."

When he returned he had an older nurse beside him. She was one of the Catholic Nuns that run the hospital and immediately started fussing with straightening my bed sheet.

"Well now, thank the good Lord you're back with us." She said in an American Accent. "How are you feeling dear?"

I looked around at Dare who was once again pacing the floor.

"Better than him," I whispered making her laugh out loud.

"Don't mind him, he's been on the pay phone over an hour," she said and leaned down, "no cell phones in the hospital."

"Will I be able to go home soon?" I asked wondering why I hurt so badly. I asked the nurse what was done to me and she gently pushed Dare out of the room.

"Well hon, they did a D&C, cleaned you up - inside and out. You had some nasty scrapes on your knees as well as you elbows, a bump on your forehead. You'll be stiff and sore for several days, but you're young, healthy; you and your husband will have more children, God willing."

I started to tell her he wasn't my husband, but decided to let it slide. At least I could say we were married for a brief time, at least on my admittance form. She motioned for Dare to come back inside and then said, "I'll get the Doctor to sign your release forms, you've paid the bill, now all that's left to do is take your bride home, and give her some TLC. Your clothes are hanging in the closet, a little dirty but still serviceable, come out when you're dressed and we'll get you dismissed." She said and closed the door behind her.

"Do you need help getting dressed?" he asked reaching inside the small cupboard for my clothes and once again checked his watch.

"No just give me a minute and I'll be ready to go." I said hating him at that particular moment for being so insensitive.

Once I was dressed I opened the door before he had a chance to, walked over to the nurses' station, signed my name on the release form and walked out the front door as quickly as I could, even though the movement was killing me. I opened the car door, climbed in holding a small bag of bandages, pain relievers, and my jewelry.

The muggers took my bag, but thankfully my wallet was at home along with my keys and passport. Parking on the street out front of our place Dare quickly got out of the car, ran around the hood and assisted me out. He held onto my arm as we walked up the front steps. As I reached the landing of the first floor he scooped me up in his arms and carried me the rest of the way. He was so impatient that he already has his door key in his hand. Setting me on my feet he opened the door and ushered me inside. He hadn't said one word to me since we left the hospital, and I'd reached my limit.

"What is the matter with you?" I demanded, "Are you late for a meeting, am I keeping you from something or someone?"

He looked down at his shoes but not before he looked at his watch. He was meeting someone. What little bit of love I still felt for the man just died.

"Just leave," I snapped at him, "I'm fine, apparently you want to be somewhere else, anywhere else but here, with me. So take off."

He held out his hands to me and I saw such indecision in his eyes. He wasn't talking to me, so I had no idea what was going on in that mind of his. I pulled out the pain medicine they gave me, slowly walked over to the sink and filled a glass of water, tossed back the pills and rinsed the glass out and left it in the sink.

Turning to face him I knew we we're through. He was going to leave me and from the look of things, with in the next few minutes. He took out his cell phone and checked his messages.

"I have to go back to the states," he said, "My father needs me, something has happened, and my father needs me, there's been a family emergency..." I swore for a second I saw tears in his clear blue eyes but knew I was mistaken when he turned to look at me; Steel as cold and strong as his name gazed back at me, no light, no spark, just a blank stare.

I wanted to shout 'and I don't need you?' But I nodded my head and turned to leave the room. He followed me inside our bedroom, picked up his suitcase and walked over to where I was standing.

"I don't know how long I'll be gone, but I'll handle everything, you don't have to pay the rent, I'll take care of it. Try to get some rest and good luck with your final presentations." He said, and kissed me on the forehead. "I know you'll ace them. I'll call you when things settle down."

"Have a safe trip." I told him and turned around so he didn't see the tears start to fall.

I could hear the door close behind him and I knew he wouldn't be back...

10

I slept for almost two hours and feel great until I recall what brought on that migraine - Dare and his son. I slide off the bed, head to the bathroom and in a couple of minutes' walk downstairs. No one is around so I pick up the tablet I was working on, type in a search engine and in no time I'm staring at Dare, his father and his son. I can't seem to look away from the photo. He doesn't appear to be resentful, being a father, so who is the mother? I know it's not Rhonda Starr, super model wanna be. Who was he seeing behind my back? Hell he could have been married the whole time he was with me, like a fool I trusted him, but I don't recall asking him point blank if he was married...

BJ walks into the room smiling then looks over his shoulder and there's Mokie Joe. I feel my heart swell at his coming and know my staff called him. I scoot my chair out from under the table and fly into his arms. The tears start to flow and he simply holds me like only he does.

Once we're alone he walks over to the sofa where he pushes me down and once again wraps me tightly in his arms as he sits next to me. It dawns on me he hasn't spoken a word, neither of us has. When I'm cried out I lift my head and he kisses me on the lips, softly, fully, but once again, with no passion.

"Better?" he asks, resting his cheek on the top of my head.

I nod and feel his smile, "I wish they hadn't called you but I'm so glad you're here."

"I'll always come running, you're my family you goober." He says making me laugh at his silly name calling. "Tell me what set you off or is it the photo on the tablet over there?" he asks, "you have got to either work that man out of your system or talk to him, because you're driving yourself mad with holding everything inside."

I know he is telling me what I need to hear, but I just can't face Dare, especially now that I know he has a family of his own.

"How long can you stay?" I ask slipping out of his arms and pulling him to his feet.

"A couple of hours," he says, "I'm on my way down to LA to appear on some morning show. Come with me, we'll take a few days and play hooky."

Laughing at his expression I shake my head and say, "I can't, someone has to run the place, Roz is in Oregon still, and won't be back until next week, hopefully."

"Is her Father alright? Did something else happen?" he asks with such concern.

I remember how bitchy Roz sounded when she asked if I spent the weekend with Mokie, and now he is showing a bit more concern than I'd have expected. Are they seeing each other behind my back? They do throw sparks off each other when they're in the same room...

"Well, I think her main problem is her cranky old man and her no show sister." I tell him, smiling when he nods his head in understanding.

"What can we do for the next couple of hour?" He asks, "Shall we go see a movie, talk about Steele and your feelings, or maybe pound a little flesh over at your place?"

I always enjoy sparring with Mokie, he is quiet, lethal, and never pulls his punches. Saul always has to be careful with me and Gina, but Mokie knows how to land a punch. Maybe I should invite Gina, make it a threesome. I laugh at how that sounds.

"With the options you listed, I choose the beating." I tell him and he cracks up laughing. "I just hope I don't knock out one of your pearly whites, or black an eye, no wait a split upper lip. That would give you a sexy snarl..."

"You will pay dearly for all those insults. Let's head out." He says picking up my tablet, deleting the photograph and putting it back in the built in slots that were designed to organize our equipment.

Three hours later I'm waving goodbye to the best stress reducer known to man, well the second best stress reducer and the only one at my disposal. I tried to get in my licks, mess up his pretty boy looks but his reach is so much longer than mine. Thankfully my head gear is top of the line or I'd be sporting the split lip, black eye, or missing tooth.

As I crawl in my bed later in the evening I decide Mokie is right, I need to confront my demons, namely Dare and get past that part of my life. Reaching over for my cell I punch in his number.

"Carrie Anne? Are you alright?" Dare says in way of greeting. "Why are you calling so late?" I can hear people talking in the background as if I caught him at a party.

"I wanted to see about meeting up with you, maybe have that coffee and talk about old times," I tell him hoping he doesn't hear the pain in my voice.

"Um, now is not a good time, but let me check my calendar and get back with you, okay?" he asks and I hear a woman's voice in the background telling him to hang up the phone.

"Don't bother, once a cock hound, always a cock hound." I hiss in the phone, "Tell Rhonda I said she's welcome to you." And I hang up the phone.

It rings immediately and I know it's a pissed off Dare calling me back. I switch the ringer off and toss the phone across the carpeted floor, punching my pillow I flip on the TV and soon I drift off to sleep while a sitcom marathon plays in the background dreaming of using Steele as my sparring partner.

11

Wednesday morning my crew and I are putting the finishing touches on the Chamber of Commerce's luncheon. We're serving a seafood menu of Cioppino with fluffy rice, spinach salad with croutons, crusty French bread and a lemon sorbet with our famous shortbread cookies.

Nana has already made the cookies, and is stacking them in the portable containers. BJ and Gina have all the ingredients for the seafood soup ready to go, but since it only takes about a half hour to prepare, we'll cook it in the small kitchen in the Chambers' basement, like we do every year. The salad is ready to dress and the bread and croutons are done and sealed up as well. The lemon sorbet was made yesterday so it's good and set. All we have to do is load up the van with the food, linens, dishes, and my coffee urn. I always use my own equipment when possible, that way I know it works and will taste perfect. The studio kitchen is cleaned up, and all that's left to do is get into our chef whites and head on over to the site, but we've got about an hour to kill, so we're sitting around the bull session table playing a card game of spades when the front door bell rings.

Saul looks up and smiles, taking his cards with him so we can't peak at his hand. He returns with a strange look on his face. Walking over to my chair he bends down and says, "Steele is at the door, do you want me to send him packing? I left him on the step."

I kiss his jaw and say, "Thanks but I need to put 'an amen' to his sermon."

They all laugh at my joke, as I intended but they also know how deeply this man hurt me. I feel their strength circle around me and know I can handle this on my own. Walking to the front door I hold it open for my old lover. He looks so good, for the two timing lying trouser snake that is. His gray Dockers and rust colored crewneck t-shirt make his blue eyes pop, the blue plaid shirt he is wearing open reminds me of the times I would put on his shirt after we made love. He puts his sunglasses on top of his head, and I notice a handmade yarn bracelet on his wrist; A gift from his son no doubt.

"Sorry about Saul, he tends to get protective of his employer. Come on in we can use my office, straight through this short hall, I'll just be a moment." I tell him and walk back to the bull room.

My workers stop whispering when I walk through the door, in total synchronization they turn towards me and wait for me to speak.

"Load up the truck in half an hour if I'm not through." I start to turn but stop and say, "Oh, if you hear an ambulance, it's not for me, so don't be late for the luncheon." I wink at them and they start cracking up.

I walk back down the hall and take a deep cleansing breath before I open the door to my office only to be grabbed around my shoulders, pushed up against the closed door and kissed, roughly and quite thoroughly. It takes me a second to respond then a full minute to pull out of his arms.

My heart is racing, my loins are throbbing, and my conscience is screaming at me, he's married, he has a son, and he left you alone in a foreign country! Shaking my head I hold out my arms towards him, knowing if he wanted to he could force me back in his arms.

Because I was cooking earlier, I'm still wearing my soiled black Chef Coat and black striped pants. I hate clogs and wear white or black cross trainers but from the look on his face I wouldn't be able to outrun him no matter what shoes were on my feet. My hair is falling out of the messy bun it was in and I now have that man's taste in my mouth. God I want to jump him right here, right now, but that's not an option.

"Dare, keep your distance please," I tell him, walking around my monstrosity of a desk.

It is an ancient piece of solid oak, with a horrible paint job of probably thirty coats of high gloss black enamel; there are six drawers on each side of the double desk. Its eight feet long, four feet wide and I'd swear it weighs over five hundred pounds. Keeping the piece of furniture between us as a defense move is a sound idea.

"Why, I'm a cock hound, right? This is what you expect of me, right? I'm giving you what you want, so why not take me up on it?" he says moving closer and closer towards me.

"I want nothing from you, not anymore." I tell him straightening my spine, "You've lost your trustworthiness when you ditched me in Paris; then came home and started your own family."

He stops in his tracks and stares at me, reacting as if I'd slapped him.

"What did you say?" he whispers and I can feel the anger radiating off his body.

"You heard me," I tell him, "I was shocked when you didn't return any of my calls, but now I understand, you got back to the states, met someone and started your own family. Your choice, but what I can't understand is why hit on me now, after your 'plan' has come to fruition. And what the hell are you doing with Rhonda Starr; she's always in the tabloids, according to Nana."

I pull out my desk chair and sit down. He continues to stare at me like I'm speaking gibberish, but he knows he's busted.

"Where's your wife? Does she know about your extracurricular activities? Or does she not care, now that she's completed your stupid plan?" I tell him and even I hear the bitchiness in my tone, but now that I've let go I can't seem to shut up.

"Is she the reason you left me? Or were you married the whole time we were together?" I demand, crossing my arms under my breasts.

That one puts him on the move. He prowls over to where I'm sitting, pulls the chair out from beneath the desk, braces his arms on the armrests of the chair and leans into me until we're eye to eye.

"You will be eating those words; I'll probably have to perform the Heimlich maneuver on you. Get up, we're going for a drive," he says tugging on my arms, practically propelling me out of the seat.

I break free of his grasp and stand my ground.

"Wrong, I'm going to the C of C Luncheon I've prepared, and you're going to head back to your world, and play house some more. But just so you know, I never stopped dreaming you'd come back for me, never stopped loving you or hoping you'd come to your senses until Monday, when I discovered you had a son, how old is he five maybe six years old? He looks just like you, and your old man too. Nice article. Now get out of my sight and don't ever contact me directly again."

I open the office door and step aside to let him pass; Man oh man does he smell good… He stops in front of me, takes his glasses off his head and slips them back on his face.

"We're not through until I say we're through," he whispers in a seething voice and I see the fear in my own eyes reflected in his dark lens, "your company is handling our picnic, a contract is a contract…" he grins thinking he has one over me.

"En Bonnes Catering is incorporated; one of my employees will handle your requests, not me. I have better things to do nowadays. Go home to your family, the one you made after me." I hiss at him and before he can retaliate like he wants to Saul and Kit walk around the corner and just stand there waiting on him to leave.

"I'll be in touch," he says softly, "and baby will I ever punish you for everything you said back there, count on it."

I shake my head at him but refrain from any more comments since my self-appointed bodyguards are within ear shot.

"Let me show you out," Kit says while Saul silently asks if I'm alright.

"Good to go," I tell him, "let's go get changed and head over to the Chambers."

A couple minutes later we're loaded in the van and heading down Main Street when I look out the front passenger side window and see a black Land Rover pull out of the local gas station and head in the opposite direction. Good, maybe now I can get on with what's important, of course a part of me really did hope he'd come back for me even up until Monday. What a silly dreamer I've been.

12

The luncheon was a success, but with that fun menu it's hard to do anything wrong. Willow is one of those small, tight communities that love tradition more than progress. Mayor Olney always goes on and on when thanking us and today was no different. She advised me to pencil the luncheon for next year, as well as the City Councils Christmas brunch to be served at her house the week before the holiday. I happen to know Roz already has those dates on the books, thanks to her hairdresser's brother who works on the Town board.

After we clean up the small kitchen and put away their three long folding tables and thirty six chairs, we're tired, but in a good way. I love doing small functions, you really get the feeling the guests enjoyed themselves. I even gave them the extra cookies, but everything else was consumed by the hungry crowd. That is one great feeling. The Chamber's office is located on the corner of Main Street next door to the hardware store. The downtown merchants make up the members of the C of C and they're waving at us as I turn the truck on to the wide empty street and head two blocks over to the studio on Arjem Street.

The crew and I unload the pots and pans, dirty dishes, and linens. Since it's only three o'clock we make short work of the cleanup and by five o'clock I'm walking into the back door of my home through the garage. Stopping in the laundry room I shed my Chef whites and kick off my shoes and socks, I leave my clothes on top of the washer to add to my other dirty laundry. Right now I want a glass of wine, a hot soak in my tub, and the soothing sounds of Michael Buble.

I walk into the kitchen and smile at the homey space all around me. My house is my safe haven. It needed some work done but I didn't want to destroy the comforting atmosphere of the place. I kept the original floor plan and only upgraded the equipment and countertops. The care worn white porcelain sink with built in back splash is now resting on top of new Carrera marble counter top with the base cabinetry painted a dove gray. The appliances are commercial grade and cost more than the house did when it was built. All the flooring throughout the house is wide plank yellow poplar so the orange and yellow flowers, hand towels and fruit bowl adds to the coziness of the room. Giving Grandma Kate's glass fronted hutch a loving stroke I take down one of my stemware and set it on the farmhouse table sitting in the center of the room with six old press back oak chairs nestled underneath.

Pulling a bottle of White Orchid Merlot from my wine rack in the pantry, I fill the balloon glass and take the bottle along with me. Since I'm out in the middle of nowhere I feel comfortable walking through my house in my bra and panties, and head through the living room where I set the stereo to play three of my favorite singer's CDs. Kit wired my house for sound, and when I get so angry at his childish behavior, I remind myself of his other gifts. A house full of soft easy listening music is worth putting up with the handsome devil and his irritating quirks.

The rest of the house is untouched and has only one drawback. There are two staircases leading to the second floor and they're not connected. The one in the corner of the kitchen with red painted steps leads to the guest room and my secret dojo I created in the side attic. The other enclosed stairs is in the living room and leads directly to the master bedroom and those steps are painted a bluish gray. Walking across the small landing in front of my bedroom I enter the bath and light my favorite lemongrass verbena candle letting the soft, fresh scent waft over me and my over loaded brain. The walls are a soothing pale green with white woodwork and I always feel relaxed when I enter the space.

The bathroom has a narrow walk-in shower behind the door I tiled myself but for now, I need a good long soak. Setting my wineglass on the open window sill and the bottle on the white shelf beside the tub, I turn on the old porcelain knobs and thank God the plumbing was upgraded. I decide to treat myself to a bubble bath at the last minute. I clip my thick blonde hair on top of my head; roll up one of my russet colored bath towels for my pillow. Removing my undergarments I place them in the hamper, then gingerly step into the old ball and claw cast iron tub and sink into a frothy oblivion. Reaching for my glass I take a sip and softly moan in delight as the smooth liquid slides down the back of my throat. This is what every woman deserves after working eight and ten hour shifts.

As the 2nd CD starts playing, I enjoy the soft breeze blowing through the window, and refill my glass. The leaves from the mature maple tree that shades my back patio rustle in the background of the dozen wind chimes I hung in the lower branches. Jonathan and I have great memories of that massive tree as we used it as a free zone when playing tag, a ladder to climb out of the house as well as a courage barometer to see how high we could dare each other to climb, when Grandma Kate wasn't watching of course. Closing my eyes I feel my troubles slide away until I hear a bump on the stairs. Mouser must have gotten inside through the open bedroom window, or maybe he slipped in to the garage as I pulled in. Either way he will not leave me alone until I end up putting him outside. But until he starts making a nuisance out of himself, he can wait. I take another sip before opening my eyes and nearly drop the entire glass when I see Darius Steele standing in the middle of my bathroom, watching me.

"What the hell are you doing in here? Get out!" I scream looking down to see if there's still enough bubbles to hide my nakedness from him but he shakes his head and lowers the lid on the commode, leans over and takes the glass from my hand and sits down like he was invited to tea.

"I'll wait until you're finished," he says taking a sip from my glass, "Unless you're inviting me to join you, which being a cock hound, I'm game."

He's making fun of me, but what the hell is he doing here? How did he get inside my house? What does he think he's going to accomplish, breaking and entering?

"You have until the count of three to get out of here, and leave my house before I call the cops." I warn him, "One, two…"

"Did you want to borrow my phone to make that call? I doubt if you brought yours with you." He says, pulling his cell phone from his back pocket and handing it over to me but not before he looks over the edge of the tub and grins. I reach for the phone and start to dial Saul's number but Dare snatches it back, and laughs at me again causing those brackets to appear on either side of his mouth. I always loved drawing my fingers down the narrow creases when he'd smile like that…I shake my head to clear those kind of thoughts.

"I should have known you'd call my bluff." He says reaching for the wine bottle and refilling his glass. "This is an excellent wine, where can I get a case?"

I snatch the bottle from his hands and tip it to my lips and take a good pull.

"I have several cases in my studio; I'll give them all to you if you'll get out of my bath." I offer before lowering my shoulders under the rapidly dissipating foam.

"Why so shy, I've seen you naked countless times, even got you naked a time or two if you'll recall. Finish your bath and then we'll talk about why I'm here." He says.

"Fine, I'm finished," I tell him reaching for the cinnamon colored bath sheet and wrapping it around my torso, the suds start shifting and sloshing over the sides of the tub. I usually rinse off in the shower stall behind the door, but no way am I standing naked in front of this fiend, so I stomp into my bedroom, slam the door and lock it, then grab a pair of jeans, a blue and gray baseball shirt and a pair of white converse court shoes and dress as quickly as possible. I stomp back into the bath only to find Dare naked in my bath water, sipping my wine and enjoying himself immensely, even using my loofa sponge on a stick to wash his back.

"Have you gone mad? Get the hell out of here, Dare." I shout at the infuriating man who winks at me before continuing scrubbing his muscular back. "What do you want? An apology, you got it. I'm sorry for having met you, for sleeping with you, for getting pregnant and ruining your stupid plan…" I shout until I feel the tears start to burn in the back of my throat. Before I can escape the room he leans out of the tub, hauls me over the side and sets me back down into the still warm bathwater, fully clothed and totally pissed off.

I start to fight him when he drapes his long legs over my thighs, scissoring me between his loins, then he wraps his arm around mine preventing me from striking him. All that's left is for me to head butt him but he captures my jaw in one of his hands, bends my head backward and kisses me with such fervor I can't catch my breath, and when he softens his kiss I'm lost. He coaxes soft moans and whimpers from my throat and soon I'm kissing him back, reaching my freed hands around his neck, trying to meld my mouth to his.

He breaks free and says, "Just like old times Cam. I need to be inside you, now."

His words have the effect of a cold shower on my libido. I twist free and sling my legs over the edge of the tub and shove off the side, making a hell of a mess on my bathroom floor. I pull my wet shirt over my head and pull off my wet jeans and shoes, throw them at the demon who is laughing at me.

"Come on Cam," he taunts me, "You were enjoying me a few minutes ago; nothing's changed, well, just your mood…"

I hear him laughing his fool head off while I grab another pair of jeans, T-shirt and a pair of sandals. I race down the stairs, grab my purse and car keys and hit the automatic garage door opener, but nothing happens, the door isn't moving. Whatever is wrong with the panel, I know it's Dare's handiwork; I can still open the doors manually. Once I get my bay door open I climb into my Mustang and turn the key in the ignition but it only makes a clicking noise.

"I hate you Darius Steele," I whisper to myself.

He disabled my car too. Then I remember he always had a bad habit of leaving the car keys in the ignition. Maybe he left the keys in his rover. I quietly shut the Mustang's door and race over to his black Land rover and sure enough, the keys are dangling in the column. Fair is fair. I turn the key and the fantastic vehicle roars to life. As I put the truck in reverse Dare comes running out the back door, naked as a jaybird, yelling at me to come back gone is the mirth from earlier when he had me in his clutches.

Waving at him I spin the wheels in the gravel and wave as I pull out onto the highway, laughing my head off as he turns and runs back inside for his clothes. He'll have to fix my car in order to drive it. I guess I have about a fifteen minute head start. Having grown up in this area, I know a couple places he'll never be able to find.

Turning off the highway I take the second dirt road on the right, now grown over with brush giving me a natural camouflage to cover my tracks. The lane loops back around my place by way of the neighbor's field. It's not a true 'road' but a cattle crossing. Steele's rover will enjoy the bumpy terrain. I decide to wait a couple minutes, give him a chance to leave and comb the back roads for me. Unable to help myself I start snooping through his truck. After about twenty minutes I pull the rover onto the dirt trail and make my way back down the secondary road that leads to my house with no Darius Steele in sight.

I pull into my drive and see my mustang is gone, so I try to figure out how he disabled the automatic door opener. I feel foolish when I discover all he did was unplug the motor from the power source, so once it's plugged in I open the second bay, and pull his vehicle inside the garage again. Closing just that bay door it looks like it did before. I race inside my house and lock the door, do a quick check to see how he got inside.

I hear a car slowing down on the road out front and look out the living room window being careful not to move the curtains and see Dare looking around for his truck. He keeps looking down at his lap so he must have a GPS module in his rover but he drives on down the road in my red convertible. He makes two more loops past the house, and in that time I have secured my back screened in porch, pulled the winter shutters closed from the inside since that's how he got inside.

On his third trip he pulls into the drive and parks the car in the drive way, gets out and walks into the garage. He pulls out his phone and I hear my phone start to ring. I walk over to my bag sitting on the kitchen table, pull it out and answer it on the fifth ring.

"Hello?" I say.

"You are so going to pay for that little ride in the park." He hisses. "Open the door."

"Who is this?" I ask having to cover my mouth with my free hand to keep from laughing he is so pissed off.

"Open the God damned door Carrie Anne or I'll break it down." He shouts at me using his 'I'm out of patience' voice I remember so well.

"Why would I let you inside my house, a man who disabled my car and garage, broke into and entered my home then stood watching me bathe. Oh and tried to have his way with me. Why would I let a conniving, lying, cock hound, trouser snake, like you inside my house? And since I have your car keys, you better start walking, it gets dark out here pretty quickly, and it's a good five mile hike into town. Thanks for a totally exciting evening, goodbye."

I hang up the phone and know he is going to try something and he doesn't disappoint. As I'm racing around the house, trying to see where he's at I hear him upstairs, and then I remember the open bathroom window and the big tree beside it, but by then it's too late. He is already down the stairs and running into the kitchen.

"Gotcha," he says as he stalks me around the kitchen table with a look of unholy delight shining out of his crystalline eyes. "Pay backs are so enjoyable, aren't they?"

"I'll give you back your keys but only when you're standing outside." I try to reason with him as I side step the tabletop and try not to look directly into his triumphant eyes, "that way you can leave here without the cops escorting you out of town and I can fix myself some supper, deal?"

"No fucking way," he laughs and circles the table using his long muscular arms to push him along the surface, shifting every time I start to move.

"You started this skirmish, I simply gave you a little small town justice, we're even, so cut it out and leave my house, please." I tell him but he just shakes his head.

"You took it to a whole new level Camy, one that I never realized you would even have thought of, you're devious, mean spirited, and need to be taught a lesson." He challenges me.

I smile at him and say, "are you sure you want to play in my league?"

"Oh hell yes," he says and once again feints to the right.

This time I've got enough clearance around the table so instead of shifting away from him I run past him up the flight of stairs that leads to the guest room and my private dojo. The door to the play room is hidden in the wainscoting. There is no door knob, just a strong magnetic catch with a rope handle on the other side of the panel. I run into the room and pull the door shut. I can hear Dare running up the stairs laughing as the game is afoot, looking in the guest room and the bath, and I'm sure he is looking out the open windows and in the closet.

"Come out come out where ever you are?" he sings then starts tapping on the walls trying to find my secret door, but I'm holding the rope taunt, so there's no give on the magnetic latches but I shift my weight and the floor board creaks giving away my position.

13

"Gotcha" he says through the wooden panel. "I can wait all night; I've got the bathroom on my side of the door."

He starts laughing and I hear him drop to the floor, leaning up against the wall, waiting me out. I lean back against the padded walls, knowing Dare is going to have his say now that I'm a captive audience. He is so arrogant, but also so much fun to be around when he's playful.

"So tell me Camy, where did you get your information concerning my family; the tabloids; the girl's locker room; certainly not from me. Let me correct a few erroneous facts you were spewing earlier," his tone becomes a bit snide.

"First, I've never been married, came close to a lovely girl in Paris before she flipped out on me. Second, I have a son, he's six years old, and he's also my nephew. My brother died from injuries he sustained in an automobile accident; he was a passenger in the car driven by my son's mother, Rachel. She was arguing with Jared, wasn't paying attention, ran a red light, and a tractor trailer T-boned the passenger side door. Jared lived long enough to tell us what happened, but he died three days later. His girlfriend was nine months pregnant; she delivered a healthy little boy the next day.

Four days later, the day of my brother's funeral she handed me the baby at the gravesite and walked away.

"Her body was found two days later in the Russian River, she threw herself off the bridge, leaving behind this tiny little boy. I was needed here, to raise this child, our baby was gone before he even had a chance, Sammy was dropped into my hands, what would you have expected me to do, give him up? I couldn't do that."

He clears his throat and continues all the while my heart is breaking at his story, "Once I had my father's house squared away, I did look for you, I assumed you came back to the states, but you never mentioned where you lived. I racked my memory, trying to recall if you said where in California you were born. But I couldn't find you and I had to get Sammy legally adopted; even though his mother left her son in our care it still had to go through the courts so I decided to wait, hire a private detective to do the leg work since I couldn't just take off."

He shifts his weight against the door panel and I swear I can feel his heartbreak. "Are you still with me? Are you even listening?" he asks, but he keeps talking, ripping the sorrow from my chest with every new piece of the puzzle.

"When Sammy was legally mine I thought about looking for you again, but three years had passed and I figured you'd already found someone who could make you happy, no strings attached, no instant family to saddle you with." He sighs and says, "God, I used to dream about our days together in Paris, the trips to the banks of the Seine, the cabarets we'd discovered, finding a flea market to investigate, even eating some experiment that went south on you, and you know, with the exception of the last couple of weeks, those were the greatest times of my life."

I close my eyes and let the tears fall unchecked down my cheeks. How could I have misjudged him so badly? He had no choice, he had to step up and take care of his nephew. I know I've done him a grave disservice. There's no way I can make it up to him, but I have to try, if he's even willing to let me. He is still talking about how much he missed me, how he would have loved to have had my help, but he was overwhelmed with grief, over his brother, dealing with his despondent father, and all I did was condemn him for leaving me.

I jump up, push the door open and fling myself on him where he is sitting cross legged on the floor. I tumble him backwards, kissing his face, his eyes, his lips, trying to absorb him into my body. He laughs as he pushes me away to look deeply into my eyes. I nod my head just before he kisses me with such longing, such need I'm defenseless against him. He stands up, grabs my hand and quick steps us into the guest room. I reach up and grab a hold of his shirt front, give him a tug and he crashes down on top of me.

"Make love to me Dare, like we used to." I whisper to him, "I want to feel you inside of me, all of you, please let's pretend we're back in Paris, in our squeaky iron bed and let's walk that sucker across the floor."

He laughs at the memory and starts removing his clothing for the second time tonight. I kick off my sandals, unsnap my jeans and roll over onto my back, lift my hips and shimmy out of them. I didn't take the time to put on panties or a bra, so I'm lying totally naked, on top of the red, white, and blue quilt my Grandma Kate made me for high school graduation waiting on the love of my life to ditch his clothes.

He sits down on the side of the bed, removes his watch, then turns and climbs into bed, reaching for me until I'm lying halfway across his body. We lay facing each other, stroking and caressing until I can't wait any longer. I rise up on my elbow and kiss his lips.

"I'm so sorry," I begin, "I should never have jumped to those conclusions…"

He covers my lips with his index finger and says, "Apology accepted, now get over here and give me six years' worth of sex."

I can't help but laugh and soon we're romping around in bed like a couple of teenagers, until I need to feel him inside me. I straddle his hips and looking down into his sexually aroused face I reach between our bodies, and guide his swollen shaft into my waiting channel. Inch by inch I lower myself onto his staff, looking at his face as my body draws him from within, stretching and filling me as I continue to accommodate his girth. Once he is seated to the hilt I feel complete, like the last piece of a jigsaw puzzle has been put in place. He holds himself still, giving my body a change to get accustomed to his invasion.

We both release a sigh, and hold our next breath as I raise up an inch then lower myself back down. Needing to move he grabs ahold of my hips and starts rocking me as I raise and lower my body. Soon I'm starting to feel that deliscious pressure I crave build inside of me. Dare starts to push up off the mattress while I press down on his pelvis. He reaches between our bodies, pressing the small nubbin hidden in my cleft. As he teases me with his fingers I feel myself come unwound, just like before I soar across the open spaces in my mind, racing to that point where I'm freefalling.

Dare is whispering to me, encouraging me to let go and soon his body quickens and he joins me in his release, shouting my name into the rafters of the old house. He continues to rise and meet me until there is only one body, one single quivering pile of vibrating nerves. I collapse on top of his sweaty chest, feeling exhausted and sated. He strokes my damp back with his fingertips, trying to slow his breathing to normal. I smile into his soft chest hair and decide this is where I want to spend every evening for the rest of my life.

But every good time has to end, at least for now. He shifts me over and picks up his watch trying to read the time. The sun has set and since we're on the east side of the house, it's dark and we didn't turn on any lamps. I can see the glowing dial of his watch and it reads a little after eight.

"Are you hungry? I can fix us a quick bite before you have to leave," I offer wincing at the pain shooting down my lower extremities as I start to get up.

He sits up, throws his legs over the side of the bed and looks over his shoulder at me.

"Kicking me out already?" he grins making me want to push him down onto the mattress but I know he has to get back home, or at least call and see how Sammy is doing.

"Never, but I know you have responsibilities, so if you can't stay I understand." I explain running my fingers up and down his spine. "Do you want me to fix you anything to eat? Last chance before the kitchen closes for the night." I tease him.

He leans over and kisses me long and deeply. Then he groans when I start returning his kiss.

"God you are one hell of a temptation. I guess you better fix me something or we'll never get downstairs, at least not tonight." He teases, "Let me call home and see what's going on, I'll be right back."

He steps into the bathroom and closes the door, which is a good signal for me to head downstairs and give him some privacy. I slip on his blue plaid shirt and grab my clothes, then walk downstairs to the laundry room.

I remember my wet clothes and the wet towels in my bathroom upstairs so I walk through the living room and climb the steps to the master bath. God, what a mess he left when he realized I was stealing his rover. I silently laugh as I pull the drain plug on the tub, releasing our bathwater and gather the wet towels; I'm as much to blame for the catastrophic condition in here as he.

Out of the blue I hear Dare raise his voice at someone shocking me out of my daze. The master bath and the guest bath share an interior wall and the ventilation system makes Dare's voice carry.

"I'm visiting a friend Rhonda, who is none of your business," he says rather loudly.

He is quiet for a couple of seconds then shouts into the phone.

"You'll do no such thing," he says, "where's Sammy? Don't give me any shit about her, put Sammy on the God damned phone, now!"

He is quiet again then says in a softer voice, "Hey pal how's the big sleep over, that bad? Well I'll make it up to you tomorrow, okay? How's Buddy's paw? Is it any better?

No… we'll only take him to the vet if it's not better by the end of the week."

He laughs and says, "don't call her that, at least not to her face," then he laughs again and says, "where is Papaw? Will you hand him the phone? Hey, before you go, tell me who loves you more than anyone else in the whole wide world… that's right, now hand the phone to Papaw and then get to bed, and don't forget to brush your teeth. I love you Sammy, good night."

Listening to Dare speak to his son makes me long for a family like that. He was so sweet and gentle with the little boy that I'm shocked at the tone coming from him when he starts speaking to his father.

"Get that whore out of my house, now or I'll cut you off." He demands. "I don't care… you got mixed up in that ridiculous land venture, you personally, not Steele, Inc. so for the thousandth time I will not bail you out using company funds. I'll be back tomorrow and she better be gone or I'll be kicking the both of you out when I get there." He's quiet for a bit then says, "it's my house you're living in, I pay the bills…you'll do as I say. Get rid of her Dad, I mean it."

He flushes the toilette so I missed part of what he said next but I hear him say, "Yes I found my woman, yes she still loves me and no I haven't asked her yet, so butt out and don't let Sammy hear you speaking about Rhonda like that again, he repeats everything he hears… Just watch yourself. Have Jimmie take him to school tomorrow. I'll be back in plenty of time to pick him up. Don't forget to tell her… Yeah, yeah I'll let her know it was all your idea. Goodnight Dad."

Not wanting to get caught eavesdropping I quickly gather the damp towels and start mopping up the water from the floor. I can hear Dare hollering downstairs.

"Where'd you go? Camy?" he shouts, "don't make me chase you down again woman."

I start laughing as I carry my bundle of wet towels and clothing downstairs.

"I just wanted to get these towels in the washer," I tell him, "how's your son?"

He smiles at me and says, "He's good, worried about his dog's front paw but other than that he's fine. What did you decide to fix me? Oh and good news, I'll be staying the night so be thinking about what you're going to feed me tomorrow too." He leans forward and kisses my cheek.

"A loaded pizza from Momma Rosa's for supper? How about French toast, berries, and whipped cream for breakfast?" I ask him and start laughing when he twirls me around the kitchen with the wet towels dampening our clothes.

"Great, you better wash my clothes too, since I didn't bring a change for tomorrow," he jokes and starts taking off his Dockers and t-shirt.

His jockey shorts are in the pile of wet clothes in my arms, apparently he didn't want to take the time to put his underwear on either. Dare follows me into the laundry room naked as the day he was born and once I've started the washing machine, he starts unbuttoning his shirt I'm wearing.

I look up at him and see he is grinning, "This is part of my ensemble for tomorrow, better wash it too." He says as he peels the shirt down my arms leaving me as naked as him.

"I guess we better order the pizza if we want them to deliver it. They close at ten on weeknights." I tell him a bit breathless, "Oh and ask if Cal can deliver it, please."

He laughs and says, "You chefs are even pushy when it comes to who delivers your pizzas, now that's taking things a bit too far." He jokes but calls the order in from the number on the fridge while I walk upstairs to the guest room and see if Saul or Mokie might have left some clean workout clothes behind.

I'm in luck, as Saul left a full set of clean navy sweats a couple of weeks ago. Since he hasn't been here in a while I know he's not missed them. I slip on the huge sweatshirt. Walking back down the stairs I hold out the sweatpants to Dare. He looks up at me and asks, "Whose clothes are these and why are they upstairs in your guest room?"

I playfully swat his belly and say, "Saul left him here the last time we sparred together."

He follows me into the living room and reaches out his hand, holding me still while he asks his question again.

"Why would he leave his workout clothes here?" he asks in a too soft of voice.

"Listen hot shot," I tell him poking my finger in his chest, "After getting mugged in Paris I decided to never be that vulnerable again. I have been taking Karate lessons for the last five years, I've earned my black belt and I spar with Saul when Gina or Mokie Joe isn't available. Does that satisfy your manly curiosity? Or would you rather stand around naked?"

He pulls me to his chest, tosses the pants up into the air and scoops me up in his arms, carries me over to the sofa and drops me. Dare covers my body with his and soon we're going hot and heavy, plunging and thrusting, propelling each other towards the inevitable explosion and we come crashing back down to earth. He is hell on wheels when he's in this mood. I start laughing when I see the headlights of the pizza delivery boy's car.

"Give him a big tip," I laugh up into his questioning face. "One because he is willing to make the trek out here, and two, if his timing had been off a couple of minutes, you'd have ripped him a new one." We laugh as he rolls off me and starts to walk over to the door. "Better slip on Saul's pants or you'll be the talk of the town when Cal reports back I've had company, of the naked kind." I remind him and he wiggles his naked ass at me but slips into the too long sweatpants. I can't help laugh at him, looking like he's wearing his daddy's clothes.

He reaches for his wallet and gives Cal a good tip and he turns back towards me and says, "Dinner is served, Madam." He carries the box into the kitchen and while I grab a couple of beers from the fridge, he grabs the roll of paper towels and we dig into the best pizza in the world.

When the last slice of the pie is gone, we're both tired and relaxed, I lean my chin in my hand and need to ask him the one question I've been dying to hear the answer from his lips.

"Do you forgive me?" I ask tilting my head, biting my lower lip.

He grins and nods his head while licking his greasy fingertips making my heart skip a beat at the love I see in his smile

"Do you still love me?" I ask him, starting to smile in anticipation of hearing those words spoken to me by him. But he doesn't utter a sound.

He nods his head again, but reaches across the table, takes my hand in both of his and whispers, "I never stopped loving you, you're the only woman I've ever met that makes me hungry for your touch, long to hear your voice, and crave your lips on mine. What I feel for you isn't love, it's so much more… I can't even begin to describe how I feel where you're concerned. You complete me."

I look into his aquamarine blue eyes and know exactly what he means. I let out a sigh and bend over to kiss his knuckles.

"Let's go to bed." I tell him, scooting out my chair and releasing his hands at the same time. "Just so you know, I never stopped loving you either, God knows I tried, but there'll never be anyone else but you, never." I wait for him to come around the table and together, we lock up the house, turn off the lights and head up the master bedroom stairs.

When we're lying in bed, enclosed in the dark, wrapped in each other's arms, I know we're both going to be making some changes in the near future, but as long as we end up like tonight, I'll move heaven and earth to remain in his arms. The last thought I have before succumbing to exhaustion is he's back where he belongs.

14

As the sun shines through my eastern window I roll over and come up against a hot brick wall. Smiling I remember how fantastic yesterday was. Snuggling into his warmth I place a kiss between his shoulder blades. Dare rolls over and wraps his arms around me, nestling me to his chest.

"God I hope I'm not dreaming again," he murmurs kissing the top of my head. "I used to dream of waking up like this, too many times to count."

I move back enough to look up and kiss his lips, loving the softness and warmth of his mouth.

"Believe me, I'm nobody's idea of a dream, maybe a bête noir'," I joke but he shakes his head.

"You're my dream come true. I want to continue living this dream, but I want you to get to know Sammy first, let him get used to the idea of someone else in our life, on a permanent basis, if you catch my drift." He says, nibbling on my earlobe.

"Have there been many women in Sammy's life on a 'temporary basis'?" I ask, hating myself for needing to know.

Smiling down at me he says, "no Cam, one or two, but they never even met my son, I promise."

115

Grinning up at him I can't help but feel elated knowing he hadn't met anyone else he wanted to get close to. I hug his trim waist and wrap my leg around his.

"What about you?" he asks, "Did you meet anyone else you wanted to get permanent with in the last six years?" I feel him tense up, like I did.

"No Darius Samuel Steele," I tell him, "after I finished school and started thinking clearly again, I swore off men in general, just ask Mokie how dangerous it was for anyone to try to divert my attention from my career. There might be a couple male chefs that still don't walk straight."

He laughs with me and then he moves on top of me, nudging my legs, settling between my thighs. I feel his morning erection prodding me, demanding my attention. Widening my legs he slips inside of me and slowly starts to move.

"I love you, Carrie Anne Mosier," he whispers staring into my eyes. "More today than I ever did in Paris, you complete me, make me feel invincible. Don't ever leave me again."

"Never," I softly breathe out the word, "but you left me hot shot, so don't you ever leave me again."

He smiles and nods his head, then continues to gently rock us into an orgasm so soft, so sweet it's almost too painful. Tears well up in my eyes at the intense look on his face; I know he was hurt by me, and he knows I was hurt too. His slow lovemaking is healing, to both of us, no hot flashes, just a nurturing meld. I feel him come inside of me, his life force seeping into my tissue. His smile is filled with such love I push against his motion and let go of my own release. After we wake a second time he is no longer willing to cuddle but is hungry and wants to be fed much like Mouser when he's too lazy to catch his meal.

"Come on Cam you promised French Toast and whipped cream," he whines, gently pushing me away from him, "I'm hungry, feed me…"

I roll my eyes at him and sit up on the side of the bed, "Fine, then you have to treat me to lunch, deal?" I ask and he smiles back at me.

"Deal, my choice?" he asks, climbing out of bed and heading towards the bathroom.

"So long as it doesn't include a toy in the sack, you can choose." I holler at his retreating back.

"Spoilsport," he says as he closes the door and turns on the shower.

Grabbing my robe from the closet door I quickly make the bed and head downstairs to make the coffee and start the bacon. I turn on the stand mixer, add some heavy cream and let it fly on high as BJ says. Next I start whisking eggs in a bowl for the batter. Organization is the key to preparing any meal, whether it's a seven course extravaganza or a peanut butter and jelly sandwich. Five minutes later I'm enjoying my first cup of coffee when Dare walks down the stairs wearing Saul's sweat pants. He walks over to me, leans down to kiss my lips and takes my coffee cup instead.

"Hey, kiss me before you steal my coffee, it's the least you can do," I complain.

He turns back around, takes a drink and sighs.

"Nobody makes coffee as delicious as you, and the French roast is still my favorite," he tells me as he bends down to give me the kiss I demanded, "I always think of you when I smell the dark roast."

His lips are soft, but firm on mine. I wrap my arms around his waist and snuggle into the soft chest hair. Inhaling his clean scent, even when he uses my body wash I can still smell his essence.

"I need to use your computer, is that alright?" he asks stepping over to refill his cup. "Your office is back here right?" He motions down the short hall towards the back door.

"Sure, I always leave it booted up." I tell him and get a new cup for myself. "I'm going to take a shower, so you've got about twenty minutes before breakfast will be ready," I tell him after I put the sliced baguette in the egg mixture and turn off the mixer. I slip the bowl of whipped cream into the fridge beside the dish of mixed berries I sliced and head back upstairs for my shower.

When I walk back into the kitchen wearing my favorite blue jean cut offs and a faded old blue t-shirt I smell the bacon and pull it out of the oven, take out one of my skillets and turn on the heat. Dare is nowhere around but I see the coffee pot is empty.

Walking over to the sink I see the bright pink post it note on the fridge to remind me of Uncle Walter's birthday. I need to call Jon and tell him I won't be going to the birthday party again this year. Picking up my phone I walk over to the hot skillet and start frying the egg soaked bread. When I fill the pan I call Jon, hoping he's still at home and hasn't left for the day. When he's out in the orchard, he never hears his cell, and he refuses to put the phone on vibrate, says it feels weird having his pants quiver. He answers on the third ring.

"*Hey good lookin' what 'cha got cookin'*" Jon sings every time he answers my calls. He carries a tune only a fraction better than I do and I've been known to cause birds to fall out of trees with my singing voice.

"Hey John boy," I retaliate calling him his dreaded nickname given to him by Grandma Kate. "Just calling to tell you I won't make it to Uncle Walter's party. Will you and Jess be going this year?"

"Not if I can help it." he jokes, "last year all they did was talk about Dad's and Walter's kids and grandkids, not once asking how you and I are doing. I felt like a ghost."

I understand that feeling and refuse to put myself through it again. I reach for the bottle of real Vermont maple syrup and pour the entire bottle into a small sauce pan and turn the burner on low.

"Thankfully Jessie agrees with me and no longer is insisting I try to fit in with Mom and Dad's new families. It only took seven years but she finally sees how uncomfortable it is showing up, having to pretend we care about the virtual strangers they call family." He says, summing up my feelings on the subject to a T. "What's new with you? Did you read that article about Mokie Joe?" he asks, "I was impressed with what all he's accomplished. I wonder if his father is finally proud of him."

"I doubt it," I tell him then turn when I hear Dare walk into the kitchen from the sun porch. "Hey sweetie I got to run, just wanted to tell you I would be a no-show, glad to know you're through trying to fit in with that crowd too." I tell him as I remove the last slice of fried bread and put it on the platter.

"Okay, good to hear from you sis," he says, "take care, love you."

"Love you back; give Jess and the girls my love. Bye." I tell him and end the call.

"Was that your brother?" Dare asks as he reaches for a piece of bacon. "How is he doing these days?" he asks, "Is he still in the area?"

"Yeah, right next door to your neck of the woods actually." I tell him, "He and his family are having a tough time at the moment, what with the economy, some bad crop years. I know Jessie's family has considered cashing in, but I hope they hang on; things should turn around soon, hopefully. I'd hate to see another family farm bite the dust."

He nods his head then smiles and asks, "Are we ready to eat? I need to head back to Sonoma by eleven."

"We're good to go," I tell him, "grab the platter, but be careful it's hot, I always keep it on the back burner, and the vent keeps the food warm."

"Smart girl, you really did learn something at your fancy cooking school after all," he teases.

We sit down across from each other at the old farmhouse table and dig into one the best breakfasts ever invented. The mix of berries is plump and juicy, making Dare's full bottom lip appear red and more inviting. I can't help myself, I lean over and suck his now red tongue into my mouth, making him drop his fork, reach over the table and pull me closer. I barely keep from dumping my plate on my lap but it would have been worth the sticky mess.

I sit back down feeling my legs tremble under the table, amazed Dare hasn't ignited and burst into flames, he is so turned on right now. But he winks at me, picks up his fork and plows through the rest of his meal like nothing happened.

"Wow," I whisper and reach for a slice of bacon.

"Be thankful I didn't swipe the table clean and pour maple syrup all over your naked body," he says, "but then again," he teases holding the small glass pitcher full of the rich, amber liquid, swinging the container from its white plastic hinged handle.

"Don't even go there," I warn him, "that would be one hell of a mess, and since you're going to be taking off, I'd be the one to clean it up. I'll stick with greasy lips and red tongues, thank you very much."

He laughs again but turns the subject to his son.

"Sammy's seventh birthday is coming up, October 23rd. I was hoping to throw him a birthday party. Any suggestions?" he asks. "I'd want to keep it small, but I know he has several 'best' friends and he adores my housekeeper's grandkids. Help me come up with an idea." He says, pushing his empty plate out of his way and reaching for my hands.

"I'd love to work on that," I smile and think of all the birthday parties I planned as a little girl but never had. Jon and I always got to pick our meal, and Grandma would bake cupcakes and have one gift for us. It wasn't much, but she did her best and my brother and I always enjoyed that special day.

"Hey, where'd you go?" he asks waving his hand in front of my face, "You were a million miles away just now."

"Thinking of party ideas," I tell him, not feeling like sharing memories of my childhood. "When will you want to have this party?"

"His birthday is on a Wednesday this year, and he and I have always gone out to dinner and then to the go-cart raceway on the actual day, or miniature golf, where ever he wants to go, so maybe that following Saturday, the twenty sixth. That gives you two weeks to knock his socks off."

"You're such an amateur." I tell him, "I'll have it squared away tomorrow. Depending on the number of guests we can serve a buffet or just have snacks. What kind of cake would he like or would you want cupcakes in different flavors? I'll need to coordinate with Roz, see your house and do a set up sketch. Do you want me to send out invitations? Or do you want to handle that?"

He stares at me in awe and whispers, "no, you go ahead and do it, that way I know it'll be done right. You're amazing."

"You ain't seen anything yet." I joke and reach for our dirty dishes. "When can I meet Sammy?" I ask hoping I'm not assuming too much.

"When are you free? What's your weekends like?" he asks, grabbing the syrup pitcher and bowl of left over fruit, which he carries over to the counter and turns around, leaning back against the cabinets, with his arms folded over his chest and he crosses his freshly laundered jean clad legs. I didn't even notice he had changed out of Saul's sweats and was wearing his own clothes.

"Sorry, what did you say?" I ask knowing I was concentrating on his body movements and wasn't listening to him. "You are my greatest distraction." I whisper to him making him grin.

"Thanks, right back at you." He says, "I asked what your schedule looked like."

"Well, I'll need to check, but until Roz comes back I'm stuck in Willow. You could always bring him up here, spend the weekend... no that's too soon isn't it?" I ask.

"Yeah, let's just play it by ear, see how it goes," he says walking over to me and wrapping his arms around my waist. "I don't want to share you just yet," he tells me.

"Liar, you're scared of your own little boy," I laugh and he nods his head.

"He's a great kid, but it's always been just me and him. I don't want to blow it, I'd love for him to get to know you, have you two become great friends, then I'll tell him we're a couple, okay?" he asks hoping I'll go along with his time table.

"Sure, whatever you think is best," I concede but deep down feeling a little left out again. I shake off that feeling and wrap my arms around his neck, pull him down to kiss me, long and deeply.

"I hate to end this but I have to get back," he says when we both come up for air. "I've got meetings scheduled all day tomorrow and a dinner appointment for Saturday evening, but I'll call you and we'll work out our schedules then, okay?"

Looking at his watch I have a flashback of another time when he continually kept looking at his watch. I tamp down the irritation, knowing that's not fair to hold his priorities against him. I smile and push away.

"Go ahead, take off and we'll talk later this evening." I tell him making him smile and kiss me one more time.

"I'm so happy and relieved we're back together." He says then turns away, walks out of the room and heads towards my office. "I need all your numbers just in case I need to get a hold of you."

I follow him down the hall and stop in the doorway to see him writing something on a post-it note. He takes the small yellow square and pins it to my huge bulletin board that covers an entire wall. He moves a couple of bills of lading, a work order, and a calendar page out of the way, so the small memo sheet isn't blocked by another piece of paper.

He turns around to face me and grins, "There, now you have no excuse not to call me. I wrote down all my phone numbers, faxes, email addresses, and my home address."

Laughing at his antics I cross my arms under my breasts and respond, "I can have them tattooed on me if you'd like?"

He tilts his head, as if considering the possibility then says, "No tats, nothing should leave a mark on your gorgeous skin, well except my fingerprints."

Dare walks over to me and says, "I'll call you later this evening, don't go to bed until you hear from me, okay? I want to be the last voice you hear before you go to sleep."

"Don't forget to call or I'll be grouchy the next day. According to BJ I'm hard as nails when I don't get enough sleep." I tell him making him chuckle.

"I remember," he says and shudders, "Those twelve hour days you used to do were God awful. I'm glad those days are gone."

"The nights were pretty fantastic though, if I recall." I tell him walking my fingers up the front of his shirt. "But you're right; I'd never want to do that again."

"I have to run," he says again, but this time he is walking out the back door into the garage. He turns to face me and says, "Do you still have my keys?"

Laughing I turn back inside and reach up on the peg board I always keep my keys on and toss them at him. He nimbly catches them and shakes his head.

"Yesterday was fun, last night was unforgettable, and this morning I'm sorry I have to leave." He smiles, "what a difference a day makes."

I press the garage door opener and walk over to stand between the driver's door and the seat. Bending down I lean into the vehicle, kiss my gorgeous man goodbye and whisper in his ear.

"I love you Dare, don't ever forget that." Stepping away from the truck I shut the door and walk back inside the house, watching him pull out of the garage, reverse down the driveway and turn onto the highway, all without looking back at me.

Closing the garage door I walk back into the kitchen, start to clean up the mess I made fixing the best meal I've ever eaten. I love him. I never stopped loving him, but it feels better this time, stronger, deeper, a forever kind of thing. After I load the dishwasher I walk back into my office, open up my email and see what Roz has sent me. There are three new contracts she needs signed, two proposals that need going over, and a supplier that has put us at the bottom of their list for some reason. That would explain why my latest spice order hasn't arrived yet. I pull my schedule and know I've got a big problem. The twenty sixth square has a yellow hi-lite meaning an evening dinner and there's a flag attached telling me all the notes Roz has entered for this contract. Crap!

Before I tackle the items on my computer I decide to call the studio and see if anything is worth coming in for. The phone rings twice before Gina answers it in her soft, purring voice.

"You're in good hands with En Bonnes Catering, how may we assist you today?" She says making me smile at the inadvertent sexiness that always comes across with her.

"Hey Kitten, just me, don't waste your spiel," I tell her making her laugh out loud.

"There's more where that came from, don't cha' know." She says in her best vamp's tone, her Bronx accent is coming through loud and clear.

"I was just checking in, seeing what's going on?" I tell her hoping its dead. I don't feel like getting dressed and driving in for nothing.

"Well let's see," she replies, "Saul is washing the van and looking very hot doing it I might add. BJ is in the kitchen trying out a new recipe, but I can't figure it out yet, at least nothing is burning." She teases, "And Nana and Kit are doing laundry, oh and I'm going through our table décor inventory just because I didn't want to be in the same room as Kit who is in one of his moods, and BJ wouldn't let me help. I didn't even offer to help Saul, the big control freak. I swear he's as bad as my mother's cousin Frankie."

Laughing at my dear friend I feel a thousand times better about staying home today.

"Well, continue to hold down the fort," I laugh then thinking about forts reminds me of Sammy's birthday. "When's the last time we did a child's birthday party?" I ask.

"Child as in Bar mitzvah; Sweet sixteen; or the dreaded piñata?" she asks knowing I'll understand her age group description and party type.

"Piñata, boys and girls," I reply. "Dare Steele's son is going to be seven on the twenty third and he's asked me to plan a party for that following weekend. I already promised we'd do it before I checked the calendar. We're free in the afternoon, but there's the Burchart anniversary that evening in Oakland."

"Wow Ma, you're spreading yourself pretty thin, and for a man you detest? Hmm, I think something big is going on here. Spill it sister, what gives?" she demands knowing something happened since yesterday's showdown.

"I'll tell you all about it tomorrow, at brunch." I assure her and smile when she gives me a Bronx cheer.

Every Friday we cook a different breakfast, everybody is involved and as we sit down to eat we go over the next week's schedule. I've always done this and I think it's beneficial as well as it gets the crew pumped for the upcoming events.

"I'm going to go out on a limb here and speculate you and Mr. Hard as Steele worked out your differences; did the wild thing…Ba-da-Bing, Ba-da-Bang and then you made that hunk of Steele breakfast this morning." She says making me laugh at her accurate description of the last twenty four hours. She usually cuts to the heart of any situation talking a mile a minute and waving her hands as she does.

"Careful little girl, KP duty is right around the corner." I teasingly warn her but she is not to be deterred.

"On the money wasn't I?" she asks with a smile in her voice and then starts laughing harder when I fail to respond. "Hot damn, do I know you or what? I could have made a fortune if we'd started a pool like I wanted to do, no one believed me when I said you were still hot for the man. I guess they'll believe me now."

"KP duty, next three events," I reply and before she can do anything else but sputter I say, "See you tomorrow sister" and hang up the phone. Gina is going to tell everyone about

Dare and me, but I don't care. I'm ready to shout the news from the rooftop myself.

I spend the next two hours playing phone tag with my sales rep from Spice Unlimited until finally I get the man on the phone. We hash out why he is holding my orders. It appears he has begun representing another supplier as well and forgot to enter my orders. Deciding to show my inner 'tough as nails' I threaten to use his competitor.

"You know you'll spend twice as much for their product," he whines in response, "I'll get your request expedited, but it will cost a bit more for shipping."

"No Ted," I tell him, "it will cost you more for shipping. You failed to process the request, so it's on your head, not mine. If I don't have the saffron, curry, turmeric, and Himalayan salt in three days' time, I'm cancelling all outstanding orders and will cheerfully pay the higher price and go with Angel's."

"Calm down Carrie Anne, I'll make sure you get your order," he says, "no reason to play hardball."

"This is your last chance Ted, don't blow it." I tell him and hang up feeling immensely better. The rest of the afternoon flies by with me catching up on all the paperwork Roz usually handles.

15

Later that evening I fix myself a light supper of pesto and angel hair pasta, and sit in front of my computer waiting on either a phone call from Dare or an email from Mokie. Sipping my crisp Pinot Griggio, I have to admit neither of the men in my life is thinking about me. I spent the afternoon going over the two proposals Roz sent earlier. After confirming on-line my spice order had indeed been ordered and expedited at no additional cost to me, I felt like tackling the three pending contracts. I set up two appointments for tomorrow and the third one for Tuesday of next week.

The proposals in front of me are bids Roz intended to send in for the opportunity to be included in the Wine festival's annual people's choice contest in Napa Valley. Each year hundreds of wineries compete on multiple levels and in the people's choice category there is always several tables providing nibbles and hors d'oeuvre. There is no prize awarded, but the publicity is phenomenal. You can't get that kind of exposure anywhere else. Roz is hoping we get chosen for both the savory as well as the sweet categories, but just being chosen for one is good enough for me.

Wine connoisseurs as well as the public are there to sample your wares. Over three hundred business cards were sent out last year to local caterers, restaurants, and market vendors offering the chance to be highlighted. You have to be invited, sort of audition for a spot; we've been preparing some outstanding dishes in the hope of getting a call back.

After I finish my bowl of pasta I look at the clock on the computer and see it's almost ten o'clock and I know Dare isn't going to call me like he promised. But I have his number, all of them actually, so I can call him. He probably was worn out after all the running around last night and this morning. Deciding to cut him some slack I choose his cell number first, but it automatically goes to voice mail. I decide not to leave him one. Next I call his home number and do leave a message.

"Hey there, its Carrie Anne, just wanted to tell you I know you're busy, so don't worry about calling me back. See you later, bye." I hate not telling him I love him, but I don't want to upset Sammy if he was to hear the message.

I call the other home phone he has listed and a woman with a heavy Hispanic accent answers the phone.

"Steele Residence," she says in a lilting voice.

"Good evening, Carrie Anne Mosier calling for Darius Steele," I tell her in my best business tone.

"Mr. Dare is not home, may I take a message?" she asks in broken English.

"When do you expect him back?" I ask, hating to have to question the help.

"He and MS Rhonda won't be back until much later. They go to supper then night club, like always, Mr. Derek is home... you want to speak with Mr. Derek?" She asks trying to be helpful but I stopped listening at the name Rhonda.

"No thank you, don't bother him. I will call Dare at the office next week. Thanks anyway, Good night." I tell her and hang up the phone before I throw up.

I run into the bathroom but by then the nausea passed but I still feel light headed. Walking back into the office, I start to shut down my computer when I decide to send Dare an email.

> "Hope you had a good time tonight with MS Rhonda. I should have checked with you on your evening's entertainment schedule, but once again I assumed you were being upfront with me, my mistake, won't happen again. Enjoy your dinner and the clubs afterward.
>
> Your one night stand,
> Carrie Anne Mosier.
>
> PS
> Please don't bother to call me anymore."

I hit the send button and shut the computer all the way down. Normally I wander in the office when I'm home, and like to leave my email up, but I don't want to know when he gets this note. I lock up the house, turn off the lights and leave my phone downstairs, on the desk knowing he'll call me and 'explain' why he couldn't call me like he said he would.

Climbing out of my clothes and sliding into bed, I instantly smell Dare's cologne. I hurl the offensive pillow he used across the room and roll over and cry myself to sleep. I feel like I did when he left me wondering in Paris. I swore then I'd never let another man cause me to feel this way and here it's the same guy... I'm through with men.

16

After a restless night I welcome the dawn just to get a move on the day. Unlocking the front door of the studio I let myself in as quietly as possible. Carrying my traveler mug into the kitchen I smell the French Roast I crave and know Nana is here. Sure enough she is kneading dough, whipping up dinner rolls just like Grandma Kate used to make.

"Good morning dear," she says looking up from the arduous task and tosses a bit more flour on the board. "You're looking exceptionally lovely this morning, anything new you'd like to tell me, something different going on? You look sophisticated and polished and your outfit is very nice."

"Watch it Grandma, you can still do KP duty the old fashion way, right beside Gina." I snap at her then feel instantly contrite when she gets that questioning look on her face.

"I'm sorry honey," she apologizes, "Gina said you're be walking in the clouds, but that will teach me to listen to gossip won't it." She punches the bread a little harder than necessary letting me know I hurt her feelings.

"No, Nana, I'm the one that's sorry. I shouldn't take out my bad mood on you," I tell her walking around the island and hugging her from behind. "I just popped in to pick up a few menus and theme options, for the Red Bluff Art's Guild dinner and the Lower Lake Yacht Club Regatta so I'll be heading out shortly." I tell her, letting her know where I'll be for most of the day. "Fill in for me on the Friday breakfast meeting will you?"

"Sure, no problem, and honey if you need to talk, I'm right here." She offers, "Maybe when you get back from your appointments we can beat the tar out of some bread, bake enough to put Costello's Bakery out of business."

She makes me laugh, and I hug her again, careful not to get flour on my sky blue blazer I'm wearing over my camel sheath dress. I was in my kitchen at the crack of dawn, and after baking three loaves of bread, two dozen cupcakes, which I frosted using an Italian butter cream recipe I love, and the six dozen orange flavored Madeleine's, I was all baked out and in need of a distraction.

The reason I look a bit more polished than usual is due to the fact I needed some confidence building after last night. There's nothing better than seeing good results from spending an hour on hair, make-up, and selecting a sharp outfit. For the amount of time it took me to get dressed I know I look damn good. The woman that stared back at me this morning was strong, beautiful, and more than a bit determined according to the gleam in her smoky made up eyes and the high color across my cheekbones. The bright red gloss on her smirking full lips made me think of BJ's description of me: 'hard as nails' Mosier.

"I should be gone all day, but if Roz calls tell her where I'm at and to take all the time she needed. Have Saul place the order for more booze and make sure BJ and Kit weed the herb garden; it was looking a bit shaggy. Oh, and tell Gina to keep her mouth shut." I tell her and in sync both nod our heads. I refill my cup and walk into the office.

My phone's voice mail light is red, but I don't want to see who left me a message, but then my professional training kicks in. What if one of my appointments called to cancel and I end up making the two hour trip for nothing. I drop my purse and attaché case on the desktop, twirl my chair around and press the button for new messages.

One is from Ted; sucking up, assuring me my order will ship in two working days. Chalk one up for the Tough as nails Mosier. The second call is a hang up. The third call is from the man I sent to Perdition. Do I listen or delete? In fairness to him I promised to trust him, but when the servant tells you he's out as usual that's a little hard to do… Looking at my watch I decide to listen.

"Camy, I'm sorry but I couldn't get to the phone last night, Sammy was insisting we spend the evening together, my father needed me to look over some contracts, and Rhon…well I had a thousand things to do, but I'll make it up to you. Sammy is going to be staying over at Jimmie's house Saturday evening, so I'm free if you are, call me back and we'll set up a date, Love you, Bye."

He almost admitted he was with Rhonda but thought he caught the slip. He lied to me and not for the first time either. I delete his message as well as the other two and change my voice mail message.

"You've reached 555-3377 leave a message." At least that way he knows I've received his voice mail and decided not to return it; passive aggressive behavior accepted.

I wave to Nana as I walk out the front door, locking it behind me. Looking at my watch I have plenty of time to reach my first appointment in Lower Lake. I hit my play list, roll the windows down just enough not to lift the hair off my head and fly down the highway, refusing to think about the two timing son of a bitch that got my hopes up and then dashed them.

The drive up to the yachtsman clubhouse is uneventful taking I-5 all the way. With half an hour to spare I slowly drive past the Lower Lake Yacht clubhouse. The three story building reminds me of a summer cottage belonging to the filthy rich in South Hampton with six dormer windows across the roof line, a wraparound porch supported by countless white columns, and twenty or thirty cane seated rocking chairs all currently vacant at the moment. I park my car in the visitor parking space and pass the next couple of minute's people watching. There are a lot of potential clients milling about the stately manicured lawns. I can see row after row of expensive boats lined up in their slips peaking just out of full view from behind the building. Even the air smells expensive to me. I'll have hit pay dirt if I can get this contract signed. Taking a deep, cleansing breath I decide to wander around the place. Reaching for my purse my cell phone starts ringing. Sighing I pull it out of my bag and am not surprised when I see Dare's number light up on the screen. Knowing he is going to be relentless I answer the phone.

"En Bonne Catering, how can I help you?" I say knowing he knows this is my private cell not a business phone.

"Hey, you should really look at your screen before answering the phone; you never know who might be calling you." Dare jokes, "Where are you?"

"I'm working, and you?" I ask not letting any warmth in my tone at all.

"So am I, is something wrong? You sound funny, distant." He asks, "You got my voice mail right? I'm sorry for missing your call last night, Jimmie said someone called but she couldn't remember who, but I knew it was you." He sounds a bit smug.

"You should check your other numbers as well. Oh, and your personal emails. I was a busy girl last night, since I sat up waiting on you to call, which as we've already established, you were busy." I tell him and know he isn't happy with my tone.

"What's wrong? So I missed one call, I've already apologized, but my kid wanted to spend some time with me..." he starts to lie to me.

I interrupt him before I have to listen to that lie one more time.

"Did you take Sammy out to dinner and then the clubs, you know, like you normally do with MS Rhonda? Gee, you're a great dad. Check your email Mr. Steele, and then advise your help not to be so truthful. Goodbye." I hang up and know he is checking his computer as sure as I'm sitting here, fuming.

I take a couple deep breaths, turn my ringer off and check my makeup in the rear view mirror. No one would know by looking at me that my hair is seconds from catching on fire. I open the car door, reach across the seat and pick up my attaché case and lock up the car.

I know this is going to be a tedious meeting, but I need to gather my patience, reach my inner calm before I walk into the building. I hate this part of the business, that's why

I pay Roz's superfluous salary so I don't have to deal with the indecisiveness of choosing what canapé goes with what wine, which cheese to choose and how many desserts can they order at the rock bottom cost.

The super-rich can be the most difficult clients sometimes, but as long as they pay my bill on time, I know I'll learn to deal with them, or make sure Roz is in the office before I schedule the next meeting. An hour and a half later I walk out of the Yacht Club with a signed contract and fifty percent of the bill represented in this lovely fat check I'm carrying. Honestly it wasn't as bad as I expected, but I'll be glad when Roz is back. Smiling at the final price we agreed on I know I held my own much to the good old boys' dismay. Walking into the place I felt my inner Rottweiler just below the surface and it must have shown through, or they were too busy looking at my legs, either way... I won.

Deciding to reward myself for the tedious meeting I drive over to the local pub and order a blue plate special. When Mokie Joe and I were younger, we'd spend our weekends driving around local diners, ordering whatever was on the blue plate special and we'd share our thoughts and opinions on how we would fix the same dishes, or offer changes due to our ever evolving palates. We worked our way through some nasty patty melts, and horrendous chicken a la kings... so many that neither of us will ever create those dishes.

I walk into the charming retro diner and sit down in a booth. The waitress who appears to be in her eighteenth month of pregnancy waddles over. Empathy rushes out of me and I smile at her, loving the way her eyes light up when she asks, "What can I get for you today?" as she sets a small glass of cold water in front of me and hands me a plastic covered menu.

Smiling back, I ask for the special and she nods her head, looks over her shoulder and turns back towards me and whispers, "I'd order the chili and a grill cheese if I was you. The special today is tuna patty melt and fries." She makes a face, and then shudders before nodding at one of her regulars as they leave their table and tell her they'll see her tomorrow.

Laughing at her honesty, which I find refreshing after last night I nod my head and take her up on her suggestion. She smiles, takes the menu she brought me and shuffles back to the counter and calls out my order. Looking around I love the red, black, and white décor. The small jukeboxes on the table with condiments setting in front remind me of a simpler time in my life. My mind wanders back to the days where I worked in an establishment very much like this one; only in France they're called bistros. I had some wonderful learning experiences from those types of eateries. The clientele was very much the same, regular patrons that looked forward to their meal and a touch of camaraderie only in France even a light repast could take several hours instead of a quick half hour break we here in America call lunch. My phone has been vibrating constantly since I sat down so I check my messages and see I have five and all but one from Dare.

Listening to them I know nothing has changed. He insists he didn't lie to me, he really was with his son, at least part of the evening, and then he suddenly remembered he had a meeting with a buying group his father was involved in. I delete them as I listen to them, knowing I don't believe him. The last one sums it up.

"If you can't trust me going into our relationship, how in the hell do you expect us to make a go of it? Call me back, dammit." Then a pause and he softly says, "Please," before he ends the call.

My heart says he's telling the truth, at least partially but my gut says to walk away before I'm reparably damaged. I look up and see my waitress coming towards me carrying a cup of chili and a beautifully grilled sandwich. She smiles when she sets it in front of me.

"This looks great," I tell her and she beams with pride. "Is that your husband behind the counter working the grill?" I ask knowing right away it is but I don't want to think about my current situation at the moment so I strike up a conversation with the girl.

"Yeah, we're working our way through school and now I'm about to bring another twist into the mix." She says, rubbing her distended belly lovingly.

"When are you due?" I whisper taking a bite of the creamy cheese sandwich perfectly grilled.

"A week and a half ago," she laughs, "They want to induce me day after tomorrow if I don't go on my own, so either way I have to work up to the minute."

"Well tell your husband his chili is three alarms good, and the grilled cheese is the best I've ever had. I mean it. What are you both studying?" I take another bite of the soup.

"Hotel/Restaurant management at the local community college," she says, "well I need to see about that couple that just sat down in my station; enjoy your meal."

I watch the happy young woman walk over to her next customer. I feel a touch of envy at the simplicity of her life at the moment not that I'd want to trade places with her. I finish my meal and fish out one of my business cards, write a note on the back and take out enough cash to pay for the meal, plus a hefty tip for her excellent service. I pick up my purse and wave at the young woman and her husband, who nods at me like I'm crazy, but I feel lighter as I walk outside and climb back into my car and speed off to my next appointment.

I'm on a roll as the Arts Festival have everything lined out, chosen the menu they want, the wine and cheese course as well. Since we're supplying the cake, I make a note to Nana they want her red velvet cake with traditional cream cheese frosting, a no brainer in my opinion.

Thirty minutes later I'm sailing down the highway, two contracts signed, sealed, and ready to be delivered. Not a bad day after all, with the exception of having to deal with an angry Dare when I get back, but I still had a good day in spite of all the drama.

At a quarter after five I pull into my driveway and am not surprised to see Dare's rover parked in front of my garage. Dressed in a beautifully tailored gray pinstripe suit, white shirt and pale yellow tie he is every secretary's dream boss, gorgeous from the top of his wavy dark hair all the way down to his brown wing tips. His sunglasses shield me from his piercing stare but I can feel it just the same. The man is still pissed off. He is leaning against the driver's side door talking on the phone, and when he moves I see someone else in the vehicle, a little lighter haired boy that must be his son.

Sammy is pretending to be driving the truck and he smiles and waves at me as I pull into the open garage.

Dare brought his son with him, but why? I thought he wanted to take it slow, meet the boy later on? I lean over and grab my purse and attaché case. Before I can open my door Dare and the handsome little boy are standing in the garage. Sammy reaches over to open the door for me, steps out of the way, and allows me to climb out of my car. I look over at the miniature Dare and see the twinkle in his eyes, so like his father's, and apparently every other member of the family. He holds out his hand and introduces himself.

"Hello, my name is Sammy Steele, and I'm very pleased to meet you." He says mimicking perfectly what he was taught to say. He is dressed a bit more casual than his old man. His blue jeans are cuffed at the ankle, his red canvas sneakers are scuffed, and the T-shirt he is wearing has what appears to be chocolate ice cream streak running down his belly.

Shaking his hand I tell him, "The pleasure is all mine young man."

He looks up at his father and Dare nods his head, he did a good job. I look at the man responsible for all my pain and pleasure and know this is going to be a long evening. I close my car door and walk up the step, unlocking the back door and walk inside, knowing there's no way I could turn Dare away, not with his gorgeous little guy standing beside him.

"Sammy, may I call you Sammy or do you prefer Sam?" I ask him, waiting on his response.

Again he looks up at his Father who shrugs his broad shoulders at the question. Sammy tilts his head to the side and says, "Sammy will do."

I laugh at his matter of fact tone but nod my head.

"Well Sammy, would you mind to press the long white button on the other side of the door, I need to close the garage bay door please." I ask him and he smiles up at me.

"Cool, I'll be right back Dad," he says and walks over to the garage door and standing on tip toe he pushes the button, holding it down unnecessarily until the bay door closes and the area becomes dark.

He walks back over to where we're standing and says, "All done. That's pretty loud," he tells me, "we have four of them at home, but I've never pushed the buttons before, I have to say it was neat. Hey Dad, maybe when we get home I get out and push our buttons?"

Dare smiles and ruffles his son's strawberry blonde head, "We'll see, but you might be asleep by the time we get home, but if you're awake, it's a deal."

I look down at my camel colored pump, anywhere but at the honest look of fascination on Sammy's face and the loving look on his father's. Walking down the hall towards the kitchen I set my bag and case on the table, turn to my unexpected guests and start the ball rolling.

"Well gentlemen, to what do I owe this unexpected visit?" I ask, rubbing my hands together.

Dare walks over to stand in front of me and says, "We needed to talk, and I wanted Sammy to meet you, so here we are, such as we are, right Sammy?"

The small boy looks around the place and asks, "Do you have a dog? I do, his name is Buddy but he hurt his foot, I mean paw. He'll get better, but if he doesn't Dad says we'll take him to a vet, that's a dog doctor."

I bend down and smile at Sammy. Good thing I made all those cupcakes.

"I don't have a dog, but I do have a cat, well sort of…his name is Mouser, because he catches mice for me," I tell him, "he's usually lying on the patio table out back, why don't you go see if he's back there while I speak with your father, it'll only take a minute or two, okay?" I ask.

"Sure, but don't let Dad yell at you like he does MS Rhonda," he says as he walks towards the back door. He turns around with his hand on the door knob and says, "Sometimes Dad uses words that would get my mouth washed out with soap."

I start laughing at the child's sincerity and then the faker winks at his dad and opens the back door, and goes off in search of the cat. Before I can put some space between us Dare is on me. Forcing my hands behind my back he swoops down and starts devouring my lips and my neck. I try to struggle but a part of me is dying inside to touch him, hold him to me.

"God you're driving me crazy," He murmurs against my lips. "I want to throttle you then throw you over my shoulder and make wild passionate love to you, and I intend to do exactly that, first chance I get."

I push out of his arms and put the kitchen table between us like a couple of days ago.

"No Dare, you're not going to do either," I tell him. "You lied to me, and were still lying to me even after you were caught, I won't play these games, I just can't. And then you bring your adorable kid out here as a shield? What the hell Dare? That's a cheap trick and you know it."

"God dammit Cam I'm desperate here," he snaps running his hand through his thick hair, "I'd have brought my father too if I thought he could help me out, but he's part of the problem, but that's another story."

He looks frazzled, tired and tense, but is that because of me? I want to believe him but how can I when his own staff turned him in.

"What do I have to do to convince you I was not out on a date with Starr? Name it and I'll do it, please, I'm dying over here." He says slowly working his way around the table, trying to get within arms distance of me.

"Did you go clubbing after your dinner meeting?" I ask slowly walking around the table.

"Yes," he says, "but it's not what you think. I want to explain things but I can't just yet, but I swear on my child's life I didn't take her out to eat, or take her dancing, or want to spend any time with that whore. She's poison and will be gone soon, but that's all I can tell you, you just have to trust me on this, please baby, don't ruin what we have, I need you, love you with all my heart, I swear."

He reaches over and pulls me into his arms, pressing the softest kisses along my forehead, down my cheek until I can't stand not touching him. I reach up and pull his lips towards mine, and once we connect I know I'm lost. He is so dear to me; every time we kiss I feel the electricity flow through my body. I kiss him back with all the pent up frustration and anger I felt from last night. We're both grinding our lips and our hips into each other, groping and pressing our bodies together in a fit of angry passion. If we hadn't heard Sammy yell we'd probably have ended up flat on the table.

"Daddy!" he shouts and Dare jerks away from me and races to the back door wrenching it open and rushing outside taking in his surroundings. The brick pavers are laid out in about a twelve by twelve foot square with Grandma Kate's wrought iron table and four chairs taking center stage. A brick fireplace complete with a built in stainless steel grill creates a wall and a I've been growing fresh herbs in large terra cotta pots which line the perimeter of the deck; But no Sammy. I can hear him whimpering but I can't locate him.

"Hey pal, where'd you go?" Dare asks frantically looking all around for his son.

"Up here," a little voice says and we both look up and see a pair of red sneakers dangling from a tree branch pretty far up in the tree. The frightened boy is desperately hugging a good size branch from the same tree his father climbed to reach my bathroom window, only he's out on the edge of the limb. If either of us tried to climb up there I'm afraid the branch would break.

"Come on down son, I'll catch you." Dare urges the boy walking over to stand underneath the massive tree.

"I can't move Dad, I'm scared." He whispers, and then looks over at me and I can tell he's embarrassed as well as scared. I feel his fear and shame as if it was my own.

"Hey Sammy, when I was a couple years older than you, I got stuck up in that same old tree," I tell him, "my brother Jon tried to talk me down but I couldn't move either, so you know what I did?"

"No, what'd you do?" he asks rubbing his tear stained cheeks on the sleeve of his dirty T-shirt. He stares at me with such a hopeful look in his teary eyes I almost loose it myself.

"I hugged that old tree branch, scooted my butt over to the edge of the porch and climbed into the bathroom window. See, it's open." I look over at Dare and say, "Didn't you do this recently too Dad?" I ask making Dare dart a glance at me then smile.

"Sammy I've climbed this tree before so believe me," he laughs making his son look down at him, "If I can climb in through that window, I know you can do it. Just take your time and you'll do fine."

"If you'd like I'll go inside and open the window wider for you and your Dad will stand right below you, just in case you'd rather jump," I tell him, not using the word scared, or fall.

Dare nods his head at me and I race up stairs, kicking off my shoes as I go until I reach the bathroom. Stepping into the tub I open the window as wide as I can get. Leaning out the window I can almost touch his arm but he's too far out.

"Sam come on inside and we'll have some orange cupcakes with an Italian cream frosting I think you'll really like." I tell him distracting him from looking down at the ground. "Maybe you can give me your best opinion, see if they're sweet enough, you know from a kid's point of view."

"Yeah, I could do that, cause' I'm a kid and I know how sweet things are supposed to be, cause I sneak lots of Jimmie's cookies when she's not looking." He tells me all the while scooting closer towards the open window. Dare is holding his breath down below but remains silent not wanting to distract the little guy since he's on the move.

"What kind of cookies? Does she make them or buy them?" I ask trying to keep him talking for a little longer; I can almost reach him now. Looking down I see the frantic look on Dare's face and pray I can reach the boy soon before he starts to panic or get tired from gripping the tree branch so hard.

"She takes them out of the fridge and scoops them on a pan, then bakes them, so I guess she makes them and buys them." He tells me and is finally close enough to put his dirty, sweaty hand in mine and I haul him inside. I swing him over the tub; rubbing his dirty shoe across the front of my cashmere shift leaving a perfect sneaker imprint as he goes. Dare is racing up the stairs and once he reaches the bathroom he grabs Sammy up into his arms and hugs him tightly. I climb out of the tub and start to leave, wanting to give them some privacy when Dare reaches out his arm and pulls me into his chest and hugs me hard to his heaving side.

"Thank you," he whispers and kisses me on the lips, Sammy watches us with a smile on his lips.

"Gross Dad," he says, "but thanks for opening that window, I'd hated to have to pay for it when I kicked it open, right Dad?"

Dare shakes his head and starts laughing at his son's assessment of the situation. I look up into his eyes and see the relief. I stare at his lips and want to feel them on me in the worst way. Dare must be feeling the same because he keeps staring at me with such longing.

"Sammy, I'm going to really kiss Cam this time so you better close your eyes," he jokes with his son but is looking so intently at me I feel my heart rate accelerate.

"Just tell me when it's over, okay?" the boy says squeezing his eyes shut as tightly as he can.

"Hurry up and kiss me so Sammy can have a cupcake," I tell my love.

"Cupcakes," Dare shouts, "Sammy hop down and go down to the kitchen and find those cupcakes."

He sets his son down and the little guy takes off like a bolt of lightning. His dad is just as quick when he pulls me into his arms and starts devouring my mouth.

"God you feel so good," he says, "I need you something fierce. Feel how badly I need you."

I rub my belly against the strained fabric of his slacks and know if Sammy wasn't downstairs I'd me flat on my back on the bathroom floor by now. I press his aroused flesh through the fabric. Rubbing my hand up and down the front of his trousers Dare groans into my mouth. Then we both freeze when his son starts shouting.

"Hey Dad, I found them! I can't reach them!" Sammy hollers and I hear him running back up the stairs.

Dare turns away from the door adjusting the front of his pants, so I step in front of him, blocking Sammy's view.

"I put them up high so Mouser wouldn't get into them," I tell the excited little boy who stops in front of me when I block his path. "Let's get the step stool out and you can climb up there and hand the container down to me. It will be just like climbing the tree only not as tall."

"I like tall things," he says walking in front of me, heading back down the stairs.

I look over my shoulder at Dare and he blows me a kiss, but waits for a few more minutes before joining us in the kitchen. Sammy helps me put the cupcakes on my milk glass cake stand, and arranges them to his liking. I look up and see Dare leaning against the door way, watching us.

"Hey Dad, look what Cam is letting me do, ranging cupcakes, like she does. But I want the tall ones on my side, you take the short ones." He says, touching every cake with his dirty little hands.

Dare looks over at me and says, "I hope these weren't for a customer, or we're in trouble pal."

Sammy looks over at me with concern, "did I ruin somebody's Burt-day?" He asks in such a sweet voice I lean over and hug his narrow shoulders.

"No sweetheart," I tell him, "sometimes when I'm upset, or angry, or waiting on a phone call I bake, and that's what these are."

He grins and says, "If you'd bake this many for me, I'd never call you so you'd keep making them." He licks the cream frosting off his hands and looks over at his Dad. "Can you upset her and maybe she'll make some more?"

"Sammy, I think I upset her enough for one day, don't you, Cam?" He asks using his nickname for me more and more.

"Sometimes I might burn them if I'm really upset," I tell them, then lean over and start tickling Sammy until his giggles fill the room when he looks up at me with such mischievous delight.

I fall in love with Sammy at that exact moment. Something inside me snaps and I feel the tears welling up in my eyes. Thankfully the boy is too busy counting all his tall cupcakes to notice I stopped talking, but his father knows, and nods his head for me to leave the room, just to get myself under control.

"Excuse me Sammy but I need to get something from my office," I tell him and scoot back my chair and all but run out of the room.

I can hear Dare talking to his son, but I can't tell what they're saying, which is probably a good thing, because that little boy's honesty and goodness is breaking my heart. I want to snatch him up and take off for the far reaches of the earth, anything to protect that innocence, that charm. But I know he's not mine to have so I wipe my eyes, blow my nose on a tissue from the box sitting beside my desk. Having got my hormones under control I walk back into the kitchen to find Dare standing at the sink, washing the sweet cream frosting off his hands.

He turns to face me when I pull out one of the kitchen chairs. Dare walks over and pulls out a chair and sits down beside me, drapes his arm around my shoulder and pulls me into his chest.

"I know how you feel," he whispers, "and I know you're thinking that should be our kid, and he can be or will be if you agree to marry me. He can't help but fall in love with you, just like his old man."

I start crying all over again and know that's the sweetest proposal I've ever heard. But I know we'd be rushing things so I shake my head and lean up to kiss his lips.

"I'll say yes, one of these days," I tell him smiling into his clear blue eyes, "but we both know it's too soon, like you said earlier. I'm okay, really I am, it's just he's so precious and easy to love."

He kisses the top of my head and pulls apart when Sammy walks back inside, immediately concerned that I'm crying. He walks over to me, lays his dirty hand on my shoulder and gives me a pat.

"What's wrong with her Dad? Did you make her mad again?" he asks in such a way only truthful little boys can. "Kiss her again, maybe then she won't be so sad."

"I think that's a good idea, Pal." He tells his boy, "pucker up Camy, I'm about to make you 'very' less sad."

I can't help but laugh out loud at the Father and Son tag team. They must be hell on Dare's dates. But I know that's not true, since Dare's never introduce any of his 'dates' to his son, before me. That makes me feel infinitely better so I lean over and wink at Sammy then take Dare's face in both of my hands and kiss him hard and quickly making Sammy start laughing again. Dare takes the lead and soon we're both breathless and Sammy is back to counting cupcakes.

17

Having decided to stay for supper I put them to work. My two sous chefs-in-training are about to commit mutiny from the sounds of their grumbling and whining but they're so funny, chopping up vegetables they both swear they won't eat, picking up the bits of carrots and celery that keeps falling off the chopping blocks. I've never used this many vegetables for one meal even in my buffet dishes. Finally for the sake of expediency as well as economics I relieve them of their duty as I continue with my cream sauce. Father and son head to the sink and wash their hands, putting more water on the floor than in the basin. They start splashing and flicking water at each other, laughing and shouting. They're making a mess, but melting my heart in the process.

"Guys, stop it you're making a mess all over my floor." I tell them in a firm voice, and drop a dish towel on the floor and use my foot to start mopping up the puddles.

Suddenly Dare hollers at me, "Cam, look out!"

Startled I look up and get squirted in the face with the spray hose attachment in Dare's hand, the dastardly duo laughing and whooping it up at my expense. I take the towel and use it as a shield until I reach the sink and wrench the hose out of his grasp. Then turn the water up and send a downpour over their heads, making them run for cover.

"Come on Sammy; let's get out of here while we still can." Dare says, grabbing his son around the waist and running into the living room. "Call us when suppers ready," Dare shouts.

"Yeah, let us know so we can wash our hands before we eat." The sneaky little boy says and starts giggling at the thought of getting his hands back on my sprayer.

Thank God I took out some puff pastry from the freezer before I started supper; at least it should be at a workable temperature by now. I look at the messy table and all the odd sized pieces of vegetables and start laughing in spite of myself. Kit and Saul could do a better job than those two. I heat up the stock pot, dump the chicken breasts and the vegetables inside and get them on the boil while I clean up every surface in my usually pristine kitchen.

An hour later I'm brushing the tops of four white lion head soup bowls with egg wash, and slide the sheet pan into the oven. My guests are awfully quiet. I wipe my hands on a dry dish towel and walk into the living and find father and son sound asleep, having watched the carton channel all this time. I love how natural they are together, and can't wait to be included in their lives. They look right at home in my cozy living area with the fire in the hearth burning down, their sock feet resting on the white slip covered sectional. I turn on the lamp setting on the end table and leave them to their slumber. Walking into the office I check my emails and see Roz has sent me a new contract to get signed. I fill out the pertinent information and print it out, knowing I'll have to wait until Monday to contact the wedding coordinator's office.

That reminds me, I thought Dare was scheduled for meetings all afternoon and this evening? I'd bet the farm he is playing hooky. Well for once I'm glad he lied and decided to come see me. I log off my computer and set the table, loving the smell of chicken roasting in the oven. The pastry smells so good and the scent takes me back to my cooking classes and my practice presentations Dare gobbled up, saying he'd give me an A+ in all categories. Lost in the memories I jump when I feel small arms wrap around my waist. Looking down at the little charmer I can't help but smile.

"You really like my Dad, don't you?" He asks looking up at me with such a serious look on his face I realize I could never hurt this child.

"Yes I really like him and you too." I reply, "How do you feel about that, you know me and your Dad liking each other? Does that bother you?" I ask, praying he's okay with it.

"No, it doesn't bother me, but I just don't want you to make him angry, like Rhonda does." He informs me, "Papaw says she's a stick and needs to eat a donut or six."

I start laughing at his candor and feel the need to hug him. He looks up at me and grins knowing he isn't supposed to be saying things like that. He walks over to the table and pulls out a chair and sits down, lightly drumming his hands on the surface. I see a perfect opportunity to delve into his psyche and find out what he wants for his birthday.

"Tell me something, if you could have any kind of a party, what kind would you like to have?" I ask, hoping for inspiration on his upcoming party theme.

"Well, super heroes are good, and *X-men* are one of my favorite comic books, but I think I'd like a cowboys and Indians party, maybe have a bunch of real Indians come over and we could play games, like cops and robbers. No wait, what about a hunting party, you know where you get a list of things and you have to find them by reading stuff off the paper?" he asks unsure what they call it.

"Scavenger hunts?" I ask, "Is that something you like to do?"

"Yeah, my friend had a party and we dressed like pirates looking for a buried treasure chest, full of gold, and candy, and bones."

He goes on to describe the latest pirate movie his Papaw took him to see, but he didn't like the skeletons all that much, he wasn't afraid, he just didn't like them. My timer goes off and as I open the oven door and bend down to reach for the pies, I hear Dare tell Sammy to get back. I set the hot baking sheet with the dishes on the empty front burner to cool.

"Leave Camy alone while she's by the oven," he says, "get washed up, it smells like supper is ready."

"Can I wash up here in the kitchen?" he asks his father who knows why he wants to wash up at the kitchen sink and not the bathroom.

"No, use the bath in Camy's office, and step on." He tells the boy. "Man that smells great, is that the chicken pot pie Sammy and I made?"

Laughing at how silly he is I turn around, wrap the dishtowel around his neck and pull him down to my level. He kisses me and makes my toes curl. I can't get enough of him. Sammy runs back into the room and opens the refrigerator door.

"Can I have a soda?" he asks me so I look over at Dare who is shaking his head.

I nod back to the parent before I reply to Sammy, "May I have a soda?"

Sammy looks over at his father and who shrugs his shoulders like earlier.

Again I say, "May I have a soda? Not can I have a soda?"

Sammy nods his head and smiles before asking, "May I have a soda?" and he reaches for a can of pop.

"No you may not," I tell him making the father laugh and the son groan. "But you may have chocolate milk if you'd like."

Sammy lights up and tries to reach the milk carton on the top shelf but can't reach it. Before the he tries to use the crisper drawer as a step stool Dare quickly reaches around him and pulls out the milk, setting it on the table he looks around for a glass.

"Go over to Grandma Kate's glass cupboard and you'll find a drinking glass on the bottom shelf." I direct him but Dare holds up his hands.

"He usually drinks out of a plastic cup, for safety sake, plus those glasses look old, irreplaceable." Dare explains. "We wouldn't want to damage your set."

"Nonsense, if children are ever to learn what to do and what not to at the table, they must learn from example. Now Sammy you're not going to break Grandma Kate's old glass are you? You'll be careful, and act like a gentleman at the dinner table, won't you?" I ask him.

"Yes ma'am." He says making my heart swell and his Father's too from the look on Dare's face even though he still looking doubtful.

"There, that's settled," I tell them but Sammy shakes his head at me and crooks his finger for me to bend down so he can whisper something in my ear. He cups his hand around his mouth and unwittingly whispers loud enough for Dare to hear what is being said.

"Dad sometimes smacks the table with his hand and makes all the dishes jump, at least he does when Papaw or Rhonda are eating supper with us. I think you need to ask him if he's going to break Grandma Kate's glasses too."

I whisper back, "Good point, if we have to be good, he does too, right?"

He has a mischievous grin on his face and says, "Right."

"Well Mr. Steele it's been brought to my attention you sometimes behave in a less than gentlemanly fashion at the dinner table." I tell him playfully admonishing his previous behavior and loving that he is having a difficult time not laughing at the two of us. "There will be no table slapping, no yelling, shouting, cursing, or ..." I look over at Sammy and wink, "tickling at the supper table, do you agree to behave yourself?"

He wraps his arms around my waist and says, "Yes ma'am, I agree to that."

I look down at Sammy, who is giggling at his father having to promise to behave, but then he launches his body into ours and we end up with a group hug.

"Okay, let's get the chocolate milk made, the wine poured, and the coffee brewing for later. Chop chop boys," I order them about and love it when Dare starts pushing and pulling on Sammy hindering his progress in bringing me the chocolate syrup from the pantry.

Fifteen minutes later we're setting down to this wild and crazy meal, just like a family. I pick up my napkin, drape it across my lap and wait for the guys to do the same. Dare rolls his eyes and rocks his head from side to side which make Sammy start to giggle. Next I pick up my soup spoon and tap on the top of my crust covered dish.

"Do you hear how hollow that sounds? That's a sign of a good, flaky crust, go ahead, gently tap on the top of your pie, but be careful the filling is hot." I advise them both.

Dare taps on his crust then 'accidently' pushes his spoon through to the filling.

"Oh no!" he jokingly cries putting his hands on either side of his face in mock alarm; "Now I'll never know if it was a great pie crust or just a good one."

Sammy starts laughing and does the same thing, poking his spoon down deep into the center of his dish and pulls out a steaming spoonful of creamy chicken and vegetables. He carefully takes a bite and starts chewing, and when he swallows, he reaches for this chocolate milk and takes a big drink leaving a milk mustache. Dare motions with his fingers for his son to wipe his mouth on the napkin and nods his head when the mustache disappears. Sammy remembers to put his napkin back on his lap.

"That was dee-lish-shus!" Sammy says, "But it was hot."

He points at his half empty glass of milk, licks his lips and says, "Camy that is the best drink I've ever had!"

Dare rolls his eyes at his son's antics but I can't help but be charmed by the little bugger. We finish our meal without a hand slam, a curse word, or a broken dish. I can't remember the last time, if there ever was one, I enjoyed a meal more than this one. By the time Dare and I are ready for coffee, Sammy is starting to nod off.

"Were you planning on driving back tonight or staying over?" I ask hoping he wanted to stay the night. We're holding hands and watching the munchkin fight his exhaustion.

"I'd have to sleep in the guest room with Sammy," he softly says, "but once he's out, he's out for the night. Let me get our bag out of the truck and we'll get him settled in for the night."

"I'll get your bag, you take him on up," I offer knowing his keys are in the ignition.

He carries his son upstairs to lay him down on the full size bed, the same one Dare and I made love on only two days ago? It seems longer than that. I pull the rover into the empty bay next to my Mustang and close the bay doors. Hefting their black overnighter I lug it up the step and into the kitchen. Dare removed his shoes and socks and silently walks down the stairs and picks up the suitcase like it was empty.

"What's in there a load of bricks?" I ask following him up the stairs and joining him at the foot of the full size bed where Sammy is already stretched out and sleeping.

"You don't know anything about little boys and the toys they have to have, even on an over-nighter. You're such a girl." He says and nudges my shoulder with his.

"Fine, this girl is going to have a cup of coffee and a Madeline, care to join me?" I ask.

"Can I have a cupcake instead?" he asks raising his chin and tilting his head to the side.

"Fine, you're such a baby." I huff and turn to walk back down the stairs.

"I'll show you who will be crying 'baby' when I get him to bed." He warns me.

"Promises, promises Mr. Steele." I tell him and walk back into the kitchen finally understanding the joys of having someone around, even doing the mundane things like putting a child to bed, cleaning up the dishes, or enjoying a simple dessert. I can't believe the feeling of joy I'm experiencing at the moment and know there's more to come in this evening's entertainment.

18

Fixing coffee the next morning I can't help but smile at what a great time I had last night. Once Dare came back downstairs we sat around the kitchen table, eating dessert, drinking coffee, and talking for hours. He told me about Rachel and how troubled she was, how he felt when she handed him Sammy, how afraid he was about his family and their future. He shared his past so openly, not only about his family but his business, where he wants to take Steele, Inc. We laughed, I cried, and we bonded like never before. When we finished our coffees he took our cups and rinsed them in the sink, then he turned towards me and I knew we were going to make love.

Instead of walking into my bedroom, he took my hand and led me to the bathroom and started filling the tub with water and then added some bubbles for good measure. I told him we had to be quiet, because the vents acted like speakers so we quietly bathed together, and then made love in my bedroom until we were both so exhausted we crashed.

A little before dawn he kissed me awake, slid inside of me from behind and we made love so softly, so sweetly it was magical, until he left me and went downstairs to slide into bed with his son. I slept for another hour or so, but then needed to get up. I didn't want to waste one minute of my precious time with my guys sleeping. I threw on my favorite cut offs, a pair of leather flip flops and a brown and gray striped T-shirt, pulling my hair back into a pony tail I'm ready to start the day.

I hear footsteps on the guest stairs and know my little guy is awake and on his way down.

"Good morning Sammy," I tell him smiling as he rubs his eyes.

Wearing his blue pajamas, X-men of course, he walks over to where I'm standing and wraps his arms around my hips, and whispers, "morning."

Hugging his small body to me I lean down and kiss the top of his head.

"What would you like for breakfast?" I ask figuring Dare will be coming downstairs any minute.

"Cereals good," he tells me and walks over to the table, pulls out his chair and rests his head on his hand; apparently he isn't a morning person.

"What's wrong Sam, didn't you sleep well?" I ask hoping that's not the case.

"Yeah, but Dad is a blanket hog." He complains, "And he sleeps sideways in the bed, taking up all the room. Plus he snores when he sleeps on his back, or is really tired."

Smiling at the fact I'm the reason he was really tired I decide to make it up to the little man with a special meal.

"How does pancakes and bacon sound, no cold cereal in this house." I inform him, "Do you like pancakes and bacon?" I love to hear him tell his opinions so I encourage him to talk with me.

"Everybody loves bacon," he says then smiles, "Dad and Papaw always fight over the last piece, sometimes they even steal it off each other's plates. But Jimmie gets angry and tells them she's not going to fix lunch if they don't behave, and sometimes Papaw tells her he's not going to pay her celery if she doesn't feed him."

I laugh out loud at Sammy's misunderstanding of celery and salary. He laughs with me and together we start making breakfast. Dare comes downstairs, showered and dressed in a pair of navy walking shorts, a grey striped V-neck T-shirt and a pair of brown boat shoes. His arms and legs are both tanned and on his left wrist is his ever present watch and on the right is that homemade yarn bracelet. He looks as relaxed as I've ever seen him. He laughs when he sees Sammy standing on a wooden step stool, wearing one of my old chef's coats, and whipping something in a small bowl with a wooden spoon.

"Good morning Dad," Sammy says looking up from the mixing bowl, "I'm on batter duty." He looks over at me and nods his head and smiles.

"Good morning son, what kind of batter?" he asks looking over Sammy's shoulder and kissing his son on the top of his head.

"Pancakes and their not from a box, those are disgusting." He informs his father repeating what I told him earlier. "Everything's better if you make it from snatch and love."

We both laugh at the little boy and his catchy turn of phrase.

"I think you meant to say 'scratch' but I agree, everything is better when it's made with love." Dare agrees and looks over at me leaning up against the counter sipping my coffee.

He walks over to me, takes my cup and helps himself to the hot brew. Setting the cup on the counter behind me he pulls me into his arms and kisses me like we've been apart for longer than a couple of hours. I kiss him back and love the taste of coffee on his tongue. I groan into his mouth.

"Dad you're hurting her with your kiss," Sammy says without turning around from his work station. "Maybe you should only kiss her on the top of the head, like you do me. That never hurts."

We start laughing at his crazy suggestion and Dare playfully swats the seat of Sammy's PJs just barely showing beneath the bottom of his chef's shirt making Sammy giggle.

"Let me get you some coffee, and then I think Sammy here will be ready to start the griddle, right Sam-a-lam?" I ask my helper.

"Right Cam-o-lam," he replies making his father chuckle at our easy camaraderie. "Dad you have to set the table, use Grandma Kate's dishes, but be careful, remember last night?"

Shaking his head at being out numbered in the kitchen he opens the cupboard and counts out the number of plates and glasses needed, and adds a coffee cup for himself. Setting the table seems like a small price to pay in order to enjoy this feast we're about to prepare.

Thirty minutes later, I have one boy covered in batter, maple syrup smeared all over the counter, a couple burnt pancakes, and one laughter filled room, we're starving.

"This is the best breakfast ever!" Sammy declares reaching for his chocolate milk. "Don't you think this is the best breakfast ever Dad?"

Smiling at his son's enthusiasm he agrees, "Yes it's the best - The best food, the best chefs, and the best family."

I start to choke up and have to use my napkin to hide my emotions. I love having them here and will miss them terribly when they're gone. But until then, I'm going to enjoy every waking moment with my two guys.

After breakfast, the cleanup, and Sammy's shower, Dare agrees to take us to the Studio, for a grand tour. We climb into the rover and fifteen minutes later we arrive at my favorite place in the world, my domain.

From the number of vehicles parked in the drive I see Nana's here as well as Saul which is unusual for them to be here on a weekend with nothing scheduled. They're up to something for sure. I unlock the front door and usher my men to the kitchen where I find BJ, Kit, Nana, and Saul working at the counters, wiping down the cabinets, and organizing the pantry.

"What are you guys doing here, on a free Saturday no less?" I ask looking at their surprised faces and my two guests.

Nana straightens up from wiping down the base cabinets and smiles at us.

"Well, Roz is coming back tomorrow and we wanted to have everything in tip top working order." She says, "Since we don't know what kind of a mood she's going to be in, we decided to give the kitchen a good once over, just to be safe."

"She sounds like a terror," Dare says trying to ease the tension that suddenly has filled the room. "I thought you were the Queen Bee."

Nana and BJ laugh and Sammy walks over to stand in front of Saul who was wiping off the top of the commercial refrigerator.

"Are you a giant?" Sammy asks the big man with a look of awe on his face.

"No, are you an elf?" Saul asks bending down at the waist having to fight back a smile at the precocious young man.

Sammy laughs and says, "of course not, I'm a kid, and we're supposed to be short, but you're huge!"

Everyone laughs at his comments and the air is no longer crackling with tension. Kit and BJ walk over to Sammy and introduce themselves as well as Saul. Nana shakes hands with Sammy and asks if he'd like a cookie.

"Yes thank you," he replies and lets Saul pick him up and set him on one of the wooden counter stools. Sammy is busy looking around the place, fascinated by the stainless steel appliances that are bigger than normal. Seeing the work area from a child's perspective I follow his gaze around the kitchen. There are large expanses of counter tops with heavy free standing mixers, blenders, fryers, and ice cream makers. The massive pot racks hanging over the islands and dozen crocks of all shapes and sizes holding utensils and spatulas big enough to flip ten burgers at a time. It looks like a giant's kitchen. "Everything is huge around here, except you guys." He says to Kit and BJ.

"We're bigger than Nana, and Carrie Anne, and especially bigger than you squirt." Kit jokes and ruffles Sammy's hair.

Nana hands him a chocolate chip cookie the size of his head, causing his eyes to widen and his mouth to drop open.

He takes the cookie with both of his small hands and holds it up for us to see.

"What do you say Sam," Dare encourages his son to use his manners.

"Gee Whiz that's huge!" the boy replies, then laughs and says, "thank you, Nana."

"You're welcome, Sammy. Would you like some milk to go along with that monster?" She asks nodding for BJ to grab the carton from the fridge behind him as she gets him a glass. He looks a bit disappointed the glass isn't on the large size as well.

"Are these glasses Grandma Kate's too?" he asks and confuses Nana with his question.

Smiling at him I say, "No, these are cheapies, don't worry about them," and he nods his head making me and Dare smile at last evening's antics.

Saul grabs a couple more glasses and holds them for BJ to fill them up. He looks over at Dare and asks, "Do you need a glass?"

Dare smiles and squeezes my waist, letting me know he's cool with the guys and nods his head.

"Yeah, and I'll take a giant cookie too," he replies and accepts the glass of milk from my self-appointed body guard and the cookie from Nana.

She motions her head for me to follow her into the pantry, away from the guys.

"Are you alright?" she asks, "I'm not prying, but it appears you're in a much better place than you were yesterday."

I smile and hug her practically giddy with delight making her laugh out loud before covering her mouth with her hand.

"Oh my God Nana, you have no idea…" I reply and we both start laughing like school girls.

"Since you're here," Kit hollers loud enough for me and Nana to hear, "maybe Sammy would like to help us finish the inventory, if you two need a moment alone, you know a little private conversation in your office." He winks at me as I return to the kitchen, making me want to clobber him over his head. But Dare takes control of this conversation.

"No, we've spoken quite a bit, last night and again this morning," he says in a 'none of your business' kind of voice. "We're just here for the Grand Tour then we have to get back to Sonoma, but thanks for offering, we might just take you up on your babysitting offer, but not today."

Kit stands there, shocked that Dare thought he was offering to babysit. He quickly looks over at BJ, who is grinning at how the joke back-fired on him. Saul laughs out loud and shakes his head at the joker.

"When will you ever learn to keep your mouth shut?" Saul asks taking a bite of cookie.

Sammy is mimicking every move the big man makes. He looks up at Saul and shakes his head as if he too can't believe Kit would say that, even though Sammy hasn't a clue what Kit implied. He is just going along with his hero of the moment.

"You know that wasn't what I meant," Kit says looking scared at the possibility of having to watch over a child.

"What exactly did you mean then?" Dare asks tilting his head to the side, knowing Kit can't admit to trying to embarrass us.

"Forget it, a slight misunderstanding on my part," he mumbles and turns to grab a roll of paper towels and the glass cleaner. "I'll clean the pantry cabinets," he says and walks out of the room to the sound of everybody laughing at him.

19

The rest of the morning seemed to fly by. We spent an hour at the Studio, were I finally got to give my guys a peak into what we do as caterers. Sammy loved every minute, asking all sorts of questions, some silly but most your typically curious six year old questions wanting to know why, or what if… I enjoyed every minute, and so did Dare.

We left there and headed to the local convenience store to pick up a couple items we'd need for our picnic, which was Sammy's idea. He wanted to give me a break he said.

"You fixed supper last night, and breakfast this morning, let us cook something for you." He offered much to the surprise of both Dare and me.

"What did you have in mind Pal," Dare cautiously asks, "we don't know how to cook, remember Jimmie, she does the cooking for us."

He leans over the back of Dare's seat and cups his hands over his mouth and whispers, "but Dad we can buy stuff for a picnic." And he pats his father's shoulder as if to say, 'I got this covered'.

I stare at the two and have to turn my head towards the window in order not to laugh out loud.

"Alright, lunch is on us guys," my love tells me having a hard time not laughing as well. "Where's a good spot for a picnic?" he asks me and right away I know the perfect place, and it's not that far way.

"On the back of my property runs a creek that my brother Jon and I used to play in when we were Sammy's age. It's perfect, secluded, and all ours."

"Lead the way," Dare says, "Or would you rather drive?"

"Dad! You never let anyone drive the rover," Sammy squeals from the back seat, "can I drive too?"

"Yeah, in about ten years," he replies then looks over at me and waits for my answer.

"Yes please," I tell him, "I loved what little bit of time I spent in here the last time."

"Don't go there," he tells me and looks in the rearview mirror at his son, but he's no longer listening to us, just watching the scenery going by. "I'll pull in here at this gas station, I need to re-fuel anyway." He says and pulls up to the self-serve pump and gets out of the truck.

"Anybody need anything? Soda or maybe a trip to the restroom?" he looks pointedly at Sammy who suddenly nods his head and opens his door to get out. "Wait for me Sam," he shouts as his son starts to take off across the parking lot.

"Go ahead; I'll pump the gas while you help Sammy." I offer and open my door and walk around the hood of the vehicle.

"Thanks here let me get my credit card and we'll fill it up." He says and kisses me after he swipes his card and punches in his pin number. "We'll be right back."

Then puts his hand on Sammy's shoulder and soon they disappear into the convenience store. I look around and see all sorts of families out and about and feel such joy being one of them. Once the pump shuts off, I replace the nozzle and tighten the gas cap, then grab the windshield squeegee and clean the bugs off the glass. It's a small gesture, but one I'm happy to do plus I can't stand to look through a dirty windshield when I'm driving. The guys make it back to the truck a couple minutes later carrying a Styrofoam cooler, a bag of ice and a six pack of cold beer. Sammy is holding a whiffle ball set and a bag of green plastic army men. I pop the back hatch and climb back out of the truck to help.

"I thought you forgot I was out here," I tell the two guys and both laugh at me.

"Not likely, right sport?" Dare replies opening the bag of ice and emptying it into the cooler. "Hand me that grocery store bag with our sandwiches and potato salad; along with those drinks and we'll keep everything cold, I'd hate for our spread to go bad. It's the first meal we've made for you." He tells me and leans down to kiss me on the mouth.

"Look what I got," Sammy says holding up the plastic bag of men. "This is for me after we eat," he tells me, "but the ball and bat are for all of us to play with before we eat."

"Good ideas, work up an appetite, eat, and then send you off to war." I tease him and he smiles and nods his head.

"You got it." he quips making both Dare and me laugh out loud at his comment.

I slide behind the wheel, adjust the seat and mirrors and soon we're back on the highway, on our way to what will be the best picnic I've ever been on. We pass by several small farms, wave at oncoming vehicles and I point out things I remember from my childhood. Sammy starts up his twenty questions again and I answer them just as quickly.

"Who owns those cows?" he asks, pointing at several cows in the field.

"Farmer Jones," I tell him, making up names as I go. "That's his prize bull Mortimer over there in the fields, see him?"

"Where does that road lead to?" he asks pointing his finger to a gravel driveway.

"That goes to Betty Jo's house," I tell him making Dare smile at my answers and get in the spirit of the game.

"Who is she?" Sammy fires back.

"A sweet little old woman, probably a hundred and three by now, she makes great cherry pie and always has clothes on the line to dry," I tell my little one.

"Where is that tractor heading?" he asks as we have to slow down for the slower moving vehicle in front of us.

"Why that's Marty Brown, he owns all these fields on both sides of the road." I tell him, "it's been in his family for years and years, and his children will farm the land too, when its' their time."

He's quiet for a spell then says, "I hope they get a lot of money when they sell it."

I look over at Dare who shrugs his shoulders and then I look in the rearview mirror at how sad Sammy sounds.

"What's wrong Sam-a-lam? You seem sad." I ask him again looking over at a suddenly distracted Dare. He is looking out the window at nothing really.

"Papaw says when farmers don't make money they need to sell their land to him." he tells me suddenly leaning around the edge of my seat, he pats my arm and says, "but don't worry, Dad always pays them top dollar, right Dad?"

"Right, hey why don't you tell Camy how far you can hit a whiffle ball." He says changing the subject in exactly ten seconds not wanting to discuss the down side to his business; the selling of family dreams that never made it to fruition.

Sammy regales me with his record breaking hits until we turn off onto a dirt path at the back of my property. Coming in from the back, neither of the two guys realizes how close to home we actually are. It's about a two mile hike, straight through the woods, but I'll save that surprise for later.

After a rousing game of Whiffle ball, which the two guys mistakenly believe they won, we set up our picnic underneath a huge live oak tree. The three of us tackle our sandwiches and potato salad within seconds of sitting down on Dare's red and green plaid blanket he always keeps in the back of his rover. We forgot all about dishes and utensils but luckily I found one individually wrapped knife and fork packet in the bottom of my purse, left over from some outdoor event most likely. Sammy even shared the salt and pepper he proclaimed to be his.

Dare and I take turns using the fork while Sammy is enjoying playing pirate and using the plastic knife trying scoop up his share of potato salad. We're breaking all catering rules and eating out of the plastic container and it tastes great. After my first beer I'm relaxed and so comfortable, leaning up against the trunk of the tree, Dare's head resting on my lap and Sammy playing around the other side of the same tree.

After a full twenty minutes of quietly playing, Sammy leans around the trunk of the tree, looks over my shoulder and sees his father is napping. The young boy rests his back against the trunk and softly starts to speak.

"Is your real name Camy?" he asks out of the blue making the two army men in each of his hands jump onto my shoulder.

"No, your Daddy calls me Cam or Camy because that's what my initials spell. My real name is Carrie Anne Mosier, remember? What do your initials spell?" I ask him.

"Nothing, just S.D.S that doesn't spell anything does it." He asks sounding sad again. "I'm just Samuel Darius Steele."

"Well, what if we make up a special name, sort of like a secret code." I suggest and he moves closer to me, interested in my thoughts and the army men are now hiding in my ponytail.

"Like what? What can you make out of SDS?" he asks.

"Let me see, what if we make the first S stand for "Special" like special agent." I tell him, "The D could stand for Dangerous," I whisper with a hint of awe in my voice.

"Special Dangerous what?" he whispers getting into this game tossing his toy men back in the plastic bag where he was playing earlier.

He slides down the trunk and lifts my arm around his shoulder, nestling against my side. He looks up at me and grins before saying, "finish the name."

"You have to help," I tell him, "think of all the cool things that start with an s."

He's quiet for a second or two then starts listing everything he can that begins with the letter in question.

"Snakes, snails, sugar, salt, salamander, shit but I'm not allowed to say that but Dad says Papaw is full of it." He pauses then continues, "Ships, spiders, stumps like a tree stump, Saul... I could be a secret, dangerous, Saul."

"No, you don't want to be called Saul, believe me one of him is enough." I tell him and laugh at the strange look on his face.

"But what can the last S stand for?" he asks starting to sound worried.

Dare rolls over on his back, looks up at me, winks, and says, "Spy."

"That's it!" I tell Sammy, "Your Dad is brilliant, let's get him."

Together Sammy and I start tickling Dare until he rises up on his knees, grabs ahold of Sammy around his waist and lifts him over his head. He starts squealing and laughing so hard I can't help but roll over on my back, holding my sides. Dare lowers Sammy to the blanket and shares a secret nod with his son then they pounce on top of me. I wiggle and struggle trying to escape but they're too much.

"I give up, you win." I shout breathlessly, laughing so hard I can barely breathe.

"That's right, we win, Brilliant Dad and Special Dangerous Spy rule!" Dare says high fiving his son and together they fall back on top of me, exhausted from our wrestling match. Sammy is using my chest as a pillow and he once again draped my arm across his body.

"Do you really like my new name Dad?" Sammy asks his father, who is resting his head on my stomach too. Sammy turns his head and looks up at me and grins.

"Yes, I think it suits you to a T." he tells Sammy and they both cross their arms and relax.

Soon Sammy is asleep and I assumed his father was too but Dare looks up at me with such love in his eyes it takes my breath away.

"Now will you marry me?" he softly asks, his eyes sparkling with love and desire.

I comb my fingers through his thick hair and tell him, "Yes, I'll marry you. Any time, any place. I love you." I can barely get the words out my heart is so full of joy. "But I thought we needed to wait, let Sam get to know me, you know...your plan."

He grins at me and carefully rises up to kiss me, mindful of his son sleeping beside him. Deepening the kiss he murmurs on my lips.

"No need," he says, "he loves you, look at him. That's trust let me tell you. He is outgoing, but he doesn't like to share his space, at least he never has before. I want three maybe four kids total," he says, "are you alright with that?"

Laughing inside I nod my head, so happy I'm going to cry.

Dare kneels in front of me, reaches under his shirt collar and pulls out a long gold chain with a beautiful solitaire engagement ring attached to it. Unhooking the necklace he slides the ring off and into the palm of his hand. He gently holds the spectacular diamond ring up to his lips kisses the stone and slips it on my finger. It shimmers and sparkles as the sun suddenly shines through the leaves as if even the heavens approve of the union. I'm breathless, speechless, and ready to jump up for joy but instead I smile at the man I love most and kiss the ring as well.

"I bought this ring when we were in Paris, actually the first weekend we spent together, but it never felt like the right time, you know," He confesses, "I knew I wanted to spend the rest of my life with you, but I guess I was afraid I would come between you and your dream, your plans for your own future… then we got pregnant, I became an ass… well you recall the rest of the story." He stares at me then smiles, making me cry even harder.

"Dad, what'd you do to make Camy cry?" Sammy asks having just woke up from his catnap.

"I asked her to marry me, and she started crying." Dare whispers still watching me.

"I thought you liked my Dad," Sam says turning over on his stomach and looking up at me. He becomes protective of his Father. "You told me you like him."

"I love your Father," I softly say to the little champion and then I hold out my finger and show my soon to be son my ring. "I said yes, I can't wait to marry him."

"Then why are you crying? Oh, wait is this one of those times girls cry `cause they're happy?" he asks surprising me with his youthful insight. "I don't get that, do you Dad?"

Dare laughs and pulls his son to his chest and gives his head a rub and they start wrestling on top of me.

"Nobody gets it, well… except girls." He says in such a derogatory fashion I pull his hair, making him yelp, "Sorry, but it's the truth and you know it."

I push both guys off me and stand up, ready to clobber both of them when Dare says, "Hey Sammy, did you know Camy has a black belt in karate?"

"Cool, just like you Dad," he says and leaps into my arms and knocks me into Dare.

We crash back down on to the blanket and start laughing.

179

I rise up on one arm and ask, "When were you going to say something? When did you start martial arts?"

"When I was a teenager, and then once I returned from Paris, I started going back to class as a stress outlet, but now that we're getting married, we can spar with each other, if you're game." He challenges me.

"Brother I was born game," I reply, "but I'm sure Saul would be only too happy to fill in for me if I was unavailable or even Mokie Joe."

Dare pulls me to him and says, "I'd love to test both their mettle, but I'm your only sparring partner from now on, well you and Gina can still go at it...two girls, kickboxing each other, WOW! What a world."

Before I can retaliate Sammy asks, "Who's Mokie Joe?"

I look at Dare and he nods for me to explain.

"Well, Mokie Joe is my best friend, I've known him forever it seems," I tell him. "He is a chef and also the best swimmer you'll ever meet... which makes him twice as fascinating, doesn't it. He'll want to meet you for sure."

"When can I meet him?" he asks and I turn to his father and wait for him to respond and then the questions really begin...

20

We're exhausted when we arrive back at my place but ecstatic as well. Dare and Sammy leave a little after four, promising to call me when they get home. Earlier we packed up our picnic trash, cooler, and toys and drove back to my house. I hated to see them leave, but Dare had a banquet he couldn't get out of going and Sammy was spending the night at Jimmie's grandson's house.

As I wave goodbye from the driveway I glance down at my ring, my engagement ring and start squealing with joy. I quickly run into the house, grab my phone and dial Mokie Joe.

"Hey there Baby doll, what's up?" he asks sounding sleepy.

"Can you talk? I've got the greatest news." I tell him. "I'm engaged."

"To whom?" he asks in a girlie breathless voice.

"You're an asshole. You know it's Dare." I tell him, then start laughing at the great feeling I get every time I think about becoming Mrs. Darius Steele.

"Congratulations," he says, "I guess I don't have to ask if you're happy since you're practically jumping up and down on your sofa, aren't you?"

Laughing even harder because that is exactly what I'm doing I miss the next part of what he said.

"…because I'd beat the shit out of him if he did," He is saying, "So would Saul."

"What? I'm sorry I must have missed something, what did you say about hurting him?"

"I said he better give you lots of kids and make you as happy as you deserve or Saul and I would beat the crap out of him," he repeats. "Of course, you could probably take care of that light-weight yourself." He says laughing at the thought.

I decide not to mention Dare's karate training but continue telling my best friend what a wonderful time the Steele's and I had together. I also tell him about the ring, and how long Dare had been holding onto it. I feel myself tear up just remembering the look on his handsome face when he slid the ring on my finger.

"…happy to do it, just tell me when and where," he says and once again I missed the first part of his sentence.

"Happy to do what Mokie," I ask, "I'm having a hard time concentrating right now. Repeat the last sentence please."

"Why'd you call me if you're not going to listen to what I say?" he snaps then lets out a long, heavy sigh. "I offered to cater your wedding as a gift, just let me know when, where, and how many."

I start to cry at how sweet that is; my best friend handling my wedding reception. Oh my God, how big a wedding will it have to be? I'll be marrying into Sonoma finances… Man oh man does that scatter my brain.

"I'll have to get back with you on that," I tell him and soon we end the call with him reminding me of the Cartwright Gala and what kind of accommodations should he make.

"I'll have to get back with you on that one too," I whisper, "Sorry Mokie, but I guess now I have to clear certain items with Dare, you know, I'd expect the same courtesy from him. I'll call you Monday and let you know, okay? Is that enough time or will we be sleeping in Balboa Park?"

"There would be no sleeping in there," he jokes, "I'll reserve two rooms, if we need them we have it, if not I can always cancel the second room. Take care Doll, and I'll wait to hear from you on Monday."

"I love you Mokie," I whisper, knowing our lives are about to change irrevocably, and I can't wait. "Hey, Roz is coming back tomorrow, so I'll leave word with her. She always does a better job of organizing my life than I do."

I know he's dying to ask more questions, but I decide to let it go.

"I hope he's everything you dreamed he'd be Cam," he says, "I'm truly happy for you kiddo, take care. Have Roz give me a call."

"See you soon Mokie." I tell him and hang up my phone then realized he used Dare's nickname for me without even thinking about it.

Next I call Jon and have to leave a message as he's probably out in the fields, I email my crew to meet me bright and early Monday morning and tell them I have important news to share. I know they'll be guessing what I'm going to say, but I don't care.

I email Roz and see if she's back yet. I'd love to get her in on the ground floor of our wedding. I flip through my resources and contacts for the next couple of hours until my stomach starts to growl. Flipping on the kitchen light the clock reads eight o'clock so I walk over to the fridge and wonder what sounds good for supper when my cell phone rings. I pull it out of my back pocket and see Steele, Inc. on the screen.

"Hi sweetheart" I answer the phone, "are you having a good time?"

"No," he replies, "I'd rather be there with you, eating something, anything besides rubbery chicken and oily pasta salad. What are you doing?"

"Getting ready to cut into a thick, juicy, medium rare New York strip, a huge forkful of creamy twice baked potatoes, and popping a stuffed mushroom cap into my mouth," I tease him, "what did you say you had for supper?"

"You're evil and must be destroyed," he tells me making me laugh out loud. "I have to go in a minute but I wanted to hear your voice, to tell you again how much fun I had today, and to let you know Sammy wants the Scavenger Hunt birthday party, and he listed off the friends he wants there, so I can email them to you tomorrow."

"Great, I'll get with Roz and we'll start right away. I still can't believe we're going to be married," I tell him, "Any kind of time frame flash through that brilliant mind of yours?"

"Well, I thought maybe June or July would work out best, don't you?" He asks.

My stomach starts to cramp at the thought of waiting eight or nine months to get married. But he has as much say in the planning as I do so I hide my disappointment.

"Sure, there's no rush," I tell him and then hear him laughing in the phone.

"Gotcha," He laughs and says, "I'd have paid money and a lot of it, to have seen the look on your face. 'Sure, there's no rush' my ass," he barks, "I was thinking Christmas, how does that sound?"

Thank God he's almost a hundred miles away right now or I'd be tempted to drive over there and flip him over my shoulder, hog tie him and call the preacher.

"Darling, paybacks have always been my forte." I tell him in a soft purring voice, "when you least expect it, expect."

"Come on that was funny and you know it." he cajoles me. "Besides, do you really think I could wait that long to make you my own? Get real Cam."

Feeling better after hearing that last sentence I decide to forego the revenge plotting until further notice.

"Good, because there's no way I'd be able to last that long not being able to see you and Sammy every day, let alone every night- big or small?" I ask.

"I beg your pardon?" he says then chuckles, "You already know the answer to that question…"

Laughing at his joking attitude I reply, "Hey smart ass I need to know if you want a Cathedral wedding or a chapel wedding."

"What's the difference?" he asks.

"The number of people, the amount of food, and the length of time it takes to organize and prepare the reception.

And just so you know, Mokie Joe wants to do the cooking for us." I tell him and laugh when he is quiet. "It won't be submarine sandwiches and chips sweetie, I promise."

"Fine, I'm leaning toward Chapel, without a lot of fanfare." He says, "Are we on the same page?"

"Even on the same paragraph. I'll start checking out venues, but I need a date, check your schedule and let me know when you're free, okay? And don't put it off, it takes some fine organizing to pull off the Steele Wedding as we'll be referred to, so I want to make it as quick and painless as possible."

"Thanks, I appreciate that. I'd like to have the reception here, at the house, but I guess you need to see the place first. What's on your schedule tomorrow? Feel like a drive? Want to come spend the day with me and Sammy?" He asks with a tone of hopefulness in his voice.

"I'd love to but I'd have to drive back that night, I have scheduled appointments all day Monday and a charity organization luncheon on Tuesday. I think I'm free on Wednesday and Thursday but I have a cocktail party on Friday in Mendocino, plus an anniversary reception in Lucerne on Saturday. Those are just the dates I remember and the closer we get to the holidays the crazier it gets."

"Hell, we need to sit down and do some head banging but I have to go, they're calling my name from the podium. I love you and will call you tomorrow. Sleep tight Baby." He says and before I can respond he's gone.

Letting out a heavy sigh I check my emails and see Roz has not responded yet so I walk back into the kitchen and reach for a block of gruyere cheese, some grapes, and walk into the pantry for some crackers, take it all over to the kitchen table and have a late supper.

A little after midnight I log off the computer, turn off the lights and lock up the house when I see a car pull into my drive. Thinking someone is simply turning around I'm surprised then elated when I recognize Dare behind the wheel of a luxury sedan.

I run out to the porch and down the steps and throw myself into his arms, kissing his neck, his chin, and finally his lips.

"What are you doing here? Tell me you didn't walk out on a business banquet just to spend the night with me? God, I'm so glad you're here, I missed you so much." I know I'm rambling in between kisses but I can't seem to stop.

"Slow down honey, let me get inside and I'll fill you in, okay?" he says and steers me back inside.

I close the door behind him and launch myself at his fine form. He looks fantastic in his black tuxedo, white shirt and tie. I reach over and start unbuttoning his shirt, then remove both the jacket and shirt at the same time. His black tie was already hanging untied around his neck and it falls to the floor as I start stripping the man.

We make it to the living room then he picks me up and carries me over to the sofa, drops me and follows me down. Limbs entwined, we race to finish undressing, all the while kissing and nipping on each other. Finally when there's nothing but air between us he slides into me and makes me his once again.

Each time we make love it feels new, like it's been years since we were connected not hours, tonight is no different. Like minks we quickly reach our summit and both cry out our release. The ride might have been short and hard, but we reached our climax together, now both sated and exhausted we lie back on the sofa and enjoy each other's presence.

"I'm glad you're here." I whisper in the dark, running my hands over his soft chest hair.

"Me too," he says and I can hear the smile in his voice when he asks, "did you eat that whole steak or is there any left?"

"Crap!" I mutter under my breath and know I have to confess to the man.

21

Sliding the hot juicy steak onto Dare's plate I wrap it in foil to rest while I sauté the mushrooms. Since there's no time to make the potato dish I teased him with I fry two eggs in a pat of butter and soon I'm ready to dish up our 'two in the morning' meal.

"God that smells great." He tells me walking into the kitchen, wearing nothing but Saul's sweat pants after he grabbed a shower. "I expect you learned your lesson on teasing a hungry man, huh?"

"Yes, for the thousandth time I'm sorry for teasing you, geesh." I whine, "I could have just said there were no leftovers and let you continue dreaming about that meal. I learned my lesson all right, not to confess my crimes…"

"Hey, that's not what I meant." he laughs leaning around me and snitching one of the cremini from the paper towel lined plate and popping the hot mushroom into his mouth before spitting it back out immediately. "Damn that sucker's hot."

I smile and consider that instant Karma. We sit down at the table, and I pour a glass of wine for each of us. The man is in heaven, moaning and groaning as he chews his meat.

"You are the best cook ever... oops, make that chef." He winks and takes another bite.

"What made you decide to make the drive and come over?" I ask, "Not that I'm complaining, just curious." I steal one of his mushrooms and pop it in my mouth before he can stop me.

Waving his fork at me he warns, "That's your one freebie, don't do it again," and then goes back to shoveling the food into his mouth. He appears to be starving...I wonder how bad that rubbery chicken meal was that he consumed. Maybe Sonoma could use a touch of En Bonne Catering on a permanent basis...

"Earth to Camy," he jokes, "where'd you go? You didn't even hear my explanation for coming to see you did you?"

"Guilty." I tell him and smile, "I'm sorry; tell me why you made the late night trip?"

Dare reaches for his glass of Merlot, takes a sip, and says, "I couldn't stop thinking about that meal you described."

I know he's joking so I stick out my tongue at him, making him laugh and say, "Is that an invitation?"

"Dessert," I reply and he winks at me and says, "you're on, but I think I'm starting to slow down," he motions to his almost empty plate and then tells me, "I'll take a rain check on dessert, maybe have it for breakfast."

I hide a yawn behind my hand and nod my head, "you got it. How late can you stay tomorrow... correction, today?" I joke looking at the clock on the wall.

"Sammy won't be back until four, they're going to the matinee and it's a double feature, so until one or possibly two." He wipes his mouth with his napkin and pushes his plate into the center of the table and stares at me.

"What's wrong?" I ask starting to think I've got something stuck in my teeth, or maybe I should have checked my mascara after our hearty romp on the sofa.

"Nothing, I just can't believe that in less than a week I found you again and we're going to finally get married. What are the odds?" he says.

"You're the speculator; you should know all about these things... speculate." I tease and he starts laughing.

"Let's go to bed, crunch some numbers, and work your figure... I mean the figures." He says taking his plate to the sink. "You must be exhausted too."

"I am," I tell him reaching out for his hand. "I love sleeping with you; it feels so right, doesn't it?"

"Yeah, I love knowing you'll be there, beside me, even when we sleep." He says making me pull him towards the master bed room stairs.

We brush our teeth, get ready for bed, and as we turn off the lights I lean over and lie across his naked chest. He is so warm, so solid; I place a soft kiss over his heart.

"Keep that up and I'll be getting a second wind... otherwise, let's sleep on it and have a late breakfast... French toast is my favorite, but you already knew that..." he says starting to yawn.

"Goodnight Baby," I tell him and kiss his lips.

"'Night," he replies already slipping into a soft, dreamy, place. "I love you Cam."

"Love you too Dare, I'm glad you're here," I whisper and he holds me tighter as we both start to drift off into our own dreams.

22

We slept until nine, made hot, scorching love and showered together. After breakfast Dare and I start making lists; arguing about venues, time frames, work schedules; and generally creating a mess of paperwork in my office until I call Roz who agrees to come over and help organize our plans. Everything was going semi-smoothly until we hit a snag on how a big of wedding to have.

"We're not going to go to City Hall," he informs me as he leans back in one of the two metal chairs I purchased from a closed down bistro in Monte Marte, "I don't want Cathedral, but I certainly don't want Civic."

"Dare, you can't just whip up a wedding in six weeks, at least not the kind you keep describing." I try to reason with him, and that's when he threw the paper lists he was working on up in the air.

"Hire someone to make it happen." He shouted running his fingers through his hair in aggravation, losing his patience at me explaining why one after the other scenarios he put forth wouldn't work.

I fall back laughing at him losing his cool when he scoots his chair back and lunges for me, making me jump out of the way and slide across the carpet of papers on the floor before I escape into the kitchen. I can hear him growl in frustration, but he won't believe me you can't have extravagance without planning in advance.

"Roz will be here in half an hour," I holler down the hall, "We'll let her explain what we can accomplish in less than two months' time, okay?"

"Fine! But don't bitch at me when it's not what either of us wants." He shouts back.

I just finished cleaning up the kitchen from our breakfast mess when he walks back into the room, talking on his cell phone.

"… Are they alright?" he asks walking past me and into the living room.

Something is wrong so I follow behind him when he turns and covers the mouthpiece, "Sammy and Jimmie's grandson Toby were accosted at the movie theatre by some strange man and both kids are pretty upset. I need to head back to Sonoma."

Nodding my head I race upstairs and grab his clothes and carry them downstairs and place them on the sofa, wanting to help in any way I can.

"Jimmie it's not your fault," he's telling the woman who took the kids to the movies, "those God damn perverts are everywhere. The main thing is the kids are alright, so calm down."

Feeling helpless I stand off to the side and wait on him to fill me in. He is pacing, and only stops when he tells his housekeeper he's on his way home.

"Stay put, don't worry about anything," he tells the distraught woman, "Did the theatre call the cops? Why the hell not?" he demands and then holds the phone away from his ear. I can hear the woman crying and quickly speaking in Spanish.

"Jimmie calm down, I'm not angry with you dammit." He shouts into the phone, looking so angry and exasperated.

I walk over to him and hold out my hand for his phone. He willingly releases the item and walks away, rubbing the back of his head with his hands. Poor baby is beside himself not being able to fix the problem immediately.

"Jimmie, hi my name is Carrie Anne," I tell her and hear her take a couple deep breaths, "Dare and I are going to be heading back to Sonoma within the next half hour, please have the boys cleaned, fed, and waiting on us, okay? I know you're upset," I tell her in my calmest voice, "but if you're calm, they'll be calm, right?"

"Si, Si you are right," the distraught woman says, "please tell Mr. Dare I'm sorry, I didn't know there was anyone around them. They wanted to go to the bathroom before the show; I couldn't go in there too," then she breaks off into rapid fire Spanish and I'm unable to keep up.

"Jimmie, you did nothing wrong, and Dare is grateful you called to let him know what happened." I assure her, "now try to act normal, take care of both boys until we get there, I know you know how to do that, right?" Making her concentrate on being proactive and not focusing on what could have happened is my goal, and she starts thinking like we need her to.

"Yes, I know how to take care of my boys, you are right." She says and I can hear the smile in her voice. "Please tell Mr. Dare to hurry, but to drive safely, goodbye Carrie Anne."

I return his cell to him and notice he is completely dressed in last night's finery and ready to walk out the door. Knowing how upset he is I walk over to him, take his hands in mine and put them around my waist, slip my arms around his neck and kiss him soundly on the lips. He takes over, finding an emotional release by grinding his mouth onto mine; pressing our bodies so closely together I'm waiting to hear our bones snap. When he begins to soften the kiss I know he has himself back under control. Pulling away I look up into his eyes and see the clear, Caribbean blue shining back at me.

"Thanks, I guess I needed to regroup," he acknowledges, "but I couldn't get Jimmie to stop crying, and I could hear the boys in the background and knew my son would be on the verge of crying too. I got to get back."

"We'll both head back to your place," I tell him knowing his ordeal is only beginning, depending on how Sammy reacts to this situation. "I'll call Roz, cancel our meeting and have her take over for me tomorrow, it was just a couple of confirmations on three receptions, and she'll follow my notes, no problem."

He hugs me to his body and whispers, "thanks Cam, I appreciate your willingness to drop everything and help me out," he smiles and kisses me quick and hard, "grab a couple days' worth of clothes, what you don't need you can leave there, and when we come back I'll leave a couple outfits here as well, deal?"

"You're brilliant Mr. Steele, give me ten minutes and I'll be ready to fly." I tell him grabbing my cell phone out of my jeans pocket and call Roz on my way upstairs.

She answers it on the second ring.

"I didn't forget," she says in lieu of a greeting, "but I got a call from Desiree and it was good news for a change, give me half an hour and I'll be on your doorstep."

"Change of plans Roz," I tell her and then fill her in on what happened with Sammy, she naturally goes into take charge mode.

"Okay, the consultations tomorrow are a piece of cake, so don't sweat that," she assures me as I fill my overnight bag with underwear, khaki capris, white t-shirts, black jeans, ballet slippers, a couple blouses, a blue cardigan sweater, and sandals, as well as my jewelry bag and facial kit.

"The charity luncheon is a repeat of the C of C luncheon minus the Chioppino, we're replacing it with lasagna, and face it Gina's lasagna is to die for, BJ and Saul will help Kit serve, and Nana already has the dessert done, so go, I have things under control," she instructs me.

"Thanks Roz," I tell her, "will you be my maid of honor?"

"Oh hell yes," she laughs, "like I'd let anyone beat me out of that position. Now be back by Friday, we still need your skills on preparing the cocktail party for the Senator from Mendocino. That gives you four days to help the kid, set a date, plan for the reception, and calm down that hunk of yours. You go girl and leave En Bonne in my capable hands…"

"I love you," I tell her, "would you please let Mokie Joe know what's going on? He'll worry if he can't get a hold of me at the studio…"

"Will do, take care and hug that kid of yours." She tells me and I hear the longing in her voice for a family of her

196

own, "There's a special place in hell for psycho's who prey on children."

"Thanks again. See you Friday." I tell her and carry my luggage down the stairs and see Dare is on the phone again.

"...tighten the security around the stables as well, just in case this was no random attempt, and Tanner, make sure you change the security codes at all gates, today, don't tell anyone and be at the gate when I get there, we've got a leak..." He says then looks up and smiles at me. "Gotta go, see you in a couple hours" and ends the call.

"All set?" he asks, taking my suitcase from me and carrying it down the hall towards the garage door. "Grab your laptop and anything else you might need," he says and walks out into the garage.

Picking up the lists and notebooks he strew about the place I tuck them into my attaché case, and then start locking up the house. Five minutes later I pull the back door to, lock it tight and walk out of the garage door and over to the luxury sedan Dare drove down last night.

As far as cars go, this has got to be one of my favorite ones, a Jaguar XK8, charcoal gray and sleek, waiting to pounce and eat up the road. I toss my bags into the trunk, open the passenger side door and slide into the perfect interior. Again it's all black, the leather seats, the carpet, and even the windows are darkly tinted, I feel safe, secure, and incredibly powerful sitting here waiting on Dare.

Once he climbs behind the wheel, wearing his tux pants and white shirt he slips on a dark pair of sunglasses, he leans over and smiles, kisses my lips and says, "Let's go check on our boy."

"I'd love fifteen minutes with the scum that tried to take the boys," I whisper vehemently and see the same look of retribution in his eyes as he nods his head.

"Me too," he says and grins while he turns the key and makes this wild beast of his roar to life.

We eat up the highway and in no time we're pulling onto the freeway and soaring towards what's soon to be my new home. We're both quiet for a while until Dare breaks the silence.

"I need to explain about my household, and the rules we all live by, just so you're not shocked at what you might find." He tells me.

I laugh and reply, "Sounds intriguing. Go ahead and 'explain'."

He grins and begins, "My father, Derek is a widower, my mother died from breast cancer when I was a senior in high school. Since then it's always been my father, Jared, Jimmie or Jimenia, and me. She has three kids and they have a couple kids each. Her only son Jorge was one of my best friends, still is and his son Toby is Sammy's best friend. Jimmie is technically my father's house keeper, lives over there, but she works for me."

"I pay all the bills, legally own all the properties as well as controlling interest in Steele, Inc." he tells me and I know there is a reason, it's not like he's bragging.

"Dad got mixed up in a real estate scam five years ago, and I bailed him out. It would have cost him his home, his stock in Steele, Inc., as well as his reputation as an honest developer. I took control over Steele, Inc. in payment for saving his ass, and to assure that he'd never put our company in financial jeopardy again. Suffice it to say he learned his lesson, or so I thought." He says, watching the traffic start to pick up as we get closer to the city.

"Two months ago he was approached by Sammy's Aunt, Rhonda Starr, and asked to help pull together a sweet deal and they'd both get rich. But it was another scam, this time Dad used his own personal monies and of course it went belly up. He's practically broke, and constantly demanding I bail him out with Steele collateral, namely some prime real estate I own. I've refused, making us adversaries instead of father and son. He is relentless, but I know if I bail him out again, he'll do the same thing over and over," He continues. "He lives on his dividends, nothing else, except an allowance I have set up for him through my accounting firm."

"I'm telling you this first so you can avoid any dealings with the man, secondly, I want you to understand why my father and I don't get along, and third, why I've forbidden that bitch Starr into my home. She is not to be trusted." He tells me.

"And no matter what she says, she and I have never been intimate, not even a goodnight kiss, even though there have been a lot of reporters speculating on our relationship." He switches lanes and continues, "Rhonda has a knack for being in the right place at the right time, like the Stone Reception, you and everyone there thought she was my date, but she just seems to know where I'm going to be and just shows up and hoards into the scene. Frankly I'd love to find a deep hole and dump her in it, but that opportunity hasn't presented itself, yet."

"Good to know," I smile and tell him, "So you'd have no objection to me laying down the law, marking my territory with her?"

"None what so ever; Just don't underestimate that tramp, she'd do anything to continue in the lifestyle she is living, thanks to Rachel's lack of a will. She was Rachel's next of kin, except Sammy, but her life insurance named Rhonda as sole beneficiary and honestly the policy wasn't enough to go to court over, and since Jared's name was on the birth certificate as father, and she legally made me his guardian, I let it go."

"Jared and Rachel intended to get married after she gave birth; Rachel insisted on a pre-nuptial agreement, but Jared wouldn't hear of it, so Sammy's aunt has been trying, quite unsuccessfully I might add to try to get her hands on some of Sammy's inheritance. She's unbelievable, and I'm in the process of eliminating her from my son's life, but it's taking more time than I thought it would..." he seems to be thinking out loud on that last part.

"The gist of this discussion is not to trust anyone from the Starr family, not to loan your father any money, or agree to his schemes, and to know you're on top of the situation and to trust you to handle it, right?" I ask putting the last hours' worth of conversation in a nutshell.

"You're beautiful and smart," he says lifting my hand from my lap and placing it on his thigh. "A deadly combination and one I look forward to spending the next sixty or seventy years enjoying at my leisure."

"Me too," I tell him and smile when I get my first glimpse of my soon to be new home.

23

We pull into the gated drive lined on either side by blue and deep purple California lilacs and silver bush lupine leading to a two story white stucco modern style home. The gold sedum and Sonoma sage creep across the gravel while Pacific reed grasses rustle in the breeze on either side of a ten foot tall wooden gate creating a majestic feel to the entrance. We stop at a small gate house nestled in a bank of western red twig dogwoods where a man walks out and nods his head at us. He is ruggedly good looking, in his mid-thirties, dark hair and skin, short clipped brown hair and he is as tall if not taller than Dare and built on the lean side. He is wearing wraparound sunglasses and a pair of blue jeans with a striped t-shirt covered by a blue sweater and boat shoes.

Dare rolls down his window and holds out his hand, they shake and the man bends down to get a look at me, putting his sunglasses on top of his head. He smiles and his whole face changes in a blink of an eye. He has warm, chocolate brown eyes, lashes a woman would kill for and the most amazing dimples on either side of his smooth shaved cheeks.

"Hey there, I'm Tanner," he says in a hoarse throaty voice, "so you're Paris huh? I understand everything now

Dare, sorry for the ribbing." Then he straightens back up and motions for us to go through the wood and steel barred gate that is automatically opening and sliding across the paved driveway where it gently brushes the silvery green junipers flowing out of the stone wall surrounding the house.

"We'll check on Sammy first," Dare says as he turns towards me and smiles before he slowly steers the car up the drive and around to the back of the house where multiple garages and even a horse barn are situated. "I'll have Tanner bring in your bags and park the car. I need to see Sammy."

I nod my understanding, unfasten my seat belt as he puts the car in park and opens his door. Dare looks over his shoulder at me, extends his hand and once I've grabbed a hold of his he pulls me through a seven foot wooden gate and hollers for his son.

"Sammy! I'm home, and I brought Camy." He shouts and soon I hear Sammy's shouts from a distance.

We walk through an outdoor family room complete with kitchen then Dare slides open a huge glass door and we end up inside another kitchen. A woman I assume to be Jimmie is standing at the kitchen sink, peeling potatoes and from the looks of it enough to feed an army. I smile and nod at the woman who has tears in her eyes. She is in her late fifties early sixties, on the heavy side and extremely short in stature. But once she sees Dare and Sam together she relaxes a bit and I notice a sweet smile cross her coarse features.

Father and son come together in a rush, hugging and kissing each other, communicating in a private, silent way I don't want to intrude upon. Tears well up in my own eyes at the tenderness Dare shows his son, and finally when they're through bonding Dare turns around with his son in his arms and motions for me to join them.

Sammy leans so far out of Dare's arms when he wraps his small arms around my neck. I feel his tears and take him the rest of the way out of his father's embrace and walk over to the huge wooden island and sit him on the counter top. When I step back I see him look up at me. He wipes his eyes on the back of his hand and smiles at me in that precious way that is Sammy.

"Hey Sam-a-lam," I say, "good to see you again."

"It's only been a day, Cam-a-lam, but 'long time no see back' atcha." He jokes and we all laugh at the silly greeting. "Dad is Cam living with us now?" he asks when he sees the luggage Tanner brought in side and looks over at his parent for an answer.

Dare doesn't hesitate but says, "Yes, she is going to stay with us, at least until Friday, and then she'll be back for your big Scavenger Hunt birthday party."

"That's the best news I've heard all day." He says then hollers over my shoulder, "hey Toby, come meet my new mom, she'll be my new mom… when are you getting married Dad?"

I look over at Dare and see the fire burning in his eyes at the mention of me being his son's mother. If we were alone he'd have burned my clothes off of me with that intense blue stare, then he smiles and I melt on the spot.

He replies to his son, "Soon Sam, real soon," and then winks at me while we wait for Sam's friend to join us in the kitchen.

A small little boy comes running into the room, with auburn hair, dark brown eyes and a smile as bright as the sun. He is dressed identically to Sammy in cuffed blue jeans, red, white and blue striped t-shirt, and dirty sneakers, except he is wearing small gold wire rimmed glasses. He stops short when he sees me and looks over at his Grandmother.

"Hello, it's nice to meet you." He says as if he's been practicing all day.

I bend down to his height and shake his proffered hand.

"And you must be Toby," I guess, "Sammy's best friend, am I right?"

"Yes ma'am," he grins then gets elbowed by Sammy and they scuffle and laugh as little boys do.

"Don't call her ma'am, call her Cam." Sammy laughs at his rhyming phrase and soon Jimmie walks over and joins us.

"Hello," she says, "I'm Jimenia Torres, and this little varmint is my grandson Tobias Torres. We are both pleased to meet you, and glad you came back with Mr. Dare."

"I've heard a lot of wonderful things about you Jimmie, from both my guys, and I look forward to working beside you." I tell her, hoping she is calmer than before. "You'll have to give me the grand tour later, if you've got the time."

She smiles and nods her head then looks nervously up at Dare who is leaning against the island counter, waiting on her to finish speaking with me. I can feel her anxiety and know she is beating herself up for what she perceives as negligence on her watching the boys, but Dare removes the cloud of doubt with his next words.

"You seem to have everything under control here," he tells her, hugging her rounded shoulders to his chest, "Thank you for looking after the boys, but why don't you take the rest of the evening off, go home to Juan and kick back, leave the boys here."

She looks over at me then back at Dare and says, "Thank you Mr. Dare but I don't want Toby to be a bother, since this is your first night here with Carrie Anne."

I smile at her and say, "No trouble at all, what where you planning on fixing to go with all those potatoes?"

She smiles and says, "I really hadn't thought that far," she laughs at the pile of peeled spuds, "when I'm nervous I cook, so I guess I could use a little time off, like you said. I could use some time alone with Juan. Jorge has taken Cindy and Julia shopping in Sacramento, and won't be back until late, so if you're sure it's no trouble, Toby would love to stay over, but don't forget they have school tomorrow."

"Toby can wear something of Sam's, so go on home and we'll see you tomorrow. I'll run them to school, and that way you can pick them up, okay?" Dare asks hugging the woman again.

"Si, Mr. Dare that is a good plan." She says then turns to me and says, "Welcome to your new home, I hope you enjoy many happy years in this house, with your 'boys'." And then she and I laugh, breaking the tension even further. I hug her goodnight and holler for the boys.

"Sammy, Toby come tell Jimmie good night, you're having another sleep over." I stand back and let the two rowdy youngster's hug the woman goodbye.

Once the woman leaves the boys race back upstairs and I walk over to Dare watching me and how I reacted to the boys.

"Want a grand tour?" he asks, pulling me into his chest and kissing me slow and deeply. "We can start with the master bedroom which is just down the hall, the only bedroom on this floor…"

"Put it away Mr. Steele," I tease him, "you can save that room for the last stop of the tour, but right now I'd love to see the rest of the house after I put these potatoes on to boil."

He laughs at me but I know he'll love the Pommes Dauphine I'll be fixing him later, maybe with a roasted chicken or a pork loin, I need to see what he has in his freezer. Looking around the kitchen, I love the open space, and the high end appliances, all in matching stainless steel, commercial grade. The ceilings are vaulted with roughhewn cedar planks, copper pendant lamps that extend down to the island which is at least eight feet long and five feet wide, done in gorgeous walnut butcher block. A beautiful gas range top sits directly under a large stainless steel exhaust hood and there is plenty of work space on either side of the stove. There are five wooden stools with white canvas woven seats and backs lined up against the island and the white cabinets encompass one entire wall with floor to ceiling glass front doors tinted in a smoky gray.

On either side of the extra-large sink are open shelves painted white filled with every day dishes as well as several much loved potted herbs. There is also a double oven built into the wall with a prep sink and a nice size wine fridge built into the wall too. This will be my favorite spot in the house. Everything is streamlined, no extra knick knack items on the counter tops, but it doesn't feel sterile, or too sparse. Even the natural tiled floor is soft in color, a pleasing taupe and cream palette. I love it. Dare has been watching me all this time, taking in my new surroundings and has a look of satisfaction on his handsome face. I walk over to him and lean into his body.

"I feel like this is my kitchen, right down to the last detail of the design," I tell him and kiss his lips.

He grins and wraps his arms around the small of my back and says, "It is your design. When we would lay in bed, late at night and talk about our futures, our dreams, you mentioned this layout a thousand times. I could visualize it as clearly as if you drew me a blueprint. I always thought of you when I'd come in here. So this is your kitchen, and has been all along. Welcome home."

I feel the tears start to fall down my cheeks at his sweet confession.

"I love it, like I love you… both of you are perfect for me and I intend to get a great deal of use out of each." I smile when I feel him stir, "but the kitchen gets my attention first."

"Figures, I get second billing over a kitchen." he pouts then says, "let's check out what you can fix to go with that ton of potatoes cooking over there," and opens the freezer door.

He sifts through the freezer wrapped packages and shakes his head, reading what is labeled on the paper but not picking anything out. Walking over to the fridge I see Jimmie has two whole chickens cut up wrapped up in plastic so I decide to roast the birds, make a root vegetable medley along with half of the potatoes I've got cooking.

"Why don't you go check things out with Tanner, maybe see if he'd like to join us for dinner while I get supper going," I suggest to Dare. "When I'm through here I'll take a fifty cent tour on my own."

"Are you sure? I hate to leave you alone but I really need to speak with Tanner about today, then I thought the two of us, now the three of us can question the boys, without Jimmie's emotional response tensing them up." He says and kisses me again, "how long before supper?"

Smiling at his hopeful expression I tell him, "about an hour and half, so run along and let me get started. Do you still like chocolate mousse?" I smile, knowing he used to devour my practice renditions.

"Yes, I would love to sample your mousse again," he smiles, "it was always my favorite dessert you made."

"Enough flattery I'll make a double batch, since I'll bet all four of you will want extra." I tease him, "I'm going to be very busy keeping up with your demands, won't I?"

"Yes and just wait until we enlarge the household…" he teases and starts laughing as he walks out of the room in search of Tanner.

24

An hour later I'm sitting on one of the white sofas in the formal living room, enjoying the sound of the fountain located in the foyer, trickling water in a peaceful and serene way, I almost fall asleep. The house smells great with supper in the oven; the mousse is in the fridge so I poured myself a glass of a crisp local Chardonnay and relax in my new digs.

Looking out the large glass window that faces towards the front of the house, I'm amazed at the hard landscape. It looks like a botanical garden of every kind of succulents known to man. There is no grass only gravel and pavers, but it doesn't seem harsh or too edgy. The entire house has white walls throughout, black steel framed windows, soft taupe colored tiled or hardwood floors. The open floor plan makes the place seem cozier than I expected. The rooms are well defined, but still flowing. Each room feels inviting with a different accent color to help designate the space.

The living room has a large canvas painting in gradient shades of teal to deep turquois hanging on the wall between the open two story foyer and the living area. Splashes of color from glass bowls and vases are scattered around the room with glass top end tables and an oversized cocktail table done in iron and walnut. A couple of open weaved wicker accent chairs flank the opposite side of the sofa and two small black leather cubed ottomans sit up next to the table as well.

Wandering into the other side of the room a huge walnut dining table with eight matching chairs reigns supreme. Their seat cushions pick up the soft white, gold, and teal from the painting. A large hanging glass orb is suspended above the table, looking like a hug sculpture done in amber glass.

I walk down the corridor and find myself in what will be mine and Dare's rooms. A large walnut encased king-sized bed takes center stage with built in night stands and attached head board; the colossal bed takes up the entire north wall. The large furniture fits the room scale perfectly, and the duvet at the foot of the bed looks inviting. A massive floor to ceiling fireplace clad in pale beige and gray marble slabs nestles between two large windows covered with sheer beige curtains. A matching set of oversized barrel chairs upholstered in light toned linen have a matching ottoman between them and are positioned in front of the hearth inviting conversation or a game of chess, and there happens to be a gorgeous glass set on the bookcase across the room. The floor is a soft light wood that blends with the entire color palette, making the room restful and serene.

The entire space makes me feel pampered, almost decadent and I can't wait to sleep in the bed tonight. As I turn toward the double doors that open out to the patio and the in-ground lap pool I stop when I see the large canvas painting on Dev's side of the bed.

I'm shocked to see it's a painting of me, from a photograph Dare took of me in Paris one morning when we were sleeping in. I had just rolled over and had been dreaming of him when he snapped my picture and laughed when I tried to get his phone away from him. Looking closely at the canvas I see dark lashes hiding my blue eyes giving me a sensuous, happy, and almost ethereal appearance. The artist used a light touch as there is nothing bold or sharp about the entire painting. It looks like it's about a four foot by six foot canvas, and I'm touched to the core that Dare wanted to see my image every morning, and every evening... even before we met up again.

I hear the boys laughing and giggling all the way upstairs, so I decide to go check on the little mischief makers. Walking into the foyer I glance out the window and see Dare and Tanner walking down the drive, pointing at the lights that line the pavement. Wondering what they're talking about I start to open the front door when I hear a loud crash and then glass breaking from upstairs. Turning around and running up the curved stairway I race down the hall and see an open door at the end of the corridor. Stepping into the large room I see it's a playroom full of every toy imaginable. The two little boys are carefully picking up a lamp that got knocked over and broke.

"Careful guys," I warn them walking over to take the broken glass from them. "What happened, and don't lie to me, I'll know if you do."

They look at each other and then back at me when Sammy says, "I was showing Toby a new karate move I saw my dad do and I hit the floor lamp."

Toby steps forward and says, "It was an accident," as I hold out a small trash can for them to put the broken light bulb pieces.

Smiling at their concerned faces I nod my head and say, "you'll have to tell your father, but I'm glad you told me the truth. Now are you supposed to be rough housing in here? Maybe you should go outside and practice your moves, where there are no breakable things around."

"Will you show me how to get a black belt?" Sammy asks and nods his head over at his friend, "Toby says girls can't get black belts, only colored ones."

I smile and cross my arms under my breasts and look over at the shy boy.

"Toby, anybody can earn a black belt," I tell him, "boys and girls alike. If you'd like I'll show you some moves, but only if you agree I can get a black belt."

"My Dad says girls should be girls, stop trying to be like us." He says defending his views.

"Sweetheart, girls and boys are different, and we're made that way. But if I want to do something, I'll do it, and no boy is going to tell me any differently." I tell him and start to tell him to change his attitude when they start smiling at something behind me.

I turn and see Dare leaning up against the door jamb, arms crossed over his chest and ankles crossed. He is smiling at me, waiting on me to continue.

"Please continue Cam," he smirks, "so no 'boy' can tell you not to do something? That should prove interesting, don't you think?"

Walking past him I lean up and kiss his cheek then reply, "well the 'boy' can try…" and walk around him, saying over my shoulder, "they broke the lamp make sure the glass is picked up before you take them outside and show them your black belt moves, I've got to check on supper."

"Cam what are you talking about?" he asks and then I hear him reprimanding the boys for breaking the lamp.

Smiling to myself as I walk into the kitchen I see Tanner leaning against the cabinet next to the refrigerator, eating one of my mousse cups.

"That's for supper," I warn him, "don't make me send you upstairs with the other naughty boys."

"You're just a girl," he teases, "you're not the boss of me."

I grab the white ceramic ramekin from his left hand and snatch the spoon out of his right hand as well. Taking a large scoop I put the creamy concoction in my mouth before I run around the island to escape him. We're both laughing like kids when Dare walks into the room carrying the broken lamp.

"Don't make me have to separate you two as well." He says in a frustrated tone, making us laugh even harder.

"Hey, you're the dad, remember?" I taunt him, "and like Tanner says, 'you're not the boss of me' so there."

"Oh, I'm the boss of you alright," he grins dumping the broken glass in the trash container hidden in a built in cupboard, then takes out the broom and dustpan. "Here, take this upstairs and clean up that mess."

Tanner and I look at each other then back at Dare and start laughing again.

"I've got to go check out the new filly at the stables," Tanner says and scoots around me, snatching the dessert from me and walking out of the room. "She started it... Dad," He says and I can hear him laughing until he's outside.

"Well, well, well..." Dare says slowly stalking me around the island, "so I'm not the boss of you, huh?"

I start backing up around the counter, making my way out of the room but he pounces on me from behind and wraps his arms around my waist, kissing my neck, nibbling my collarbone until I start to squeal.

"Alright, you win," I laugh, "but if supper burns, it's your fault… boss."

He spins me around and kisses me with all his passion that I forget I'm supposed to be mad and start climbing up his body. I need to be with him, right now and apparently he forgot we weren't alone in the house too because he pushes me away making me fall backwards in the island when we hear giggles coming from the hallway.

"Come on in guys," he says wiping the corners of his mouth with his thumb and forefinger. "Its allowed, Cam and I can kiss anytime we want."

Sammy and Toby walk over to the island and stare at both of us until I feel a blush coming on.

"But you're not married yet," Sammy says, "Don't you have to wait until the preacher says 'I do' and then leave the church?"

Grinning at Sam's reasoning I raise my eyebrows at his father, silently letting him know this question is all his. He glares at me and then looks down at the curious faces of the two boys, bites his bottom lip and says, "Camy made chocolate pudding" and he quickly leaves the room when the kids turn towards me.

"Cowards aren't welcome at my table." I holler at him and then look down at the boys still waiting on their answer. "Well guys, it's like this. When your Father put his ring on my finger, I agreed to marry him, we're already a couple, and so we're just waiting on the wedding and of course the party afterwards… hey speaking of parties, I still need you two to help me with the food list."

I hear Dare laughing in the other room at my changing the subject.

"I guess you won't be eating at the table tonight either," he hollers and this time I hear him run up the stairs with the broom and dustpan.

"Forget about that," I tell them and start open drawers looking for a note pad and pencil.

"Let's start with the important stuff first, the cake." I tell them, "What kinds do you like best?"

Thirty minutes later, after much pondering, and questioning, we come up with the guys' best idea of a party and it's time to set the table. With their help we are ready to sit down, all we have to do is call Dare and Tanner to the table.

"Run and tell the men supper is ready, okay?" I ask them and they take off like a flash trying to beat each other to the task.

Carrying the platter of hot roasted chicken with herbs to the table in the dining area I turn to find Dare staring at me with such longing and a hint of contentment. I smile as I walk over towards him, wrap my arms around his neck, feeling him draw me into his body with his arms around my waist.

I lightly bite his ear lobe and whisper, "you can fill your plate and take it back outside, scaredy cat," and bite his lobe a touch harder and step away from him.

"Fat chance of that Mama," he says and swats me on the behind, making the other males in the room laugh at our play.

"Come on Cam, let Dad stay," Sammy says laughing, "he can do the dishes as his punishment."

"Yeah, and take out the trash too." Toby chimes in giggling at the faces Dare is making at them.

Tanner pulls out a chair for me, "After you dear lady," he says, "Any one that can make chocolate pudding like that deserves to be waited on. Get over here Dare and wait on her."

We all start laughing and soon we're quiet, eating the simple yet hearty fare in front of us. The boys regale us with what all they're going to find on the scavenger hunt. When the time comes for dessert, Sammy and Toby jump up and offer to bring in the tray of ramekins from the fridge.

"I'll help," Dare says wiping his mouth with his napkin, "did you make coffee?" he asks and leans over to kiss my lips.

"But of course," I tell him in a bad French accent, "we must have café' with chocolate."

"Your French hasn't improved any has it?" he asks and steps out of my reach, laughing and telling the boys to wait on him, and then he leaves the room.

"Dare is so happy," Tanner says, "Thanks for putting his life back on track. He's been a demon for so long; I forgot he used to be a bit more carefree, like now. You're the reason, so for what its' worth, welcome to the family... there's no going back now."

We both start laughing and when the waiters appear all three have chocolate around their mouths and there seems to be a ramekin missing from the tray the boys are holding.

"I could have sworn there were nine dishes in the fridge," I look at the guilty faces of my crew, "did something happen to the ninth one?" I ask.

Toby and Sammy both look up at Dare who is shaking his head at them, warning them to be quiet, and as one voice the boys tell us, "He ate it."

Dare and Tanner start laughing and when I join in the kids do too.

25

After the dishes have been cleared away, the pudding fought over, and the coffee drank Dare ushers all of us into the family room, which is towards the back of the house. The wall leading out onto the patio is all glass and I can see the tall evergreens and juniper ground cover of the side yard the boys obviously use as their playground since there are bikes and a couple toy trucks on the sidewalk.

A built in bookcase blends into the rich wood paneling covering the walls, and it's loaded down with DVD's and CD's, a large flat screen TV, and state of the art Stereo system, books, picture frames, and glass jars of rocks and shells. The furniture in the room consists of a beautiful large round table with six 'mid-century' modern wooden chairs, two mismatched wooden and woven cane chairs done in a neutral fabric scheme and a an L-shaped sectional that is basically wooden boxes with plush linen cushions for seats and a ton of various shapes and sizes of throw pillows, one is from a pair of pillows that I remember Dare and I purchased from a flea market in Paris. He catches my eye and nods his head, letting me know he remembers where it came from as well. The mate to that pillow is in my bedroom in Willows, and I cuddle with it every night. Smiling back at him I walk over and take the chair Tanner is offering me.

Soon the boys climb up on the rest of the chairs and with dangling feet wait for the grown-ups to begin. They know we need to know what actually happened earlier today at the theatre, but they have no idea why.

"So, now that your Grandma Jimmie isn't around, she worries like grandma's do, can you guys tell us what really happened in the restroom?" Dare begins.

Toby leans over and whispers in Sammy's ear and he nods his head in agreement, then looks over at me and says, "I don't want you to be afraid, Dad and Tanny will keep you safe, but the man asked us about you Camy."

Dare and Tanner both turn their heads and look at me in surprised unison.

"What did he want to know Sam-a-lam?" I ask hoping my fear and confusion isn't showing.

"He asked if you were going to marry my dad, and I said yes. Then he asked if you were going to adopt me and I said I didn't know." Sammy looks over at his Dad, knowing how tedious a process adopting him was.

"Yes," Dare and I say together, and then smile when he and Toby pump their fists in the air.

"What did the guy look like?" Tanner asks, "Was he tall like me? Old like your Dad?"

Dare frowns at that last statement but reaches over and takes Sammy's hand.

"Think back both of you, just close your eyes and imagine the theatre." Dare directs them.

"Hey, I'll bet you can smell the popcorn and hotdogs?" I ask knowing the sense of smell is the strongest memory trigger we have.

"Yeah, but Jimmy wouldn't let us have a hotdog, only popcorn and a drink." Sammy complains, "And then she was angry because she had to hold them when we went to the bathroom."

"Did you see the stranger in the lobby before you walked into the restroom? Did he follow you guys in there?" Tanner asks, "Think back when you chose which stall to go into."

"I saw him in the mirror before I closed the stall door." Toby says, "He was talking to someone on his cell phone."

"Way to go, Toby," I tell him, "was he alone? Did you hear anything he might have said, listen to the noise in the background, I'll bet there were a lot of guys in there weren't there?"

Sammy shakes his head, "no he waited until the man with the little boy left before he walked over to us. I tried to shut the door but he held it open, asking me questions."

Toby opens his eyes and says, "He wanted to know if Sammy was going to be a big brother, and did he think his Dad would still love him when he had a bloody son of his own."

Dare looks over at me and I know Toby meant a son of his own blood. Thankfully Sammy hasn't a clue what the man was referring to. I lean over and put my arm around Sammy's shoulders and he opens his eyes, leans his head on my shoulder and sighs.

"Did that guy want to take me and Toby with him?" He asks, knowing that's what Jimmie thought and he must have overheard her say that to Dare on the phone.

"We're not sure hon," I whisper and kiss his forehead, "but that's why you guys have to be careful, not run away from Jimmie when you're out shopping, or playing alone on the playground. I know she couldn't be with you two inside the restroom, and you two stuck together like you're supposed to, but promise you'll keep an eye out for people like that, okay?"

"I wish I knew a karate kick that would have made that man leave us alone," Sammy says and looks over at his Dad. "How old do I have to be before I can fight?"

"Let's wait a couple more years, get a few more belts before we try to compete, okay?" Dare says looking over at both boys for their agreement.

Toby nudges Sammy's shoulder and says, "tell them about the woman you saw in the parking lot, you know your Aunt Rhonda."

"Oh yeah, I forgot," Sammy says, "I thought I saw Aunt Rhonda get in the car with this guy but Jimmie pulled me away from the window before I could be sure."

Tanner and Dare freeze knowing this is a major clue as to the identity of the stalker. I shake my head at them, asking them to let me ask the questions now and lean over to address the boys.

"What was she wearing? I just love clothes, don't you?" I ask them and they shake their heads no but I continue, "Was she all dressed up, looking like she does when she's being photographed in the newspapers?"

"No, she was kind of ducking down in the seat, like she was hiding from someone." Sammy says letting us know his aunt was involved in the set up. "She had on a hat and no makeup," he laughs and covers his mouth, "she is an ugly stick without her makeup, just like Papaw said."

Dare is seething mad and I know it wouldn't take anything to make him go after that woman, but for the boy's sake I wrap my arms around Dare's shoulders and give him a firm squeeze.

"Stay calm sweetheart," I whisper in his hear and he nods his head, and then covers my hand with his.

"I think it's time you boys give Cam a tour of the stables, but stay away from Casper's stall, okay?" Tanner asks, "We'll be out in a couple of minutes."

I know they're going to discuss what they discovered so I smile and take both of the boys' hands and we head outside, through the outdoor living room and down a lovely paved sidewalk that leads us through a small landscaped garden and then opens up to the out buildings hidden from view of the house. Immediately a large black and white dog joins us, with both boys leaning down to hug and scratch his ears.

"This is Buddy," Sammy says, "remember his paw? It's all better now, just like Dad said it would be. Bend down and let him show you his paw."

I kneel down and before Sammy can give the dog his command Buddy knocks me over and starts licking my face. The boys are dying laughing at me, flat on my back and soon with their help I'm back up on my feet and petting the huge dog's head. The tour continues.

The horse barn isn't that big, only housing maybe eight horses, but it's so well-tended, I'm impressed at the entire spread. I love the smell of hay and even horse manure when it's not on my shoes. My brother Jon's in-laws have horses. I used to ride with him and Jessie before the girls came along.

It's been three or four years since I rode, but I know I'll be picking up that hobby once again. They lead me into the barn and introduce me to the tenants.

"This brown one is Hester and that's her brother Hercules." Sammy says pointing to two beautiful matched palominos poking their heads out of the wood and steel barred gate.

"Poncho and Echo are next to them," Toby says, "they do everything together, like me and Sammy, huh? Do you think they're best friends? Do horses have best friends?" he asks.

The next stall is empty so we walk across the aisle and the next horse I see is a beautiful Arabian filly; she is almost all white with a hit of gray in her coat. She tosses her mane back and forth, stamping the dirt and straw, demanding attention. Leaning over the gate I reach for her halter and nuzzle her nose. She is unbelievable.

"What's her name?" I ask and the two boys snicker.

"Carry me away," Sammy says and looks behind me and sees his father and Tanner walking into the barn. "Hey Dad, Cam likes Carrie me away."

Turning to look at Dare he is laughing and says, "her name is Cara mia not Carry me a way, you knuckle head," he says stooping to pick up his son and start tickling him, "I tell you that every time."

Tanner grabs Toby up and starts tossing him in the air amidst their peal of laughter.

"Good, tickle them both for me while you're at it." I tell him, "I thought they were telling me the horse's name was Carrie Anne."

They all start laughing at me so I turn to check out the next stall when Dare walks up behind me and says, "I named her Cara Mia Mosier" and he twirls me around the aisle, making the boys giggle.

Tanner nods his head at Dare and takes the boys back to the house leaving me and Dare alone in the stable. He presses me back against an empty stall gate and starts kissing me.

"I want you so badly," he whispers, reaching out, caressing my breasts, pulling my T-shirt up and over my bra, unfastening the front clasp and softly licking my nipples, "let me have you, here, right now before I go crazy."

I open the gate and walk inside the empty stall, knowing we're well hidden from view. Reaching out I caress the front of his jeans, loving the feel of his rapidly growing aroused flesh. I grab ahold of the edges of his plaid cotton shirt and give it a yank, releasing the snaps and exposing his gorgeous chest.

"Take me here, in the stall while the kids are busy." I whisper running my hands over his chest and belly making him go wild at the suggestion. His hands are all over me, pulling and tugging, driving me crazy with his need.

A few minutes later he unbuttons my jeans and strips them down my legs along with my panties and frees his burgeoning shaft from his own jeans. Lifting me up I wrap my legs around his hips and he walks us back to the corner. Bracing my back against the wooden slats he swiftly enters me, all the way to the base and holds stock still, giving us both enough time to adjust.

"You feel so good, so tight," he groans and tentatively starts to move, but stops when I let out a gasp, "are you alright? I didn't mean to rush you and I'm sorry but I need to move…"

He pulls almost all the way out of me, and then slams back into my body, making me hold back the screams as he works his body inside mine, over and over until I feel the coiling sensation in the pit of my womb. I dig my nails into his back, urging him to continue the ride and he takes off like the stallion in the next stall over.

The smell of horse, hay, and sex is in the air, the soft whinnies and shuffling of hooves blends in with our groans and muffled shouts. Soon we're reaching the zenith of our desires and I feel him quicken, shout my name and start spewing his life force inside me. Once I feel him jettison his semen I'm lost, letting go and riding out my own climax. A couple minutes later when our breathing and pulse rate returns to normal he slides out of me, kisses me long and deeply, making me want to climb back up his body.

"Thanks for helping us question the boys," he whispers, rubbing my quickly distending nipples and he leans down and suckles me making me gasp at the returning passion. "I could make love to you all day, all night, and all the rest of my life."

I kiss his neck, leaving a love bite and reach inside his jeans but he catches my hands and says, "the boys are about three minutes from finding us in a clench, hurry up and get dressed, then we start the dreaded nightly ritual of bath, bed, story, and then merciful sleep."

He laughs at my disappointment and says, "I promise to nail you to the wall once they're asleep, okay? I'll even check your backside for splinters."

I lick my lips and start devising the quickest way to get the boys prepped for bed.

26

Thursday morning arrives with a light drizzle, making our bedroom feel cozy and dark, inviting us to sleep in, but I know from the last three mornings that is an unlikely occurrence. Rolling over in the huge bed I press a kiss to Dare's naked back and climb out of bed by scooting to the foot of the monstrosity. The wide bed is fun for playing, but it takes some maneuvering to get out.

"Wake up sleepyhead," I tell him reaching for my robe and sliding my feet into a pair of flip flops. "Coffee's already done, and Sammy has to be at school early, he has his science project and Jimmie is off today."

"How important is science, really?" he muffles into his pillow making me chuckle as I walk towards the bathroom.

"You can shower first and I'll wake up Sammy," I tell him as I leave the room.

He's still mumbling so I go ahead and take care of my pressing needs. I love this room with its' cool tiled floor, double marble vanities and humongous walk-in shower. But my favorite spot is the chrome plated slipper tub sitting in front of a wall of glass that looks out into a totally private Zen garden. Bamboo trees are planted in clusters along a redwood privacy fence. Gravel and pavers provide a foundation for a beautifully tranquil spot. Dare built backless benches and a fire pit in the center of the space and he put a fountain where water pours down large sheets of thin copper; it shimmers iridescently, like a wide waterfall.

I hear him climb out of bed so I need to get a move on. Walking into Sammy's room I'm amazed at how tidy he keeps his sleeping quarters and how messy he leaves the playroom. Checking to see if he is sleeping in the top or the bottom bunk – I'll either gently shake his shoulder or tickle the bottom of his foot. This morning he's in the bottom so I bend down and start the long process of waking the child. He takes after Dare on that character flaw.

"Come on Sam-a-lam, time to wake up, tell me what you'd like for breakfast?" I ask knowing food is the only thing that will get him out of bed without too much complaining.

"Pancakes and bacon," He says like he has for the last three mornings. "Yours are ten times better than Jimmie's, and a hundred times better than Dad's."

Dare walks into the room in time to hear that and he holds up his finger to his lips quickly sneaking over to his son's bunk. Quick as a cat he grabs Sam and starts tickling his feet, making the boy squeal in laughter.

"Help me Camy!" Sammy shouts squirming and kicking to get away from his Dad and the punishment his father is doling out for insulting his culinary talent.

"She can't help you brat," he jokes, "plus now you have to eat whatever I fix for you…maybe Buddy will share his chow, what do you think about that?" Letting Sammy sit up, his hair standing on end, he looks like he went through a cyclone. He looks up at his dad who is still kneeling by the bed and pats his father's shoulder.

"It will still taste better than your pancakes," he says and jumps to the end of the bed and escapes Dare's reach as he races into the bathroom, laughing the whole way.

"Cam, fix him wall paper paste, and rainwater." He jokes and stands up to kiss me good morning.

"Let's spend the morning together, going over our schedules again, so we can get our wedding plans on the books for Roz." He suggests, "Then we'll have the afternoon to spend canoodling."

Kissing him back I finally pull away and say, "Sounds like a plan."

"Hurry up sprout!" Dare calls over his shoulder as we walk down the hall and head downstairs.

"Tanner will be by this morning to go over added security for Sam's party, so let him know how many of your crew will be in attendance, that way he'll be able to prepare dossiers on each of them." Dare informs me, casting a shadow on an otherwise fun morning.

A half an hour later I'm flipping the last pancake onto the warming platter and sliding Dare and my country omelet onto our plates when Tanner walks into the kitchen.

"Good morning Carrie Anne," he says smiling as he pinches a piece of bacon I piled high beside the pancakes. "Is there any coffee left?"

"I just made a fresh pot," I tell him and hold out my own cup for him to refill. "Thanks, would you like pancakes or an omelet?" I ask.

"Seriously?" he asks coveting Sammy's plate, "I'd love some more of your pancakes, they are so much better than

Jimmie's and don't even compare to the clay pigeons Dare serves." He jokes making me laugh out loud when Dare puts down his copy of the *Sonoma Index-Tribune* and glares at both of us.

"For your information," he begins, "I've only made pancakes maybe three times in my life and they weren't that bad. Besides, you ate enough of them, you back stabbing freeloader."

Sammy comes in and sits down at his usual place at the island counter and takes a huge gulp of his milk. Without putting his paper down Dare tells Sammy to slow down.

I look over at Sammy who is in a sneaky mood this morning and he tosses one of his green army men over the top of Dare's paper. It quickly sails back over and lands in a puddle of maple syrup on Tanner's plate causing Sammy and me to burst out laughing.

"Steele, I'll put up with a lot of your craziness, but don't send your men to reconnoiter my chow." Tanner says then picks up the plastic toy, licks the syrup off him and sends him flying back over to Dare.

"Children, let's put our toys and newspaper away and eat while the food is still hot," I tell them being the only responsible adult in the room.

I pull out my stool only to have the well-traveled military man end up in my glass of orange juice splashing me in the face and the front of my shirt.

"Dammit Dare," I yell at him mopping up the splashed juice from my chin with my napkin. "You are going to be eating with Buddy if you don't behave."

"Sorry, it was an accident," he says laying his paper to the side and handing me his napkin. "I promise no more hijinks, we'll behave." He says looking at his cohorts who are still chuckling at my breakfast invasion but are refusing to look at me.

We get through the rest of the meal and when it's time for Sammy to leave for school, Dare leans down and kisses me goodbye as I hold the back door open for him.

"Call Mokena and remind him there will be two sleeping over at his place tomorrow night," he says, "I'm even willing to help serve, or whatever so long as you pay me the standard rate."

Shaking my head at him I reply, "fine but just so you know, I don't sleep with the help," and close the door on him and watch as he laughs all the way through the outdoor family room and then out of my sight.

Cleaning up my breakfast mess I decide to call Mokie and advise him of the change of plans. It goes to voice mail immediately.

"Hey Mokie, wanted to see if you can put Dare and me up for the night tomorrow after the Mendocino cocktail party, let me know if having Dare with me is going to be a problem, love you call me back soon." And I end the call.

Wandering back into our bedroom I start to make the bed when I hear someone in the house. Cautiously walking down the hall into the living room I see an older man and a young woman heading into the kitchen. I recognize the woman as Rhonda Starr so I assume the man must be Dare's father. Not wanting them to know I'm here I creep over to the family room and can hear their conversation without them seeing me.

"You said that last one would be it," Derek Steele says and from his tone I can tell he is upset. "What the hell were you and your good for nothing brother thinking?"

"We needed information, and took the only opportunity we had to find the boy alone, no big deal... the house keeper didn't even insist they call the cops, don't sweat it old man." She says opening the fridge and helping herself to Dare's food.

"It is a big deal you stupid little idiot," he snaps, "Dare was livid, calling me on the carpet for something I didn't know anything about, and it's a good thing I didn't. The man is so protective of his son; he would have taken me apart if I had been involved."

"Then you're welcome," she laughs, "but I need to know what your son is doing, is he really marrying that cook? What the hell for? She's crazy for him, anyone could see that at the Stone affair," she pauses for a second, probably eating or drinking something then she continues.

"I have to know the plans for Sam's birthday party," she tells him, "it might be our only chance to turn the tables before the hearing next month. I have to win this case or you're going to have to foot the bill for the next thirty years or however long you live..."

"God, you're such trash, how the hell did I not see through you I'll never know." He says in disgust.

She laughs in a hateful manner and says, "You weren't actually looking at my character at the time, remember? You got your ashes hauled so stop complaining."

"Shut up you slut!" he hisses at his tormentor, "I've paid you all the cash I have and I will not let you harm my grandson."

"Calm down Papaw," she taunts, "I won't need your cash if I can prove I was never notified of the legal adoption of my 'dearly departed' sister's only child. I'm entitled to the money that bitch denied me by postponing her marriage to Jared. She was always so sanctimonious, a little straight arrow ever since she was brought to the Starr's house. Why the hell she would want a pre-nup I'll never know."

My cell starts vibrating in my pocket; thankfully I accidently turned the ringer off last night otherwise they would have caught me eavesdropping on their schemes. I run upstairs and hide in the playroom. The call went to voicemail and I see it was Mokie returning my call. I decide to call Dare and let him know his father and Starr are here but I hear the front door close. Tip toeing to the window facing out front I see the two racing to their car, a silver Jaguar that looks like the vehicle Dare was driving Saturday when he showed up at my place.

They almost make it out of the drive before Dare's rover blocks their retreat. He slams out of his truck and walks over to confront the pair. I can hear him shouting and cursing until Tanner gets out of the passenger side and pushes Dare away from the car. He shrugs off Tanner's grip and points his finger at his father, but I can't hear what he is saying but from his rigid body stance, he is reading him the riot act. Dare runs up the front walk and I hear the front door bang open and he starts shouting for me.

"Carrie Anne? Where are you?" he yells and then I hear him on the stairs.

"In the play room," I tell him.

As soon as he enters the room he pulls me into his arms. I can feel him trembling, fighting the rage he is experiencing at having his father and that woman in his home. I run my hands up and down his back, soothing him until I feel his muscles relax.

"What did they say to you?" he asks. "I can't believe that son of a bitch had the nerve to show up here with that witch. Why'd you let them in?" he demands holding me at arm's length and giving me a shake.

"I didn't Dare," I snap at him glaring into his glacier eyes. "I was making our bed when I heard the front door open, and when I heard them speaking I decided to hide and do a little eavesdropping." I try to push out of his arms but he refuses to let go.

He hugs me to his chest and kisses the top of my head, "I'm sorry, I'm sorry for snapping at you. I should have known better. Come on, let's go back downstairs and you can fill me in on what you heard."

When we join Tanner in the family room I tell them what the two said; Dare is frighteningly quiet and Tanner begins asking me all kinds of questions.

"How long where they here?" he asks, "Did they go into any other room?"

"No, but they did open the fridge." I tell him, making him smile, "They were here maybe ten minutes."

"Sorry for the third degree but we need to know all we can. You said Derek said the stranger from the movie theatre was her brother? She doesn't have a brother, only a sister on record... I wonder who he is," Tanner says.

Dare is lost in his own thoughts when he suddenly comes back to the conversation.

"You said Rhonda mentioned Rachel was a straight arrow and then something about 'ever since she was brought to the Starr's house'… that might mean she and Rhonda weren't really sisters." He says and then turns to Tanner, "We need to look into children that were fostered or adopted in or around the Arbuckle area. You'll have to go back at least twenty years. Contact Russell and have his people get on this right away." He says finally looking at me.

"Girl you just gave us the best lead we've had yet," he tells me and kisses me hard on the lips.

He scoots his chair out from the table and follows Tanner out of the room. I wonder if Dare even thought about how many other times his father or anyone for that matter might have just walked into the house. He could have been robbed if not killed. He is going to have to remember to lock his doors, just like he now does with his vehicles. I take my phone out of my back pocket and call Mokie back.

"Hey Carrie Anne," he says sounding so cheerful, "glad you called me back. I had an unexpected job fall into my lap so I won't be able to join you tomorrow, but feel free to stay at my place anyway, you've got your keys, right?"

"Sure, but what kind of job would make you leave me in a bind like this?" I tease knowing he was only going to tag along like he did at the Stone's reception.

"Well, I've been playing phone tag with this restaurateur over in Lake Tahoe. They saw the article in *Bon Appetite* and want me to fill in at their resort…" he goes on to say it's a dream come true, he's sorry their chef hurt his back but he is thrilled to be working in a hot spot like that, and with carte blanche as well. We talk for a couple more minutes until he says he has to go and pack but he'll fill me in later. I wish him luck and end the call. I hope it works out for him; he is really an amazing chef and deserves his time in the sun.

I spend the rest of the morning doing light housework, wanting Jimmie to have very little to do when she returns tomorrow. Sammy is staying with Toby's folks for the weekend, they're going to San Francisco to visit Toby's mom's family, and he is so excited. Hopefully Dare will still let him go after what he found out this morning.

Fixing a rice pilaf with ham and almonds for lunch I realize how little time I've been spending in the kitchen lately. I miss coming up with new recipes and menus. I lose myself for the next hour and jump when Dare says my name.

"God you scared me to death," I snap and throw a dish towel at him when he starts laughing. "I was in my zone and now it's gone."

"You were definitely zoned out," he agrees as he walks around the island and hugs me from behind and starts to check out what's cooking on the stove, "what smells so good?"

"Don't lift that lid mister," I warn him not wanting to spoil the surprise inside the pot.

"Tell me what's for lunch," he smiles and steps away from the range but steals a couple of raspberries lying off to the side.

I tell him, "Pilaf Au Jambon Amandine and it's in the oven already. I'm going to surprise you with dessert. Give me fifteen minutes."

"Sounds good, call me when you're ready and I'll come running," he jokes.

"Is Tanner still here? Will he be joining us for lunch?" I ask as he stops in the doorway leading to the family room.

"No he's on his way to a meeting with a private investigator named Mason Russell out of Vallejo so he'll be gone for the day, possibly the night." He informs me, "It's just you and me kid."

"Sounds like my idea of a good time." I reply making him laugh as he leaves the room.

Once I've sliced the fresh peaches and added them to the raspberry sauce I turn off the burner, set them aside to go with the ice cream for dessert. The casserole is done so I remove it from the oven and place it on a hot pad between our plates. Opening a bottle of Pinot Griggio I fill the stemware and call Dare to lunch.

We're both enjoying the meal and discussing our wedding plans when it dawns on me, will this morning's drama end his relationship with his father? I need to know so I don't say or do anything wrong.

"Dare, what are you going to do about your father?" I ask taking a sip of my wine.

"Nothing," he replies, "I told him he was no longer welcome in my home, and that he has to pay his own bills from now on. I'm no longer willing to support him."

Understanding how he feels I can't help but wonder how Sammy is going to react when his Papaw doesn't show up for his birthday party.

"Dare?" I ask, hesitating because I know he'll probably lose his temper at my questioning him.

"Hmm?" he asks looking at me over the rim of this wine glass.

"Won't your father not being at the birthday party upset Sammy?" I ask and like I thought, he loses his temper.

"God dammit Cam I can't take the risk of the old man trying something," he snaps at me pouring more wine in his glass. "That bitch will stop at nothing to get her hands on 'her share' of her nephew's inheritance including using my old man to get to the kid."

"Calm down Dare," I tell him sorry for upsetting him, "I was just wondering if his grandfather's absence would upset him," I tell him. "I wasn't suggesting you invite him and his date to the party, only wondering what Sam's reaction might be."

"Date?" he snaps at me, "what the hell are you implying? Surely you don't think my father and Starr are lovers? God tell me that's not the case."

"He mentioned it to her when they were here earlier, but maybe it was a one-time deal?" knowing I'm not making this any easier for Dare to deal with. "I'm sorry I brought it up," I apologize climbing down from my stool and collecting our empty plates.

"No, I'm sorry for taking my anger out on you," he says looking deeply into his wine glass, twirling the pale liquid in the glass. "Things went to hell real fast for Dad once Jared died. He hasn't been the same. He wants everything given to him, he's no longer trustworthy."

Walking over to the freezer I take out the ice cream and start scooping out the frozen treat onto a saucer, press the metal scoop into the center of the ball making a well and then I slide a peach half into the indention and fill it with raspberry sauce and sprinkle slivered almonds on top.

"Here, this will make you feel better, remember?" I ask recalling how much fun we had serving each other this dessert in our tiny apartment. "Try not to make a mess this time, okay?"

He grins and says, "I cleaned it up if you'll recall."

Laughing I take my dish back over to my spot and enjoy the rich taste as well as the memory of Dare eating the raspberry sauce off my naked belly. I still can't smell raspberries without thinking of his hot tongue, swirling into navel as well as other nooks and crannies.

"We'll deal with Sammy's feelings concerning his grandpa later, okay?" he asks, "right now I just want to concentrate on finding evidence against that tramp and sending her packing for good."

"Sounds like a plan," I tell him, "Oh, I spoke with Mokie and he's not going to make the cocktail party tomorrow night, he's going out of town so now we have the run of his house, just the two of us."

"Thank God," he laughs, "some good news for a change."

We finish our desserts and he goes back to the family room where he is working on some land deal. He agreed to work from home while I was here, but he'll be back in his office next week while I'm back in Willow.

The rest of the afternoon flies by and soon its' time to pick up Sammy from school. I offered to fetch him back and originally Dare said that was fine, but now he's changed his mind, being a bit more on his guard. We pull up in front of the school just as they're letting the kids out. I glance around liking the looks of this facility when I happen to see Rhonda Starr get out of a white car parked a couple vehicles behind us. She waves at Sammy as he exits the building and he waves back.

Dare instantly gets out of his rover and heads towards his nemesis but the car she is a passenger in speeds away before he can reach it. He jogs back over and slides back behind the wheel, reaching in my purse for something.

"Quickly I need something to write on," he says rooting through my leather bag.

He pulls out my date planner and removes the pen I keep in the spiral down the side. Jotting down a number I see it's the license plate number for the white sedan. I get out of the rover and open the rear passenger door for Sammy who is waiting on Toby to catch up with him.

"Smart thinking," I tell my fiancé through the open window. "Are you sure you're a realtor and not a secret agent like Sammy?"

"Smart ass," he mumbles and tears out the page from my binder. "Tell the kids to move it; I need to have this checked out before they can ditch the car."

"Yes sir," I tell him and he looks up at me over the top of his sunglasses.

"It's a good thing you can cook." He tells me making me laugh at his old comeback he'd use when I'd one up him. He used to say that was why he put up with my smart aleck mouth.

The boys are chattering a mile a minute when they climb into the rover.

"Tell them about the science fair," Toby says smiling from ear to ear. When Sammy doesn't tell us fast enough Toby shouts, "He won!"

Sammy turns to his friend and whines, "I was going to be the one to tell them,"

"Sorry but you were taking too long," his friend explains; "besides now I can tell them I came in second."

"Great job boys," I tell them, "this deserves a special supper, what would you like?" I ask, ready for anything from Pizza to chicken strips and fries.

"Hunter's Chicken," they both say together making me laugh out loud.

Dare smiles at them and says, "You've conquered the finicky eater in both of them."

"Boys we had that Monday, remember?" I offer to fix them something else, "is there anything else you'd like to try?"

"No," they say again at the same time.

"Tell us again what that means in French." Sammy says, "We're going to learn different languages, to help us become better spies."

I smile at their logic.

"Poulet Saute chasseur, chicken, hunter's style," I tell them and they whisper it out loud to each other, liking the sound of speaking in French.

"It was delicious," Dare says, "I'm okay eating it again if they are."

"Thanks, you're a lot of help." I tell him making a face at the man. "You'd eat anything you didn't have to prepare yourself."

"We're a match made in heaven." He jokes and pulls back into traffic.

27

Friday morning I'm back in Willow with my crew plus one. Dare is spending the weekend with me and helping at Coulton's tonight in Mendocino as well as driving to Lucerne for the huge fiftieth wedding anniversary reception on Saturday.

Saul and Dare are loading up the van; since we don't need the box truck Dare and I are driving up separately from the crew. Nana, Roz, and Gina are not going tonight. They're working on the finishing touches for tomorrow. A cocktail party is a snap compared to preparing a sit down meal for one hundred guests. Thankfully Roz has hired some students from a local cooking school. We don't pay much but it looks really good on a resume to work, even part time, for an established caterer.

Nana has outdone herself with the canapés. Together we made several different nibbles; from bleu cheese, walnuts, and ham wraps to the standard but slightly upgraded deviled eggs. Loading up the containers takes some time so I leave that job to those not going and make sure my working staff is dressed appropriately.

Our standard uniform is black dress slacks, black vest, and a simple solid colored tie. Everyone working looks alike, creating an image of high-end waiters. The only time I defer is when I'm acting as hostess, which I will be doing this evening. Thankfully Gina picked up my go-to black sleeveless sheath dress from the cleaners. It's a cocktail party for twenty five to thirty guests, so nothing as formal as the Stone Reception.

Dare walks back into the kitchen and winks at me making me catch my breath. The man is too good looking by half even dressed in low riding jeans worn in the knees and a simple black T-shirt.

"Where do you want me to shower, here or at our place?" he asks making me want to scream with joy at that one little word, "our".

"There's a full bath here, upstairs or we've got time built in if you want to go home." I tell him, "Gina brought my clothes here so I'm set. Besides if we both end up back at our place we'll for sure be late."

He joins in laughing with me knowing the more we're together, the more often we make love. Like last night after Sammy went to bed, we went outside to our private pool located off a small patio from the master bedroom and made hot scorching love, yet this morning we came together like we'd been apart for years, not lying next to each other for eight hours.

"You're zoning out on me again," he whispers in my ear. "I'll head on over to our place. That will leave the shower open for one of the guys. I'll be back in about an hour try not to miss me too much." He says and bends me over backwards, kissing me long, slowly, and incredibly deep. When we come up for air I hear the sound of applause coming from the pantry. Gina, BJ, Kit, and Nina are all smiling and clapping their hands at us.

"Good job," Kit says, "that ought to loosen her up for the evening."

Nana smiles and says, "Or makes her walk around in a fog all evening, stay away from open flames honey."

BJ laughs and says, "Jealousy is a disease, don't listen to them."

Gina walks over to us and hugs us both, "Thank God you're back together," then she turns around to face the trio and says, "Pay up."

They each hand over twenty dollars apiece making Gina laugh and fan the cash in front of her face.

"Nobody believed me, but I guess they'll not doubt me again, huh?" she smirks.

"No, you're right Gina," I tell her, "but that also means you're on KP duty for the next three events, including tomorrow night's sit down, for gossiping about me. Did I mention 'hand-wash'?"

It's everyone else's turn to laugh and she flips them all off as she stomps out of the room mumbling, "It's going to take every bit of my winnings to pay for the freakin' manicures I'll have to get."

Dare kisses me again, still chuckling at the easy camaraderie we share and he heads over to our place to get cleaned up. Kit and BJ dash upstairs to get dressed while I use the full bath in my office. I can only imagine the ribbing Dare and I would have received if we'd shared the shower here. I'd probably have to fire them all.

When everyone and everything has been loaded into the van I turn to pick up my overnight bag I packed earlier.

We'll be leaving from Mokie's house heading to Lucerne tomorrow so I've got both of our evening clothes in a suit bag and a change of casual clothes for each of us. I'm waiting on the man to arrive having sent the crew on ahead. I like to have two hours set up time even for a cocktail party. Since we're about an hour and a half away, we're cutting it pretty close. Hopefully Dare will get here within the next fifteen minutes or we'll be cutting into my prep time.

"Ready to go?" he asks leaning up against my office door jamb.

My jaw drops at the vision of masculine grace, charm, and flat out sex appeal he is emitting. Dressed in a beautifully tailored gray and white tweed sports coat, black silk shirt opened at the neck, and a pair of perfectly fitting black trousers he makes me think of all sorts of racy, lewd, and lascivious deeds I'd like to do with him. I feel myself blush at the erotic pull he has over me.

"Penny for your thoughts," he teases walking over to stand in front of me.

"Speak of the devil and the devil appears…" I tell him, reaching up to kiss his freshly shaven cheek. "God you smell delicious. I could eat you for supper young man."

Laughing he asks, "Do we get a fifteen minute break sometime tonight?"

I shake my head at him, "no way, that's all I need, to get caught sexing it up with you in a broom closet. We'll have to wait until we get to Elk."

"If you can keep your hands off me for that long." he teases moving his sports coat up over his tight behind, bending over with his hands on his knees, looking over his shoulder, he starts gyrating.

"Hot damn girl if you don't take it I will." Roz says from the doorway, making us both look up and notice the tall, willowy brunette dressed in a navy blazer over a white blouse and khaki dress slacks, in her idea of business casual attire.

I start to laugh and Dare, not to be put on the spot walks over to the stunning dark haired woman where he twirls her around and dips her low over his arm. He barely touches his lips to hers and says, "sorry, but all that belongs to Carrie Anne, but this is just for you."

He presses her full bottom lip between both of his and sucks hard, making her swoon. He sets her upright and walks over to me, slings his arm around my shaking shoulders.

"You must be Roz, I'm Darius Steele, but after what we've come to mean to each other you can call me Dare," he tells stunning her even further at his carefree behavior.

"Nice to meet you," she whispers touching her thoroughly kissed mouth. "Man oh man," she says fanning herself. "Honey, get those wedding contracts signed a.s.a.p. ... Damn I'm in need of a drink, or a repeat." She leers at him raising her perfectly arched eyebrows up and down. Her velvety brown eyes twinkle with mirth as she licks her dark red lips in a sexy invitation.

"Sorry Roz, but we're on a time table here," I tell her hugging her hello and goodbye at the same time.

"I'll wait for his return." She says smiling at both of us. "Have a nice time after the event. What time will you be arriving at Lucerne?"

"Around noon," I tell her grabbing my black clutch and charcoal gray silk shawl. "You're going to that one, right? I'll be working so I'll need you to man your battle station."

"I'll be there, unless studly here makes me a better offer…" she jokes.

"Nope, one guy, one gal; that's the rules, right Cam?" he teases placing his hand in the small of my back and leading me towards the front door.

"One to one is the only ratio that works for me. See you tomorrow Roz." I tell her then remember to mention Mokie not coming tomorrow. "Mokie is in Lake Tahoe for the weekend, he's going to be filling in for some chef that is down in his back. Call him and congratulate him, he's in heaven."

"Good for him." she says a bit too nonplussed to fool me. "I'll catch up with him later."

"Goodnight and a pleasure to meet and dip you." Dare says making us both laugh as we walk outside to my convertible mustang.

"Keep the top down," I tell him, wrapping my silk shawl around my head to protect my hair from being ravaged by the wind. "I love this drive; it always makes me feel free."

"You got it," he says slipping on his sunglasses and puts the car in reverse and pulls out onto the road, and soon we're both enjoying the crispness of the breeze.

28

We hold hands across the console as we make our way towards Lakeport at the edge of Mendocino National Forest. Dare drives like he does everything else, with ease and confidence so I sit back and enjoy more of the rugged Pacific coast scenery flitting past me. The day is warm and the air smells of the pine and fir trees stretching for miles. Dare enjoys the drive as well taking in the naturally landscaped highway and all too soon we're pulling into the gated driveway of Jack Coulton, an agent for several top music bands and performers. I've never met him, but Roz says he's sort of 'greasy' but his check was good and that's all I care about. Dare and I drive up to the rear entrance once we explain who we are and get the security guard to let us pass. I smile at Dare knowing he is thinking the same thing I am.

"It always amazes me how silly these affairs can be, I mean, it's drinks and snacks for crying out loud," I laugh and he nods his head in agreement.

"But it pays the bills so we smile and play nicely," he finishes for me.

"You're right," I agree and wait for him to open my car door for me.

As he hands me out of the low slung car I notice he is staring at the long expanse of my leg exposed, he wraps his arm around my waist and whispers in my ear, "I can't wait for those sexy legs to squeeze the life out of me later tonight."

I stumble and he catches me, laughing at my distraction. I reach for his hand and take his index finger into my mouth and suck hard on him until he swallows hard enough for me to hear.

"There, that's better." I joke evening up the sexual scoreboard a bit.

We turn to walk into the ultra-contemporary modern style home that feels a bit cold and depressing; everything is cement- gray in color. The two story split level house is too jagged in design; it isn't aesthetically pleasing to the eye, almost jarring in fact due to the stark angles of the structured concrete. The hardscape yard looks as if someone actually removed any flora. It reminds me of an old WWII bunker I recently saw on a PBS documentary. Hopefully the interior is a bit more pleasing than the exterior. Once inside we run straight into Saul who appears to be arguing already with the hired staff.

"… I don't care what your employer says, we're supposed to set up the bar, as I'll be bartending, I have a certain way I do things…" Saul is telling the angry red-faced man whose head barely comes up to Saul's chest.

"Mr. Coulton likes things done his way, he hates change. I know what he likes and I will tell you once more, you can't set up the bar in the living room," the little man is practically screaming.

"Maybe I can help," I step in, trying to keep a silly temper tantrum from becoming the last act this staffer makes.

Saul is getting pissed off so Dare nods for him to leave me alone with the pint sized tyrant.

"Tell me what the problem is and I'm sure we can fix it." I assure him.

Looking me up and down in a totally inappropriate manner he says, "Yeah, you can probably make Mr. Coulton do whatever you want, after he's had another drink that is."

"Mr.... I'm sorry I didn't catch your name," I tell him.

"Tunks," he says puffing out his slender chest barely moving the dark fabric of his jacket, "my name is Tunks and I run the household and what I say goes. Tell that Neanderthal to stop setting up his bar in the living room, like I told him."

"Where would you like for us to set up the bar, in which room?" I ask diverting his anger into something more positive.

"Well, I thought you could use the den, or the family room, that way it's out of sight. The photographers always make it a point to shoot how much alcohol is served at Mr. Coulton's parties, and it angers him the next day when the articles start appearing in the tabloids." He huffs his indignation.

"Surely a man of Mr. Coulton's stature doesn't worry about what is being written in those rags?" I ask knowing he now has to defend his employer's insecurities.

"No, no of course not," he back tracks, "but he's the devil to live with when he does get bad press, and something always goes sideways at one of these infernal affairs."

"How about this," I propose walking over to the bar set-up, "Let's keep all the bottles, even the tonic and seltzer bottles underneath the bar or behind it anyway. We'll put a couple platters and tiers of appetizers on the bar top and my guys will keep the surface clear of those incriminating items, okay?"

He ponders my suggestion for a couple more seconds, and then nods his head in agreement. We shake on the deal and he leaves to harass his own household staff.

"One fire down, nine to go," Dare jokes and I can see he's proud of the way I handled the little snipe. "Remind me to take you to my next land negotiation; you're a killer at turning the tables."

"Thank you my good man," I tell him, "but I'm off to let the troops know of the silly concession we're making. Care to join me?"

"No, I hate to see grown men cry." He teases and wanders over to the tables being loaded down with my food. "Holler if you need me to kick somebody's ass, I'm here for you," Then walks into the other room. I turn and run into the host and his son who appears to be an identical but younger version of his father. Hopefully the younger won't become as dissipated as his sire. Senior Coulton is balding and his jaw line is going soft, his expensive Italian suit doesn't quite hide his paunchy middle, and he already appears to be a bit unsteady on his feet.

"Good evening Mr. Coulton and Mr. Coulton" I smile, "I'm Carrie Anne Mosier your caterer." I hold out my hand and the elder motions for the younger to leave, which he does with a nod to me. Coulton Senior takes my hand in both of his, which appear damp, and a bit too soft.

"It is a pleasure to meet you Carrie." He says in a slightly oiled voice, "perhaps it will be your pleasure later on."

I blink at the inappropriate insinuation and am grateful Dare isn't within ear shot.

"Thank you but no, I'll be too busy making sure your guests are taken care of." I tell him letting the cold into my voice ring out but like a lot of men in powerful positions, whether they've been hitting the bottle so early in the day or not, he hears what he wants to hear.

"Good, I'll hook up with you later then," he says dropping his gaze to my breasts, "looking forward to you taking care of my needs."

Knowing he is impossible already makes me worry about his condition by the end of the evening. Thank God Dare and Saul are with me tonight.

"Excuse me while I help set up the food," I tell him and feel his beady little eyes watching me walk away.

I close the kitchen swinging doors and take a couple of deep, cleansing breaths before I approach the extra staff hired for this evening.

"Everyone, please make note who is on the floor and who is in here. I run a tight ship so mind your p's and q's and look lively." I give them the speech I use at functions like this when I add to my crew.

"Do not put empty glasses on trays with full ones; don't leave an empty glass sitting on any piece of furniture. Make sure no one lights up inside the house, and I mean it." I emphasize this strongly as the last one of these affairs something besides cigarettes was being passed around much to the dismay of the hostess.

"Do not nibble or drink out on the floor, be courteous, but not too friendly. If you see anything out of place let me know." I tell them as the small tyrant Tunks makes his way over to me.

"Tell them about the bar," he snaps at me looking over at Saul and giving him a smirk.

"I've already set things up with my man, so you go mill about, make sure the additional staff is following your orders and we'll start this party off with a soft, unpretentious bang." I tell the littler pisser making him look over his shoulder at me in question. I wave at him and turn to get with Saul who isn't happy at the changes made.

Two hours later the party is in full swing, no problems so far. The food is a big hit according to the guests, especially the baked eye-of-round with rosemary and Gina's special pesto spread. I mill about making sure everyone has something to eat as well as drink. Holding my glass of seltzer water I accidently get bumped into by a slightly inebriated man that looks faintly familiar, but I can't place him.

"'Scuse me," he slurs his words, "hope I didn't hurt you pretty lady."

The words pretty lady makes me think of a song I used to love and that's where I recognize him from. His name is Fitzgerald, part of the old band Fitz-Simmons, but they broke up years ago and I seem to recall he went into the movies. He apparently is high as a kite tonight.

"No problem," I tell him and he just stares at me. "Are you alright?" I ask trying to keep him from spilling his neat bourbon down my arm.

"Susa? Is that you?" he asks and leans into me trying to rest his head on my shoulder. "I've missed you baby."

Before I can push him off Dare is beside me taking the drunken man by the arm and propelling him out of the room. I discreetly look around and see Jack Coulton watching me, smiling that greasy smile, making me feel like I need an acid bath to come clean. I get stopped several times on my way to the kitchen where I hope Dare is keeping the actor out of trouble. BJ catches my eye and motions for me to get in there but before I can take two steps Jack Coulton pulls me up against his body from behind. I can feel his erection pressing into me and I suddenly have had enough manhandling. I turn in his arms and quick as lightning I raise my knee striking him in the groin, making him double over in pain.

"Are you all right Mr. Coulton?" I ask loud enough for others around me to hear my question. "Could someone help Mr. Coulton, he seems to be feeling faint all of a sudden," I put enough concern in my voice to keep the attention on the host and I walk away when a crowd gathers around the jerk.

Smiling at me Kit walks over and says, "Your concern was a nice touch, the sofa hid the racking you gave that slime ball."

"Don't let Dare hear about this okay?" I ask him but see him smile and shake his head at me.

"Too late," Dare says from behind me. "What happened and what did you do to remedy it."

Kit starts laughing and says, "Balls to the walls brother," and walks away to refill a tray of canapés.

"He had it coming, I'm not sorry, but hopefully he won't remember what happened tomorrow, besides he's already paid in full for tonight." I lean up and kiss an irate Dare on his jaw because I know he's thinking back to the

Stone reception and my having to fight off the two drunken groomsmen.

"Are you always fighting off drunks at these affairs; because that's not going to fly anymore?" He tells me leaning over and nuzzling my neck making me laugh out loud. "Well, your lovesick pretty boy is outside by the pool hurling your cheese straws and about a fifth of bourbon," he says smiling as a senator walks by and nods his head, "let's hope they think it's the booze and not your food that's making everybody sick."

"That's not funny Dare," I scold him as I push out of his arms and head back into the kitchen but have a hard time not laughing at his joke.

An hour later we're wrapping things up in the kitchen when Fitzgerald walks through the swinging door. He sees me right away, mistaking me as someone named Susa. I motion for BJ to find either Saul or Dare. By the time he staggers over to me Dare is by my side, wrapping his arm around my waist.

"What seems to be the problem," Dare asks in a soft but cold voice.

"Sorry," he mumbles as he leans forward to get a better look at me, "I thought she was Susa, but she couldn't be my Susa… she's gone back to that small hell whole she crawled out of." I swear I see tears in the man's eyes.

"You need to have someone drive you home pal, sleep it off." Dare says then gently pushes me out of the drunken man's line of sight. "Come on let me call you a cab."

The two men walk out of the kitchen together and I get back to packing up the unused linens and utensils. BJ returns with Kit and they start hauling the packed bins out to the van.

"Finally, alone at last," I hear that creepy voice behind me. "Sorry about our interruption earlier, oh and by the way, you'll pay for that little act of aggression upstairs in the master's chamber, and I don't mean that word as a euphemism. It really is the master's chamber."

I set the crate of clean stemware down and slowly turn to face this jackass who is practically salivating at the thought of punishing me for the earlier racking he received from me.

"First off, you had the whole knee in the groin thing coming from the skanky behavior you've shown me since I arrived. Second, the only 'master' thing you'll be doing tonight is masturbating, and third, I'll lay you flat on your back, with you ending up in a fetal position if you don't back away from me right now."

I cross my arms under my breasts and count to three, if he hasn't moved back a step or two, I'm slipping the noose.

"Who the fuck do you think you're talking to," he snarls at me leaning in so his hot breath blows over my cheek. "If I want I can have you detained, accuse you of stealing from me, and ruin your shitty career all within five minutes."

His balance is precarious at best, but he keeps leaning towards me bringing his pudgy index finger close to my breast.

"Step back Coulton," I warn him again and see Saul walk into the room, then Dare enters behind him and starts to interfere but Saul holds out his massive arm to waylay Dare's interference.

"Let's take this upstairs and we'll see who wins." The drunkard says placing his hand around the back of my head trying to pull me into his wet, sloppy kiss.

I lean into him and bring up my elbow sharply into contact with his stomach making him jerk back in pain. Grabbing a hold of his wrist I turn my body into him and place my leg between both of his then twist and pull up, flipping him over my hip and landing the drunk flat on his back. Stepping between his shaking legs I gently press the toe of my shoe to his crotch making him flinch.

I lean over his whimpering body and whisper, "Don't you ever touch me again. En Bonne Catering will no longer be accepting your business and I will be informing my colleagues to do the same. Plus I've got a contact at one of the rags you desperately read, I'll mention your overzealous need for booze and how you walked around all evening exposing yourself."

I look up and see my crew, the extra staff along with Dare smiling at the spectacle lying on the granite floor in the predicted fetal position. A young woman with black hair, wearing a mini dress two sizes too small runs over and kneels down beside the man, offering him assistance. Several people have their cell phones out snapping photos of the downed Coulton. Dare holds out his hand to me and I race over to him, breathing in his clean scent.

"Good job baby," he says, "now let's finish loading up and getting on to our next party tonight."

I smile and kiss him, then walk out of the kitchen and check to make sure everything is as it was when we arrived. I swear I hear laughter and Kit say, "see you in the funny papers," before the swinging door stops moving.

29

Dare is sleeping in this morning, after the grueling party, then the comfort sex last night plus early this morning. He is dead to the world. I take my huge tumbler of coffee out on to the deck, lay back on one of the two Adirondack chairs, prop my feet on the deck railing and watch the gorgeous movement of the rugged seascape in front of me. Large boulders take a beating as the surf crashes against them. Glancing toward the edge of Mokie's property I watch the Pacific reed grass sway to the melody created by the ocean's tide and in turn soothing my soul.

When we got here last night I was expecting an argument from the man. Something along the lines of 'there are too many drunks for you to have to deal with, or it's too crazy of a business for you to handle, or 'it's not safe for a woman to be out there dealing with scum like Coulton' but he said nothing except he was tired.

I honestly thought we weren't going to make love but when I leaned over to kiss him goodnight he came alive. He flipped me over onto my stomach, parted my legs from behind and pushing my rear end up in the air he proceeded to prove me wrong. Each stroke he gave me went deep, raking his swollen member across my nerve center, making me moan in tortured delight. Whispering dark encourage into my ear I was primed before he was half way there. He took great delight in making me wait on him, telling me he could do that all night, and didn't it feel good not to rush things.

When I reached the end of my rope I grabbed a hold of his arm and tried to flip him over but even though I couldn't budge him, he did lose control at my losing control and he started hammering away, putting me out of my sexual misery. We came together both shouting our release. When he was depleted, he collapsed on top of me, kissing the damp hair at my temples.

"God damn you always make me feel so good," he whispered and slid out of me, rolling over onto his side and swiftly fell asleep.

Smiling at his stamina he woke me up at the crack of dawn by suckling my breasts and lightly stroking his long fingers between my folds. Opening my thighs wider he kissed his way down my body until his wide shoulders nestled between my legs. He was tender and gentle and laughed as I spun out of control. When I settled back down on the bed he slid into my body with one fell swoop, then came after the third stroke. Once again we fell back to sleep. I woke up to the sound of gulls calling to each other and the pressing need to use the bathroom.

Now, enjoying my time alone I feel each ache and pain, every twitch of a muscle makes me wince but it was worth it. Standing up from my seat I set my traveler on the deck and use the railing as a ballet bar, slowly working the kinks out of my muscles. After ten minutes of stretching I bend down to pick up my cup but it's gone and Dare is sitting in my chair silently watching me.

"Good morning," he says in his sexy hoarse voice. "Nice view and the ocean ain't bad either."

I walk over to the chair and straddle his legs, parting my robe showing I'm naked beneath.

"Just trying to stay limber enough to keep up with you," I whisper and start to kiss his lips but instead I grab my tumbler now almost empty of coffee. "What time is it?" I ask wondering how long I've been out here.

"It's eight thirty," he says and refuses to let me get up, "I like this position very much." He whispers and unties the drawstring of his black silk pajama bottoms, and low and behold he has a massive morning erection.

"I'll bet you're in need of something besides coffee and a lovely ocean view, huh?" I tease.

"Yes please," he says and scoots his hips lower in the wooden chair given me greater access to his throbbing flesh.

I scoot off his thighs and grab a cushion off the matching chair and toss the pillow on the floor.

"Remember all those lessons on oral sex we had," I tell him smiling at the bright light shining in his azure eyes, "well let's see if it's like riding a bike, shall we?"

He starts laughing and reaches down to shuck his pants off and lay back, his arms behind his head and winks, ready for me to show him what I remember. And in the end, it appears I forgot nothing. Resting my arms on his tight thighs I love him in all the ways he showed me when we were in Paris. His soft groans and moans encourage me and I pull, tug, and draw him farther, deeper, and harder into my mouth until I feel him quicken.

"Climb on top," he groans and when I don't stand up fast enough he reaches down and picks me up, sets me on his hard staff and rises up to meet me. I feel the top of my head start to come off from the force he is using to ease his need.

"Move Camy, God don't just sit there," he half jokes, but my inner muscles are so sore from last night and this morning that I give up and let him take this one on his own. When he can talk without gasping he grows concerned.

"What's wrong," he demands, "you were the one that started the oral refresher's course. Why didn't you let go, you held back and you've never done that before."

I start to stand up but he is not letting me go, "Tell me Carrie Anne, what's wrong?" he yells.

"My whole body feels like it got ran over by a damn truck, okay?" I yell back at him, still trying to bring my thighs back together to take the pressure off those muscles. "You practically broke me, there are you satisfied?"

"For the moment," He whispers and draws me to his chest, running his hands up and down my spine, massaging my aching lower back muscles. "You always got like this right before your period, are you due?" he asks in his usual straight forward manner.

"Yes, next week." I admit to him making him smile.

"All you had to do was tell me you felt sore," he whispers, "I know you always cramp hard at first, so in the future, I'll watch the calendar closer and leave you alone," he jokes, "how does that sound?"

"Like you'll forget when the mood strikes." I tease him back. "Besides, this started out as oral sex; you took it too far, not me."

"Agreed, it's my entire fault, and I thank you for remembering everything I taught you." He jokes, "we need more coffee, and a long hot shower, slowly slide backwards and we'll start the day right."

After we shower, I fix a lovely quiche Lorraine and we eat every bite having worked up quite an appetite. He offers to clean up while I call the studio and make sure everything is running on schedule. BJ answers the land line.

"Good morning La Capitaine," he jokes, "how are you feeling today slugger?"

"Like I have one too many employees," I reply knowing BJ is grinning from ear to ear. "Is everything on schedule, any problems?" I ask

"Just a horde of pesky paparazzi knocking on the front door, wanting to take a couple close up shots of the caterer/ kick boxing queen that set Jack-off Coulton on his ass." He jokes at least I hope he's kidding.

"Tell them to talk to my agent, Mr. Darius Steele." I joke, "Seriously, everybody up and running?"

"You bet," he assures me, "Nana's cake is in the carrier and loaded in the van. Roz has confirmed the hotel has their service laid out for us and the tables and chairs set up in your configuration as well." He laughs and says, "We all love it when you rent all the equipment, it's so nice not having to lug all that furniture, makes my muscles sore just thinking about it."

I laugh at the mention of sore muscles, much to his confusion and say, "Dare and I will be there at noon. Make sure everybody is wearing their black ties tonight, its very high end and we don't want to stand out as individuals, but as a collective. Senator Anderson is going to be very good for our bottom line."

"And that's what it's all about, huh?" he teases.

"Little man you're starting to sound way too much like Kit." I warn him and see Dare motioning for the phone, "hang on BJ, Dare wants to say something," and I hand my cell over to him.

"Hey BJ, go on line and see if there is a mention of last night's knock down drag out fight with our resident Bruce Lee, I'll hold." He says and winks at me. "I just want to be sure we don't end up in any more embarrassing situations like last night."

"Ha ha you're so funny Steele," I tell him and walk over to the huge bank of windows facing the sea and sit down on one of the long gray sofa's and wait for my comedians to get through.

"No shit? Wow who knew there were that many cell phones at the ready?" He laughs and says, "No, she's already mad at us, I'll tell her later. See you in a couple of hours. Bye."

"Well, Coulton's 'down for the count' photo ops are all over the internet so be prepared for a backlash." He says, "I doubt he remembers any of it, but just in case I think I'll call our attorney and give him a heads up."

"Do you think I'm going to be sued?" I ask hoping he's just being overly protective of me. I can't afford bad publicity.

"He doesn't stand a chance, not with all the witnesses that were there last night." He assures me, "he's probably worried you're going to file a sexual harassment case against him, which you would definitely win." He leans over me and says, "Don't sweat it. I got your back."

He kisses the tip of my nose and turns back around and heads into the bedroom to get dressed.

We're on the road in less than an hour, with our evening clothes lying neatly in the back seat, our luggage in the trunk, and a lighter mood since we spoke to Sammy before we left.

"I'm glad Sammy is having a great time." I tell him, "He and Toby really are closer than most brothers aren't they?"

"Yeah, they remind me of Jared and me when we were that small." He says and tells me far-fetching stories of the Steele boy's triumphs.

I feel like I laughed the whole trip. We pull into the parking lot of the Regency Hotel where the big bash is unfolding. Getting excited at such a huge banquet I start to get jittery.

"Relax baby, this will be a cake walk compared to last night." He teases me and he is right. I love big fancy parties like this, it gives me and my team the chance to really shine.

With the whole En Bonnes crew working we sail through the preparations of the meal. Nana's cake has been set up just off to the side of the four long banquet tables that will hold our feast. Senator Anderson's wife wanted a buffet line that way everyone would be able to feed themselves and not have to wait to be served.

The floral arrangements were outsourced due to their size and the cost of producing the extravagant bouquets. With over a hundred and fifty guests the vast number of tables, china, crystal, cutlery, and linen is enough to send me over the edge. Thankfully Roz has it all lined out and all I have to do is prepare enough food for the masses.

The perfect meal for this occasion is Steak au poivre, herbed fingerling potatoes, sautéed green beans, mushroom pastries, Salad Normande, crusty French bread and demitasse to be served with the cake Nana spent two days making.

It is so elegant, with its multi layered fillings, fondant ribbons and gorgeous edible flowers; it is Nana's masterpiece.

Kit is busy with the special effects and lighting, Saul is unloading cases of liquor and champagne. Gina is busy with the seating chart she and Roz spent several days filling in and the placement cards were picked up yesterday morning from the printer, talk about cutting it close.

En Bonnes got a deal and a half on the price due to Roz and her ability to make others see her side of the situation. I wouldn't be surprised if our printing service man was in tears after she got off the phone with him. He'll never assume he knows what looks better than my girl. She wins every time.

Dare is looking over the hotel waiters that the Anderson's required, making sure they measure up to En Bonnes high standards. He is practically using my speech from last night, words changed here and there but basically he is laying down the law. My goodness he looks good laying it down too.

He is wearing one of his tuxedos, masterfully cut to his lean frame. The black velvet vest and bow tie he has on sets him apart from the rest of the crew, they're wearing their black silk ties without a vest. Honestly he'd stand out in a room full of people wearing the exact suit; it's the man, not the clothes.

We complement each other in dress. I chose a matte silver/gray form fitting dress that drapes horizontally down the front, and tied around the waist with a matching grosgrain ribbon. Silver strappy sandals and small silver fleur de lis are dangling from my ear lobes. They were a gift for my graduating top of my class. My Grandmother and Brother went in together and bought the extravagant gift, and since the fleur de lis is part of my trademark I always love wearing them to big events such as this. They make people remember us. I'm wearing my ruby and diamond ring on my right hand now that Dare's ring is resting on my left ring finger.

30

The meal is prepared, the bar is open, the candles are lit, and there are over a hundred people milling about. As I walk into the room I feel a great sense of pride and accomplishment. Dare is talking to Senator Anderson over by the bar so I head over to say hello.

Dare is in mid-sentence when he turns and sees me walking towards him. He stares at me like he's never seen me before. The senator laughs and nudges Dare's shoulder breaking his trance. He looks down at his shoes then back to the powerful older gentleman and they laugh at something the older man said.

"Senator Anderson, allow me to introduce you to my fiancée, Carrie Anne Mossier, owner and operator of En Bonne Catering," he says and kisses my temple when he pulls me to his side, "Cam, this is Senator Everett Anderson, I believe you've been working through his office and assistant James Hood who is over by the bar trying to convince Roz to go out with him."

Laughing I turn to look at my crew, who are head and shoulders above the rented staffers and once again feel proud. I take the senator's hand and say, "it's a pleasure to finally meet you sir, and on behalf of En Bonne Catering, congratulations on the first fifty years."

"Young lady, you're charming as hell, but don't think I'm going to stick around for another fifty. You'll have to find someone else to cater to." He says making us laugh.

"She already has found that someone, haven't you Cam?" Dare teases giving me such an intense look I feel a blush coming on.

"If you'll excuse me, I need to go check on the meal," I tell them needing to cool my jets around that man of mine.

I walk into the kitchen, grab my chef coat off the hook and walk through all the different stations. It is a hive of well-organized activity. Gina is in her element and has BJ to back her up. Every dish has been tested and found perfect. The waiters are loading up their appetizer trays they'll be carrying as they mingle through the crowd as well as the waiters with the wine trays.

Kit's lighting extravaganza is amazing. He under lit all the tables skirts, the floral arrangements, the stationary fountain as well as he hung sheer curtains from the ceiling and back lit them with rope lighting. It's a magical room. I turn 360 degrees and take in the whole room.

"You out did yourself again," says Blake Stone who walks up beside me with his wife draped over his arm. He looks fantastic in his dark evening attire.

Tonight she is dressed in basic black too, but manages to stand out in this crowded room of black tuxedos, little black dresses, and dressy black pants suits which more than half of the matrons here tonight are wearing. They resemble a murder of crows.

"Thanks," I tell them, "even I'm impressed with my crew."

"She's being modest," Dare says coming up behind me and handing me a tall flute of sparkling water. "Congratulate us; we're to be married come Christmas."

Both Stones look at one another and then she laughs and holds out her hand, palm up waiting on her husband to do what? Then I feel another blush heat my cheeks when Mr. Stone reaches inside his jacket, pulls out his money clip and whips out two crisp one-hundred dollar bills and lays them in his wife's hand.

"Do you have to be right about everything Phyl?" he sneers and turns to explain, "She said there was something between the two of you when she saw you together at our daughter Randi's wedding reception and apparently my psychic wife was right. Consider that part of your wedding gift Steele." He places his arm around his wife's narrow waist and says, "come on Mrs. Money bags you can buy me a drink." They move along leaving me and Dare staring at each other.

"I love you," he whispers, "When I saw you walk into the room while ago I forgot what Anderson and I were talking about. He said I'd have this defect for at least another fifty years."

Smiling at him I lean closer and say, "all I can think about is seeing your tuxedo lying on the floor and you lying on top of me..."

"Dammit Cam, you're making my pants too tight," he complains but pulls me into his side and kisses my temple. "I'm proud of you and all you've accomplished in six short years. I'm even more proud to tell everyone you're about to become my wife. God I'm going to black out if my blood circulation doesn't stop pooling below my waist."

Laughing at his delicate situation I kiss his lips and sigh, "I've heard of people getting too big for their britches, but I thought that was just a figure of speech…"

I stand in front of him and push my backside slightly into his groin, hearing him swear under his breath.

"Behave Cam or I'll take you behind the fountain and nail your ass to the lighted walls." He threatens and pushes me away.

"I'll remember who pushed who away later on, when I'm alone in our hotel room, stretched out naked on the queen sized bed, massaging the kinks out of my back and legs, sort of like this morning and the deck rail." I tease him.

Dare motions for another flute of champagne, and hands his empty glass to me.

"Here take that into the kitchen and leave me and these ball crunching pants alone until I know I'll be able function again. I'll pay you back a little later," he says and turns away and slowly tries to adjust his burgeoning crotch without anyone noticing. I cover my mouth with my empty hand as he walks into the crowd.

31

The next morning Dare opens the hotel room door to receive the coffee and croissants he ordered as well as the morning newspaper. Scooting up in bed I reach over and pick up his watch off the nightstand. Wow, it's already ten o'clock. I know I could sleep another couple of hours, but we have to head back to Willow, get the studio back to normal. Dare is staying the night with me but then he'll leave first thing tomorrow for Sonoma.

The smell of coffee makes me smile. I put his watch back and shift the bed pillows and lean back waiting to be served breakfast in bed. He grins as he walks over to me, sets a cup of hot coffee on the night stand and steps up into the center of the bed, sits cross legged in his black silk pajama bottoms and smiles while he touches his coffee cup against mine in a silent toast.

"According to the society page of the Lucerne Ledger last night was a huge success and your company gets mentioned three times. Oh and there are several pictures of those who attended, coming and going." He leans over and kisses me on the lips, "congratulations."

He has folded the paper in such a way I can read it one handed and sip my morning elixir with the other. There are three photos, one of Senator and Mrs. Anderson dancing, another of several of his political cronies, and one of Dare and myself talking with Blake and Anita Stone. As I take another sip of coffee something in the photograph catches my eye. I almost spill my drink when I recognize Rhonda Starr in the back ground of the picture. Looking up at Dare, I feel queasy. She is diabolical, how did she get inside the room?

"What's the matter?" he whispers setting his cup on the table and taking mine from my shaking fingers, "are you going to be sick? Cam, tell me what's wrong."

"Look at the photograph, behind your left shoulder," I tell him pointing at the profile of his archenemy.

"Son of a bitch," he hisses then leans over and picks up his cell phone off the nightstand as he steps off the bed. "Tanner, call me back immediately." He says letting me know he was talking to voice mail.

"Hurry up, get dressed." He tells me, "We're leaving as soon as we can get checked out."

Dare on the move is a sight to behold, a virtual whirlwind. He pulls out a pair of worn jeans and a black crew neck sweatshirt from his overnight bag and tosses the items on the end of the bed. He slips off his pajama bottoms and pulls on a pair of jockey shorts then his jeans. Bending over he slides his bare feet into his leather driving moccasins in the time it takes me to get out of bed.

"Move it Cam," he snaps tossing my overnight bag on the bed, "I'm serious – we need to be on the road in ten minutes."

Not understanding his sense of urgency I start to question him when his phone rings. Pulling it out of his back pocket he points to the bathroom and stares at me when I fail to comply.

"Tanner? Yeah thanks for responding so quickly," he says then looks over at me again and waits for me to move. "Starr was there last night, at the reception," he says and then is quiet, listening to his friend.

"…because I saw her face over Cam's shoulder in the morning paper," he replies.

I take off Dare's white dress shirt I slept in and walk over to the suitcase, take out a pair of jeans, clean underwear, and a long sleeved wine colored T-shirt. Once I'm dressed all but my ballet slippers I turn to see Dare staring at the newspaper. They've been communicating for a couple of minutes and only when I hear my name do I start to pay attention to Dare's responses.

"… Was by invitation only, who the hell let her inside?" He is fuming, "she was so close she could have reached out and touched her. No, I didn't mention her to her crew, but it looks like I should have," he says glancing over at me and nodding his head when he sees I'm ready to go.

He covers the mouthpiece and says, "Grab our things out of the bath and we'll go."

Mindlessly I do his bidding still not sure why he is so upset. Sure she crashed the party, and yes she is practically stalking us, but she's just one crazy broad, not an army. Dare snaps his fingers at me, drawing my attention back to him as he writes down a number on a piece of paper.

"Great, the sooner you can pick him up the better," he says, "just don't scare him. Tell him we're spending the next few days in Willow, that way we won't have to worry about him being taken at school. And don't say a word to Derek."

Dare is no longer calling his parent, father. That's a bad sign. I grab our luggage, fill my traveler mug full from the carafe sitting on the small table, sling my purse strap around my shoulder and give the room a once over. It's not neat, but everything we brought is in our arms. I walk over to the door and wait for Dare to join me.

"We're heading out now, so keep in touch." he says not even looking at me when he walks out the door. "Wait," he says, "do you have Cam's cell number? Good. If you can't reach me, call her, okay?"

He walks down the hall carrying our evening clothes bag over his shoulder, the newspaper under his arm and the cell phone still to his ear. I reach the elevator car right after he does and step over the threshold. He is listening to Tanner and totally involved in whatever he is being told. I start to think about what all I have to do this afternoon and in seconds it seems like the lift doors open out onto the lobby.

"Cam, go check us out, I'll get the car," he orders, "be on the lookout for Starr.

His sharp tone is starting to grate on my nerves but I grab the receipts and turn in the key card and turn towards the lobby when I get the feeling I'm being watched. Casually I turn and look behind me and could have sworn I saw a man duck behind the large marble columns but when I lean around the pillar, there's no one there. Great now I've got the jitters thanks to Dare's hysterics.

"Carrie Anne, stop playing around," Dare snaps at me standing directly behind me, scaring the crap out of me and making me jump. "The cars out front, let's go." He snaps and turns on his heel, leaving me to follow like a trained dog.

That cuts it. I refuse to run after the arrogant jerk so when I reach the car he is in a full blown temper.

"What the hell is wrong with you?" he hisses at me grabbing the luggage from my hands and tossing them in the trunk. "We're in a bit of a hurry, in case you haven't picked up on that," he says in a snide tone of voice, "get the lead out."

I remove my shoulder strap and swing my purse, hitting him hard on his bottom making him turn around and gape at me. I've got a death grip on my traveler, seriously consider dumping it over his head, but then again, in the mood he's in we won't be stopping for coffee so I resist the temptation.

"Good," I tell him walking over to snatch the keys out of his hand. "Now that I've got your attention, listen up Steele. I'm not your servant, your child, your employee, or your dog. Stop ordering me about and tell me what's got you so riled?"

"Get in the car," he snaps at me, looking around the portico. He is about to explode.

"No. Not until you tell me why you're in such a hell-fire hurry to leave." I counter crossing my arms under my breasts and lean against the rear panel of my Mustang.

"Carrie Anne," he growls, "you better get your ass in the passenger seat or so help me God I'll pick you up and toss you in it." His eyes narrow to slits and I know he is about to go ballistic and would probably enjoy tossing me around. "I'm driving," he says and grabs the keys from my fingers.

Opening the car door for me I raise my chin in open defiance then quickly slide into the white leather interior, buckling my seat belt then turning away from him and staring out the window. If he doesn't want to explain his actions, I don't want to talk to him. He pulls out into traffic, opens his phone and hits speed dial.

"Hello Jorge? It's Dare." He says, "Good, everything went well I think, but what do I know, right?" he maneuvers into the turning lane and continues to speak to Toby's father.

"I know he's having a great time," he says in an even tone of voice, "something's come up and I sent Tanner to pick up Sammy. He won't be spending the evening at your place, so apologize to Toby and thank your in-laws for their hospitality but Carrie Anne is having a family emergency, so I'd like for Sammy to be with us, you know how good a distraction those two are. Since they don't have school tomorrow for teachers in service, I want him to be with us."

He talks for a couple more minutes and then ends the call. Finally he turns to look at me. But before he can say anything his cell phone starts ringing. Dare reads the screen.

"What's up Saul?" he asks and at the mention of my friend I turn to openly listen to their phone conversation.

"We'll be at the studio in about an hour and a half." He says looking at his watch.

He smiles at something my employee says and replies "Have everyone meet us there, no excuses. We need to have a family meeting, there are some things going on you and the others need to be let in on, so meet us there." He laughs again and says, "I don't care, tell Gina to fix whatever she'd like, but make a lot, we're expecting Tanner and Sammy."

He ends the call and just as he signals to switch lanes a driver who appears to be texting on his phone nearly side swipes us. Dare has to use a great deal of driving skills to keep us from careening into the semi-tractor trailer on his right. Swearing under his breath he looks over at me.

"Are you alright?" he asks looking into the rear view mirror and signaling another lane change.

"No, I'm not." I tell him without looking over at him, "I will be when I get home, away from you and your God damned high-handedness."

"I'm sorry sweetheart," he says patting my knee but keeping his eyes on the traffic around us. "I got a little edgy and took it out on you, it won't happen again, okay?"

Sensing he is lacking any remorse for his behavior I decide to remain quiet. I take out my cell phone and call Roz.

"Where are you? Saul said we're to hightail it back to the studio for some POW WOW with you and Dare, what gives?" she says as a greeting.

"Don't ask me, I'm just along for the ride," I tell her. "Would you mind looking after Sammy when he gets there? He and Tanner have a head start on us and I don't know what excuse Tanner gave the boy," I say once again I feel Dare staring at me but I continue talking to my friend.

"Help Gina with whatever she needs, but my main concern is for Sammy." I tell her and she assures me she'll look after him, not to worry.

I end the call and know right away Dare is angry at me. I don't particularly care but he is not going to be ignored.

"Spill it," he says implying I'm holding out on him. "Get it out in the open, so we can discuss what's pissed you off."

"You," I tell him without elaborating.

"What the hell did I do?" he snorts and nods his head in understanding, "so I didn't treat you with kid gloves, I'm sorry. If I snapped at you, again I apologize for upsetting your delicate sensitivities, but we're on a time schedule and your dallying about wasn't helping," he says still keeping an eye on traffic.

"Like I said, you are the reason I'm pissed me off," I tell him crossing my arms under my breasts and staring straight ahead, seeing the traffic has spread out some so the driving isn't so intense.

"Are you really going to sit over there and pout? For God's sake, grow up." He snaps and stomps down on the gas pedal, making up for lost time.

32

Hunkering down in the seat I rest my head on the back of the seat and close my eyes, and doze off to sleep only to be awakened by Dare kissing me. We're no longer moving and he's got me caged in his arms.

"Kiss me, take your anger out on me," he whispers licking the seam between my closed lips, "I really am sorry I upset you, and I'll explain what is going on once we're inside, but please don't create anymore tension. Sammy is going to be scared, your crew is going to be protective of you, and I'm going to go nuts if you start pretending I'm invisible."

I stare at his grinning face and then he makes me laugh when he screws up his lip in a trout pout worthy of a supermodel. Staying mad at him is proving to be more difficult the longer we're together. I hope this isn't setting a precedent for our behavior in the future; Best to nip it in the bud.

"If we're going to be a pair, a couple, man and wife," I begin and grab his ears pulling him closer to my mouth, "you better start acting like we're partners. Don't keep me in the dark, talk to me."

I kiss him with all the pent up anger and frustration I felt for the last two hours. He returns the kiss and soon we're moaning and groaning, trying to climb into each other's skin. If Tanner hadn't shouted from the front porch for us to come inside, we'd probably have had a lot of explaining to do.

"Let's go," he says "while I can still walk."

Opening his door he gives his pant legs a tug, trying to make room for his swollen member and then walks around and opens my door, handing me out and pressing me into the mustang's rear panel.

"I love you," he says and grinds our hips together, "partner. And I promise not to hold out on you in the future, deal?"

I can't help but smile at his playfulness now that we're back in Willow and apparently out of harm's way. Interlocking our fingers I grab my purse and we walk into the front door, as a solid front and join our team. Sammy runs into his daddy's arms, wrapping his small arms around Dare's neck squeezing him tight.

"God I missed you squirt," Dare says, kissing the boy's cheek.

Sammy leans over and hugs me around my neck and practically jumps into my arms, making me step back to keep my balance. Sam has a death grip on me and I feel him trembling in my arms. I nod at Dare and turn to take Sammy down the hall into my office; Dare follows behind us.

"Close the door Daddy," I tell him and carry Sammy over to the massive desk, sit him on top of a bunch of contracts and legal pads and brush his hair off his forehead.

He looks up at me and then over at Dare who pulls out my desk chair and sits down, pulling me onto his lap.

"Are you guys okay?" he asks with a hint of fear in his voice, "Did something bad happen? Tanny said I had to come back with him but he wouldn't say why?" he continues talking faster as he goes, "we were going to go to Candlestick park tonight, but he pulled me into his truck and that's all he said. We did go through the drive thru and I got a kid's meal. Look at this really cool magnifying glass," he says like any other six year old.

"I'll bet that's going in your spy kit, huh?" I ask smiling at his normal demeanor.

He smiles and nods his head, "I've already got a string tied to a dollar bill, that's my lure. Three really cool bottle caps," he cups his hand over his mouth and whispers, "they're from Jorge's beer but don't tell Toby's mom."

He grins at his secret then in a rush of enthusiasm continues, "They're going to be make believe tear gas stink bombs. I have a whistle, a metal box that Tanner keeps those hot mints in. I filled it with band aides and a compass. Toby gave me a really neat rock and Papaw gave me two nickels and a quarter."

"You're on the right track," Dare says and rests his chin on my shoulder. "Did you have a good time, up until Tanny arrived?"

"Yeah, but Toby's cousins, twin girls, kept following us around." He says shaking his head from side to side, totally disgusted. "We had to let them play with us, but you know girls don't get it when it comes to spy work."

I can't help but laugh and lean forward to hug him. "I'm glad you're here, now we can walk the woods, looking for new things to add to your kit."

"Hey, that's right," he says remembering I told him we'd go hiking in the pasture the next time he was in Willow. "Can we go now, tonight?" he asks.

Dare chucks him under his chin and says, "Not tonight pal. We need to have a meeting, just us grownups, so I'm going to ask Nana to take you into the kitchen, and see if she has any cupcakes you can have, okay?"

"Can I help her frost them?" he asks jumping down off the desk and running towards the closed door. Looking over his shoulder he says, "I promise to put more on the cake than in my mouth."

"Go ask, but be nice, act like a gentleman," Dare tells him, "One Neanderthal in the family is enough." He says grinning at me.

I stand up and pull him to his feet.

"He seems alright, unaware what's happening, don't you think?" I ask and wrap my arm around his narrow waist as we walk out into the hall.

"Surprisingly enough," he agrees. "He's used to Tanner being direct, so I guess he didn't get his nose out of joint, you know like some people did…" I pinch him hard enough on his side to make him flinch, "Hey, that hurt," he says and squeezes me harder into his side. "Say you're sorry."

"Fine, you're sorry." I tell him and squirm out of his arms and quickly walk into the kitchen to find my entire crew waiting on us.

"Dad says if you have any cupcakes that need frosting I can help." He tells the grandmotherly figure dressed in her chef's coat leaning against the stove. "I promise not to make a mess."

"Well, that's more than I get from Saul or Kit," she teases, "let's shoo these guys out of our bakery and get to work on frosting some cookies I made for us instead," she says wrapping her arm around his slight shoulders and nodding for us to leave them alone. "They're a new recipe I'm trying; maybe you could give me your opinion on them, hmm?"

Sammy nods his head and puts his hand in Nana's, already forming a bond with her. He needs a grandma in his life, one that makes him feel important, special... like mine did, in her own way.

"Mind if I stay and help?" BJ asks, "I'm a whiz at the pastry bag, hey Nana, why don't we show Sammy how that's done?"

We leave them to their distraction and walk into the bull session room, closing the double French doors behind us, closing off the laughter from the kitchen.

Dare pulls out a chair for me and soon, we're all seated around the eight foot farmhouse table waiting on the two men to explain what is going on. Tanner leans against the door frame, waiting on his boss to begin.

"First off let me say you all did an amazing job this weekend, with Coulton's gig and then the Senator's fiftieth... I know Carrie Anne was beside herself with pride. You're the best team imaginable. The Senator's wife booked three more parties off you last night, didn't she Roz?"

My office manager smiles and nods her head, "she said we were the 'slam dunk' in her never ending battle to one-up the other senator's wives."

Once the high fives, the nods of self-congratulations, and laughter dies down; Dare gets serious.

"There was one flaw in last night's reception and I blame myself." He says nodding at Tanner. "We failed to tell you about Rhonda Starr and the potential danger she is causing for my family. She has been trying to win a court case concerning Sammy's inheritance. She's crazy, but persistent."

He goes on to explain about his brother and Sammy's mother Rachel; Rhonda's supposed sister and the lack of a prenuptial agreement.

"The courts ruled sole custody to me and because no one came forth at the time of the adoption, it went through, albeit slowly, but binding." He tells the quiet room. "Sammy's mother committed suicide, even though I'm starting to have my doubts. This brings up why this woman has to be caught. She'll stop at nothing to get what she feels is her due."

He looks over at me and I shake my head knowing he is going to mention his father's involvement. Nodding his head at me he continues.

"My own father has on occasion sided with the bitch, letting her bring him to the brink of financial ruin. I have refused to bail him out this last time, so for all I know he's now working with her."

I hear the pain in his voice; see the sadness in his eyes at how he not only lost his brother in the wreck, but his father as well. He explains about my over hearing Starr and Derek talking about getting a hold of Sammy. When he finishes I reach out and take hold of his hand and he squeezes mine in return.

"What do you want us to do?" Saul asks ready and willing to go to battle for us. "Just name it, it's yours."

Kit and Gina nod their heads in agreement, willing to jump into the fray at Dare's request. I feel my heart swell with love and pride that my crew, my adoptive family has taken to Dare and Sammy like they're part of our unit… which now they are.

"Look at this photograph, try to remember if any of you saw her last night?" Tanner says opening the folded Lucerne Ledger and laying it on the table.

"Yeah, she was with an older guy," Roz says, "I thought she was too hot for the old man, but hey whatever floats your boat. But I couldn't say I saw her after that one time. She's pretty but nothing that would stand out in your mind, you know."

Gina looks up at me and says, "She was in the restroom the same time I was, talking on the phone, but all I can remember was she was angry. I think she yelled 'find the mark' or something like that. But I didn't see her after that one time either."

Dare straightens up and Tanner walks over to stand behind my sous chef's chair and then leans down close to Gina's ear and says, "think back hon, could she have said, 'find them Mark'?"

She looks into the Tanner's ruggedly handsome face and says, "Well Slick, I wasn't paying that close of attention, but yeah, I guess she could have said that."

Nodding his head Dare smiles a sigh of relief.

"That means she and her brother Mark had no idea where my kid was over the weekend, and that the family Sammy was staying with are not in any danger." Dare says,

"But my son is, I need each of you to keep a close eye open for strangers in the area, if you see anything suspicious let us know."

Kit looks over at Saul and nods his head, and then they turn to me and start to look uncomfortable. Tanner touches Dare's shirtsleeve and motions his head for the two to speak up.

"Hell if we'd known she was dangerous we'd have tied her up and hauled her out back." Saul says looking uneasy at what he's about to say. "Even the senator commented on her looking out of place dressed like she was a low budget movie star on the red carpet. He said if his wife saw that trash she'd raise a ruckus for sure. But I heard her say..." he stops and looks over at Kit.

"Saul, go ahead, we need to know everything," I encourage him. "Did she speak to you?"

"She told the maître'd she was waiting on Dare," Kit says, "and by the way she was wheedling her way inside the hall, you know pressing her boobs into the ushers, giggling at them... Hell I thought as long as she was messing around with them she wouldn't be causing trouble for you."

"What the hell are you talking about?" Dare asks raising his voice and scooting his chair out of his way, trying to get over to where Kit is leaning over the back of one of the metal seats.

"Hey dude, she was with you at the Stone gig, I thought maybe she was crashing the party," Kit says and gives Dare a little smirk. "You know, at your request."

In the blink of an eye I see Dare lunging at Kit, angry as sin for being accused of cheating on me; Saul quickly steps in front of Kit while Tanner and I try to hold Dare back.

"I'd never cheat on Cam," he hisses, "Never! Have you got that man?"

I wrap my arms around his neck, feeling his heart pounding, his chest moving like bellows.

"He didn't mean anything by it baby," I tell him, kissing his rigid jaw, running my hands up and down his stiff spine. "I know, we all know you'd never cheat on me," I softly say.

"Kit, why don't you go upstairs for a bit, go cool off," Roz says standing beside the startled man who has his hands out to his side in surrender. She turns to Dare, points her finger at him and says, "Knock it off; we don't have time for any more drama. We know you love her, would kill for her. So let's get back on track. Tell us what you intend to do to end this craziness."

I smile at my ever-pragmatic friend and at Kit as he turns and leaves the room at her request. Nobody ignores Roz when she's in her 'take charge' mode.

"Sorry," Dare whispers, hugging me to his body, "I was never with that woman."

"I know, you told me that first time you called, remember? I never doubted you for a minute after that." Kissing his lips I feel him relax a bit.

Tanner puts his hands on his lean hips and says, "We expect her to try to grab Sammy at his birthday party Saturday, and we've increased security around the entire compound, but I still need to know if you'll have extra staff there? I'd hate to create an incident just because I wasn't informed of additional workers." His tone of voice doesn't set well with my manager.

"I emailed you the list of names but I'm sorry I don't have headshots available for you to memorize..." Roz snaps, hearing the censor in the man's voice, "it's a kid's party for crying out loud, complete with a scavenger hunt, a piñata, birthday cake and ice cream."

"Sorry, I meant no offense," he says and smiles at her, "just trying to think of every scenario to keep the little guy safe, along with the other twenty rug rats that will be crawling about the place."

She nods her head and turns back to Gina, "Have lanyards with photo id made up of all the staff, he's right. Sammy is what's important." Gina stands up and walks out of the room to start her new task.

Saul walks over to Dare and says, "Kit always says what he thinks, but he's not mean or petty. He'd never hurt Carrie Anne, and in his own way thought he was protecting her, from you. Can't blame the man for caring, can you?" Saul leans down and kisses my cheek. "Let me know what you need us to do, but I think the planning would be better left to you guys. We're available whenever and where ever you need us. Just let us know," he says holding out his hand to Dare, and nods his head at Tanner.

They shake hands and Saul turns to leave, "I can take Sammy with me tomorrow. I have to visit Phyllis, and nobody would mess with that old gal. Even with a bum leg she's still hell on wheels."

I laugh knowing his description of his mother-in-law is accurate.

"Thanks Saul, we'll let you know. But you and the crew have tomorrow off, so enjoy." I tell his retreating back, making him raise his massive arm in a wave, and then the front door closes.

33

Monday evening, the three of us are heading back to Sonoma after I cleaned up our supper dishes and Sammy had his shower. Dare insisted he put on his pajamas because it was going to be late when we arrived home. Sammy regaled us with all the things he was going to do with his newly discovered treasures from my woods.

He and I spent Monday morning traipsing through the back section of my land, stopping to inspect a rusty piece of metal, a possible piece of flint – from an arrowhead he assured me, and the whole time his mouth is running a mile a minute.

"… Why do they call it a 'creek' and not a mini river?"

"Did you plant all these trees when you were a girl?"

"Do bears live in your woods?"

"Why are we following this trail, did deer make this path?"

He never stopped with the questions, but when he'd pause long enough for me to answer, I'd share bits and pieces of Jon and my childhood journeys.

"Jon and I would hide from our Grandma Kate, making her come looking for us was hilarious. She always carried along a stick to tap in the high grass… looking for snakes." I told him.

"Once I wandered too far from our usual spot we played in and got lost," I tell him making him stop walking and look up at me.

"Were you afraid?" he asks, "because I know that's a scary feeling, I got lost in the mall one time."

"I was scared, but I simply followed the creek and sure enough, it led me back to our house, at least to the edge of Peterman's pasture and from there I could see the roof of my house." I tell him, "all roads lead home, remember that Sammy."

He smiled at me and said, "I will. Can I have a snake stick?"

We spent a good half hour looking for the right stick. We found a sturdy one and together we knocked the bark off of it and when we got home he asked his dad for his pocket knife. Sammy carved his initials in the wood very carefully with Dare supervising, well he was actually on hold, working in my office trying to get caught up on his own business.

Now, as the wind is whipping my hair across my face, my arm around Dare's shoulder I glance over the back of the seat and smile when I see Sammy, wore out and sound asleep covered in the red, white, and blue quilt off his bed. He informed me as we made up the guest room bed this morning that it was his room now and he wasn't a guest.

"What's your schedule like tomorrow?" I ask Dare hoping he'll be working from home.

"I've got a client coming in to look at some properties," he says "so I'll be out all day and probably late in the evening as well."

"Well, I'll stay close to the house, maybe try out a couple new recipes," I tell him wondering if Roz got the dossiers for the staff over to Tanner.

Dare looks over at me, places his wide palm on my thigh and gives me an affection squeeze.

"This will all be over soon baby," he says, "I promise. Then we'll start to work on those other three kids you promised me."

Laughing at his positive outlook I nod my head.

"The sooner the better," I tell him and rest my head on his shoulder. "You're a wonderful father. I've been meaning to tell you that and know Sammy is a lucky little boy."

"He's a good kid, and I'd like to think Jared is pleased with the job I've done, but sometimes, I wonder what would have happened if Jared had lived." He says, "We'd have been together for over six years, married, with children, a mortgage, and a heap of debt." He jokes.

Smiling at him I kiss his jaw and say, "all things happen for a reason, or at least I'd like to think they do. But the main thing is we're together, we've got Sammy, and our future is what we make of it."

"I believe that too. No 'its destiny or fate' for me," he declares, "everything I own I've worked hard to get; even Steele, Inc. Now that it's going public, I'm wondering if I should maybe bow out a bit, travel less, spend more time here, in Sonoma."

"I'd love that, but only if it's what you want. Don't make any sacrifices on Sammy and my accounts. We're set." I assure him and love the grin that crosses his handsome face.

"I can't tell you how pleased I am you and my son is thick as thieves." He says, "I used to lie in bed at night dreaming you'd come over, and never leave once you found us... I spent a lot of nights praying for just that. And now you're here, in the flesh, and willing to be saddled down. I must be doing something right..."

"Oh, you're doing a lot of things 'right'." I tease him running my hand over the front of his jeans, "so right."

"We're almost home," he says, "then once the munchkin is in bed, you're all mine."

"Why wait?" I ask and start unfastening his belt.

"Hell no," he says pushing me off him, "You get back over on your side, stop distracting me, plus teasing me too."

"Really... Are you sure you want me to leave you alone for at least fifteen minutes?" I ask, "You're driving like an old lady. I hope I'm still awake when we pull in the drive."

I yawn real loud emphasizing how sleepy I'm getting when slides his hand between my thighs, rubbing my core with the side of his palm making a great deal of friction. My head lolls back onto the seat and I open my legs wider, giving him greater access to me.

"You're already wet, aren't you?" he whispers, pressing his fingers further down between my thighs, "you'll be primed by the time we pull into the drive."

Grabbing his hand I pull him away from me, now that I'm all hot and bothered.

"Just get us home before I self-destruct." I whisper and can't help but smile at the knowing look on his face.

"Don't worry," he teases me, "I can always get you back up and running, should you succumb to my fanciful touch."

Laughing at his playful mood I sigh when we turn into the drive and he uses the new key pad to open the sliding gate. He pulls my car around back and parks on the back lot. He'll move it to the garage after we bring in our luggage and a sleeping Sammy.

Following Dare upstairs, Sammy draped over his shoulder and still sound asleep I help get the boy in bed, turn on the nightlight he prefers which is an exact replica of the solar system. It casts the spinning universe on his ceiling. We hold each other as we watch him sleep, amazed at how angelic he appears when sleeping and then we head downstairs.

I slip on my night gown, brush my teeth, and climb into the enormous bed waiting on Dare to finish putting my car in the garage. I must have dozed off because I feel him slide under the sheets a while later, nuzzling my neck and shoulder.

"Go back to sleep," he whispers, "We're both too tired. I love you Carrie Anne, kiss me goodnight."

Smiling at how good he feels I roll over and push him onto his back.

"Let me show you how tired I am." I whisper on his skin, "just lay back and let me do all the work."

Straddling his hips I hike up my gown and let him feel my wet bottom. From his quick, indrawn breath I know he is not too tired after all. Reaching between our bodies I feel the truth in his rock hard staff. I caress him and slip his fevered flesh into my tight sheath, again making his breath catch in his throat.

"Let me take us the rest of the way home," I tell him barely touching his lips. "I need to feel you inside me, burning for me…" and start to slide back and forth, making it a slow drag and pull. However, neither of us last too long, especially when he grabs my hips in both his hands and rises to meet me. A couple hearty slams and I'm soaring into space followed closely behind by Dare. We fall asleep still connected and I barely recall him pulling out of me and rolling us onto our sides, spooning each other before I slip into a deep sleep, totally satisfied.

34

Our Sonoma household developed a routine over the next couple of days, with me or Jimmie running Sammy to school and back, Dare and Tanner working in town at their office during the day, and all of us sitting down for an entertaining evening meal. Jimmie gratefully relinquished that chore, as she hates to cook. She and I compromised, with her doing the cleaning up, as usual, and me doing all the grocery shopping.

Sammy and Toby are always together, and only apart at the end of Jimmie's shift. When Dare is working at home, which he has been doing every night trying to catch up on his backlog, Sammy and I work on his homework, or watch TV, or we bake together.

For Sammy's birthday he wanted the three of us to go out, which was breaking tradition. Dare always made Sammy's actual birthday a private celebration, for the just the two of them, but at the last minute Sammy asked if I'd join them playing miniature golf at the local putt putt course. So we dined on tasteless pizza, flat soft drinks, and the world's best ice cream sundaes. He was thrilled at the present I gave him, his very own 'spy' kit complete with plastic credentials, a real magnifying glass, a note book and pencil, fake mustache and glasses, fake money, and a play passport.

I laughed until I cried when Dare put on the fake mustache and glasses, then he started 'detecting' things on me until Sammy hollered he wasn't playing right and grabbed up his toys and stomped upstairs to his playroom. That's when Dare kissed me and ran up after his son. The two played with the gifts long after Sammy's bedtime. The next morning as I placed Sammy's breakfast of scrambled eggs and bacon in front of the hungry boy Dare came into the kitchen with a pinched look on his face.

"I've got to fly down to LA and meet with Tucker's people," he says holding out his phone and reading a text message. "Someone is pitching a fit over last year's numbers, so I've got to run. Tanner is dropping me off at the airport," he tells me bending over Sammy's chair and kissing his son's head then snitching a piece of his bacon.

"Take care of Cam while I'm gone, okay pal?" he rubs his hand across Sammy's hair.

"Am I the man of the house?" he asks making me wonder where that came from.

Laughing Dare says, "Yes, until Tanner gets back, you're it."

Pumping his fist in the air he turns to me and says, "I'm in charge, so I'll be staying home from school today, I want chocolate chip cookies for my mid-morning snack, and Toby to spend the day with me."

Rolling his eyes at his precocious child Dare chucks him under the chin and says, "Maybe I should take your spy kit with me, how about that?"

"Uh, no I'll go to school, I want to show Toby what I got," he back tracks and slips out of his chair, eats his last bite of eggs and says, "bye Dad, be careful and don't forget to give us a courtesy call when you're on your way back," and he races out of the room to get his 'kit'.

"Alone at last," he says pulling me into his body, "I hate to leave you and Sam, but Tanner will be back in a bit, and Jimmie said she'd trade her day off for another time, if you're uneasy about being alone here."

Kissing him hard on the lips I say, "I'm not afraid of being alone sweetheart, I'll just miss you, that's all. Now take the traveler I filled for you and head out."

"I love you," he says and kisses me tenderly on the lips, "be careful, and I'll give you that courtesy call our son mentioned when I'm on my way back."

"Deal, and I love you too." I tell him pushing his hot body out the back door.

He looks like a million bucks dressed in a sharp gray suit, white shirt, charcoal gray silk tie with white polka dots and his russet brown leather wingtips. He's holding his brown leather attaché case in his left hand and reaches for the traveler in his other.

"Thanks, call me if you need anything. Hopefully I should return late this evening or worst case scenario, first thing tomorrow morning, but I'll be back as soon as I can." He opens the back door and says, "Keep your cell phone with you at all times. Don't hesitate to call Tanner if something doesn't seem right, okay?"

Kissing him again I murmur against his lips before he can think of anything more to say, "I promise, we'll be fine, but I'll keep my cell with me. Now go so you can get back."

Once he's gone I holler for Sammy to grab his backpack and get a move on or we'll be late for school. Since Jimmie isn't working today, Toby is catching the bus at his house. Sammy and I are on time as I drop him off and watch him enter the building. I wave at the teachers that have entry duty and turn my car around and head back home. It's only a twenty minute drive each way, so I'm back in the kitchen in no time. I spend the day trying out a couple new menu items, which should be great for the upcoming holidays and lose track of time and almost forget to pick up Sammy. I happen to glance at the clock on the microwave and see I'm going to be pushing it if I don't leave now.

Wiping my hands on my blue jeans, I slip my feet into my tan moccasins, and pull on a sleeveless honey colored cardigan over my long sleeved white t-shirt. Not even bothering to tidy up my hair I pull it back into a pony tail and race out the back door, hoping Sammy is one of the last kids out of the building. Luck is with me and I pull into the parking lot just as my charge is coming out the door. He smiles and waves at me and then quickly looks over his shoulder as if someone spoke to him. I get out of the car and race over to him just as I see a dark haired man slip in the driver's seat of a white minivan and speed out of the parking lot.

"Who was that Sam?" I ask wrapping my arm around his shoulders and ushering him quickly to my car, "did that person say anything to you?"

"He said my Papaw wanted to talk to me about coming to my party," he says, "but he looked at you and said, 'later kid' and ran off," and climbs into the front passenger seat and buckles up, "it was the guy at the movie theatre."

I'm shocked at the overt move made by Rhonda Starr and her cohort but I play it cool, simply nodding my head as he tells me this news. We pull out onto the highway and for the next twenty two minutes he tells me how impressed the kids were with his spy kit. We are about to turn into the front gate when the same white minivan cuts us off and slams on its brakes preventing us from going any further. A strange man gets out from the driver's side and starts stalking over to us. He has a baseball bat in his hand and a mean look on his face that tells me he is willing to use it, but on whom?

"Sam, climb down onto the floorboard and stay there until I tell you it's safe to get up, okay?" I tell him, "Cover your head with your back pack."

He does exactly what I tell him to do. Thankfully the top on the car is up and the fast approaching man doesn't see Sam take my phone from my hand.

"Take my cell and call Tanner," I tell him, "tell him a white van is blocking the road out front of our drive and to come outside and get us."

I put the car in reverse and start slowly backing away from the bat wielding jerk. I pray there isn't any traffic coming up behind me. I hear Sammy repeat what I told him to Tanner and immediately feel better until Sammy tells me what Tanner said. The man keeps advancing towards us.

"He's not at the house," the boy says in a frightened voice, "he's in town. He said, 'get the hell out of there' and go to the mall, where lots of people are… Camy I'm scared, what if the stores are closed? Or what if that guy beats us to them, what do we do then?"

"Don't borrow trouble little man," I quote my Grandma, "we do what we have to do in order to be safe. Now get back up into your seat, put on your seat belt and hold on tight, 'cause momma's about to come undone."

Sammy looks up at me with frightened eyes, but once again does what he's told and he sits staring out the windshield as 'bat-man' is talking on his cell, waving his arms in agitation. I push my foot on the gas pedal and my little mustang gives me all she's got. I reverse down the road until I'm around the bend and slam on the brakes, shift into drive, and whip the car around just like they do in the movies, or at least that's what it felt like. We're out of the thug's view but I imagine he is going to be chasing after us any minute.

We speed down the two lane road until I see the city limit sign, we speed past a gas station, a branch bank, and bodega when I see what I need and turn into an automatic car wash that has closed stalls. Sammy is looking over his shoulder for the white van but so far there's no one following us. I put in the proper amount of money and let the conveyor built take us to the best hiding place available. I pick up my cell phone from the floor board and hit redial. Tanner answers immediately.

"Where the hell are you?" Tanner shouts at me. "I'm at the mall but don't see your car."

Sighing in relief that the cavalry is here I laugh and say, "We're across the street at the auto car wash, getting our rims polished."

Sammy taps me on the arm and points out the back glass that is no longer obscure with suds, "they just drove by," he whispers, "I don't think they saw us."

"Sweetheart, you don't have to whisper, they can't hear or see us, okay." I ruffle his hair and speak into the phone again. "Tanner they just drove past us, heading north in a white minivan. We're almost through the hot wax so tell me what I should do, wait for you here or go over to the mall?"

"Stay put," he snaps, "they're coming through the parking lot and I want to get the license plate number, then I'll follow you home."

"Okay, Sam and I are sure glad you're here, aren't we pal." I ask him and end the call.

He nods his head and I see his bottom lip start to quiver and his eyes are tearing up; I unfasten my seat belt and open my arms wide for him to climb over and let me hold him. He doesn't hesitate and hurls his small trembling body onto my lap, pressing his face in my neck. I feel myself lose it as well and together we have a good, cleansing cry. We both jump when the conveyor belt moves us and when the hot air dries the car to a spotless shine we both smile at each other and feel better for having had our little melt-down.

Tanner is just pulling into the car wash lot so I pull the car forward and pull up beside him. He notices our red rimmed eyes but doesn't comment. He nods his head and waits for me to pull out into traffic, and then he positions his red jeep behind us and follows us all the way home. Once the gate is open I start to pull in the drive when I notice Tanner getting out of his vehicle and walking over to the black skid marks my car left when I burned rubber getting away from the thug. He gives me the thumbs up sign and climbs back in the jeep and passes through the gate, activating it to close. Sammy and I are already out of the car when Tanner pulls into the empty space beside us in the large garage.

"Woman you are some kind of driver," he says hugging me to his chest. "That was a pretty impressive maneuver you did back there, right Sammy?"

Sammy, now safe and sound, comes to life. He relives the frightening experience, even remembering what I said about 'momma coming undone'. Tanner's phone starts ringing and he pulls it out of his back pants pocket, notices the caller and walks out of our earshot. I know it's Dare and Tanner is sparing Sammy and probably me too, the details he found out concerning the mystery van and the man that wanted to grab Sam. Tanner walks back into the room and hands the phone to Sammy.

"Your father wants to talk to you pal." He smiles down at the boy and says, "I told him how brave you were, he's proud of you, and so am I."

Sammy grins in the phone and once again relives the incident, elaborating on his part of the getaway. I dread hearing what Dare is going to say to me so I walk over to the island, reach for a plastic container of chocolate fudge brownies I made and open the lid, taking out a good sized one for myself I pass the dish over towards Tanner.

"Thanks," he grins and takes two of the gooey treats. "You are one hell of a cook, and a driver, and a mother... I expect you to leap tall buildings in a single bound..." he laughs and I make a face at him.

"Dad needs to talk to you Cam," Sammy says, handing me the phone and trying to reach the container of treats but is unable to grab one so I hand him mine and we trade sweets for the sour.

"Hi sweetheart, how's your meeting?" I ask hoping to stall the chewing out I'm expecting.

"Not nearly as exciting as your trip to into town," He says in a tight voice and waits for me to speak.

"I'd hope not," I joke, "One psycho chasing us around the countryside is more than enough, leave the LA nuts where they are."

"Are you alright?" he asks in a soft voice, "I know this wasn't your fault, so don't blame yourself, okay? But maybe next time keep a closer watch on the traffic around you. You should have called Tanner to pick up Sammy from school; he was already in town…"

"How was I to know that?" I snap starting to resent his tone as well as his implication I could have avoided today's scare. "That's not fair and you know it."

"Calm down hon," he says, "I'm just pissed off I wasn't' there to take care of you and Sammy."

"Don't worry about it Darius Steele," I hiss at him letting my temper loose, "I was there, I did handle the situation, and now I'm hanging up."

I end the call and hand the phone back to a grinning Tanner. Before I can leave the room the phone is ringing but I shake my head when Tanner offers the ringing cell to me to answer.

"No thanks, my nerves have been beat up enough today," I tell him, "I'm going to have a soak. Tell Steele he can spend the night in LA for all I care."

I walk down the hall towards my room and grab my white bath robe and holler up the stairs for Sammy.

"Sam, come to the top of the stairs please," I shout.

"What is it?" he asks all of a sudden nervous again.

"Sweetheart, I just wanted to tell you I'm going to take a bath, not to answer the door while I'm in there okay? Tanner is in the kitchen or the family room watching over us so we're safe, okay?"

"Okay, Cam why was Dad mad at you? You didn't do anything wrong, did you?" he asks sitting down on the top step, dropping his chin in his hands, elbows resting on his knees.

"Sometimes, when we get scared, we snap at one another, because we're scared too, or angry that we're not there to protect our family from harm. He's not really mad, just... anxious." I tell him hoping he lets the topic go since I'm still ticked off at the man for jumping me about today.

"Don't tell Dad I was scared, or that I cried, okay?" he says refusing to look me in the eyes, "he won't think I'm big enough to be the man of the house if he knows I cried."

"Samuel Darius Steele, look at me," I snap at him making him jerk his head up at my tone. "There is nothing wrong with being afraid, or crying if you feel like it. Feelings are what make men and women powerful. Soldiers are afraid, but they still do their duty, right?"

He nods his head and smiles, "do you think spies get scared?"

Laughing I tell him, "I bet they're shaking in their secret compartment shoes when they get their assignments. Working through your fear is what makes you strong and brave, remember that."

"Yes ma'am, I will." He tells me and runs down the stairs towards me, throwing his arms around my waist and says, "I can't wait to call you mom."

Then he turns around and runs back up the steps to his playroom leaving me stunned by his admission. I feel tears falling down my cheeks and know what a mother's love feels like.

35

Dare didn't make it home in time for supper, so Sammy, Tanner, and I enjoy the pot roast I prepared along with baked potatoes, green beans, and crusty French bread. A house always feels like home when you can smell freshly baked bread. We plow into the brownies for dessert and turn in early. Dare has spoken with Tanner several times on the phone, but only asked to speak to me once, but I was still too upset to say more than a couple of words, then he said he'd see me later and hung up the phone.

Rolling over in bed, I notice the digital clock reads 2:44 a.m. - something woke me, a sound out of the norm, so I get up and walk down the hall. The house is dark, quiet as a tomb. Deciding to check on Sammy I climb the stairs and walk down the hall, careful not to wake Tanner who is sleeping in the spare bedroom.

Opening Sam's door enough to see in side, he is sleeping in the top bunk, sprawled out like his father. The gentle swirling atmosphere glowing on the ceiling continues to spin. I walk back down the steps, enter my bedroom and suddenly know I'm not alone. A dark figure stands in front of me, and a split second later I feel Dare's arms encircle my waist, lifting me off the floor in a hug that threatens to break me in two pieces.

"God, I'm so sorry for yelling at you." He murmurs in my hair, "I didn't mean to piss you off. And later when you wouldn't talk to me, I nearly lost it."

He picks me up, gently closes the door and then walks over to the bed. I slide down his front as he eases me to the floor.

"When I got home and came straight in here, you weren't in bed and I panicked." He whispers letting me know how upset he is.

"I heard something, a noise and went upstairs to check on Sammy." I tell him caressing his shirtsleeve, trying to calm the nervous energy I feel coming off him. "Relax Dare, everything's all right sweetheart," I try to gentle him but he is too upset. "Come to bed, make love to me and we'll talk in the morning."

He quickly undresses and joins me in our bed; we kiss with a hunger, a driving need to be closer to each other. He is rough, yet gentle, insistent; and soon I'm reaching for that blazing star, I lift my hips off the bed as he pummels me, urging him with dark, earthy suggestions I feel him slip the noose and come unwound.

"I'll never leave you alone again," he pants, "squeeze me tighter, pull me deeper."

Raking my nails across his taunt buttocks and pulling him closer to my body I quickly spin out of control and like the swirling universe displayed on Sammy's ceiling I float through the miasma of my mind, until I hear Dare shout his release into our sexual cosmos. He kisses my damp forehead and drops his head on my chest.

"I love you," he whispers, "please don't be mad."

I cup his beard stubble cheeks and whisper, "I'm not mad, not anymore."

He grins down at me, and as exhausted as he must be from working all day, then flying back to me I feel his sex start to twitch inside me.

A few minutes later, I hear a knock on the bedroom door, and as he slides out of my body Dare shouts, "It's alright Tanner, I got back later than I thought."

"Dad?" a small, excited voice asks through the wooden panel. "You're home!"

The door slams open as I grab the sheet to cover our naked bodies. Reaching for my discarded nightgown I slip it over my head while Dare distracts his son.

"Hey pal," he says patting the spot on the bed next to him. "Come on over and tell me how glad you are to see me," he teases.

"I heard a noise and thought it was the bat-man, so being the man of the house I knew I had to check it out." He grins and hugs his dad by throwing his arms around Dare's neck. "Are you done with LA? Can we help Saul and Kit set up for my party? Can I sleep in here?"

"Sure, how about I let you sleep on my side of the bed, that way you really are the man of the house." He says much to Sammy's delight and scoots over in the massive bed.

"Great, thanks Dad," he says, "I'm glad you're alright Cam, that noise was just Dad," he says and yawns patting his Dad on his arm, "I would have karate chopped that bat-man for messing with Mom."

Dare grins and looks over his shoulder at me, there are small crinkle lines around his eyes and I see his beautiful smile, he is that pleased with Sammy calling me his mom.

"Sam, you're the best body guard a gal could ever have," I whisper at the happy little boy. Leaning over Dare's naked shoulder I add, "Whatever you want for breakfast, you got it, except brownies and chocolate chip cookies."

"Mom sort of sucked all the fun out of that didn't she pal?" Dare teases his son, making the boy start to snicker?

"She can't help it," Sammy says trying to hide another yawn, "she's a mom, it's what she's supposed to do."

"Goodnight Sam-a-lam," I tell him and roll over onto my side, facing away from Dare.

"Goodnight Mom," he says and rolls onto his side, and facing away from his dad.

"How did I get stuck in the middle?" he asks and then rolls over on his side and whispers in my ear, "grab me a pair of pajama bottoms from the dresser," he laughs, "I wasn't prepared to receive visitors, especially overnight ones."

I slide out of bed and pad over to the huge chest of drawers and pull out a pair of white silk pajama bottoms and toss them at Dare.

"Thanks," he whispers and quickly tugs the pants on while Sammy is quietly sawing logs. "He is worn out," he whispers again and then holds out his arm for me to come back into bed.

He spoons my back to his front and softly says in my ear, "I can't tell you what it did to my heart when he called you Mom."

Smiling at the feeling I've been reliving all evening I look over my shoulder and says, "He has made me the happiest woman in the world, to be his mom is an amazing feeling."

I roll over to face my love and kiss his soft lips, "Make me a mother," I tell him.

He wraps his arms around me and says, "I want a ring on your finger and then nine months to the day, you got it." He lays his head on my breast. "I can't wait to increase our family," he tells me placing his large hand over my lower abdomen, "I want them close together, like Jared and I was," he says in a dreamy tone of voice, "that way they're never alone, even when we can't be there for them…"

He drifts off to sleep and I follow right behind him, thinking of becoming pregnant, having Dare's babies, and making Sammy my legal son.

36

I wake up Friday morning with the loss of feeling in my left arm and a hot rock touching my back, and somehow I'm lying in the middle of the bed. Sammy is lying on my shoulder drooling down my neck and Dare is pressed up against me. Raising my head I look over to see what time it is when Tanner quietly opens the door, sticks his head inside and whispers, "Good Morning mommy."

Smiling at him I look down at my new son and he starts to stretch and wake up. He yawns and looks up at me with such love in his eyes. His hair is standing straight up and dimples appear at the corners of his mouth, like his dad's.

"Good morning, Mom." He tells me, making my heart swell twice its normal size. "Can I still have anything I want for breakfast?" He sits up and looks over at his sleeping father and starts to laugh.

Tanner steps into the room and picks up Sammy from the bed and says, "Let's go start some coffee, leave your folks alone, huh?"

"I want Bulging Waffles and sausage," he tells me over his shoulder as Tanner closes the door.

"Are they gone?" Dare mumbles from behind my back. "I thought they'd never leave."

He flips me over on my back and parts my thighs and starts untying the drawstring on his pajama bottoms, freeing his morning erection. Bracing his arms on either side of my head he softly kisses my lips.

"I want to be inside you, first thing, every morning, without fail." He says and presses into my waiting channel, sliding in to the hilt. "Nothing feels this good, absolutely nothing compares to you, and your tight, secret tunnel," he says, "you complete me."

He stops talking but continues to gaze into my eyes as we softly rock each other into orgasm. Once we shower, dress, and head downstairs I start to feel the aches and pains of sharing my bed with the Steele men.

"What's wrong?" Dare asks when I reach the bottom of the stairs and rub my aching back. "Are you cramping?" he asks and starts to massage my lower back.

"No, but that feels great." I tell him and hug my arms around his waist. "I won't start until Monday, but I think my back hurts because you sleep sideways in a bed large enough to play football on, and our son likes to sleep on top of me."

"Family togetherness," he jokes, "ain't it great?"

I can't help but laugh at his easy going manner this morning. We walk into the kitchen and immediately I smell freshly brewed coffee. Tanner is handing Sammy the carton of milk, and he's holding the package of sausage links in his one hand and a carton of eggs in his other.

"Good morning guys," Dare says and reaches into the cupboard for a couple coffee mugs. "How'd you sleep?" He grins looking down at me and pours us both a cup.

"After the house settled down a second time, around three thirty, I slept like a log." Tanner says, teasing me and Dare with our late night lovemaking.

Sammy takes a sip of his orange juice and says, "I heard Mom shout and thought she was being hurt by bat-man, so I went on patrol, and checked out the house."

"Liar, you ran into our room wanting to share our bed," Dare says, making Sammy giggle at being caught exaggerating his late-night patrol.

"Well, Dad, what startled Mom?" Tanner mischievously asks looking over the rim of his coffee cup, waiting on us to come up with a good reason for my shouting, without admitting we were in the throes of a passionate interlude.

"I surprised Cam," he says and winks at me, "she was startled to find me home already, that's all, Tanny." He says using Sammy's nickname for his best friend.

"Huh? So you scared your fiancée in the bedroom?" Tanner teases, "good thing she's a brave girl, isn't it Sammy."

"Yeah, I guess," he says having gotten lost in the adult teasing. "I'm hungry."

"So am I," Dare says, "Can we have 'bulging' waffles and sausage links, like you promised?"

Smiling at the silliness the three males are displaying I walk over to the cabinet, pull out the large cast iron skillet and set it on the front burner.

"Hand over the sausages, step aside and let me do my thing," I tell them and they scatter out of the kitchen like dust in the wind.

I locate the waffle maker and whip up my favorite batter, adding more cinnamon and allspice. When the griddle is hot I start pouring the batter and soon the house smells delicious. The sausages are almost done, the counter has been set, and I grab the bottle of maple syrup from the fridge.

Right before I call the guys, my cell phone rings and see it's a call from En Bonne.

"Hey En Bonne," I answer wondering who is calling me this early.

"Good morning to you," Roz says, "we're pulling into your drive, we're in need of sustenance, and coffee."

Laughing I ask, "Who is we, how many are we talking?"

"Saul and Kit are in the box truck with the tables and chairs, BJ, Gina and Nana are in the van." She says, "I on the other hand am sitting in the passenger seat of Desiree's brand new Tahoe Explorer."

"Good God the whole team is here already?" I ask in surprise. "What's the deal? And how did you manage to hook Dez into this gig?"

"Well, I told you last week she had good news," Roz says, "she sold her photos to a national magazine; they're using some of her shots of the rugged Oregon coast she has been taking for the last six weeks, plus she found out last night her agent sold her series on rural America and she is sitting on a hell of an advance. She wanted to celebrate but I told her we'd have to wait until after tomorrow evening. Can you believe Dez is in the coffee table book genre?"

"Tell her congrats, and I'll have Tanner open the gate." I advise her, "I guess I better keep cooking if you're all hungry, huh?"

"Hell yes," Desiree Cannon says into the phone, "I like your country omelet the best."

"Great, you can help me fix it while I feed my boys; one has to go to school yet." I joke, "come on up," I tell them and end the call. I walk into the family room to find Tanner reading the morning newspaper.

"Where are Dare and Sammy?" I ask, "Breakfast is ready."

"Dare is helping Sammy get ready for school and I'm about to let Jimmie in the front gate," he tells me, "and what sounds like a caravan of beatniks inside as well."

"Thanks, but hurry, your waffles are getting cold." I warn him and walk into the foyer.

Dare is starting down the stairs with Sammy right behind him. He smiles at me and chucks me under my chin when he reaches the bottom step. He is dressed in a gray Henley shirt, brown chinos, and his brown lace up boots. He has blue jeans jacket over his arm. Sammy is a miniature version of his father, except he is wearing sneakers.

I'm glad I dressed in comfortable clothes too; we're all going to be busy today and tomorrow morning as well. Looking down I smile at my worn jeans, red tank top and the plaid snap shirt I threw on, as well as my old leather ankle boots. I look like a female lumberjack.

"You look good enough to eat," he whispers and then says, "but I'm glad you're not on the menu right now, we're starving."

"Yeah, we're starving," Sammy says, "is Toby here yet?"

He runs to the kitchen and out onto the outdoor living room and hollers, "Dad, Mom! They're here already."

"Let them inside son, and then you need to eat, so Tanner can take you boys to school." Dare says and immediately Sammy starts to groan.

"Can't I stay home with you guys and help get the place ready for my party?" he whines walking over to his place setting and climbing onto the stool.

"No you can't," I tell him, "now sit down and eat your breakfast or I'll let Saul and Kit fight over it, which they'll do anyway."

"Yes ma'am." He says surprising both Dare and Tanner, "Better make a plate for Toby."

Smiling at his thoughtfulness I walk around his stool and kiss the top of his head. Dare stares at his son who is happily digging in to his requested meal.

"Let me make you guys some more waffles, let's give those to Toby so he can hurry up and eat." I tell Dare but Tanner has already started in on his plate.

Before Dare can argue Toby rushes into the room, making a bee line to the empty stool beside his best friend. He looks at Sammy's plate and then up at me through his wire rimmed glasses and grins.

"Good morning Camy," he says, "may I have a bulging waffle too?"

"Good morning to you Toby," I reply, "of course you can, and guys they're called Belgium waffles not bulging waffles, hey maybe we can look up the country of Belgium later."

I slide Dare's full plate of waffles, sausage, and a lake of syrup over to the small boy laughing at Dare's face. I pat his cheek and walk back around to the stove and mix up another batch. One by one my crew files into the room, amazed at the large, open floor plan of the house. Roz and Desiree are the last to enter and they're the first to comment.

"Geeze Louise," Desiree says spinning around on the heels of her worn cowboy boots.

Tanner and Dare both stop and stare at the gorgeous young woman taking in the place. She has that effect on people, but once she opens her mouth they forget about her stunning good looks and start to open up to her as a human being, as well as a top rate photographer.

She is wearing the polar opposite of her older sister. Dez is wearing scuffed boots, tattered jeans, and a teal plaid shirt that is so old you can see through it in places, a white tank top underneath, a khaki baseball cap that has seen better days rests on her head, aviator sunglasses hanging off the front of her shirt, and a couple heavy bracelets, mostly turquoise. Her bomber leather purse looks like its a hundred years old but I was with her when she bought it just last year.

She takes off her hat and holds out her hand as she introduces herself to a shocked Tanner. Her dark brown hair is cut in a layered bob and her clear gray eyes rimmed with thick black lashes shimmer with friendliness.

"Hi there, I'm Desiree Cannon, Roz's much younger sister," she grins and shakes Tanner's hand making her bangle bracelets tinkle.

"Nice to meet you," he says looking over at Roz and seeing the family resemblance.

"No we're not twins, and I'm only two years older than Despicable Dez." The older Cannon sister says walking around the island for a sip of my coffee.

She is dressed in her typical casual outfit. The skinny white jeans she is wearing makes her legs look twice as long, the caramel colored t-shirt and multi colored silk scarf around her neck is as relaxed as she gets when she goes out in public. The light tan sandals with gold beads is very chic and her leather bag looks brand new, but I gave it to her as a Christmas gift the first year we met, six years ago. She also favors aviator glasses but in an amber shade which are nestled on the top of her brunette head.

"Hey, I'm Dare," my fiancé says starting to act like the other goof ball men in the room and I can't wait to see his reaction to the real Dez.

"Nice to meet you," she says with a sweet grin on her light pink glossed lips, "So you're the one that broke Carrie Anne's heart, and here she is fixing a meal in your lovely kitchen. You must be one mover and shaker in the bedroom son," she says laughing at the man, "'cause I'd have castrated you with a dull spoon if you'd left me behind, in another country no less."

Tanner and Dare both look like they're shocked this lovely creature would be so blunt and forward after having only met them mere seconds ago. Dare looks over at me and while I shrug my shoulder and try to keep from laughing at him.

"Dad, what do you move and shake in the bedroom?" Sammy asks finishing his waffle and reaching for his usual glass of chocolate milk.

"Furniture, son," Dare replies giving me a look like 'control this woman' but again all I can do is laugh at his expression.

"Sweetheart, you get used to her blunt style, trust me." I assure him as I start cracking two dozen eggs into a bowl.

Kit walks in with Saul and says, "Don't believe her man. You forget what a sharp tongue she has but she reminds you within minutes of meeting you again. It's traumatic every single time…"

"She makes Roz seem sweet and docile." Saul says dodging Roz's hand on the back of his head.

"Don't bother feeding the male animals," Roz says, "they insisted we go to a fast food joint so they can't possibly be hungry."

"Come on Roz," Saul says, "you know that's not real food, we need sustenance if we're to put in two days of work in only twelve hours' time."

"What is he babbling about?" I ask my office manager as I begin whisking cream into the bowl of eggs. "We're not scheduled to show up tomorrow evening until five o'clock."

"Well, the Burchart wedding planner is insisting we have someone at the reception hall, which is technically a renovated barn for security sake." Roz says, "but they need us to have the place decorated earlier than we agreed so they can take their 'pre wedding' pictures, right Dez? Isn't that what they meant?"

"Yes, they want those insipid canned shots right down to the kids running through the grass, shocked when they come upon the couple embracing… blah, blah, blah…" the elite photographer says.

"What does that mean?" I ask then notice Sammy and Toby are still here trying to follow the conversation, and will be late for school if they don't leave in the next five minutes.

I dump the eggs in the hot skillet and start to stir them. I reach for the left over French bread from last night and butter the tops of the slices, put them on a sheet pan and slide them into the hot oven to toast. I take a deep breath and let it out slowly and turn to organize the chaos. It's time to play boss.

"Tanner, load the boys up and get them to school. Saul move the box truck around to the side of the garage, you're blocking the bay doors," I tell him, "Jimmie would you come over here for a second?" I ask the housekeeper who is cleaning up even before I've begun to cook.

"Yes Miss Camy," she says, "what can I do to help?"

"Roz, take Jimmie into the family room and map out the areas we'll be using for the actual party. Kit you can start unloading the table and chairs, and do not get into the landscaping; where are Gina, Nana, and BJ?" I ask trying to get this day organized and still get breakfast on the table.

"Right here," Gina says walking through the outdoor room, dressed in her usual uniform of tight dark jeans, bright orange t-shirt and sandals. "Nice place Steele," she says looking around the room.

"Hello everybody," Nana says carrying her purse and a plastic container of cupcakes. "I tried out a new recipe, butter pecan with maple cream cheese frosting." She says holding up the carrier. BJ silently waves at me and smiles at Sammy and Toby as they walk past him and out the door.

Dare walks over to me, kisses the back of my head and says, "I'll grab something in town."

"Wait, where are you going?" I ask, "I need you to help set up tables, chairs, blow up balloons…"

He grins at me and says, "No, that's what I'm paying En Bonnes Catering to do, make sure I get my money's worth," and swats me on my backside as he hugs me goodbye.

He evades the soft back kick I send his way and he wags his finger at me, "behave or I'll tell Nana on you." He tells me and kisses the older woman's cheek as he walks past. He grabs two of her small cakes and runs out the door.

"BJ, come stir these eggs, Gina add more sausages to the pan, Dez get the tableware out and we'll eat in the family room and stop taking photographs for crying out loud." I tell her making her laugh but she doesn't stop. She has the uncanny ability to produce a massive camera out of thin air when she wants to photograph someone or something, which is what she's doing right now.

"Come on Carrie Anne," she says behind the telephoto lenses, "you know the camera loves you, just like me. I can't wait to do an exposé on the gritty side of the catering business.

She continues to snap shot after shot, the camera whirring and clicking until she decides she has enough and sets the expensive camera on the back counter and grabs a stack of plates and heads for the family room.

"Calm down Carrie Anne," Nana says, "everything is going to be fine. Roz worked it out and I know it's going to make perfect sense to you, once you listen to her."

"Fine, but first will someone bring me a cup of ..." before I can finish my request BJ hands me my coffee mug and I can tell he made it, not Tanner who apparently thinks as long as you can't see through the coffee pot that means it's a good cup.

"Thanks, BJ." I tell him and stand back, enjoying the coffee and trying to organize things in my head.

Normally I don't stress about these kinds of things, that's what Roz does. But this is personal, and I need for everything to be perfect, no better than perfect. Ten minutes later Roz walks back into the kitchen, refills her coffee mug and leans on the island counter and lays her ever present spiral notebook down in front of her. She doesn't like to rely on her IPad just in case it crashes and she's left in the dark. She is fond of saying 'a pencil and paper will never fail you'.

"Are you ready to hear my plan?" She asks over the rim of her cup, "or do you want to wait until after we eat?"

"Let's eat, and then talk." I tell her and we start dishing up the scrambled eggs, sausage, and a loaf of oven-toasted French bread. BJ doctored the eggs, making them spicy and with cheese too.

Saul and Kit walk in at that exact moment and wrap their arms around my shoulders, both at the same time, nearly pushing me into the floor and start kissing the top of my head.

"Oh alright," I tell them, "You can eat with the rest of us."

Immediately they release me and help carry the huge platters of eggs and sausage into the other room. Jimmie just stares at my crew, shocked that this is how we work. This is similar to the Friday brunch we usually do at the studio, and I know we'll get a lot accomplished today, my only worry is whether Sammy will like what we're doing or not...

37

Soaking in my tub later that evening I can't help but smile at all En Bonne accomplished. After our brunch, Roz explained how we needed to split forces, cover more territory by delegation, so we did, and I have to say, it was a brilliant plan. Roz would have made a wonderful military leader, except she probably would have met with friendly fire. She can be every bit as brutal as Dez.

We worked with Jimmie marking off the different 'zones' for the party. She said Dare always did his entertaining on the side patio of the four car garage. It has a fire pit, a charcoal grill large enough to feed a small army or twenty, six and seven year old kids. Plus there is a large carport we can set up the food tables, keep everything in the shade.

Saul set up tables while Kit and Gina organized the cooking area. Roz and I set up chairs and started stacking up plastic containers that hold our linens, tableware, and beverage dispensers. Since this is an outdoor BBQ we're going with two beverage stations; lemonade, cherry limeade, and ice tea at a self-serve spot, then Gina will tend bar at the liquor station which will be in the outdoor kitchen. Jimmie suggested we store the food tables and utensils in the empty bay of the garage, that way we can carry the loaded table out tomorrow.

Nana started assembling her cupcake stands, minus the cakes which again we'll add tomorrow. All the food that hadn't been prepared yet is in the huge chest freezer out in the garage, the soft drinks, liquor, and beer are in ice chests chilling on the outdoor living room counter. All the sides, potato salad, slaw, pasta salads, as well as the baked beans are in the outdoor fridge. The rest of the snacks are in our special tins, waiting to be dished up.

I hear laughter coming from the kitchen and wonder which one of my workers is in there but I'm too tired and too comfortable to get up and see. I reach for my glass of merlot sitting on a small intricately cut wooden table and lean back, letting the hot, scented water work its magic. I started cramping again after supper, which was a build-your-own- pizza party, and Sammy was having a ball.

Dare and Tanner arrived after six, both amazed and relieved at the progress we made. Unsure of what kind of welcome he would receive, Dare hung back, taking all the ribbing my gang dealt him about leaving me to do all the work, and how the betting pool was going, my favor or his that we'd be turning in for the night earlier than normal.

I smiled at his chagrin, loving the fact that he can take a joke, but also give back as good as he received. Gina and Dez were betting I'd hold out, make him pay for bailing on me, but Roz and Kit said I was a softy and would cave. Even Sammy, not really understanding what the adults were talking about placed his 'spy' dollar on the books telling everyone his Mom and Dad always go to bed early but their

TV sure gets noisy, and he joined in on the laughter his comment created.

There's a knock on the door and then Dare says, "can I bother you a minute?"

"Come on in," I tell him and smile when his eyes light up at seeing me still enjoying my bath.

"I, uh… just wanted to tell you, ohm, what Tanner and I found out on the van." He says kneeling down by the side of the tub and skimming his fingertips across the warm water. I wait for him to continue but he seems to have lost his train of thought.

"What did you find out?" I gently ask squeezing the soap from my sponge down my throat and can't help but smile at his having to shake his head, almost as if the clear his thoughts.

"The van is registered to a Vivian Starr," he says tracing circles on my arm with his wet fingers, "she is also a foster mother for four children. She and her husband have been fostering kids in the area for almost twenty years. She fostered Sammy's mother and three other kids at that time."

He stands up and walks over to the door, turns the lock and starts to undress. I wonder who won this time slot. When he is naked he steps into the tub, pushing me to the middle so his long legs can slide around my hips, and he presses me to lie back across his chest.

"This feels great," he murmurs kissing my temple and reaching for my wine, "we should do this more often."

"Good idea," I agree enjoying his body heat, "you were telling me about Vivian Starr?"

"What? Oh, yeah, she and her husband fostered Rachel and Rhonda, but it turns out there was an older brother, who was over eighteen and already doing a stint in the local corrections facility, serving time for armed robbery, he was never in the Starr's household."

"How did Rachel meet Jared," I ask linking our hands together. I want to learn more about Dare's family and encourage him to share his past with me.

"She came to work for us," he smiles and says, "She was a whiz on the computer, and a wonderful office worker. Within the first year Jared moved her to an office manager position, freeing him to work the client base a bit more thoroughly. I had just left for Paris and had only met with her a handful of times; Dad and I worked out of our office in Sacramento back then."

I hear the sadness in his voice and know he is thinking back on the dark days after the wreck and his brother and Rachel's deaths. Turning to rest my head on his chest he takes the wine from me and upends the glass, then leans down and kisses me, long and deeply until I get up on my knees, and straddle his hips. I have a burning need to be connected to him, on all levels.

"Make love to me Dare," I whisper, "Make me come apart like you did last night."

Removing the glass from his hand, I place it on the small table and reach under the now lukewarm water for his rapidly swelling member.

"Let's not think about anything but just the two of us, how we make each other feel," I tell him as I fondle his flesh, and lean into his body, kissing his chest, neck, and lastly his lips.

"Ride me, hard." He says and slides down in the tub until his chest and shoulders are under the water line. "Mount up," he says smiling that million dollar smile of his.

Smiling back I slide onto his hardened tool and start to gallop. His smile fades and he becomes intense, using his hands on my hips to help me rise up and down, creating a mess on the bathroom floor with the displaced water like we did in my bathroom in Willow. Neither of us cares as we stare into each other's eyes, losing ourselves in the wild, passionate moment. Soon we reach the point of no return and skate over the edge; free-falling into a sensual world we can't seem to stay away from. We rest against each other and I wonder how long we'd have stayed in the chilly water if Sammy hadn't knocked on the door.

"Mom, Dad… did you guys forget to tell me goodnight?" his little voice asks through the locked door. "Dez and Gina said you better not make them loose their twenty… whatever that means."

"Sweetheart, we'll be right out," I tell him and kiss Dare across his lips and feel the loss when he slides out of my body. "Go on to your room and we'll be right there."

"Is Dad in there too?" he asks, "because Roz says you're the man that is if you're in there."

He laughs and replies, "I'm here Pal, but go on to your room like Mom says and we'll be there in a few minutes."

"'Kay but don't forget me," he tells us as he walks away.

"I'll make sure Sam wins the bet," he tells me and we both get out of the tub and dry off using a couple huge white terrycloth bath sheets.

"Let me get my robe from the back of the door," I tell him, "yours is in the bedroom closet."

Less than five minutes later we're tucking Sammy into the bottom bunk, while he tells us about his exciting day at school and how he was the most popular boy because everyone was talking about coming to his birthday blowout. We kiss him goodnight and amazingly enough he falls right to sleep no doubt dreaming of his big day tomorrow. Dare and I walk downstairs and notice the kitchen lights are still on so we turn and walk into the room.

"Hey Mom, Dad," Roz grins, "did I win the prize? Why look here Dez it appears big sister won the time slot, pay up all you non-believers."

She holds her hand out, palm up and soon one hundred forty one dollars is lying across her hand. Starting to close her fist I snatch the pile of loot and hold it up in the air.

"Sammy won this money, fair and square." I proclaim amidst a whole lot of snickering and Roz's bitching and moaning, "He will be looking forward to spending the cash prize, thank you all for playing." I tell what's left of my crew.

I turn to kiss Dare and say, "And thank you for your generous contribution as well."

He laughs out loud and kisses me hard on the mouth, whether he was sexually moved or just wanting me to stop talking, I'll never know.

"We're going to bed," he tells Dez, Roz, and Gina. "You can use the guest room since Tanner went home and Saul took BJ, Kit, and Nana back with him."

Smiling at us, Roz and Dez say at the exact same time, "goodnight Mom, goodnight Dad."

We laugh at their silliness and walk down the hall to our room. Sliding out of our robes we both slip into our pajamas, just in case we need to get up quickly and slide between the sheets, cuddling like children.

"I'm so happy," I breathe, "I'd like to talk to you about opening a franchise of En Bonne here in the Sonoma area."

"Great idea, less travel more down time," He says and yawns, "We'll talk about it Sunday, when you get back from Willow."

"Deal," I whisper and soon we're both sound asleep.

38

I wake up to the smell of bacon frying and fresh hot coffee. Dare is already up and out of bed, and I hear laughter coming from the kitchen again. Debating on getting up and seeing who is in my domain I'm interrupted from my decision making process by Dare bringing me a cup of steaming hot java, following closely behind his dad is an ecstatic Sammy.

"Did you hear I won the game last night?" he asks, laughing and jumping onto the bed. He has on a pair of jeans, a striped t-shirt and no shoes or socks.

He squirms his way underneath the blankets and throws his arm around my waist.

"This is going to be the best day ever!" He proclaims, "And I know exactly what I'm going to buy with my prize money." He says looking at me, then over at Dare who is grinning at his son's antics.

"Kiss Mom good morning and then head out," he tells the over enthusiastic seven years old. "Tell Gina I want three eggs, over easy and my bacon crisp."

Sammy kisses my lips and cups his hand around his mouth and whispers, "Dad's been picking a fight with the girls," and he jumps out of Dare's reach and races out of the room laughing. "Hey Gina," Sam shouts down the hall, "Dad says he wants three…" and then he's out of range.

"She's not going to like that," I whisper then see the devilish glint in his blue eyes.

"Good," he says walking around to my side of the bed, "those three witches have been blasting me for over an hour," he sulks and takes a sip of coffee before he hands the mug to me. "They're even planning when we should get pregnant, for crying out loud. And Roz wants to organize the event," he says and when I start laughing he takes my cup away and says, "not The Event, but the baby's shower, announcement, first haircut… the woman is a nightmare to have to work with."

"She has her good points," I tell him, "like she might not be able to boil water, but she can organize fifty cooks in the same kitchen to do it for her, and they'd all jump at the chance. She's a tresor'."

"Your treasure, not mine." he pouts and hands me back my cup. "Please get up so I don't have to listen to their cackling and taunts… They're mean."

I hand him my cup and scoot out of the bed, take my cup back and walk over to the closet. Opening my side I smile at the number of outfits that have made their way here from Willow. Roz packed a large suitcase of clothes she deemed acceptable and I put them away last night. I pull out a pair of dark jeans, a white T-shirt, a black cardigan sweater and my favorite black ballet slippers. I close the doors and find Dare standing behind me, grinning like the Cheshire cat.

"I love seeing your clothes in my closet, well our closet now." He says and kisses me behind the ear. "All your jars, tubes, and brushes in the bathroom make it feel permanent."

"I know, it feels right, doesn't it?" I tell him and hug him, "you look right too."

He actually looks like a stud wearing blue jeans, an old navy t-shirt that's been washed so many times its now a faded bluish gray and as soft as flannel. He's wearing a pair of brown driver's moccasins and if there wasn't a mess being made in my kitchen at the moment, I'd be all over that man.

"Come on, let's get some breakfast," I tell him and steer him out of the room, "I'll be there in a few minutes." And I close the bedroom door in his face.

"Hurry up." He says through the door panel, "They'll probably tie me up and walk all over me with their pointed witchy shoes."

"Dad who are you talking to?" Sammy asks from the other side of the door and I can barely hear Dare's reply.

"Mom, who has officially left me out to dry," He says.

"Why are you wet?" Sammy asks but they're already out of ear shot.

I get dressed, brush my hair and teeth, then stop to make the bed, pick up the dirty laundry, and slowly make my way into the kitchen, knowing Dare will be pissed off I took so long.

"Good morning sleepy head," Gina says from the prime position of top chef which is directly in front of the stove. "Your munchkin says you make him pancakes and bacon every single morning, isn't that right Special Dangerous Spy," she teases.

"Well, almost every morning," he grins, "don't you Mom?"

I nod my head as I pour more coffee into my mug, "that's what Spy's eat, whether they're special or dangerous."

Sammy smiles at me and turns to Gina, "see, I told you she did."

"Okay, okay… I get it but how about we make some crepes or French toast with berries?" she asks only to be met with a stoic expression from both of my men.

"Fix the guys whatever they want," I tell her and sip my coffee some more. "Besides, the sooner you feed them the sooner they'll start their chores, right guys?"

"Yeah, sure, chores… whatever you say." Dare teases and pulls out the counter stool, sits down, and takes his paper away from Roz who has been reading the local news and enjoying her coffee.

"Excuse me Steele but I wasn't through reading that." Roz snaps trying unsuccessfully to retrieve the paper. "Is this how you treat all your guests who stay over?" She asks crossing her arms under her breasts, starting to rise to the occasion.

"You're on the clock, hardly a guest," he says evading her hands. "But if you were a guest, you'd be hers, not mine. The morning paper is off limits until I've read it, and if you take the last cup of coffee," he narrows his eyes at her, "you better make damn sure you start the next pot. I've already made two pots this morning and only drank one cup."

Roz looks great this morning in her white skinny jeans, chambray shirt and black loafers. Her long dark hair is pulled up in a top knot and she is wearing her black framed reading glasses. She looks over the top of her readers and gives him her best withering stare, which he gives right back. It appears to be a stalemate.

Dez walks into the room snapping her camera at the group, and says, "I'll title this one, 'Roaring Roz crashes into man of Steele,'" she laughs, "What do you think?"

"I think I'd like my eggs and bacon in the family room." He asks me, "Would you mind? I suddenly don't trust the other cooks in here."

Smiling at their antics I nod my head at him.

"I'll call you when they're ready, Sammy too." I tell my guys and they grin back at me.

"Thanks, you're the best." Dare says and he puts his arm around Sammy's shoulder and steers his son clear of the three 'witches of Willow' as he called them under his breath.

Once breakfast has been eaten, the dishes cleaned up we head outdoors and start the tedious task of arranging and rearranging the seating area. Since Saul went back to Willow last night, Gina will be tending bar; I'll be manning the grill while Roz and Dez work the crowd, making sure everyone has all they need.

The invitation said the party starts at two but the first guests arrives unexpectedly and one uninvited, around noon. I just started the coals of the massive grill when I hear raised voices inside the house. Dare is yelling at someone, hopefully Sammy is nowhere around. After I lower the grid over the coals I walk inside and see who has made such a fuss.

I stop in the doorway of the kitchen and see Derek, Dare's father holding Sammy in front of him with the older man's arm across the boy's chest, preventing him from moving. The frightened look on my son's face sets me in motion. I walk past an angry Dare and stop in front of the elder Steele. He and Dare resemble each other, and while Dare looks hot and sexy in his casual attire, his father is dressed in a gray sports coat, black slacks, and a French blue shirt. His black leather loafers look brand new.

"Hi, my name is Carrie Anne Mossier, and that's my son you're manhandling." I tell him, "You have ten seconds to release him before I send you across the room. One, two, three…"

Derek Steele laughs at me and says, "Where'd you pick this one up Dare? She's a riot."

I continue my count, "four, five, six, seven…" and his smile fades from his handsome face.

"Stop this nonsense right now," he snaps at me, "I'm his grandfather, a blood relative for crying out loud, and you're certainly not his mother."

"Eight, nine, ten," I tell him. "You were warned."

I smile down at Sammy and while the older man is distracted I slip behind his back, position my leg between his expensive navy dress slacks, wrap my arm around his neck and shoulder and use my own weight to send him to the floor and Sammy runs over to his Dad. The elder Steele starts shouting at Dare to get me off him.

"God dammit Dare get this crazy woman off me, now!" he shouts, making Dare and Sammy start laughing at the sight of me and the less than dignified man wallowing on the kitchen floor.

"She warned you old man, you should have listened." Dare says walking over to help me to my feet. "This is Sam's mother; she won that title when she rescued my son from Rhonda and Mark Starr's kidnap attempt. If I could prove what happened, and I found out you were involved, or even knew about their plans, you'd be sharing a jail cell with them. Carrie Anne and I are getting married, legally but she is already my wife, in every way, so don't you ever disrespect her again, or I'll be the one tripping you to the floor."

Sammy runs over to me and wraps his arms around my waist, "are you alright? That was way too cool! Can you show me how to do that? Spy's need to know that kind of stuff, don't they Dad?"

"Later Sam," he answers the boy, "right now I need to show your Papaw out."

"How did he get inside the gate?" I ask looking around the room and suddenly I see we're not alone. With all the commotion I sort of developed tunnel vision and only focused on getting Sammy away from his grandfather.

"Well Cam, you certainly put your best foot forward on that one," Mokie Joe says, leaning against the door jamb. "Unfortunately I'm the Trojan horse, he walked inside the gate before it could be closed behind my car, sorry about that."

I run over to him and throw my arms around his neck, thrilled he could make it. He looks wonderful dressed in a pair of khaki cargo pants, white t-shirt with a black V-neck sweater. His hair is braided down his back and his eyes are sparkling like black diamonds.

"Oh my God am I glad you're here," I tell him, "how was Lake Tahoe?"

"Perfect, absolutely perfect" He says and turns towards Dare, holding out his hand my fiancé greets my best friend in a cordial manner. "Mind if I steal away your girl, for a couple of minutes?" he asks Dare who is still seething at his old man showing up.

"No, go ahead and take Sammy with you," he says nodding his head at me, "I'll be out to help you in a couple of minutes."

"Happy Birthday Sam," Mokie tells Sam, "I didn't know if you were opening gifts now or waiting until later, so it's your call little man."

He hands Sammy a huge black and silver bag loaded with tissue paper. Sam looks up at me and I nod my head he can open it now. We walk through the kitchen and out into the outdoor living room where Dez is setting up a tripod for her telephoto lens aimed out at where everyone will be eating their meal.

"Desiree? Wow I can't believe you're here," Mokie says, "and taking pictures of something as pedantic as a child's birthday party; my how you've grown."

She looks up, gives him the finger, and then quickly looks over at Sammy who is busy with his gift. She looks up at me, shrugs her shoulders and then smiles before she goes back to her work.

"She's still as lovely and sociable as ever, aren't you darling?" he teases her.

"Mokie, stop picking on her," Roz says walking over to the built in fridge and taking out a bottled water, "she's doing this as a favor, so don't piss her off and make her leave."

"Hey Roz," he says looking her up and down; "still looking a bit up tight, but then that's your normal stance, isn't it?"

He takes the water bottle from her hand, untwists the top and hands it back to her. She nods her thanks and walks over to look inside the bag.

"Stop it you two," I tell them and motion for Sammy to use the reclaimed lumber coffee table to set his gift bag on. "This is Sam's day, so either be nice to one another or leave."

She looks up at me and smiles, "I thought we were being nice, right Moke?"

"For you, this has been a prime example of charm school failure, but at least you acknowledged your attempt at being cordial." He teases then turns to look at me, "don't put too much pressure on the woman, she might snap."

"Hey Joe," Roz says making him look over at her at the use of his given name.

She squeezes the water bottle and sends an arc of cold water in his face. He sputters and reaches for the bottle water but she whirls out of his reach and laughs as she walks away. Beside me I hear the whirring of Dez's camera having caught the blitz attack on digital. I know she'll be downloading those pictures on her computer media boards.

"You'll never learn will you?" Dez taunts, "You need to be faster than that if you ever want her to notice you."

Mokie quickly turns his head and looks over at me with a sheepish grin. So it's been confirmed, they're doing the prelude of teasing and pranking rituals before the real mating dance occurs. I smile back at him and say, "what are you -twelve years old? Stop acting like a child and go take care of business."

Sammy has pulled out all the tissue paper and is diving into the huge bag. He squeals in delight when the first item he pulls out is a very real looking gun, but it's a water pistol. If there wasn't an orange cap on the end of the plastic weapon I'd have had to do a double take.

"Cool!" he says and starts taking out a small black nylon backpack with his initials SDS embroidered on the front pocket. There is a pair of thin metal handcuffs with key, a pair of wraparound sunglasses, a pair of kid size black leather gloves, a couple bags of milk chocolate candies individually wrapped in foil.

"This is the best!" Sammy shouts, "Everything a spy needs… and with the other stuff I already got, I'm set. Thanks Mokie Joe," he tells his new best friend and runs over and hugs him around his waist.

Mokie not being used to children and their impulsive gestures is slow to respond, but when he does, he picks up the child and hugs him to his chest. I feel tears start to well up for some strange reason when Roz walks back under the porch.

"Moke put the kid down before you break him in two." She teases, "Besides, your gifts are 'nice' but wait until you see what Dez and I got him."

"You're trying to bribe this clever boy into liking you," he says putting Sammy back down, "how sad, but if that's the only way you can get boys to play with you, I understand."

Again I hear Dez's camera clicking away, capturing their bickering and enjoying every minute. Dare walks outside, winks at me, and sees the pile of gifts on the coffee table, reaches for Sam's hand and says, "Show me what you got?"

He is impressed with the whole secret agent theme we have going on here and looks up from where he is sitting on the sofa and nods his head at Mokie, who in return beams, and he looks over at Roz who is rolling her eyes.

"I win," Mokie says and then sticks out his tongue and crosses his eyes at Roz.

"That one is going on my computer as wallpaper," Dez laughs making Mokie look over at her.

"I'd like a copy of it as well." He tells her, "Since you're only as good as the subjects you film, I know this will be a good 'career move' for you."

"Bite me Mokena," she tells him then looks over at Sammy and says, "Don't say that."

He grins and I know he just developed a taste for snappy come backs.

39

By two-thirty the party is in full swing. The birthday boy, along with Toby and the other boys from school is running away from the girls. The older girl cousins and a few female classmates of Sammy are over at the stables with the dog, Buddy and Tanner who is with a nice lady named Tammy. They're not dating just friends or so he claims. He is the victim of multiple school girl crushes, making the rest of us snicker when he turns and trips over one of the pre-teens. I've been manning the grill, loading it down with hamburgers, hotdogs, and sausages. The spread turned out nice, very colorful and easy to please the crowd. There is music softly playing in the back ground, ice cold drinks in everybody's hands and the sound of children being children. The weather is sunny and warm, like October should be.

Dare walks over to me and slings his arm around my shoulder, beer in one hand and a flower he picked from the landscaping. He bends down and kisses me on the lips, making me grin and start to giggle when he puts the bloom behind my ear.

"You guys did a great job for Sammy," he whispers in my ear, "but have you given any more thought to our wedding?"

I take the beer bottle from his hand and tilt it to my lips, taking a sip and handing it back to him.

"Yes, but I don't want a 'spy' theme, everything else is good." I tease him, "What did you have in mind?"

"You mentioned Mokie wanted to cater it, so what if we have it here, at Christmas time like we agreed on, but make it small, private, and family only... extended families included to a point," he says.

"I like small and intimate." I tell him turning over the sausages so they don't burn. "I'd want to invite Jon and his wife and two girls, which he said they were sorry they'd miss today, but the girls have head colds and he didn't want to cause an epidemic."

"Jon still works for his father in law, right?" Dare asks and starts to say more when Doug, his cousin from Sacramento, and his wife Trish walk over and join us.

They're a nice couple, a little older than Dare, and have two pre-teen daughters, the ones stalking Tanner. Dare's other cousin's name is Thomas and he and his wife don't have kids yet. Her name is Wendy and she's a bit shier that Trish. We chit chat for a couple more minutes until Doug, who is Dare's mother's nephew starts laughing at the boys.

Sammy and his gang are sifting through the white gravel in the driveway, turning over the landscaping edger looking for God knows what, detecting like only small boys can and will do. It keeps them busy so I decide to let them alone. The stones can be straightened up later.

Trish offers to carry the rapidly filling up platter over to the food station where Roz is making sure everything has a serving spoon, and if it's supposed to be hot it is, and the same with the cold dishes. Des is silently filming the

341

day while Mokie Joe is keeping an eye on the boys. Tanner is bringing his all-girl troop back towards the house, like a mother duck and her babies. Soon everyone is filling their plates, finding a place to sit, and chowing down on our simple yet tasty fare.

We blew up fifty of the one hundred colorful balloons I bought and suspended them with strings from the rafters of the roof. A soft breeze is making them sway, along with the exterior ceiling fans. The adults all opted to sit under the breezeway, allowing the kids to take care of themselves at the long table we set up in the grass, not having to worry about being too loud or messy. Dare and I are sitting side by side on one of the sofas, our feet propped up on the coffee table, finishing our meal when Sammy comes walking over. He leans into my side.

"Hey pal" I greet him with a smile but see he isn't happy at the moment, "What's wrong?"

"Why isn't Papaw here?" he whispers with his hand cupped around his mouth, "are you mad at him because he grabbed me in the kitchen?"

I look over at Dare who is about to speak up when I rest my hand on his thigh signaling I've got this question. I put my other hand around the boy's shoulder and whisper in his ear.

"He did something that made your Daddy upset," I begin not wanting to elaborate but not wanting to lie either. "Aunt Rhonda and her brother Mark also did something bad, and we chose not to include them, in case they tried it again. Why, did someone say something?"

Sam nods his head but now he needs some answers. Kids aren't dumb, so it's best to be upfront with them, at least that's my opinion and how Grandma Kate raised me and Jon.

"Were they the ones in the white van?" he asks me, and then looks over at his father.

"Yeah, it was them." He answers the question, "Mom and I won't' risk their trying to take you, and I don't know if Papaw would help them or try to stop them."

When I see fear cross Sammy's face I try to soften the blow.

"They wouldn't hurt you," I tell him, "but they think we're keeping money from them, money they believe your mother inherited, and should be passed down to them, but she didn't want the money, she only wanted your father, Jared."

"What if I told them they could have my winnings from this morning," he asks, "do you think that would make them happy, and leave us alone?"

Dare sets his empty plate down on the table, takes his feet off the wooden surface and pats his lap, wanting Sammy to come over to him. He steps over my legs and climbs up on his dad's lap and leans back against his chest and Dare wraps his arms around Sammy's waist.

"Pal, there isn't enough money in the world for those kind of people." He says, kissing the top of Sammy's head. "Keep your money, spend it on anything you'd like, it's yours not theirs."

Grinning over at me he starts to tell me something, and from the gleam in his eyes it's a big deal, but Toby comes running over and hollers at his best friend.

"You gotta see this," Toby laughs excitedly; "the grown-ups are having a water balloon fight. C'mon."

Quick as possible he leaps off Dare's lap and the two races out of our sight. I turn to look at Dare who is smiling with anticipation and leans over and kisses me.

"I got to see this too," he tells me and jumps up and races around the corner of the house.

From where I'm sitting I can hear the kids laughing and yelling. I sit still for a count of ten then put my plate down and run after Dare; Doug, Trish and a Jorge who is sporting a plaster cast on his left arm from a fall he took a week or so ago and his wife are a ways behind me. They're curious as well but not intending to get too close to the action. None of us are prepared for the sight that greets us.

Mokie Joe has the remaining fifty balloons filled with water stacked up in the landscaping around the side of the stables, Roz and Gina are trapped in the horse barn but they have a garden hose and their reach is far beyond Mokie's. Dare and Doug are opening up a couple of Sam's gifts and reveal a couple of water blasting cannons Doug's girls were going to give to Sammy, but with his blessing his dad and cousin fill the huge containers with water and start to retaliate, at least Dare is. He has payback written across his face.

Roz sticks her head out from the door and together Dare and Doug hit her with a stream of cold water, right smack in her face, causing her to swear out loud and retreat back inside. Dare motions for Sammy to fill his new water pistol from the five gallon bucket Mokie used to fill his grenades, with the help of his dad's other cousin. Mokie motions for the rest of the boys to grab a couple water balloons and when he gives the signal, they're to let the women have it.

Dez has a free press pass, but has to agree to be non-biased and can't help the girls. She is snapping away on her camera, two around her neck and the smaller one in her right hand. Laughter fills the air when the girls sneak up and take an armload of the water balloons before Dare or Doug noticed.

They run squealing inside the barn with their new weapons and then all is quiet. The men gather the boys in a huddle and discuss a new plan of action. Deciding to get in on the fun Trish and I quietly walk up behind our guys and snatch their massive water cannons out of their unsuspecting hands.

I run as fast as I can away from Dare who is chasing me around the stables, gaining on me as I look over my shoulder. He is laughing and ready to pounce when I stop, turn and blast him in the face with my gun. I hear my partner in crime holler and know her husband must have got his weapon back. Not stopping to see if Trish is behind me I holler for the girls to open the barn and slip inside just as Gina sprays Dare in the crotch of his jeans, making him shout.

"Hey! That's hitting below the belt," he shouts, "You can be court martialed for that offense, Gina."

I'm doubled over laughing at the look on his face, and how he is walking back to the guys. We hear a round of laughter and a lot of shouting, but still no Trish.

Roz walks over to me, puts her arm around my shoulder, which happens to be sopping wet from her soaked shirt and says, "Trish knew the dangers of this mission, lets honor her memory by totally annihilating those pigs."

Gina is still laughing at her quick save and I know she is going to love telling this story over and over again. Roz is fiddling with the nozzle of the hose, unable to get a steady stream when it dawns on us the guys turned off the water from the outside shut off valve.

"Dirty Pool, old man," I holler at Dare, "that's cheating and you know it."

"All's fair in love and war baby," he replies making the guys cheer him on. "Throw down 'my' weapon and come out with your hands above your head, maybe we can talk terms of surrender... no promises, but I'm sure we can work out some form of punishment for your behavior."

We girls smile at each other and I see Trish out the back window carrying a hose connected to a different spigot. She stealthily hugs the side of the building and then nods at us, ready for the grand stand.

Gina, Roz, the young girls with the water balloons, and myself included take a deep breath and we throw open the doors, rushing outside; surprising the boys which gives our girls the advantage and we bomb the males to smithereens.

Dare gets it right in the face, Mokie slips on the wet grass and goes down, Tanner rushes over to help him up but our groupies are on top of the downed men, bombarding them with balloons. Trish is spraying her husband all over while Roz, Gina, and I rush the troops.

I snatch Sammy up in front of me and he takes a direct hit in the face from his father. He yells and sputters trying to get free from me.

"Sorry Pal, but sometimes you got to take one for the team." Is all the comfort he gets from his dad, who is retreating behind Doug, who in turn is still getting soaked by Trish.

Mokie finally gets back on his feet, laughing and gagging from the water balloons, his long hair having come unbraided from the wrestling he did on the ground. He roars out Roz's name and charges her, undeterred by the water we're pumping out of our weapons.

She squeals in delight when he stoops down and puts his wet shoulder into her stomach and stands up, tossing her over his shoulder and running off with her as his captive. She pounds on his sopping shirt laughing and cursing him at the same time.

Trish's water stream gets cut off due to the boys pinching the hose tightly, making her start backing away from her advancing husband. Gina is pulled into the boys and girls pile, wrestling each other until they're unable to catch their breath.

Dare stares at me with a look of hot desire... but for what? Playing it safe I hold onto Sam and whisper in his ear.

"Remember he shot you in the face, let's pay him back." I tell him and he nods his head and slowly pulls out his new water pistol from his back jeans pocket.

"Help me Dad," he laughs, "She's got me!"

Dare runs over and as he starts to reach out for his son, Sammy jumps down, whirls around and pulls out his water gun, aims it at his Dad and starts pulling the trigger while I hold Dare by the wrists, keeping him from raising his hands and protecting his face. He buries his head in his arms and is laughing so hard I can barely hold onto his slippery hands.

"You're both grounded." He shouts and with one hand snatches the gun from Sam, and he turns it on him while he snakes his arm around my waist, lifting me off the ground and flipping me over his hip. I hit the ground with a thud and soon Dare is straddling my stomach, dripping water all over me from his drenched hair as he leans down and kisses my lips.

"Pay backs are a bitch sweetie pie, and boy do you have a few coming," he grins and then looks up at Sam, squirts him in the face and says, "Traitor."

Sammy jumps on his father's back and holds on tightly as Dare tries to buck him off, then Toby comes over to rescue his friend by trying to tickle Dare under his arms. Dare makes a big production of wiggling and trying to get away from the boys until he finally admits defeat and they take off after the rest of the boys, who are now running away from the girls… it never really ends, this whole chasing game.

"Let me help you up," Dare offers but I don't trust his gentlemanly behavior, not after he just pounded me to the ground.

"No, I'm good, just get off me and I'll be fine." I tell him smiling at his evil grin.

"Don't you trust me?" he asks wiggling his eyebrows up and down.

"Nope," I respond making him laugh out loud.

"Okay, suit yourself." He tells me and stands up, his feet on either side of my hips, "you were a bad girl and must be punished."

"Deal, but only if I can choose the punishment," I tell him making him shake his head.

"No, but I do believe in swift and just punishments, so here's yours." He says and brings up Sam's water gun and squirts me several times in the face, making me twist and buck, trying to get away from this evil monster.

"Dammit Dare," I tell him choking on the stream of water he is sending at me, "I give up, stop -you're drowning me."

"Did I hear you say you give up," he says, "Say it again."

"Fine, I give up, you're the winner." I laugh then stick out my tongue at the bully.

"Such a poor loser, a spoilsport even, that's a shame." He says and pulls me up with his hands under my arms. "We better go get some towels or these kids will be tracking this water indoors, and you know how Jimmie is about her wood floors."

"I'll be right back," I tell him knowing there are some bath sheets in the small cabana by the pool, so I jog around to the back of the house and open the wooden gate only to be brought up short by Mokie Joe and Roz making out on one of the chaise loungers.

Backing up I bang the gate to give them a warning I'm coming in and pretend to be shocked when I see them sitting inches apart, drying off with their own sheets.

"Is it safe to return?" Mokie asks, "We've been taking asylum here at the big house," he jokes.

"We're all going to look fantastic for the rest of this evening's photographs," Roz complains but without any heat in her words.

I walk into the changing rooms and grab twenty white towels and head back around the side of the house only to have Mokie and Roz follow me. I hate that I interrupted their time together, but twenty wet kids outranks two lover's needs.

40

Waving as the last of my crew heads down the drive I turn and hug Dare around the waist. Sammy is inside going through his loot, and it was a spectacular haul if I do say so myself. Closing the front door behind us Dare hugs me and looks very pleased with today's event.

"I guess you're going to bill me extra for the water fights aren't you?" he teases pulling a strand of the messy haystack my hair dried into, grinning down at me.

Everyone dried off with the bath sheets and decided to let the sun do the rest since the other guests didn't have any dry clothes to change into. I'm still a bit damp and can't wait to take a hot shower, grab a glass of wine and relax.

"No, since I can't prove Roz and Gina were innocent victims of a provoked attack by Mokie Joe, I'll have to let this one slide." I tease walking through the foyer and into the spotless kitchen.

My team always leaves the venue looking terrific, and today was no different. Gina and I cleaned up inside while Roz and Mokie along with a protesting Dez took care of the kid's table and the breezeway. Dare and his cousins rounded up the chairs along with the wrappings of what appeared to be hundreds of gifts for the birthday boy.

Sammy is in the family room, still amazed at all the 'cool' stuff he received. Dare walks over and sits down on one of the floor cushions and leans over to see what all Sam got. Together they sit cross legged and sort through the toys, the spy gear, and the dreaded clothes.

"I love my hat," he tells his father, "it looks like the guys in the old time movies," and he cocks it low over one of his eyes.

Laughing at him I join them, laying on my stomach, ankles crossed in the air and check out his spy gear. The kids had a blast with the scavenger hunt, finding everything on their lists with the exception of something 'fuzzy' which everyone wanted to lay claim to Buddy, so in order to save the dog and his hair, we scratched that item from the list.

All in all it was one of the best times I can remember having, at least where family was involved. Dare rolls over towards me and lays back, resting his head on the small of my back.

"Well kiddo what do you think," he asks "should we hire En Bonne for all our party needs?"

Sammy smiles and asks, "Can we have another water fight at the next one?"

Dare grins and says, "We can request one, but somehow I think Mom isn't going to go for that, right dear?"

"Maybe I'll sneak it in under Roz's nose," I tease, "she really took a beating from Mokie and you guys. She's going to freak when she sees the photos of her. Dez couldn't stop laughing when she let me see them."

"Good, she deserves a put down," Dare says and makes Sammy laugh.

"What about Gina? She made you look like you wet your pants." He says and burst out laughing again. "Did Dez get a picture of that?" he asks me.

"Oh yeah, several and they were snapped so close together it looks like a movie." I tell them laughing as I remember the look on Dare's face.

"It wasn't that funny," he mumbles, "What if that had done irreparable damage to me, then we'd be stuck with only having that monster over there for children."

Sammy laughs, rolls over to his father and sits on top of his stomach.

"Am I going to have brothers and sisters like Toby?" he asks with a hopeful look on his face.

"Yes." We both say at the same time, then start laughing as Sammy jumps up and down at the news.

"When?" he asks all excited, "Will I have a brother and sister? If I could choose," he says, "I'd rather have two brothers, but if there's a girl, I guess that's alright, I like Gina."

We both groan at the thought of having a daughter like my sous chef. She's gorgeous, witty, a riot to have around, but she can be a real 'ball-breaker' like Dare called her on the way out of our place. She smiled over her shoulder, pointed at Dare's crotch, opened her palm flat out, and then quickly closed her hand into a tight fist; she laughed all the way to Dez's Explorer parked out in front. I still can see the grumpy look on his face as she waved goodbye.

"It wasn't funny," he tells me reading my mind; "it's our future."

"I guess I better start protecting you from my employees then," I tease him, "because you have set precedence on all future parties and family get –together as far as she and Roz are concerned. They don't believe in a cold war, it's full out blazing when they're involved."

"Great, just what I needed, more female drama," He sighs and pushes Sammy off and stands up. "Come on Pal; let's go see if the 'witches of Willow' left us any leftovers."

The two leave the room in search of snacks so I gather up Sam's gifts and place them on the table. I had such a good time today, and can't wait to see how the rest of En Bonnes made out at the Burkhart's reception. I'll bet Saul, BJ, and Kit will have a fit when they learn they missed out on the water fight of the century.

Later that night lying in our bed I bring up the possibility of opening a branch of En Bonnes in Sonoma unable to wait until tomorrow.

"I really want to open a second catering business here, what do you think?" I ask Dare as he slips beneath the sheets. "Know any good realtors in the area that can help me?"

Smiling he takes me in his arms and says, "I know just the man for the job, guaranteed to meet all your needs." He grins before kissing my neck and fondling my breasts.

"What's his name?" I ask making him lift his head and smirk at me.

"You can call him husband," he whispers and smiles again. "We'll check out the area but first let's see what the rest of your crew thinks. Someone has to run the Willow location, who stays behind? Who moves down here? Can your Willow business handle a cut in staff?"

Staring up at the ceiling I realize I have a lot of homework I need to do before I start looking for a location. Thankfully time is not an issue.

"You're right; I need to think about this some more before I get wrapped up in a new venture." Turning my head on my pillow I watch the moonlight play across his face. "I had a great time today, with Sammy and the crew. But you were magnificent. I believe you mentioned a swift and just punishment for my mutinous behavior."

He chuckles as he covers my body with his own, "There'll be nothing 'swift' about this punishment, believe me," he says and ends up chastising me all night long...

41

Taking Sammy and Toby back to Willow with me seemed like a good idea Sunday morning, however I failed to take into account the wild and far out questions seven years old can ask.

"Where does that road lead to?"

"Is that the same semi we passed while ago?"

"Do you think they want us to hear their music or are they deaf?"

"Can blind people drive?"

"Does Willow have weeping trees?"

"Can we stop at the next gas station, I have to pee again."

And the questions just keep on coming, and we still have over an hour to go...

I pull the box truck over at the next gas station and hop out to help the boys down. Walking into the convenience store I bend down and whisper, "no matter what, stay together in there. If someone approaches you, kick them in the jewels, got it?"

They smile and nod their heads, "We'll even pee in the same urinal," Toby says making Sammy laugh even harder.

"No monkey business in there, just do your thing and come right back out," I tell them and then remind them, "wash your hands when you're through."

"Mom," Sammy hisses at my social faux pas but he grins at Toby and the two boys head off to the restrooms.

I decide to get them a snack and a drink while I'm waiting. Walking over to the counter I pay for their treats and turn to wait on the two when I feel something hard press into my ribcage right before a hand grabs my upper arm.

"Play nice and the brats won't get hurt." Rhonda Starr whispers in my ear. "Mark hates children even more than I do so you can imagine how little it would bother him to 'take care' of the little darlings."

"What do you want?" I ask looking over my shoulder at her as I wait for my chance to break her nose, and a couple of bones as well.

"Just what's due me," she says and smiles that brittle smile she assumes is charming.

Before I can respond I see Mark leading out the boys, who are trying not to cry but the fear is written all over their faces.

"Let me go to them or they'll start crying, drawing attention to our little troupe." I snap at her and she reluctantly releases my arm.

Racing over to them and kneeling in front of the boys I feel their small, shaking arms wrap around my neck. They're trembling from whatever Mark told them.

"Hey guys, I need you to be calm, and do whatever these two say, okay? They won't hurt us if we behave." I look into both of their eyes and see they'll do whatever I tell them.

"Okay, let's go." Rhonda snaps pushing me and kids down the aisle, "Mark and the kids are going to ride in the truck, while you and I get better acquainted in my car."

I stop just before we reach the double glass doors and turn to the monster concealing the small handgun in her jacket pocket.

"No, the boys ride with me, no matter what or I'll make such a scene you'll never get out of here. Even if you shoot me, you'll still get caught." I tell her wrapping my arms around the boy's shoulders.

Rhonda and Mark both stare at me, wondering if I'm bluffing but in the end they decide to let me drive the truck with the boys and Rhonda, while Mark drives behind us in their car. This gives me time and room to start planning our escape route. I load the boys back in the truck and hand each of them their backpacks to hold as Rhonda leaps into the passenger seat and closes her door.

"Isn't this going to be a cozy ride," She says in a snide voice. "Just sit still and don't spill those drinks on me, and keep your greasy hands off my slacks."

Her outfit is very nice and I'd just love to see little handprints all over the legs of her pale blue linen trousers and maybe a dribble of orange soda down the front of her pin tuck white lawn blouse. Smiling at the image I shake my head to clear it when my cell phone starts to ring.

I look over at Rhonda who is holding my black leather bag. She reaches inside and pulls out my phone. Praying it's not Dare calling me, and she confirms it's not him.

"Who in the world is Mokie?" she asks with such disdain, "it sounds like a dog's name."

Before I can stop him Sammy comes to Mokie's defense.

"He's not a dog; he's our friend and a real Indian too." He snaps at her.

"Well, he must be that hottie I saw you with at the Stone's affair, yummy," she says and licks her bright candy pink glossed lips, "Does Dare know he's still calling you?"

"Yes, they're good friends," I tell her without looking at her smug face, "Something you obviously know nothing about. Do you want me to answer?"

"Here, but one slip of the tongue and four eyes here will find himself left on the side of the road," the black-hearted woman says making the boys flinch at her callousness.

I flip the phone open and say, "Hey Mokena, how are you?"

"What the hell is with the name calling? Am I interrupting you and your man of Steele?" he asks in a joking manner.

"No, the boys and I are on our way to Willow, but we made an unexpected stop and picked up a bug, one that's affecting the boys in a bad way." I tell him hoping Starr isn't catching on she's the bug.

"Tell me right now are you trouble?" he demands.

"You bet, and hey I'd like to have the same gift for my birthday you gave Sammy, only I don't want any orange on mine, okay?" I tell him hoping he realizes I'm talking about a gun.

"How many?" he asks, "is it Starr? Does she have a gun pointed at you?"

"My birthday is in two months, and yes I really want one." I tell him in answer to his questions.

"I'll call Dare and we'll meet you at the Studio, is that where you're going?" he asks.

"Alright, take care, see you there." I tell him and Starr snatches my phone out of my hand.

She calls her partner on my phone, which is a good thing, at least now I can trace the number, unless it's a track phone. I listen to her conversation, trying to learn anything I can.

"… Some guy named Mokena, but she kept it short," she is telling Mark. "We need to contact Derek, tell him where the switch is taking place."

"Fine, you do it, but don't bitch at me when he starts to panic when its' not me on the other end of the line. Go ahead, you know what's best…" the woman is baiting her brother for some reason.

"Okay, we've been on here long enough, they'll think she was calling Derek so we're set," she tells him, "I'll be at the studio unless there are too many people there then we go to plan B."

She ends the call, tucks my phone back in her purse and sneers at me.

"You're dying to know what's going to happen aren't you. Well, okay, I'll give you a brief synopsis like they do in my acting class." She says loving the limelight.

"You're going to the studio, just you and the kiddies, expecting your fiancé to be there, but you're shocked when he is there with me, making love in your office. You pull out a gun, shooting your lover and before I can stop you, you kill the boys and turn the gun on yourself," laughing she says, "pretty clever huh?"

Shaking my head at the deranged woman I can only hope that Rachel really wasn't related to Rhonda or her brother Mark. I notice we're about twenty minutes from the Willow exit so I nudge Sammy with my leg. He looks up at me and I can see he's upset but not as much as he was earlier. Toby is sleeping with his head on his chest so it's just me and Sammy.

Rhonda is talking on her cell to her agent, messing with her arranged windblown hairdo in the side view mirror as she speaks.

"Do you have your squirt gun?" I whisper and he leans over on my arm and nods his head. "When we get there, give it to me, okay?"

Once more he nods his head. A plan is formulating in my head and I pray I won't have to use it, that Mokie has called Dare and he and Tanner are racing down here to rescue us, but I've never been one to wait on someone else. Sometimes you have to depend on yourself to get out of trouble, so I prepare my thoughts for what I'm about to do.

"… just get me that part, and stop sending me on 'extras'. No one can see me in a crowd you idiot. And no more stupid car shows either," Rhonda yells at her agent and ends the call.

"Hey Rhonda," I begin, "my crew is going to be at the studio unloading the van from last evening's reception, do you really want to risk them finding out you and Mark are holding the three of us against our will?"

"Shut up! Mark has it under control, he knows what he's doing," she snaps not sounding too convinced.

She calls her partner and advises him of the extra people at the studio. He must be talking because she is silent, waiting on her brother to tell her his plan. Finally after five minutes she ends the call, and from the look on her face she is relieved.

"He said the crew will receive word that you're not coming after all and to go on home," she informs me, "so the place will be empty. We can take our time and wait on your fiancé to come up with the cash that is if he ever wants to see junior again."

Sammy looks up at her with his crystal clear blue eyes and says, "You and my mother weren't really sisters. She would never do anything like this especially to kids. You're ugly on the inside. Papaw was right; you're a stick and have no feelings."

"Shut the fuck up you little shit!" she screams at Sam, waking Toby up in the process.

"What's wrong? Did something happen?" the sleepy boy asks starting to get scared again.

"No honey, nothing's changed," I tell him, "but we're almost there so you needed to wake up anyway."

"Are you going to kill us?" Toby asks the in incensed woman, "you look like you are, you know, you're all angry and mean looking, like that cartoon we watched the other day." He looks over at Sam and says, "You remember the one where the monster's head blows up? She looks like him right before he exploded."

He uses his hands to show us how the cartoon character's head got bigger and bigger until it popped. We start laughing at the image and that sends Rhonda into a rage.

"Pull over! Now, or so help me I'll shoot you, all three of you Cretans." She hollers and as soon as I signal I'm pulling over onto the shoulder she is already unbuckling her seat belt and running back to the second vehicle.

"Guys, here's what we're going to do, grab my phone Sam and punch in 911, but put it the driver's seat, they'll be

361

able to track the vehicle that way. When I tell you to, run back to the car and climb inside and lock the doors. Sam I need your handcuffs and the gun, quickly honey they're coming." I tell them, "you guys have to do what I say, when I say it okay? Think of me as your handler, you're the spies, I'm the boss, got it?"

"Got it," they say in unison; placing the call to the emergency operator.

I hide the gun and cuffs in the waistband of my jeans and in seconds the driver's side door is flung open and Mark reaches in and grabs my arm. I slide off the seat with no resistance and when my feet touch the ground I shout at the boys to run back to the car before Rhonda even notices they're gone. While she steps up into the cab of the box truck I spin out of Mark's grip and mule kick him in the chest, making him fall back onto the pavement.

Pressing his carotid artery, he passes out. Pulling the gun out from behind my back I snap off the orange cap, making it appear to be real. Rolling him over I slip on the play handcuffs, making Rhonda stop and stare when she sees the gun in my hand.

"He's out of commission, and handcuffed, so you're on your own. Give me your gun," I tell her and without any bravado she does just that. Taking her real gun I slip my squirt gun in the waistband of my jeans and nudge her out of the way.

"Give me your phone." I tell her, and she hesitates but finally relinquishes it. "Don't worry; when your agent calls to tell you they need a cartoon character and you're type casted for the role, I'll let him know where you're at."

Just like I expected, she tries to attack me and I lean into her, flip her over my hip and slam her down on the pavement, hearing the bone in her arm break. She is screaming in pain and cursing me the whole time I call the 911 operator. They'll have a squad car on the way in no time the operator assures me.

"I'll be pressing charges against you and your brother, so will Dare. You'll never get this close to my family again." I tell her, and lean down into her face, "Sam will inherit his father's share of Steele Unlimited, plus Derek's stock... wow sister you really missed the boat."

"You'll pay for this," she hisses at me like a viper, "When Mark wakes up, we'll kill your family, your employees, and just for good measure, both kids, leaving Dare all alone, with his millions... but you and Sam will be dead cold by the time he finds you, I promise."

"Good point, change of plans," I tell her knowing I need to keep her with me until Dare and the cops get here. "Get in the car."

"Go to hell!" she yells, "you broke my fucking arm, I'm not going anywhere with you."

Laughing I tell her, "you have another arm and two legs, pick which one you want broken next."

She goes pale and turns towards the car. Breaking her arm was an accident, but she doesn't need to know that. I tell the boys to climb over the seat into the back and force her to slide over across the bench seat of the sedan.

"Sam what have you got to tie her hands together," I ask over my shoulder, "any rope, or duct tape in your backpack?"

He looks at me in the rearview mirror and I wink, letting him know I'm messing with the woman.

"I have some duct tape; zip ties, and fishing line." He says and the two boys cover their mouths to keep from laughing out loud when Rhonda whimpers and starts to cry.

"No, you don't need to tie me up; dammit you already broke my arm." She wails making the boys lean over the seat to see a broken arm.

"Sit back boys, we're heading home, buckle up. You too MS Starr, wouldn't want you to get injured now would we?" I tease her.

I hate leaving my truck parked alongside of the road, but at least it's locked up and Mark won't be able to drive it, unless he breaks the window and hot wires it… damn that is going to cost a fortune to fix that is if he's smart enough to even figure that out.

Turning off the exit I keep an eye on the road behind me, praying I'll see a police car or a sheriff's vehicle but it appears no one is on the road this Sunday afternoon. I decide to go to my place and pick up Rhonda's 'blinged' out phone and call Dare. He answers on the second ring.

"You fucking bitch, I'll kill you for this." He says and the savagery in his voice makes me glad I'm not the one he's angry with.

"Dare, it's me Cam, and I've got the boys too. We're safe. I'm heading to my place, come out there not the studio," I tell him, "oh and I've got Rhonda with me."

"Baby, thank God. Are you guys alright? I've been trying to call your cell, but it keeps going to voice mail. Where are you at right now?" He asks.

"At the Willow city limits sign, getting ready to turn off the highway." I tell him and suddenly I see my box truck barreling down the highway directly behind me. "Dare I've got to go, Mark is chasing us, get to my house, quick, I love you, be careful." I tell him and end the call.

Sammy and Toby are leaning over the back of the front seat, excited to be in a car chase and anxious Mark will catch us.

"Get back in the seat, and put on your seat belts, we're about to go off roading." I tell them and put my foot to the floor, making this mid-sized sedan crank up the energy.

I know I'll be able to lose the box truck on the back road, but I don't know how this old lady car will handle the pasture. I guess we're about to find out. Mark is catching up and I can even see the sneer on his face as he starts closing in on us. Spinning the steering wheel I take the dirt road on two wheels, listening to the laughter in the back seat and the hysterical screams from the front. Our car starts fishtailing, creating enough dust to obscure the truck from our view. We're almost to the pasture when Rhonda grabs ahold of the wheel with her good hand, giving it a jerk and sending the car out of control.

From the speed we are going, our car flies over a small ravine but doesn't quite make it to the other side of the ditch. The sedan's front end is buried in the dirt, and the rear wheels are spinning in the air. The interior of the car is filled with residue from the deployed airbags. Looking over at Rhonda I see she is bleeding from the contact with the safety device, so much for her picture perfect face. Waving the powder out of my face I look over my shoulder and see both boys, and they're okay, just shocked that we were airborne I'd guess.

Unbuckling my seat belt I open the door and wait for Sam to unlock his door and the two kids scramble out of the car and into my arms. Setting them down I grab Sam's backpack, and Toby's too and we start running for the tree line. No one speaks as we put distance between us and the monsters back there.

We walk past the area Dare, Sam, and I had our picnic, past where Sam and I found the fossils in the gravel, through a creek bed and into the woods where we can hide. Rhonda and Mark are both shouting, but we can't hear what they're saying. It's dark in the wooded area, which is to our benefit.

Toby is holding my hand, gripping it like a lifeline but Sam isn't scared any more, he recognized how close to our house we are. We'll be home in forty five minutes, maybe less. We don't speak out loud but in whispers.

"Don't worry Toby," Sam tells him, "our house is just over those couple of hills, right Mom?"

"Right, and when we get there, I'll bet both your Dads will be waiting on us. I wonder if they'll have something ready for us to eat," I tell them, "I'm starving."

"Hey wait," Toby says, "we still have our snacks and juice boxes from the gas station."

"Yeah we can have a picnic and pretend they're the ants." Sam laughs quietly.

"I think they're more like a pair of skunks, and man do they stink. Phew! Let's keep moving." I tell them but open their packages of cookies and punch the straw in the juice box.

"Here, you can have some of mine." Sam offers and I take a cookie from him and it tastes fantastic, I hadn't realized how hungry these guys must have been.

"Take a sip from my juice box Cam." Toby offers wanting to share his treat too.

Holding the box up to my lips I take a small sip of the sweet punch. This should give them the sugar high we'll need to make it back home. Hopefully I won't end up carrying either of them.

42

After the first mile I notice my little troopers are slowing down, and being fearful of Rhonda and Mark finding us I feel the need to push them harder. I decide to play the scavenger game with them, only making it a nature scavenger hunt.

"Why don't you guys give me your back packs and then you'll be able to run around and find the items I'm going to name off," I suggest and they readily agree.

They found something smooth – a rock.

They found something rough – a piece of bark.

They found two different kinds of leaves.

They had a hard time finding a piece of man-made litter but eventually I had to toss out a tissue and a gum wrapper from my bag, and then pretend they must have missed it. By the time we ended the game with them finding something they thought was beautiful, which was a pure bright blue feather for Toby and a small grapevine with 'spiral curls' for Sammy, I can see the rooftop of my house.

I motion for the boys to stay in the woods line while I slip into the house and make sure it's safe. Looking over my shoulder I see the fear return in their sweet faces. They're holding hands, ready to protect each other, but they're still little boys and that makes me more determined to keep them safe.

"Be quiet and I'll be back in a second." I whisper to them and they both nod their heads.

Slipping along the shrubs I sneak past the screened in back porch and try the doorknob but it's still locked. I step back and look at the upstairs bathroom window and then over at the tree but remember I bolted that window shut before I left for Sonoma. I walk over to the back of the garage and sneak a look at the driveway and suddenly all my fears are gone.

Dare is standing impatiently by a sheriff's deputy, looking tired and angry. I'm close enough now to hear him telling the officer he wasn't going to stand around idle while those two kidnapped his wife and child, plus an innocent bystander.

"Then come over here and save me." I tell him smiling when he spins around at the sound of my voice.

He literally flies to me, wraps his arms around my back and buries his face in my neck and shoulder. I feel tears running down my cheeks and then I feel then on my neck; Dare's tears.

"Officer, there are two little boys along the tree line that need to be told it's safe," I tell him, "would you mind running over there and bringing them back."

Dare carries me to the back porch and sits me down on the wicker swing suspended from the ceiling by chains. He looks at me, with such love and concern, but I know he's dying to go get Sammy.

"Go ahead, rescue our little spy." I tell him and kiss his lips before he takes off in a dead heat.

"Ma'am, we have some questions we need to ask you," a lovely female deputy says, "first, are you and the children alright? Does anyone need medical attention?"

Smiling at that question I reply, "No my kids are not hurt, but there's a man with a concussion and a woman with a broken arm and some facial lacerations, about two and a half miles due east off county road 800."

I give her directions where she can find them and wait for Dare and the boys to come back. Mokie Joe and Tanner rush to my side, both hugging me and checking to see if I'm fine.

"Roz is on her way, and man is she pissed. Kit and BJ said you left a strange voice mail about deciding you weren't going to come up, so Roz drove to Oakland with Dez, but she'll be here later on this evening," Mokie says, "Nana is nervous baking inside your house and I have no idea where Gina and Saul are at."

"Hon, are you sure you're alright?" Tanner asks kneeling in front of me.

"Back off Tanner," Dare says as he steps up on the porch carrying both boys in his arms. "I'm her knight in shining armor, right babe?"

Laughing at them I nod my head and open my arms the second he puts the boys down. They race to me and bury their faces in my neck, much like Dare did. They too are crying so I hug them hard and whisper to them.

"You both are the best special dangerous spies a girl could want as her back-up. Now let's dry our eyes and answer the questions the deputy has for us and then go inside and see what Nana has fixed, okay?" I ask and they wipe their tears with the backs of their hands and turn to face the adults.

Jorge is hollering for his son, having just arrived he is frantic to hear what happened. Saul is right behind him and walks over to me, carefully picks me up and holds me in his arms. Gina pulls up in the driveway, turning every male head as she runs up to the porch wearing what can only be described as short, black, and tight. I can't tell if it's a dress or a top, but either way she looks hot; every man stops talking as she walks over to me.

"Girl, you're going to have to watch who you let get in your car," she cheerfully scolds me.

"I think you forgot your pants, Gina Lola Brigida, either that or you're still growing." I tease her.

"Thanks Mom," she laughs and hugs me to her bosom. "Are you alright?" she whispers.

I whisper back, "I am, but they're not."

"Excellent," she responds and steps back when Dare moves in.

"Jorge was furious when he found out about the Starrs, but hopefully he'll let Toby come visit, before he turns eighteen, that is." He laughs hugging Sammy close to his side.

An hour and a half later, we're sitting around my farmhouse table, talking about what happened, eating shortbread cookies and hot chocolate. Jorge took Toby home, promising he wasn't upset any longer, not after Toby explained what happened and who the Starrs actually were. Roz and Dez showed up, frantic at first but now teasing me and Sammy about our adventure. Roz is sitting on Mokie's lap, Saul has Sammy on his, and I'm sitting on Dare's lap while Gina, BJ, Kit, and Dez are laughing at the photos she took yesterday. Nana is smiling serenely at all of us. Dare nudges me off his lap and reaches for my hand, pulling me into the living room.

"Are you sure you're alright?" he asks me for the seventh time. "God I was so scared when Derek told me what those two were up to."

"Derek told you? But I thought he was in on it," I tell him.

"He wanted them to think that," Dare says, "He came clean at Sam's party and I was going to tell you about it later, but honestly even he didn't know when it was supposed to happen. He said the brother and sister team fought like cats and dogs and was always left out of the loop, so he let them think he was game, but he has been recording all their conversations and is willing to testify against them in court."

"That's great news!" I tell him and hug him close. "Where is he now?" I ask.

"He's calling in a few favors of some pretty expensive lawyers. He still has to get himself out of hock, but I think he'll swing it, at least he'll give it his best shot." Dare says sounding proud of his father for the first time since I've known him. Yawning I rest my head on his shoulder and he instantly wraps me closer to his body.

"God I was so scared when I got the voice mail from that bitch." he admits, "she said if I ever wanted to see my son and fiancée again I'd admit to owing her an inheritance and wire the money into an overseas account. She even gave me the account number which I've turned over to the DA's office."

"She was pretty but not too bright." I tell him, "She thought she could bend Steele, but she has no idea how strong you and your family really are."

He kisses me long and deeply until I'm breathless. I hear Sam calling for us.

"Mom, Dad – where are you?" he asks with a hint of panic in his voice and then he launches himself at his father who deftly catches him up in his arms when he runs into the room.

"You weren't worried were you pal?" Dare asks smiling at the little man in his arms.

"After what we went through today," I tell them, "nothing scares this special, dangerous, spy."

"Just the thought of being without you," He says in such a poignant way I smile at his shining clear eyes so like his father's that I tear up and have to look away.

"It's alright," Dare tells his son, "mom's cry a lot, remember?"

"Don't cry Mom," Sam tells me, "we're the best team in the whole wide world, we're the Steeles, and you can't break a Steele, right Dad?"

Dare kisses me and says, "Right son, we're the Steeles."

We walk back into the kitchen in time to see Mokie and Roz trying to grab the expensive camera away from Kit, who is threatening to post the birthday pictures on his media page, Gina is laughing so hard she falls off her chair, Dez is throwing a fit at how they're handling her equipment, Saul has his head in the fridge, Tanner is on his cell getting an update of the Starr's, while BJ, and Nana sit serenely back at the table nibbling on cookies, watching the other's make fools of themselves. Everything is back to normal...

43

Two weeks later Dare and I return home from the District Attorney's office after meeting with them for the third time concerning the Starr's. Tanner's private investigator Mason Russell and his brother Isaac uncovered that Rachel was never a Starr but a Jennings, from El Cajon. She was fostered by the Starrs after her parents were killed in a car crash, leaving her without any living relatives but was never adopted legally by the couple. Rhonda and Mark are brother and sister, but their last name is Bertram out of Pasadena. Their mother was a street prostitute and an addict, their father or father's remain unknown. Rhonda was adopted by the Starrs but her brother was doing time and was never in the picture.

Going through Rachel's past was painful for the Steele family to hear, but now she can rest knowing her son is no longer in danger of being kidnapped or worst by a woman she thought of as family. Rachel refused to marry Jared until he agreed to a prenuptial agreement knowing her family would become greedy and try to share in the Steele's wealth, but Jared refused to produce a contract never realizing how manipulative his wife's relations could become. He loved her despite her upbringing, and assumed family.

Dare tried to explain these things to Sammy, but the boy doesn't think of Jared and Rachel as anything but names from the past. He considers Dare and me his only parents as it should be at his young age. Maybe later on, he'll become curious about his lineage, but until he asks, Dare and I intend to be the only parents in his heart.

"Mom, Dad?" Sammy is holler at us as soon as we walk in the door, "Come quick, it's Mokie Joe, and he's on TV."

We walk into the family room where Tanner, Toby, Jimmie, and Sammy are sitting on the sectional, watching a commercial for a chef's competition where they compete for ten thousand dollars and a prestigious title. He looks up at the camera and smiles that disarming smile as they introduce him.

"Chef Joseph Mokena, from Elk, California," the host says, "Tell our esteemed panel of judges why do you want the chance to be the next champion?"

"I've got my heart set on buying into a wonderful catering business out of Willow, California and this is my chance to show I can handle anything thrown at me. Plus it will make my girl proud of me." He grins making the panel of judges nod their head and smile.

"Good luck to you Chef." The commentator says and goes to the next contestant.

"Oh my God," I whisper, "Mokie wants to buy into my business? Why didn't he say anything to me? Or to Roz... wait a minute, I'll bet she knows all about this."

"Relax hon," Tanner says, "let's see what the boy's got, he may not be able to cook and if you're going to have him cater your wedding, I think think we need to know what he's got. I already love his idea of party entertainment..."

"No way," I tell him smiling at the grin appearing on my son and fiancé's face. "You will sign a paper stating no water pistols, cannons, blasters, squirt guns, garden hoses..."

Dare kisses me silent making the boys giggle, Jimmie sigh, and Tanner laugh out loud.

"Wanna bet," Tanner says turning back to the television program.

Right now, Dare has my full attention and I could care less if there were five gallon buckets of water perched over my head. When Dare kisses me like that, I know I'm in good hands...

Printed in the United States
By Bookmasters